Here's what readers are saying about Christine Fournier's
Gypsy Lives Series:

GYPSY NIGHTS—Lives on Tour

The first novel of the series:

*To my theatre friends and all lovers of theatre, I recommend you read
Gypsy Nights. You'll enjoy life on the road with a bunch of 'Gypsies.' I
know I did! Kudos!"* David B. Young

*Gypsy Nights is a great novel based on a Broadway tour in the 1960's.
It's a fun read for all actors and those that wish they were. I loved it!
Check it out!* Brian Kess

*Gypsy Nights - Lives on Tour" A wonderful backstage look at the lives
of Broadway performers traveling city to city in 1963-64. Fabulous
descriptions, sizzling scenes with real life drama for the adult reader.*
Andrea Brandt

*Just finished Gypsy Nights; will need more copies for other show biz
girlfriends, sure to be readers for the duration of the series."*
Jackie Steele

*A fantastic journey into the lives of dancers on a Broadway National
tour in the 60's. The descriptions are lush and made me want to go back
to my theatre roots. I can't recommend this book enough!*
Tracie Hodgdon

*A perfect balance of narrative, character development and intrigue;
look no further. I gobbled this book up in 24 hours and am hungry for
more!"* Asha Menina

*Great writing, sexy, smart and a fun journey into the world of theatre. It
was a pleasure getting to know each of the wonderful characters in this
book. I had a great time on tour. Thank you for the backstage pass—
can't wait for the next book!* Tammy Belting

*Wow . . . steamy, sexy, loved it! I enjoyed everything about Gypsy
Nights! From 60's history, to scandal, to lust. This book has it all! You
need not be a performer or have an interest in the arts to appreciate this
well-written book. This one is a must read!"* Danielle Nelson

*I thoroughly enjoyed this backstage journey of what it's like to be on the
road with a professional Broadway touring company! Well done, bravo,
and break a leg to the author! Check this one out, people!* Chuck Pekala

Gypsy Nights is hot, hot, hot! This book takes you on buses, trains, streets and the back stage of theaters across the country during one of the most tenuous and liberating movements of the 20th century and does with amazing sex appeal. The style, feel, history, and pulse of the 60's beats a drum through the entire book. Jennifer Carpenter

Gypsy Nights has everything . . . nail biting auditions in the heat of a New York summer, rehearsals that force the choreography of a hit musical into dancer muscles, eight shows a week, and life on the road. The characters and the world they live in for a year are fleshed out to perfection with Fournier's onion-peeling revelations. This is a slip-under-the-covers-and-get-comfy kind of book full of guilty pleasures. I give it twelve stars on a scale of ten. Sara Bartlett

What a great book to curl up with! Based on the author's personal life experiences, it's a fascinating look at a life most of us can only dream about. I highly recommend this book! Maris Edwards

Once I started reading Gypsy Nights, it brought back many personal memories of touring. These stories are universal to 'kids in the chorus' everywhere. Tony Vierling

Gypsy Nights is a SMASH Hit! It takes you behind the scenes into the off stage lives of Broadway Gypsies as they travel city to city. Full of twists, turns and unexpected events, it leaves you guessing and begging for more! The writing style is pleasurably descriptive and appeals to the senses . . . not to mention it's enticingly SEXY! This is a must read book for any aspiring gypsy. Emily Nies

GYPSY CITY—A New Beginning

The second novel of the series

Back to the bright lights of Broadway, the touring cast of Bravo Business from 'Gypsy Nights' does a new show for Owen Matthews. The saga of romance, intrigue, drama and suspense unfold as 'Centipede' makes its journey to the Great White Way. Jennifer Fournier

Ms. Fournier paints a vivid picture of the trials and triumphs of life as a 'Gypsy'. She puts her vast experience and knowledge of musical theatre into every chapter. Kim Carlander.

A dazzling all dance review winds its way to NYC with continued cast romantica all the way. Friendships, challenges and secret lives, side by side on stage and off. 'Gypsy City' captures Musical Theatre in the 60's as it really was; full of dreams, life, lots of sex and young love. A Great Story by and from one who really lived it. Sara Bartlett

Christine Fournier has found her muse and the right touch in bringing the world of Broadway theatre to life. She is able to successfully draw from experiences on the Broadway stage and magically tell the tales of the 'Gypsy' – the unsung hero/ine of the Broadway musical.
Kevin Rozman

Gypsy City is a unique and provocative look at the seldom seen world of the Broadway Gypsy. Christine Fournier writes from her own experience as a Broadway dancer to take the reader on a delightful and racy escapade. Tony Vierling

Another Winner . . . a page turner . . . has everything you would expect from a former Broadway performer. Ms. Fournier tells everything about the life of Gypsies when the curtain comes down. All the challenges, struggles, life on tour, heartbreaks and finally the success of a 'Smash Hit' and, of course, the Romance! I can't wait to read the next novel, Gypsy World, soon. Sue Saltarelli

Gypsy City! What can I say? Beautiful girls. Backstage intrigue. Sex and violence. All the things you need for a quiet, exciting read by the fire. I love this series. I can't get enough! Mike Tracy

I enjoyed reading Gypsy City, an amazing story about Broadway and the performers who make it unique. I couldn't put it down and am waiting for the next book. Gerri Testa

As a former Broadway and touring show performer, "Gypsy City" tells it like it was and, most likely still is. It brings to mind times of long rehearsals, try-out tours, friendships, affairs and romance. One wonders how the Gypsies did it? I still do. Thanks for the fond memories.
Bob Lambert

Gypsy City resonates with many of my own show-biz memories. It makes me long for the days when the process of getting an audition, auditioning itself, and negotiating things like life on the road was simpler and more direct than now. What great adventures we all had.
J. C. Hoyt

Gypsy City was even better than Gypsy Nights. More fun, more emotions and, more sex. Broadway stories don't get any better. Can't wait to read what happens next. Joel Thom

Want to know what it's like to be a Broadway dancer? If so, read Ms. Fournier's books! Christine guides the reader through training, auditions, and lives behind the scenes. Easy to read, hard to put down – readers become intimately involved with everyone putting on a Broadway show. A follow up to 'Gypsy Nights', this book continues stories of dancer's lives on and off stage. Challenges, drama, lots of romantica and suspense; it's all there to enjoy. Maris Edwards

Craving a titillating tale that lets your imagination run wild? Then Gypsy City is the book for you. Our beautifully crafted characters from Gypsy Nights are back! Only this time, the adventure is full of controversy, excitement, heartache, sensuality and, of course, sex!!! The gypsies are opening a new show on Broadway! Christine's writing sparkles as brightly as a Broadway marquee against the midnight sky. The erotica, lust and scandal are back, stronger than ever. So sit back, relax and enjoy the ride to - The Great White Way. Danielle Nelson

Gypsy City' proved to be as exciting as 'Gypsy Nights'. Mally and her dancer friends lead intense and complicated lives behind the curtains. It's a sexy wild ride. I'm looking forward to Ms. Fournier's next book in the series. Joan LeSiege

GYPSY
WORLD

May, 2014

For Paul Andrew :

Keep an dancing
to the muse!

Big Love,

Chrissy

GYPSY WORLD

Beyond Broadway

Christine Fournier

4 square books

Dedication

With great respect and love this book is dedicated to Tony Mordente, whose brilliant remounting of Jerome Robbins' West Side Story in Tokyo, Japan in 1964 is a treasured memory. His passion was a wonder to see, to emulate. His ability to pay it forward with clarity, conviction and knowledge of this musical theatre masterpiece was pure inspiration. For a young, aspiring dancer, it doesn't get any better than this!

Thank you, Tony

Author's Note

Writing a novel series based on persons and events in my 50 plus years in theatre has been a labor of love; challenging, emotional, energizing, as well as reflective. People often ask what my favorite project was on my show biz journey. I have to say my experience as a company member of *West Side Story*, produced in Tokyo, Japan in 1964 stands out. The cultural exposure, being touted and respected as an American artist was a unique and special experience. Performing a piece that embodies one of musical theatre's finest works was unforgettable.

Gypsy World is based on that experience.

Acknowledgment

There are individuals whose dedication, guidance, passion, support and unflinching belief in the theatrical process provides the light of creative art for those who follow. Their example and willingness to show me the way will never be forgotten. I hold each one with the deepest gratitude and love.

Among the many who personally shared their ability and skills, the spotlight falls on: Victor Stengal, Roger De Clercq, Jack Alwin, Loyce Houlton, Jerry Rumley, Larry Whiteley, Gary Shultz, Frank Whiting, Robert Moulton, JB Davidson, Neil Kenyon, Pat Carroll, David LeGrant, Abe Burrows, Frank Loesser, Cy Feuer, Dorothy Fields, Cy Coleman, Bob Fosse, Gwen Verdon, Neil Simon, Phil Friedman and Jerome Robbins.

Thank You Again—One and All.

The Centipede Casts

Broadway Company

Patricia Byrne	Joe Pinto
Catherine Andrews	Danny Bartlett
Fran Fairchild	Jim Sorenson
Cynthia Charles	Fred Norris
Kathy Olson	Ray Nordeen
Marcy White	Gerry Granger
Liz Gunther	Tim Bartel
Julie Jensen	Swing
Hal Royce	Swing

Japan Company

Mally Edwards	Chad Chapman
Nora Blake	Jeff Jenkins
Georgia Kemper	Tom Sutton
Neely Sorenson	Andy Wendt
Candy Roth	Jim Jaris
Betsy Allan	Kent Freeman
Daria Douglas	Jeff Boyd
Maddy Nichols	Swing
Terry Becker	Swing

Chapter One

A Foreign Affair

"Oh my God, look at the line, it's humungous," shouted Catherine, pointing up 45th Street. As she made her way through gridlock her side kick, Julie, tried to keep pace. Dozens of women were waiting outside the Royal Theater where *Centipede,* the biggest hit on Broadway, was playing. "Let's cross here," she said, jaywalking between cars and trucks, Julie in tow. They quickly joined the line-up.

The previous week, the trades had announced a remount of director-choreographer Owen Matthews' greatest hit, to go international for a two-month engagement in Tokyo. The project was rumored for weeks but, today, both union and open calls were being held. Hundreds of hopeful women would be put to the test for places in the new production and as replacements in New York.

While Catherine and Julie waited, discouragement reared its ugly head with each passing minute. The oppressive heat, nerves and long line of competitors, made the thought of being cast near impossible.

Catherine Andrews was from Milwaukee and new to New York. With solid technique and determination, she hoped to convince Mr. Matthews she was ready. Julie Jensen, a Detroit native, was also new to the city, hoping to land her first big job. Her technique was strong and she had an affable presence.

The line moved slowly; the wait seemed endless. "I don't know why I'm such a wreck," said Julie, combing her hair. "Have you ever auditioned for Owen Matthews?" Catherine smiled. Secretly, there was more on her mind than the audition. She met the famous director one night at the Taft Hotel bar. Owen, always the canny seducer, had taken her to bed, now insisting she audition. Proving herself worthy as a dancer would be a bonus. What better way to be with him?

Twenty-five minutes passed before the girls were given audition cards to complete. Dick Landry was at the stage door, replacing Griff Edwards, who was now organizing the Japanese remount. Having been trained by Griff for months, he was ready to take the reins.

"Please fill the card out and return to me," he said, handing them audition forms. "You'll dance in order of the number on the card. You may change downstairs, just follow the signs. Thanks."

The girls felt instant relief as they entered the air-cooled theater. Descending in the dim light, they passed others hurrying upstairs, nods of encouragement from some, cold stares from others. It would be a rumble of sorts -- only the most attractive and technically best would survive the cuts.

"God, I'm nervous! I didn't eat breakfast and my stomach is protesting," declared Julie, undressing. Her jeans and blouse stuck like glue as she pulled with great effort. Bringing a small hand towel was an asset.

Catherine wore a light sundress, allowing air to move under her skirt. She unbuttoned and slipped out. Peeling off her panties, she put on flesh-toned tights, followed by high cut trunks. Normally braless, she added one for comfort and support. A tight t-shirt followed, held in place by a wide belt. Slipping into socks and jazz shoes, she tied the laces with a double knot. A long or loose shoelace was an accident waiting to happen. The last step was to put her hair in a ponytail. When ready, both returned to the stage, quickly filled out cards and returned them to Dick.

Jonas Martin, Owen's assistant and male dance lead, was conducting the audition. Owen observed from the house, taking notes. He was reputed for clarifying his style nuances once the group was taught the combination.

"Good morning, ladies! Welcome to *Centipede!* You're auditioning for the international company. There may be a few spots open in New York as well. We are looking for those with solid dance technique who can act. We will be learning in groups of twelve and dancing in groups of three. Let's begin." The women took staggered positions, spaced so they could observe Jonas.

"Starting on the right foot, 4 single turns to stage right, step on right foot, *releve*, left leg extended in *arabesque*, arms developed and extended at angles to the sides. The counts are 1 and 2, 3 and 4, step 5, *releve* 6, hold 7 *developpe* of arms on 7 and 8. Repeat to the left. Third set of 8 begins with right leg down on 1, joining left to releve' and turning on 2, step out on 3, *pas de bouree* on 4, step on right, cross with left on 5, battement on 6 with right leg bring down, double pirouette inside on left leg 7 and 8. Hold. Last set begins on 1 with scoop leg forward from inside out with parallel leg landing in *plie* in jazz second on the right, repeating with left on 2, right on 3, and left on 4. Impulse up on 5, with a shrug, impulse on six, with a shrug, step 7 and 8 are step right, step left ending in a parallel *plie*. Arms are relaxed at your side during the jazz portion with a shrug of shoulders on after beat of 8. Then repeat the whole combination of 4 counts of 8. Let's run through it again. Ready? "5, 6, 7, 8!" The group, clearly overwhelmed, followed him, as he danced under tempo for their benefit.

"What bullshit!" A tall brunette in the front line was frustrated and vocal, causing Jonas to stop. "Is there something I can clarify?" Caught, she stammered, "It's a weird combination with so many ridiculous switches." Jonas glanced out, aware of Owen, who suddenly rose. There were murmurs and eyes glued to the director, as he moved down the aisle and up the stairs. "What is your name?" "Carol Cramer, Mr. Matthews." "Why are you here?" The air was thick as he waited. "I need a job, Mr. Matthews. Why does anyone put up with this crap?"

"Please don't put up with this crap another second, Miss Cramer. Thanks for stopping by." He gestured to Griff. "Mr. Edwards, please show Miss Cramer out. We have many other dancers to see this morning. Jonas, let's continue!"

Carol Cramer, shocked and rigid watched Griff approach. "Thank you for your time. Please follow me and to take your personal items." But Miss Cramer wasn't through. With fists raised, she lunged at Owen.

"You fucker, I know about you! Everyone knows," she yelled. Jonas was horrified. "Owen, look out!" Owen ducked too late, his cigarette airborne. Griff and Phillipe made a grab for Cramer, as she continued her outburst. "You degrade women, you asshole!" "Get that harridan out of here," yelled Owen. "Let me go, you God damned bullies!" She was strong, kicking and flailing to break their hold. As they carried her off stage and up the aisle, her screams continued. Security was called. The remaining dancers, embarrassed and shaken, waited. "Ladies, please excuse the interruption. Jonas, let's keep going!" Pulling himself together, Jonas began reviewing the combination. For the rest of the morning, scores of dancers auditioned, Owen's scrutiny in high gear. By noon most had been cut with the exception of Catherine Andrews, Julie Jensen, and four others. The girls hugged with enthusiasm. "Oh my God, we made it through the first cut," said Julie with relief.

"Wait until the final callback! You haven't seen anything yet. Personally, I'd rather have all my wisdom teeth pulled without Novocain," declared Catherine. Julie shrugged, happy to have passed the first elimination. "When do the men audition, do you know?" "Same deal. The open call is 10:00 tomorrow, the Equity at 2:00. Then everyone is called back the next day; women at 10:00, men at 2:00."

They changed and left the theatre. The heat hit them with a jolt as they walked along 8th Avenue. Julie suggested lunch, her blood sugar was plummeting. "Where do you want to eat? Want to try Mulfetta's? I hear they have the best Greek food in town." "Sure, why not?" The girls headed north looking for the restaurant. Spotting their sign, they crossed at the light and headed inside. The contrast of air-conditioning to the sultry air outside was encouraging. The host seated them by a window, handing menus to all; ice water followed moments later.

"Wow, does this cool air feel good," sighed Julie. "I hate heat and humidity. It was never this bad in Detroit." "It could get this bad in Milwaukee, near Lake Michigan and all. Downtown Chicago was worse, though. No escaping those skyscrapers holding the heat," said Catherine, taking a big swallow of water. "God, I'm thirsty!" They looked the menus over for specials. An attractive waiter approached.

"Good afternoon, ladies. Our lunch special is Mousaka. It comes with oven-roasted potatoes and a small Greek salad for $4.95. We also offer a choice of beef, chicken, or lamb Gyros, with a side of fries for $3.95." "I'd like a glass of Retsina to start," said Julie. "And for you, miss?" "I'll take a large Coke with extra ice, please." "Certainly, would you care to order now or later?"

"I'd like a large Greek salad," said Catherine, never overly hungry. "And for you?" "I'll take the chicken Gyros special with a side of fries, please," said Julie. "Thank you, ladies." As he left, he turned and smiled at Julie. "God, he's adorable! Did you notice his beautiful brown eyes and all that dark, wavy hair?" Catherine played with her fork, thinking only of Owen.

"I wonder if he's available, he's really sexy," whispered Julie. "Shouldn't you be thinking about nailing the callback rather than getting laid?" Julie shrugged. "I guess so, but I'm kind of horny. Say, what was that harangue about at the audition? It was pretty upsetting." "I have no idea," said Catherine, tossing it off. "Yes, but those accusations," insisted Julie. Catherine was uncomfortable, becoming defensive.

"Look, Mr. Matthews is the most important director-choreographer on Broadway, and extremely attractive. Women fight for his favors. She was an exception, a total bitch and obviously twisted!" "Well, I hope he hires us. We need jobs and doing *Centipede* would be a tremendous credit!" "We'll know in a couple of days, so be prepared. It's going to be the toughest audition ever." "Imagine going to Japan! I hear the Japanese revere American artists. What an honor it would be," added Julie.

The waiter returned with their orders. "Will there be anything else?" Julie smiled and winked, "We're fine for now, I think. We just need a check, please." The waiter tore the bill from his pad, placing it on the table. "Come again, ladies. It's been my pleasure serving you!" Julie couldn't resist. "What's your name?" Catherine gave her a kick under the table.

"I'm Nicholas. Stop in anytime Monday-Thursday, between 11:00 and 6:00. Hope to see you again." "God, Julie, how obvious can you get?" Julie giggled, taking a large bite.

'Obvious when I need to be,' she thought, chewing happily. Catherine, suddenly hungry, picked up her fork. "Well, let's eat and recover. We have 24 hours, Okay?"

"Agreed! Whatever happens now is anyone's guess!" Lunch continued.

During the break Owen and his team huddled, sorting through dance cards. Pulling Carol Cramer's information, Jonas shuddered. "Where did that piece of work come from?" "She looked familiar," remarked Dick, who had worked with many dancers over the years. "Boy, she's trouble on the hoof for sure," added Jonas. "Relax, gentleman. On occasion we stumble across a crazy," said Owen, unruffled. Sorting through the forms he spotted Catherine Andrew's name. Smiling, he pulled her card.

"I think we should strongly consider Catherine Andrews. She's capable enough to replace Mally, while she's in Japan." "Which one is she?" There had been so many dancers to look at that morning Jonas was cross-eyed. "The striking redhead with legs up to, well you know. She's perfect for us. The others were good, but she's exceptional." A knowing look passed between Jonas and Phillipe. "We still have union dancers at 2:00." Griff continued to pull cards of those kept for call-backs. "We'll need seven and seven, plus two swings to cover in Japan. Most of our original ensemble will stay put. We'll have to temporarily replace Mally, Chad, Nora, and Jeff."

"Keep in mind that Kaplan and Maggli are strongly considering the first national company of *Centipede* some time next spring. We will need dancers, so be on the lookout for potentials."

"What's Miss Byrne's status?" "She has decided to stay on until mid January when her contract ends," said Griff. "Well, it's a perfect opportunity to watch Miss Andrews and likely replace Miss Byrne if she proves herself." 'Catherine will soon be mine, 24/7,' he mused, already charting his course.

Following lunch, the group returned for the Equity call. Dick was again at his post, admitting only dancers showing union cards. Owen and Griff conferred in the house while Jonas and Phillipe warmed up. The long line of women waited eagerly to take a crack at the demanding work awaiting them.

Chapter 2

Decisions

The following day, the open call for male dancers began at 10:00. As with female dancers the day before, at least 100 non union men lined up in unbearable heat and humidity waiting to dance, to be seen by Owen Matthews. It was not unheard of to hire an unknown, but with this crowd, individuals had to be exceptional technicians, attractive, have the right 'look,' and endurance to survive Owen and his razor-sharp scrutiny.

Jonas placed the men in groups of 12. Phillipe took his position downstage for them to follow. In the past year, he had refined his technique, emulating Owen's style perfectly. Jonas taught a combination suitable for male dynamics, including leaps, turns, and slides -- heavy on jazz and ballet adagio. Owen looked for and selected dancers who could handle contrasting styles, the more versatile the better. Through both calls, there were several standouts. The level of talent had improved in a year. He kept at least two dozen men for callbacks and let the rest go. It was a long day, but encouraging to have such quality performers trying out.

Following the audition, Owen invited his team to the Taft for drinks. It was still hot and sticky, with no change in the forecast. Ducking into the air conditioned lobby, they entered the lounge. Happy hour was in full swing, but they managed to find a corner table. Griff arrived accompanied by Dick. Like shadows, Jonas and Phillipe stuck close to Owen, who immediately ordered scotch on the rocks. Dick chose beer on tap, Phillipe, a Dubonnet chilled and Griff, his usual, a vodka martini straight up with a twist. "I need a beer, preferably a Heineken," Jonas mumbled, easing his way into a chair. His hamstrings protested with the slightest move and his mouth was dry as cotton. "After today, camels have nothing on me!" One look at Jonas and Dick could relate. "A little dry and weary, are we?" He, too, felt the effects of aging in a youthful dance culture. "Our bodies start protesting at 30 and are relentless at reminding us we're getting older." "You're telling me." Jonas removed his shoes and began rubbing his toes gingerly. "I've hired an old man," said Owen, needling his assistant. The director was still fresh, even after the long day. He was eager to cast both productions.

"Boss, you never cease to amaze me. You must have a secret elixir somewhere. You're holding out on us!" Owen shrugged and pulled out a cigarette, taking a deep drag. Work and sex created a need for nicotine and booze, his trusted allies. "You've been great these past two days, Dick. You've handled the masses like you've stage managed for years. Jonas, your execution is nothing short of miraculous and Phillipe, you're a model dancer. Christ, we must have seen every out-of-work dancer in the five boroughs!" "I couldn't get over the numbers! They must have doubled in a year," remarked Jonas, knowingly. Owen continued. "The callback will tell the tale. We have to hire the finest of the bunch."

"I believe we've called back at least 60 men and women, nothing short of amazing," said Griff, reaching into his briefcase. He handed over audition cards. "Here are the callbacks. Do you want to take a look?" Owen looked at each card carefully, his comment codes written on the upper right hand corner of each. Dick looked over his shoulder, puzzled by the abbreviations. "What do they mean?" Jonas clarified. "The boss uses a code to evaluate each dancer. It saves time and keeps our assessment confidential. It's a great system." Dick wasn't letting up. "Please explain, will you?" "Jonas, go ahead," said Owen.

"Well, LOT means Long of Tooth. ALITL means A Little Light In The Loafers. WT means Weak Technique. DU, Definitely Unattractive; NFTS, Not For This Show; and my personal favorite, NOMS, Not On My Stage. Laughter ensued as the group sipped their drinks. "Short and sweet," remarked Dick, settling back. Griff chuckled, "If it lightens the load, it works for me." Owen insisted on another round as he reviewed the candidates, gathering opinions from his team. It had been a demanding two days for all. The final callback would bring decisions affecting the fate of newcomers and experienced dancers alike.

Next morning, the stage filled with those waiting to catch Owen's eye and approval, approval that would lead to employment. First to be tested were the combined women, selected from the open and Equity auditions, now on a level playing field. Promptly at 10:00, a group of dancers, each technically able and hoping to be cast, lined up, ready for Jonas' counts. The air was electric with anticipation and dread.

As Jonas led each group, muscles tensed, sweat flew, bodies stretched and twisted into impossible positions, making breathing loud and labored. A cacophony of curses, gasps, sighs and whispers underscored the effort, Jonas' voice breaking through the activity. The combination at the preliminary audition was now doubled in counts and technically more difficult; the detail and nuances, pure Owen. Bodies stretched, balance and control precisely noted. Double and triple *pirouettes* had to be perfect, as many as possible. Each gypsy was expected to perform with technical brilliance, including subtext, the underlying emotion let loose as they jumped, twirled, and drove through count after count. As each group danced, some were cut immediately, while others were asked to wait and repeat the combination. It was agony to stand and watch the competition, waiting with dread, but hoping to remain.

That afternoon, it was the men's turn. Around the perimeter of the stage and in the wings, male dancers gathered to wait. They were there with one purpose, to make it into Owen's world.

Dancers of every description ran the gamut. A definite asset was to possess a built-in sensuality, beyond looks and technique. Owen's reputation was controversial and uncompromising. Never had there been a director-choreographer on Broadway more sought after. To be cast by Matthews was to 'make it.'

With auditions finally over, the team gathered. Who would they choose? Attempting to put together the best ensemble was first and foremost in their minds.

Chapter 3

Two Centipedes

The casting was complete. Those hired were exceptional, chosen from heavy competitors, pleasing Owen and his team. On October first, the Japanese company would depart, rehearsals commencing within a day or two upon arrival in Tokyo. Those hired for the New York production would begin two weeks before the departing cast left town. Joe Pinto would assist Owen. He needed Joe's experience, technique and understanding of his demanding and distinct style. Jonas would remount the Tokyo production, with assistance from Phillipe. They looked forward to experiencing the Japanese culture together.

Catherine was cast to replace Mally and cover Pat. Catherine's pal, Julie, was hired as swing in Nora's place. Julie had a generic look for the show and was a strong technician, essential for a swing dancer. The men replacing Chad, Jeff, Jonas and Phillipe had to equal their predecessors. Owen's keen eyes had chosen Danny Bartlett, Ray Nordeen, Gerry Granger, Fred Norris, and Hal Royce to fill the bill, Hal as swing. Fred Norris would take Dick's spot, now that he was filling Griff's shoes until the end of the year.

The Japanese *Centipede* required ten newcomers including five men and five women, plus two swings. Making the right choice was painstaking. The Tokyo cast was headed by Mally, Nora, Chad, and Jeff, including Tom Sutton, Andy Wendt, Jim Jaris, Kent Freeman, Jeff Boyd, and Terry Becker, as swing. The chosen women were Georgia Kemper, Neely Sorenson, Candy Roth, Betsy Allan, Daria Douglas and Maddy Nichols, swing. They were all exceptional, as good as any, representing the finest in musical theatre.

For the next week, the atmosphere was heightened by super-charged activity at the Kaplan-Maggli offices. The newly hired signed contracts and were provided specifics regarding passports, inoculations and details of living abroad. During late fall and early winter, Tokyo and New York had similar climates. The company would be advised packing and weight limits for the long flight to Japan.

Broadway replacements signed contracts; eager and psyched over their good fortune. Imagine, being cast in a hit show, added to the mix by Owen Matthews himself.

Catherine waited by the phone, nervous and uncertain about her fate until Dick's phone call days following the callback. In his new position, Dick was required to notify the hired. His voice was pleasant, but professional as she answered. "Miss Andrews?" "This is!" "This is Dick Landry from Kaplan-Maggli calling. It gives me pleasure to welcome you to the New York cast of *Centipede!*" Catherine's voice bubbled with enthusiasm as she heard the words. "Oh my God, thank you! Thank you very much!" "You're welcome. Please come to sign your standard contract this week, as rehearsals will begin September 15th. You will be rehearsed for two weeks and go into the show on October 1st. Kaplan-Maggli is located in the Brill Building, 1650 Broadway, on the 15th floor. We're open from 9 to 6. Do you have any questions?" "What is the cross street, Mr. Landry?" "We're at 49th Street, west side of Broadway. The Broadway IRT line will take you to the 50th Street stop." "Thanks. I'll come in Wednesday." "Very good, we'll look forward to seeing you. Congratulations!" A dial tone was heard. A minute passed and the phone jangled. Catherine picked up quickly. "Hello?" Julie's voice was ebullient as she spoke.

"Cath, it's me! I've been cast! I can't believe it! Have you heard?" "I just got a call! I'm signing Weds. Do you want to meet at the producer's office and then have lunch?" "That sounds perfect! Cath, they've offered me the swing position! Do you think that's good?" "Are you kidding? It's only the biggest endorsement for a dancer imaginable! You were singled out because of your ability. The swing job is by far the most challenging! Wow, congrats!" "I'll see you at 11:00, the day after tomorrow. Do you have the address for Kaplan-Maggli?" "Yep, it's in the Brill Building, 49th and Broadway, 15th floor. See you!" "I can't wait!" After hanging up, Catherine winced as she stretched out some noticeable kinks. She needed to get moving and more than eager to show Owen her ability beyond the bedroom. Soon, she'd be learning his show, *Centipede*. The prospect was a thrill beyond imagining!

Monday night was the start of the gypsy work week. Pat Byrne had slept in that morning, missing her roommates, Jonas and Phillipe. She was eager to hear some good gossip, but one glance at the clock and she'd missed them. 'Damn, it's almost noon! No doubt they're doing errands.' She'd have to wait for audition details. The boys had been totally absorbed. There'd been no time to catch-up at home or the theater. She rose, feeling tight muscles protesting. One day off seemed hardly enough, considering the demanding workout eight shows a week. She reached for her bathrobe and padded to the bathroom. The need to pee was urgent after a long sleep and relief swept over her as she sat and let go.

Sunday was spent with her lover, Blaine Courtman. Today he was on his way to Montreal to seal another deal. Amazing! Blaine, a consummate business mogul, was an exceptional entrepreneur heading Courtman Enterprises, a company started by his grandfather, run by his father and passed on to him. The company manufactured shoes sold domestically and internationally, but Blaine didn't stop there. His avid interest in musical theatre had brought them together the previous year when *Bravo Business* played several locations he had holdings in. Later, an opportunity to invest in *Centipede* came through his millionaire friend and colleague, Gregory Morgan of Houston and he jumped at it.

Now he was back in Pat's life and they were inseparable. At the time of their meeting, she was head-over-heels in love with Owen, Blaine unaware of their relationship. He was no match for the director, in spite of his many qualities. When Pat ended their affair abruptly, Blaine was deeply hurt.

Owen was brilliant, compelling, complex and fatally glamorous. Pat ignored the talk of Owen's reputation with women, the repeated warnings falling on deaf ears. She became so invested in him that being taken for granted never registered. She continued to wait for his token calls, his sporadic visits and the intoxicating lovemaking he provided, leaving her totally addicted to his attention and favor. He was like a drug she desperately needed. She was boastful he had chosen her as his lover. However, she constantly worried about other women, going through periods of doubt and loneliness.

Owen's clever navigation of their affair proved beneficial to his ego and libido. His Pygmalion approach provided a career boost for Pat, positioning her in the starring role of *Centipede*. However, Owen got careless, his libido overriding his common sense. He became intrigued with Stephanie McNeil, a *New York Times* reporter. His lustful musings over the coltish young woman became intriguing and ultimately one he couldn't pass on. An intense physical affair began. As it continued, he slowly backed away from Pat, his neglect leaving her obsessing. In time she discovered his infidelity accidentally and was devastated. She now had the daunting task of trying to let him go, but had an emotional breakdown, causing her to take a brief leave-of-absence from *Centipede*. Owen's repeated apologies for his reprehensible behavior came too late. She vowed to move on given time and support from Jonas, Phillipe and Mally.

By coincidence Blaine Courtman returned to her world as principal investor of the show. He had never fallen out-of-love with her, but was resistant at first to rekindle their relationship. He had been torn up over her rejection, but couldn't deny his deep love for her in the end. They started over, establishing a new level of intimacy and trust. With Blaine's advice and support Pat decided to honor her *Centipede* contract until the end of her first year. She planned to give notice mid January, seeking new opportunities. Owen chafed at her audacious plan, her ungrateful attitude. After all, look what he'd done for her. In spite of his protestations, Pat was resolute both professionally and personally, determined to build a life with Blaine. It was time to move forward.

Chapter 4

Talent Reset

The Kaplan-Maggli staff observed many new faces coming through the door for the next few days. Appointment times were scheduled, contracts signed, an exciting fall of 1965 was about to begin. On Wednesday, Catherine and Julie met at the production office as planned and signed their contracts. After departing Kaplan-Maggli, they walked up 8th Avenue to Mulfetta's, the Greek restaurant they had tried the first day of auditions. It was noon and the place was crowded as they entered. A hostess came toward them, her demeanor warm and welcoming.

"Good afternoon, Ladies. Welcome to Mulfetta's. Please follow me!" They were led to a corner table, and handed menus. A bus boy stopped to fill their water glasses. Julie looked around furtively. Leaning close to Catherine, she whispered, "Have you spotted that cute waiter from before? I think his name is Nicholas!" "Honestly, Julie, how can you possibly be interested in a waiter? We're about to work for the greatest director on Broadway, for crying out loud!" Julie shrugged and took a sip of water. As she swallowed, she looked up to see Nicholas walking toward her. The water suddenly caught and went down the wrong way, causing her to cough loudly. Nicholas noticed and came to her aid. "Are you all right, Miss?" Slowly Julie regained control, her embarrassment covered by the napkin she held over her mouth. "She's fine, thanks," said Catherine with a grin. Give her a minute, will you?" The waiter smiled. "May I tell you our specials today?" "Yes, please," said Catherine glancing over at Julie, who by now was somewhat composed, but red in the face.

"Today we're serving a choice of Spanakopita with a small Greek salad or a Chicken Gyros with a side of Hummus, both for $3.95." Julie's eyes never left his. "I would like the Chicken Gyros. Could I get a side of fries with that?" "I'm sure I can do that for you, and would you like a beverage?" "Yes, please! I'll have a large Coke, extra ice." "And for you?" "I'll have the Spanakopita with a small Greek salad, no capers and ice tea." "Certainly, I will be back with your beverages, shortly." As he turned to go, Julie reached out and touched his sleeve. "It's very nice to see you again, Nicholas." He hurried away, slightly shaken. Catherine sat watching, bemused at her friend's lack of guile.

"You know Julie, in his culture the men are aggressive, not the women. I think you shook him up!" "Oh, I hope so! I like him! He's polite, sweet and very sexy!" Catherine rolled her eyes. "Honestly Julie, you're going to get into trouble, I swear." "Well if I do, I hope it's with him," she giggled. Nicholas returned with their drinks. "Your lunches should be up soon," he announced, gazing at Julie. She winked, causing him to blush. He returned to the kitchen. Catherine played with the basket of complimentary Pita bread, finally taking a piece, its warmth and texture, a delight.

"So, let's say this Nicholas takes a fancy to you. What then?" "Are you kidding? I'd love it! The problem is how to get him to call without being too obvious," said Julie, glumly. "Well, I can probably help. When we get the check, I'll simply write your phone number on it."

"Seriously, you'd do that for me?" "Of course, what do you think?" "Why aren't you interested in him? He's adorable!" "He's not my type, Julie. I've never been into ethnic men. I like the wasp brand; slightly older, worldly and talented," she said, picturing Owen. "Oh no, you don't have a crush on Mr. Director, do you? What a mistake that would be," said Julie, remembering the scene at the audition.

"Oh for heaven's sake, no," said Catherine, empathically. "I'm thrilled to be working for him, nothing more," she lied. Nicholas returned, placing their orders down. "Will there be anything else, ladies?" "I'll take the check, please," said Catherine, casting a knowing glance at Julie. "Very good," I'll be back in a moment." The girls ate heartily. The activity around them became a cacophony of servers ordering, cooks yelling, bus boys clearing, conversations bouncing and traffic noises underscoring the scene. The girls finished and waited for Nicholas. He returned, placing the check on the table. He hurried off. Reaching into her bag, Catherine grabbed her wallet and a pen. Carefully, she wrote Julie's name and number on the bottom of the check, placing cash on top, including a generous tip. "The rest is up to you two," she whispered, a grin on her face. "Come on, let's walk off lunch!" Julie caught Nicholas glancing in her direction as she followed Catherine to the door. Waving, she smiled and noted his smile. "We'll see," she thought, hopefully.

Owen's creative team was psyched, ready for the opportunity to remount *Centipede* for Japan and add new talent to the New York production. The staging was already in place, tried and true, so it was a matter of setting and teaching the new talent. Director-choreographers and their assistants thrived on this process. The work was all part of their wiring and what they lived for most.

The fourth floor of Dance Arts was bustling with dancers arriving, changing, sipping coffee and taking tokes of nicotine while getting acquainted. It was September 15th and newcomers to the New York production were ready to begin rehearsals. Dick Landry took a head count, noting names and faces that were unfamiliar, at least for the moment. Joe Pinto arrived and squashed out his cigarette, taking a last minute swallow of coffee from a cardboard cup. He was psyched to be assisting Owen, his long-time mentor in the business. He was every bit the seasoned gypsy, with his rock hard body and attractive looks. Setting his bag down at the front of the room, he greeted Frank Dugan, already seated at the piano. Frank would provide music for Owen, who would have no other. Frank had been his music guy for the past ten years. As the gypsies were called into the studio, tension tinged the room, anticipation heightened. Who among them would prove worthy of Owen's selection? Who would be favored? The rehearsal would bring answers as soon as they began. Now assembled, Joe faced the group.

"Good morning, ladies and gentlemen. I'm Joe Pinto, Mr. Matthews' assistant on this project. I'm a member of the New York cast and have been doing this show for the past 11 months. I will be teaching the *Centipede* choreography. First you will learn the staging as a group, then we'll break down into couples and the positions you will fill. When I call your name please introduce yourself and give us a short version of your experience.

"Catherine Andrews?" Catherine stood and smiled. She was stunning, svelte and quite tall, with wavy red hair that hung down her back, grazing her behind. Freckles popped out over her cheeks and her azure blue eyes were a knockout. "I'm Catherine from Milwaukee, Wisconsin. I've been in New York three months and have been auditioning and taking classes mostly. I've joined Equity in order to be in this show and I'm very excited to be here." "Thank you, Catherine, or do you prefer Cathy?" Catherine wrinkled her nose. "Catherine, please!" "Julie Jensen." Julie stood and looked at everyone. "I'm Julie from Detroit and this is really thrilling. I'm told I will swing the show and I'm ready to get to work! Thanks!"

Names were called, each dancer introducing him or herself. It was a great icebreaker and relaxing for all. They were an attractive group. Five men were new to the show, each young and fit, a variety of looks. Danny Bartlett, Ray Nordeen, and Gerry Granger had experience with at least one national tour credit and some off Broadway work. Fred Norris was fresh out of Oklahoma, with a twang to match. He was short and solid, with a boyish demeanor and loaded with charm. The chosen swing, Hal Royce was the most experienced; having two Broadway shows under his belt and considerable TV credits. Joe noted he was best looking of all. Joe was always on the prowl, but not today and not for two-weeks while he was assisting. Once the show opened he'd check out the new blood, see who was available and get some action. New blood was always a welcome change.

"Ok, Gang! We'll do a warm-up with Frank Dugan our accompanist until Owen arrives. Today and the rest of this week you'll be learning choreography. Next week we'll be fitting you in, matching you up our New York regulars and placing you in permanent spots throughout. Most important is to learn Owen's choreography and style as quickly as possible. The work is most challenging, but once mastered, you'll be among Broadway's best. Are there any questions? No? Ok, let's begin. Please spread out and find your own space. Frank?"

The music began, a Gershwin piece filling the room with melodious, sumptuous sound. Joe led the warm-up as dancers stretched, reaching through the space, moving with incomparable strength, ideal and fit bodies in full throttle. Suddenly the door opened and Owen walked in. All eyes shifted and followed him to the front of the room. He moved like a Panther; effortless, fluid, his desert boots skimming the floor. He was dressed all in black. Most intriguing was the stub of cigarette tucked in the corner of his mouth, the ash defying gravity. "Good morning! Welcome to my world," he chuckled, observing his new charges; all fit and ready for action. As he looked around the room he spotted Catherine Andrews. His approval was obvious as he smiled and continued. To the group, he was every bit the brilliant, glamorous director-choreographer, but to Catherine, he was much more. She shivered slightly, remembering their sexual interludes. Now she was eager to prove herself worthy of his work.

"Ladies and gentlemen, Mr. Pinto will be teaching you the staging of *Centipede* for the next week. Week two you will be placed with your partners in the production. The originals are hard to beat, having survived my demands and expectations. They are brilliant, so naturally I expect the same from you. I expect nothing less. We have two female replacements and five new men. Your counterparts are heading to Japan for a two-month engagement in Tokyo. When they return the first of the year, they will regain their former spots and you will be considered for our first national company. Others may decide to move on. For now, let's get started. I look forward to seeing how you become an integral part of our *Centipede*. Joe?" "Thanks, Owen, let's begin!" Owen smiled and walked toward the door. "Catch you later, gang," he tossed confidently. Glancing at Catherine, he winked, glanced at his watch and made his exit. Catherine's heart accelerated, watching him leave. 'Stay in the moment, Catherine,' she reminded herself.

Joe began laying out the opening number, a languid adagio, with repeated patterns by each couple. Hal Royce stood at the back learning the men's choreography. He was responsible for knowing every position in the number. Julie Jensen was expected to do the same as the women's cover. For a swing, it was critical remembering choreography with accuracy. One had to be able to transition from section to section following set traffic patterns throughout. A misstep could create chaos for the regulars, who performed the routines eight times a week. A swing position was challenging due to variation and placement from dancer to dancer. Owen instinctively had picked these two, with input from Jonas, who had a knack for spotting the most reliable and technically strong. Both Catherine and Julie had the opportunity to try lifts with all the men. Trust was a major component of Owen's staging, which demanded technical perfection, but finding ease in execution amongst partners. The work was intimate. Bringing a room full of strangers together with the same purpose took time and immense effort from all.

At six, Joe called it quits for the day, having blocked and set the opening and tropical numbers. He was pleased with the group's progress and liked what he saw. One fellow was wildly attractive and Joe, having all he could do to stay on track, had to keep a business-like pose. Danny Bartlett was every gay boy's wet dream with dark, Mediterranean looks, well cut muscles and a package too generous to ignore. As the studio began to clear, Joe picked up his gear. Making his way to the change room, he walked in and noticed several guys undressed. Danny was a standout, totally naked, his obvious attribute flaccid but promising. Joe feigned nonchalance, but was clearly distracted as he tried to undress. He felt awkward, like a school boy acting on his first sexual impulse. Imagine, the guy with the most notches on his belt, behaving like Little Lord Fauntleroy! Slipping out of dance pants, he felt a tight squeeze, a large, persistent boner. 'Damn!' Slowly turning his back, he removed his dance belt. He was horny, in need of relief. 'I'd like to nail this kid,' he thought carefully, slipping on his shorts and jeans. But reason took over. After all, he was Owen's right hand. 'Maybe another time,' he thought, slightly annoyed. The room emptied, leaving them alone. Trying conversation, Joe smiled as he sat and slipped on his socks and shoes. "So how was your first day?" Danny looked at him with a grin. "It's a ball breaker, man! Owen is brilliant, but holy shit, this stuff's difficult!" "You looked great. You work hard. I like that in a newcomer," he offered. Danny approached and sat next to him. Joe's breath slowed, his heart beating wildly. "How long have you been at this?" 'Christ he's young,' Joe mused, placing discarded rehearsal clothes in his bag. "I've been in the business for many years, worked a lot of shows." "You look good for an older guy," said Danny, offering a compliment. Joe frowned. "How old do you think I am?"

"I'd guess 28. How close am I?" Joe grinned. "Boy, you're in the will! I just turned 35 and believe me, I feel every year. I've been dancing since I was 20!" "That's impressive. I'm 24 and here in New York for three years. I did a tour when I was 21, and some off-Broadway stuff, nobody ever heard of. This job is a windfall. I'm hoping to get married next year, so I need to save money." Joe's heart sank. 'Shit, he's straight!' Without hesitation, he rose, closed his bag and excused himself. "Well, have a good evening, Danny. See you in the morning." "Yeah, see you and thanks for the feedback."

Joe entered the elevator, feeling disappointed and painfully horny, as he headed to the lobby. Walking up the street he located a phone booth and called his service. He had three messages. One from his sister in Des Moines, another from his dental office confirming a cleaning the following week and, a delightful surprise! Jordan Hendrix was back in town! Jordan dated back to high school, his 'coming out' boyfriend during his senior year. They rekindled their passion when Joe played Des Moines the previous year in *Bravo Business*. Jordan had an exquisite token wife and two perfect kids, living the straight life. He showed up backstage with his family in tow, when he learned Joe was in town. Secretly craving action, he invited Joe to lunch in his company's hotel suite. Joe willingly went along, taking advantage of Jordan's insatiable libido and need to be out. The meetings continued daily and as the week came to a close, Joe moved on and Jordan returned home, miserable. His ruse continued for a while as the straight, successful, corporate executive with a picture perfect family. However, the pain to his psyche was unbearable, his love for Joe Pinto, all-consuming.

Now, a year later Jordan was free, having come clean to his wife. The divorce was settled quickly, quietly, with Jordan agreeing to a hefty child support. The matter of Mr. and Mrs. Jordan Hendrix was closed. Jordan was now fully 'out,' accepting a job in Boston, a new career start. He would have easy access to New York. Joe Pinto was there.

The rest of the week's rehearsals continued. The new cast members learning each number under Joe's deft teaching. The group was strong as ensemble and individuals. Catherine proved a viable replacement for Mally, while Danny Bartlett proved indispensible, an obvious choice to fill Chad's spot. Chad had been Mally's partner since the beginning of *Centipede* and would continue in Japan. Joe would replace Jonas in New York, partnering Pat. Tim and Liz, Jim and Fran would remain partners, while Ray, Gerry, and Fred would be assigned to work with Kathy, Marcy and Cynthia. By Friday noon the entire show was taught. After lunch, the gypsies returned, hopeful that Owen would be pleased with their work. After all, hadn't he hand-picked each? They had already passed muster!

There was stillness in the large studio of Dance Arts. The newcomers warmed up, stretching their bodies, anticipation growing, nerves on edge. The only sound was an occasional deep breath punctuated by a sigh, soft murmur, an occasional whispered exchange. As Joe called them to their feet, the door opened and Owen walked in, the familiar cigarette tucked in the corner of his mouth. His lithe form was clothed in his usual black, a silver whistle hanging from his neck. It was rumored that when he blew the whistle, even the most experienced dancer would stop abruptly, awaiting his praise or distain. Conferring with Joe for a moment, he turned to face his new recruits. "Gang, Joe tells me you've worked very hard. Just for the record, chorus work is an exact science, no room for error. I want no less than your 150%. So let's see what you've got." "Let's begin with the opening. You ladies will run through the staging with each man, working the adagio. Let's start with Catherine and Danny, followed by Julie with Hal," instructed Joe. The girls took their places and waited for Frank. As the first notes of music flowed across studio space, the first couple danced the intensely erotic choreography. Following in tandem after 16 bars of music, Julie and Hal repeated the same routine, moving to another spot on the floor. The others watched transfixed, waiting their turn. Owen felt pleasure, gazing at Catherine, taking in every part of her. She was now the woman in his world, giving him a transfusion of inspiration. Lifting Catherine high above his head, Danny carefully positioned her body to slide down his, a slow descent that required excruciating control. They were perfect together, as though they'd been doing the routine for months. Julie and Hal kept up, utilizing each other to produce the lifts that Owen created. When the four had finished, Ray and Gerry took over, followed by Fred and Hal, to once again partner the girls. When they all had an opportunity to run the piece, Owen stopped.

"You are all working it well. Thank you! Joe, you will continue trying each man with the girls through the rest of the choreography. I've seen enough to know they're on track." Joe nodded.

A hand went up. Hal, the male swing, had a question. "Owen, will Julie and I be able to partner with some of the regulars next week, or will the time be strictly used for the blend of New York regulars and replacements?" "Good question, Hal. Next week is strictly placement and running the numbers. Judging from what I just saw, you are ahead of the game. I trust you'll be ready when the need arises." Joe jumped in. "You two are on top of it! The swing position is crucial and you've already proven you can handle it. The true test is going on at a moment's notice. You'll be fine. Everybody take five." While the gypsies took a break, Owen, Joe and Dick huddled.

"This is an outstanding bunch. They have to be to replace our kids going to Japan," remarked Owen. "I couldn't agree more," said Dick, enjoying his new post. Owen cast a look of approval in his direction. "How does the former hoofer like his new job?" "I'm enjoying it," said Dick. "It's giving these old bones a much-needed rest!" Owen smiled knowingly, thinking back to the day he stopped performing. "There comes a time when you have to throw in the towel. The body resists and too soon." "Agreed," chimed Joe, "But these bones are still going strong, at least right now!" Dick and Owen chuckled. "Well, until you start creaking, Joe, have at it. It's nice to have you aboard." "Thanks, Owen. I like teaching. Frankly, I'm surprised I do, but it's proving a direction I'd like to go. "Great! We're close to an agreement to remount a national tour of *Centipede* in spring. The producer boys are making noises to that end. When plans solidify, I will need your help." Joe brightened. "I'll be right here, Owen. You can count on it."

"Dick, call them back. I want to run the rest of the show with the recruits. Joe, please make sure they're solid for next week's rehearsal with the veterans." Dick headed for the door. Within seconds the group was back, ready to continue. Owen excused himself and smiled as he passed Catherine, about to enter the studio. Pulling her aside, he spoke softly. "Baby, stop by tonight. Come up about 6:30. I want to show my appreciation." "I'll be there, Owen." As the elevator descended, Owen pulled out a cigarette. Everything was working to his satisfaction. The newly-hired gypsies looked good, Catherine was his, on and off stage and once Pat's contract ended, Catherine would move to the top spot. 'Out with the old, in with the new,' he mused.

Chapter 5

Star Quality

Owen was high on Catherine. Her beauty, body and solid technique were all pluses. Touting her for a star turn would be a snap, his control of her offstage, a given. He'd messed up royally with Pat. He regretted their break-up, but after all, he couldn't be faithful and she expected too much. Warning her to not make demands on him had proven futile. She was needy, possessive. Eventually, along came reporter Stephanie McNeil; too big for her britches, an irresistible challenge. Becoming acquainted during an interview, a chance meeting later in a bar proved her britches could easily come off. She proved a terrific dalliance; sex with no demands, becoming the catalyst to his unraveling relationship with Pat. 'An intriguing bitch and a hot fuck,' he recalled, remembering her coltish persona. When she moved on to someone else, he took offense, ending the affair. No, Catherine was his inspiration now, the woman in his world.

At 6:30, the buzzer rang. 'There's my baby,' he thought as he lowered the lights. In seconds he was at the door, viewing perfection standing in the hall. Catherine took his breath away. He reached for her, drawing her inside. "Oh, Baby, come here," he murmured. Unbuttoning her jacket, he slipped it off, admiring the view. "You're beautiful, Baby."

Leading her into the living room, he stopped and pulled her close. His mouth met hers instantly, as his tongue explored gently. Her sweet breath held him, intoxicating his senses. Pausing for a moment, he motioned for her to sit and walked to the bar. In seconds, he was preparing their drinks. He favored scotch, Glenfiddich, which he poured into a small glass filled with ice. Next, he selected a chilled bottle of Pouilly Fuisse, his favorite. Taking a wine glass from under the bar, he filled it. 'Getting her relaxed is the first step,' he thought with confidence. Catherine sat nearby, her lush, red hair falling loosely over her shoulders. She was soft, voluptuous, her body a smorgasbord of tantalizing possibilities. Owen walked to the coffee table and set the drinks down. Sitting, he kissed her again, this time with more fervency, like a lost lover returning from war. "Baby, I've been waiting for this." Handing her the wine, he took his drink, enjoying the smoky liquid. Catherine, savoring the moment, sipped, her eyes never leaving his. "Oh Owen, I've missed you," she murmured. He moved closer. "So, how do you like dancing my choreography? Does it feel good on your body?" His hand began tracing her face, moving toward her mouth. Dipping a finger in her wine, he was playful, allowing her a taste. "God, you're so sweet!" He chugged his scotch, then took her glass. "I can't wait to have you, let's skip the shower."

Catherine's heart pounded as he carefully removed her sweater. Gently easing her down, he unbuttoned her jeans and slid them off slowly. The sound of her gasps turned him on, his shaft already hard. She was bare-chested, adding to his pleasure. Removing her panties, he caught a whiff of her fragrance. She was open, moist and ready. Moving his hands up her legs, he paused at her mound, playfully twisting her pubic hair. Gracefully, he began what pleased him most. Putting his finger inside her, moving in and out, he watched with lustful relish. Her hips moved back and forth, as she moaned her pleasure. He stopped for a moment, a smirk growing. "Do you like this? Do you want more? Beg me, Baby!" As he taunted, he removed his jeans. Like a master showman, he ran his hand over his erection, adding to the show. She was frenzied, wild with want. "Yes, yes, come inside me," she cried. Without pause, Owen braced himself and entered what he considered heaven. Colliding in massive climax, they rolled and pitched, driven in their desire to be consumed. The release was total. As the moment subsided, the two lay breathing heavily, coated in sweat. "Oh, Baby, you're the best," he whispered, playing with her hair. He felt warm tears on her face.

"Baby, what's wrong? Are you all right?" "Come on, let's have drink. I'll be right back, so don't move. He hurried off to the bathroom.

Standing at the commode was pure pleasure as he relieved the pressure build-up. While peeing, he imagined her nude, lying before him. 'What a sexy girl,' he thought. Grabbing a robe for himself and one for her, he returned. "Here, Baby, put this on. Come, sit at the bar with me," he insisted, taking her hand. Catherine felt wobbly, weak from his intensity. Pouring a refill of wine and another scotch, he watched her, mesmerized. "You're exquisite, Baby. I can't get enough of you. Silence. "Baby, what's going on?" "Owen, I love you!" No response. "Did you hear me? I said I love you!" Owen took a sip, his eyes locked on her. His tone grew serious. "Baby, relax! You're coming on too heavy. I want you with me. You're beautiful, sexy, a hell of a dancer. What could be better?" Catherine sat trembling, barely able to hold back tears. "It's just that when you make love to me, it feels deep, total." "That's how I am, Baby, happy to satisfy. Let's take a shower, continue in there," he said, pointing toward the bedroom. He noted a frown as she stood. "I'm going to make you feel terrific, so lighten up!" He reached for the light switch, plunging them in darkness. "Come on," he insisted, "Let's get started."

The following Monday the New York cast arrived at Dance Arts, a group that carried the look of a seasoned troupe. Introductions were made as couples were matched up, placed and rehearsed until 6:00. The transition proved easy, as the seven newcomers and seasoned cast members ran through the show. Pat was partnered by Joe, Catherine with Danny, Liz with Tim, Fran with Jim, Cynthia with Ray, Marcy with Fred, Kathy with Gerry, along with the swings, Julie and Hal. Rehearsals continued all week long, each day and session prepared a cohesive, exciting group ready to perform. Monday was the day for *Centipede's* newest dancers to go in. They were ready, thanks to veteran Joe Pinto. Those from the original cast were supportive and welcoming, making the transition seamless. Everyone worked to their maximum. Owen would accept nothing less. And he would be out front, a guarantee.

Chapter 6

Getting Ready

Members of the Tokyo cast were busy taking care of personal details before the trip. Their last show was Saturday, departing Wednesday for Japan. They'd have a normal dark day, plus two more to get ready. Kaplan-Maggli booked passage on United Airlines from New York to San Francisco, a brief stop-over, and then Japan Airlines to Honolulu, Hawaii. Following a two-hour layover, the flight would continue on to Tokyo crossing the International Date Line, arriving at Hanedakuko International Airport, a trip totaling 18½ hours.

Mally had obtained her first U.S. passport from a branch of the U.S. State Department in Rockefeller Center, while Griff's had been renewed recently. An updated inoculation for smallpox was required for travel outside the U.S. Following a recent outbreak in the Far East, a cholera shot was suggested as well. Griff made an appointment with Dr. Alan Nesbitt, his primary physician for years. Nesbitt had taken care of their blood tests prior to their marriage.

Griff informed Mally they would have a refueling stop in Honolulu, adding to the excitement of their impending adventure. Mally's Uncle Harry, her mother's brother, had moved his family from Massachusetts to Oahu months before. It was her hope there would be enough time for a short visit. He was a favorite uncle and she wanted to introduce Griff.

Packing entailed bringing enough apparel for two and half months. Tokyo's climate was similar to New York City, damp and chilly through the late fall and early winter, so layering was a must. Mally and Griff decided their packing should include clothing for work and play as well. Toiletries were minimal, including their personal items.

They had been on birth control from the beginning and not knowing what Japanese pharmacies carried, they would travel prepared.

At the Martin-Danier flat, the boys were in the throes of packing, when the phone rang.

Picking up, Jonas heard his father Charles' voice. He could hardly contain his delight. "Father, what a surprise, it's been ages! Are you in New York?"

It had been a year since they had reunited, following the death of his mother, Elizabeth. Her struggle ended after a long battle with cancer. At the time, there hadn't been contact for years, Charles resorting to a private detective to find his only son. During the funeral weekend, Jonas revealed a secret he had carried since childhood. At first fearful, being true to himself took precedence. He admitted he was gay. Charles embraced him, much to his shock. He guessed Jonas was gay years before, but it took his wife's death and their reconciliation to bring them together. "No, I'm in San Francisco, have been for the past six months. I retired and sold the house. I have a beautiful condo, overlooking the bay. When are you coming for a visit?"

"This is so ironic! Phillipe and I are on our way to Japan for a couple of months. We're remounting *Centipede,* the show we've been doing on Broadway, for an engagement in Tokyo."

"How wonderful, how long will you be there?" "We leave Wednesday and return the first of November. We'll head back to New York following the remount's opening." "Then I insist you and Phillipe pay me a visit on your way home. I have a lovely guest suite and I can show you around town." "We'll be able to stay for a weekend, if that's okay." "Splendid, send me a date and your flight particulars and I'll send a car for you at the airport." "This is wonderful, Father. I can't wait for you to meet Phillipe." "I'll look forward to your visit. In the meantime, safe travels and have fun in Tokyo, one of my favorite cities." "Thanks, Father. Good to talk to you." Jonas was grinning from ear to ear when he hung up. "This is the best, the absolute best!" Happily he continued packing, anticipating the adventure ahead.

Monday night arrived, as the Broadway cast checked in. At 7:30, a new voice prevailed, as Dick's announcement came through the speakers, mixing with pre-show energy and excitement. "Ladies and gentleman, half hour to curtain, half hour please!" Some had arrived an hour before to do a long warm-up, to settle nerves and ready their bodies for the workout ahead. The dressing rooms were alive with cacophonic buzz, conversations rising through the hairspray and warmth of make-up lights. Gossip prevailed, some trying to guess sexual preferences of the newcomers.

Pat sat next to Catherine, missing Mally more than ever. The fellow redhead was nervous, talkative. 'So ambitious and young,' Pat mused, reminiscent of her own beginning. She tried the personable approach, hoping to make the newcomer welcome. "How are you feeling?" Catherine looked up, smiling. "I'm okay, but a little nervous. I have big shoes to fill." Pat patted her on the back. "I watched your work in rehearsal last week. Mally is someone to emulate, but judging from your ability, you'll do well." "Thanks, Pat. Or do you prefer, Patricia?" "Pat's fine. My boyfriend is the only one on earth who prefers Patricia. I adore it." Julie, seated on the other side of Catherine, hung on every word. She had seen Pat on stage and admired her greatly. Breaking in, she added her two-cents. "I've got big shoes to fill, too. I understand Nora is top-of-the-line, the best swing on Broadway." "None better, she could cover at a moment's notice," added Pat. "I don't know how you swings do it! Your job is more challenging than doing a regular 8-show week." Julie smiled, suddenly feeling indispensable. Dick's voice cut in. "Company, please report to the green room at 7:50." Pat smiled, remembering Griff's announcements. "I have to get used to Dick, now that Griff's leaving." Catherine was now feeling more relaxed, continuing. "Is Griff going to Japan?" "Yes, he and Mally will be together! Did you know they've only been married a few months?" Julie was all ears. "Oh, that's so romantic! Imagine getting to work with your husband!" "They are true soul-mates and my best friends," Pat added.

At 7:50, the cast gathered around Dick. New faces replaced familiar as Dick took a head count. "For all you newcomers, welcome! For you old-timers, be aware of your spacing and numbers. Break-a-leg, everyone!" As the gypsies moved out, Joe caught up to Jim. "I wonder who the dip shit was who invented the phrase, 'break-a-leg'?" "I'm kind of partial to 'Merde' myself, it's less scary," said Jim. "It is risky to say, 'good luck,' said Kathy, always ready to clarify. "Well thank you,

Miss Olson. I feel so much better now," said Joe, giving her a playful poke. "Always glad to help my fellow boys out," she whispered, just as the first notes of the overture were heard.

The evening took off with fiery intensity. The new cast mates were accurate, energetic, inspired. The veterans worked well with the new blood, a fresh boost to the show. Pat and Joe led the pack, flawless together, with Joe proving an excellent replacement for Jonas. Catherine held her own in Mally's place, moving brilliantly with Danny's partnering. They were the team to watch. The newly matched couples danced as though they had for months, a testament to a seamless transition and Joe's guidance. Owen stood at the back of the house, his eyes never leaving Catherine. Her ravishing looks and facile technique only served to awaken his libido. Scarcely able to quell his need for her, he mentally began to plan their evening after the show. He always called the shots where lovers were concerned and Catherine was no exception.

The gypsies were unstoppable as they danced through the tropical number. Catherine passed Tim during a transition point from one section to the next. Her bodacious body brushed his as they made a brief exit off stage right. Tim seized the moment. Catching her eye, he moved within ear shot. As she waited for her next cue, she felt him too close for comfort. "You're all girl, Red. Want to get some later?" She could scarcely believe what she was hearing and, during a performance! Ignoring the remark, she moved into the light on cue, reaching for Danny as he approached. She was distracted and almost missed the prep for a lift. Danny's partnering was impeccable, compensating for her timing error. Once airborne, she relaxed and corrected herself. The rest of the number went smoothly. If Danny was unnerved, he never showed it. Following the number he caught up off stage. "Are you all right?" "Of course, why do you ask?" "Well, you've never had a misstep in rehearsal, so why now?" Catherine was thinking fast. "I guess I'm a little nervous tonight. It won't happen again, Danny. I apologize." He shrugged, heading to the change room.

Catherine hurried to the change room on the lower level. As you moved through the shadows she became aware of someone watching. Feeling uneasy, she entered the mass of women going through a quick change. Pat noted an obvious frown on Catherine. "You okay? How's it going?" Catherine grabbed a towel and began to dry her face, as a dresser unzipped and removed her costume. "Okay, but I was a little off in the big lift." "Oh, how come?" Catherine slipped on her next costume and reached for a hairbrush. "Must be opening, I'm a little anxious!" Pat smiled, remembering her own nerves early on. "Give it another week. You'll feel like you've done this forever." "I hope so. I never want to disappoint Mr. Matthews." Pat listened, the irony not missed. "If Mr. Matthew's was disappointed, you wouldn't be here," she reassured. "Thanks, Pat. You're so kind. I appreciate it." 'I must be growing up. A year ago, this one would have been a threat,' Pat mused. Dick's voice cut in. "Places for act two, please!" The girls hurried up the stairs.

The rest of the evening was a triumph. As the gypsies took bow after bow, the newcomers were reassured by the seasoned ones they were worthy additions. Joe was congratulated repeatedly. The cast, encouraged to meet at Joe Allen's for a celebratory gathering, hurried through the post show details. Pat turned to Catherine. "Are you coming to Allen's?" Julie, who watched the show from the back of the house, jumped in, her enthusiasm obvious. "This is so exciting, being associated with a Broadway show! Cath, are you coming?" "I'd love to, but I've made other plans. Guess I'll take a rain check." Julie, slightly disappointed, continued. "But Cath, this is your big night!" Pat undid her hair, quietly listening to the exchange. "I told you I had plans, Julie. Stop pushing!" Pat cut in. "Julie, why don't you be my date?" "Oh, wow, I'd love to! Where's your boyfriend tonight?" "He's in Houston on business. He'll be gone all week, so I'm solo. Come on, let's change and get going." "Cath, you don't know what you're missing," Julie chirped. 'Going to Allen's with Pat Byrne,' she thought, retouching her make-up.

The dressing room emptied gradually, leaving Catherine to finish. Adding a light jacket, she flipped off the light and headed downstairs. As she reached the stage, a hand touched her arm from the darkness. Startled, she gasped, peering through the dimly lit hallway. "Hi Red, nice show!" Much to her dismay, Tim emerged from the shadows, a growing smirk on his face. Backing her against a wall, he looked her up and down. Her skin crawled as she tried to move away. "Not so fast, Red, I want a close-up." "I have a date, Tim. Please, let me pass," she said, timidly. The smirk grew bigger. "Oh, some lucky guy gets some, huh?" Suddenly, he was interrupted by someone intrusive. "Hey, Catherine, been waiting long?" Danny approached, having overheard the exchange. She willingly picked up his cue. "Hi, Danny. I must have missed you upstairs." Tim stepped back. 'Nice timing, Bartlett. Fuck,' he thought, slightly pissed. "Come on, let's grab a cab. I can't wait to see your new place. Excuse us, Bartel." The two made a hasty exit, leaving Tim annoyed as hell.

Outside, the city noise was deafening. Traffic was in gridlock as theatres spilled patrons out on already crowded streets, creating a post performance clog in Times Square. As Catherine and Danny moved along, carried by a wave of people, they noted restaurants, tourist shops and bars doing high volume business. When they got to the corner, he stopped. Looking intently at her, his concern was obvious.

"Is Bartel bothering you, Catherine?" "Yes, he is! Thanks for the rescue!" "I figured he might think we're a couple and leave you alone. Will you be all right?" "Fine. I'm heading uptown. Oh look, a taxi! I'll grab it!" Catherine hugged Danny and slid into the backseat. The cab took off. Danny watched as it disappeared in heavy traffic. Crossing at the light, he headed to Joe Allen's, ready to celebrate his first night on Broadway.

Uptown, Owen was waiting. He'd chilled pate and shrimp, a bottle of champagne ready to open and had lowered lights. Tonight, he would reward her. How could he not? Such beauty, talent and potential deserved his best. And she, his chosen one. Lucky lady!

The place was jumping at Allen's. Gypsies crowded in around the bar, at tables, or at the door waiting to be seated. The mood was festive, the volume loud, a cacophony of sound permeating the popular theatre hangout. Pat and Julie spotted Joe and Jim trying to converse over the noise. Pat waved to get their attention at the bar. "Hey you two, may we join?" Joe looked up and smiled. "Hey, the boy bait has arrived! Get your asses over here." The girls pushed their way through the mob in an attempt to reach the guys. Joe continued, trying to shout over the din.

"We're waiting for a table to open up, so meantime, you can hold up here." Pat loosened her coat, Julie unwound her scarf. "What are you ladies drinking?" Pat frowned. "Joe Pinto, what do you think?" "Let me guess, a house red?" "Correct!" "And for our newbie?" For

Julie, being on the same level as seasoned Broadway gypsies was a dream! "I'll have a Rheingold and a glass, please!" "Atta girl," chuckled Joe. "You're a feisty one, I like that!" Julie blushed. She liked Joe right away. 'He's sexy and dark, just the way I like them,' she mused. Then dawn hit. 'Shit, he's too perfect. He's must be gay!'

The minutes passed, the group drank. A table at the back opened up. Leading the way, Joe zigzagged through the bustle, finding refuge in a corner. Jim sat down next to him, the girls taking the other two chairs. As they settled, a waiter approached. Joe recognized him immediately. "Dale, what the fuck? It's been ages!" The blonde server frowned slightly, placing napkins down. "What are you having?" He appeared stand-offish.

"We'll have a house red, three Rheingold's, one glass, please." "Be right back," he said, hurrying off. Pat watched him go. "He seems aloof, who is he, Joe?" Joe glanced over at Jim, wearing a slight grin. "Yeah, Joe, who's the cute blonde?" Julie was all ears and eyes.

"He's a former trick. We were on and off for about six months. He got too heavy, I wanted out."

Jim deliberately leaned toward Julie. "He's known as old love them and leave them around here!" In minutes Dale was back, balancing a full tray. "Will there be anything else?" "No thanks, just the check." Slapping down the bill, Dale walked away quickly. "Nice to see you too," shouted Joe after him. Jim watched him with interest. "He still has it bad for you!" "I guess. The man was insatiable!" Pat changed the subject. "Moving right along, how did you like the show tonight, Julie?" "It was fabulous! Hal and I caught it from the back of the house. He actually took notes! Talk about conscientious!"

"You swings amaze me," said Jim. "I honestly think I'd pee my pants if I had to go on with a half hour's notice!" "It's just a matter of being prepared, knowing the choreography. Most swings like the rush! It's intense and yet, satisfying knowing I have to be on it!" "More power to you," said Pat, clearly impressed with the newcomer. Feeling the effects of the first beer, Julie excused herself and worked her way toward the restroom. Passing through the maze she suddenly lurched. Someone stepped on her foot! "Ouch! Why don't you look where you're going?" Looking more closely, she recognized the attractive fellow. "Nicholas, from Mulfetta's!" "Good evening! It's Julie, right?"

Blushing, she almost forgot her bursting bladder, as the urge to pee intensified. "Could you wait here? I'll be right back!" "Yes, of course, I'll wait here," he said, smiling.

Hurrying off, Julie's mind was in a whirl as she rushed into the restroom full speed. Entering the nearest stall, she took down her jeans and squatted. Relief was instantaneous as she enjoyed the pressure and release. Standing, she wiped herself and pulled up her pants. 'Whew, that was close,' she mused. After washing her hands she hurried back. Nicholas was sitting at a table with three others. He rose when he saw her. "Julie, may I introduce you?" Julie paused and looked over the group. "Yes, of course. I'm Julie." Nicholas began the introductions.

"Julie is one of my customers at the restaurant. Julie, my brothers Spiro and Andras and my sister, Calista. Julie smiled; slightly relieved the woman was a relative. There was a unified, "Hi!" "It's lovely to meet you," she stammered. Nicholas continued. "Would you care to join us? I'll find you a chair." "Well maybe for a minute or two, my friends will be wondering what happened to me." Nicholas pulled an empty chair over. Julie settled, enchanted with his attention.

"What brings you to Allen's?" "I'm celebrating my first night on Broadway," she said, proudly. "How exciting," Calista said, looking her over. Spiro cut in. "You look like a dancer, a pretty one at that." Julie felt a flush. "Well, actually I'm the female swing for the show, across the street." "Oh, what show?" "*Centipede.*" "Really? I hear it's a sensation. What's a swing?" "I was hired to cover all the female dance roles. It's challenging, but a great opportunity." Andras cut in. "You must be pretty good to have a job like that." "Well, thank you!" Glancing over, she noticed Pat waving. "Oh, oh, I'm being summoned. I better go," she said, halfheartedly. Nicholas rose, pulling out her chair. "May I call you," he said, softly. Trying to stay in the reality zone, Julie smiled. "I'd like that a lot. Do you need my number?" He grinned. "Yes," he murmured, I forgot to note it from the check. Glancing at Calistra, "Papyrus?" She produced a small pad from her handbag, handing it to Julie, who wrote her number and passed it back. "It was great meeting you all. I hope to see you again sometime." "Yassou, Julie!" "Bye!" Moving through the crowd, she joined Pat and the boys. "We thought you fell in," Joe chuckled. "Nowhere near," said Julie, glancing back at Nicholas, whose eyes were locked on her. 'Greek relations have suddenly improved,' she thought with a smile.

Chapter 7

On Their Way

Departure was imminent, as the Tokyo cast gathered at Kennedy International Airport. Nerves were on edge, adrenalin high, while the troupe waited to board. Griff handed out tickets as each company member approached. A dizzying sense of adventure was on their collective minds.

A United DC-8 stood on the tarmac, ready to board the gypsies, crew and orchestra. The airline had set aside a block of seats for the *Centipede* group so they could sit near each other and visit en-route. The day was clear, the sun a welcome indication of smooth flying. When the flight was called, tickets were taken by the agent in charge. The *Centipede* team walked to the gate area and onto the field, an undulating line of bodies, gracefully ascending stairs. Larger bags had been checked upon arrival and the company advised they could bring one piece of hand luggage aboard. Griff continued a head count until each stepped through the forward door adjacent to the cockpit. Seating was open in the assigned section

Mally, Griff, Jonas and Phillipe sat across the aisle from each other, mid plane. Nora and Jeff were close by, one row back. Chad sat behind them, next to Terry Becker, the affable new swing. The rest of the company took seats nearby. The core tech crew chose to sit together, a rare opportunity to socialize. The new musical director, George Elliot sat at the rear near his pianist, Ted Benedict. Andre Crenshaw, first violin and percussionist, Jimmy Grey, settled in.

A voice was heard over the plane's system. "Ladies and gentleman, welcome to United Airlines flight 480, non-stop service to San Francisco International. Our flying time today will be 4 hours and

35 minutes; we expect clear sky all the way and will be cruising at 27,000 ft. When we are airborne, please stay seated until the captain has turned off the seat belt and no smoking signs. At that time, feel free to move about the cabin. However, we do recommend that while seated you keep your seat belt loosely fastened in the event of unexpected turbulence. Now if you will bring your attention to the front of the cabin, our crew will go over safety instructions." Two stewardesses appeared, one up front, the other mid cabin. With measured grace they demonstrated the use of seat belt, oxygen mask and referred to a card found in the forward seat pocket containing emergency instructions. When finished they walked the aisle, checking to see all seat belts fastened and personal belongings stowed. A sudden lurch on the push back surprised everyone as the plane began to move and engines came to life. Slowly, the aircraft maneuvered into the lineup joining others waiting to depart. Those next to windows craned for a view.

"Darling, we're on our way," murmured Griff, nuzzling Mally. "Oh, Griff, am I dreaming? I mean, Japan!" He chuckled and kissed her gently on the forehead. "No, my darling, this isn't a dream." Across the aisle, Jonas and Phillipe were primed to leave.

"Is your father meeting us in San Francisco, Cheri?" "Since we have so little time between planes, he'll wait until our return." "I look forward to meeting him," said Phillipe, squeezing Jonas' hand. "I love you, Cheri." Jonas squeezed back.

A hush came over the cabin as the plane slowly continued to the runway. Positioning for take-off, there were seconds of anticipation as the plane temporarily came to a halt. Then a sound of engines building power, brakes suddenly released and intense acceleration as the aircraft started down the runway, pushing everyone back into seats. Hearts beating rapidly, legs tightening, hands gripping arm rests and suddenly the moment! Lift off! "God, we're airborne," said Nora, taking Jeff's hand. He gave a reassuring squeeze as they climbed high over the ocean's edge. "Whoa, I never get over the rush," exclaimed Chad, as he savored every second of take-off. Terry was all ears. "Have you flown much?" "My dad's a captain with Northwest, so he gets employee benefits for the family, has for the last 20 years. "Have you ever flown over the ocean?" "No, this will be a first. I've never been abroad, but I'm sure looking forward to this job." "Yeah, me too," sighed Terry, his mind in a whirl. He continued. "I've been reading a lot about Tokyo since we got hired. The Nissei Theatre is only a year old! It's state-of-the-art all the way and huge. It's in the heart of downtown, within walking distance to the Ginza and Imperial Palace. There will be lots to see on our off hours." "Great," enthused Chad, ready to soak up as much culture as he could get.

Once at cruising altitude, beverages were offered from a trolley. Juice and soft drinks were free, beer and wine $0.50 and cocktails, $1.00; all with complimentary peanuts. About 30 minutes later, a choice of hot lunch or sandwich was offered. The day's selections were chicken breast with rice and vegetable accompaniments or, corned beef on rye with potato salad. A second round of drinks followed shortly after. "This is pretty fancy service" said Mally. "This is the absolute best," exclaimed Jonas, between bites of corned beef.

The flight was smooth all the way to California. Some of the cast read and slept, while others got acquainted, sharing stories. They would be together for the next 2 and ½ months. Icebreaking was the first step to a cohesive company. Save for Mally, Chad, Nora, and Jeff, they were all new and eager to blend in. They had big shoes to fill, noting the public's admiration and respect for their fellow gypsies on Broadway. The show had raised the bar for excellence and it was critical to bring that level to an international public. Upon arrival at the City on the Bay, the cast noted a shroud of rainy mist, droplets hitting the windows as they readied to get off. Then a first! A Jet way, an enclosed ramp-like bridge from plane to terminal moved into place, attaching to the forward exit door.

"Wow, talk about handy," said Nora, clearly impressed with every aspect of the journey so far. "This is great," Jeff agreed. Within minutes the company was in the terminal, Griff leading the way to their connecting JAL flight. The company manager, Sam Stewart, would arrive the next day, after tying loose ends in New York. For now, Griff was handling the whole enterprise, a job he enjoyed.

The cast gathered at the gate area of JAL, Japan Airlines, flight number 175 to Honolulu. Flying time to Oahu was 5 hours. "This could easily be the longest day of my life," murmured Maddy Nichols, female swing. "Oh shut up, Maddy, you're not going to OZ. There will be no heel tapping," teased Neely Sorenson, her best friend and fellow

cast mate. "Maybe I could just fall asleep and wake-up in Japan. I absolute hate flying!" "Hey, you could go by ship and arrive in a month!"
"Smart ass," Maddy volleyed back. "Bite the bullet, sweet pea, it will all
be worth it in the end," said Neely, reassuringly.

The flight was called at last. Boarding, the group found their
assigned seats and settled in. The crew, all Japanese, were formal, but
pleasant. "Konnichiwa!" As they passed into the cabin, Nora whispered
to Jeff, "What does that mean?" "Tell you when we're seated," he said,
knowingly. Their seats were side by side at the back. Removing their
outerwear, they put their hand luggage in the overhead and plopped
down. Thumbing through a small Japanese-English hand book, Jeff
found a page of common phrases. "Good Afternoon!" "Hey, where did
you get that?" "I picked it up at Doubleday in the travel section. I figured it would come in handy, like right now," he chuckled. Nora smiled,
stretching to kiss his nose. "I'm crazy about you, Jeffrey Jenkins."

The sound of baggage being loaded into the cargo hold intermit-
tently thumped, indicating the cast's luggage had changed planes as
well. Outside, a wash of rain shrouded the tarmac, making a gray panorama of planes, puddles, the ground crew scurrying about. Droplets
of water dotted the windows, creating a cozy effect for those on board.
Closer to the front of the cabin, the attendant crew began passing out
blankets, pillows and assorted reading matter. Their cordiality was
delightful, immediately creating a cultural behavioral difference.

"Hey look, props," noted Jonas, delighted with his discovery in the
seat pocket. Pulling out a tidy plastic package, he noted a 'one-size-fits-
all' pair of paper slippers and a sealed fan. "This is for my hot flashes,
Babe," he teased, pointing to Phillipe's fly. "Naturally I requested this
just for you, Cheri," Phillipe countered. Searching the seat pocket in
front of him, he smiled. "Voila! I have the same!" Further up the aisle,
Mally buckled in and leaned toward Griff. "I'm awfully sleepy, so I'll
probably nap to Hawaii." "Whatever suits you, my darling." "Pillows?"
They glanced up to see a sweet-faced Japanese attendant. "Yes, may
we also have two blankets?" "Hai! Mochiron desu," she replied, handing them from a small cart. "Domo, arigato gozaimasu," replied Griff.
The attendant smiled, clearly impressed with the polite westerner. "Iie,
do itashimashite!" Griff smiled back, taking the blankets and bowing
his head. From the window seat, Mally sat fascinated by the exchange.

The attendant moved on. "Griff, where did you learn Japanese?" "I've been doing a little cramming. I'm bound to work with locals, short on English, so this is a great opportunity to learn how to communicate on their turf." "You never cease to amaze me!" Griff placed a pillow behind Mally's head and unfolded the small blanket, placing it over her. "Pleasant dreams, my darling." It was then they heard the door close and felt the jet way moving from the plane.

The grey wash was heavier now, shrouding the terminal as the plane backed up and made a turn. Soon they were taxiing toward the active runway. Upon clearance, the DC-8 moved swiftly down the runway and was airborne, lifting out of the heavy mist. As the wheels retracted, a slight clunk brought Mally around briefly, but she nestled back into Griff and fell asleep. The sound of engines lulled many into a pleasant snooze. Griff pulled out the tray table and began sorting through notes. Hiri Watanabe and staff had thought of everything. A large package of information arrived at the Royal weeks before enabling him to familiarize with the Nissei's set-up; equipment, staff and logistics of operation. Though an old hand at stage management, he looked forward to a challenging new venture, one unfamiliar. Glancing over, he felt a wave of joy as he watched Mally sleeping, her head resting against him. An opportunity like this, working abroad together, was special. He embraced the notion with enthusiasm as he removed his cheaters and turned off the overhead light. His eyes had grown heavy and the notes could wait.

About an hour after takeoff, the cabin silence was broken with an announcement that beverage service would begin shortly with a meal to follow. Since a number of passengers had been dozing or relaxing, the cabin attendants came along offering hot jasmine scented towels for refreshing. "Quite a nice touch," said Mally as she slowly woke to the delightful fragrance which was filling the cabin.

Minutes later, the beverage trolley was right behind with the usual offerings of coffee, tea, juice, soft drinks and spring water. As this was an International flight, beer and wine, including sake was also complimentary. The only extra cost beverages were Champagne and cocktails. A small cup of assorted Japanese snack crackers, some of them quite spicy, came with the drinks.

The meal following was something the *Centipede* team would long remember. It started with a cup of traditional Miso soup and went on from there. The dinner choices were Beef Stroganoff or Braised Chicken in Soy Sauce on rice; a choice of three salads, Udon noodles, Vanilla ice cream, roll and butter. Upon learning what was offered, Terry Becker exclaimed, "Boy, Northwest has a long way to go to match this."

The flight was smooth all the way to Oahu. An announcement brought those napping around, while others stopped reading or paused in mid conversation, fixed on the heavily accented voice coming over the plane's intercom. "Ladies and gentleman, we will be making our final approach into Honolulu International Airport shortly. Please make sure that your belongings are stowed, your tray tables put back, locked and seat belts securely fastened. We will be on the ground in 20 minutes. Domo Arigato!"

In minutes, the plane descended into the warmth of Hawaii. Once again, the attendant's voice was heard throughout the cabin. "Ladies and gentleman, our stop will be one hour and thirty minutes. At this time, please do not leave the terminal and remain close to the gate area for further announcements. Aloha!" As the *Centipede* group taxied toward the terminal all eyes were on the magnificent beauty surrounding them; the green palm trees gently swaying, foliage of every variety including colorful flowering plants, man-made ponds, pagodas and tiny bridges dotting the airport landscape; a treasure trove of delights, so different from the concrete canyons of New York City. Once the plane was secured, a movable stairway was brought to the carrier. The door was opened, allowing the cast and crew their first whiff of island air, so fragrant! They descended the staircase, graced by warmth and tropical air.

As Mally and Griff proceeded toward the terminal, they saw a group madly waving in their direction. Moving closer, Mally recognized her Uncle Harry and Aunt Bernice as they stood with their kids. "Mally, over here," shouted her uncle as they walked through the gate area. Rushing toward her, they each took a turn hugging, including her cousins Judy, Harry Jr., Rick, and Curtis. Their enthusiasm filled the area as they placed flower leis of incredible colors and sultry fragrance, around Mally's neck. Griff stood by, enjoying the reunion. "You must be Griff," enthused Harry, extending a handshake. "We've heard raves from Paula and Frank." Griff grinned as Bernice placed leis on him as well. The children surrounded them, staring with curiosity. "You remember your cousins, Mally?" "Of course, but the last time I saw you, you were back east. Judy and Harry were in elementary school and the twins were babies!" Harry made introductions.

"Kids, this is your cousin Mally, Aunt Paula's daughter and her husband, Griff." "Gosh, it's been a long time," said Mally, taking them all in. Bernice continued. "I'd say so. The last time you saw us, was that summer at Scituate, on the coast. You and Paula came out by train and we stayed at the ocean for a week, remember?" "I do. It was one of my favorite trips with Mom."

"Moving to Oahu was one of the best decisions we ever made," said Harry. "We've all adjusted well in relatively short order." "Judy just started high school, Harry Jr., junior high and Rick and Curtis are in elementary," added Bernice, hugging the twins. Griff joined the conversation.

"How do you like island living, far from the mainland?" "We absolutely love it! This will be our first winter in the warmth. We're settled in our home in Kailua and Harry loves his new job," said Bernice. Harry changed the subject. "How is it you're Japan bound?" "Mom hasn't told you?" "No, only that you and your husband were headed there for a couple of months," said Harry, intrigued. Griff took over.

"The producers of our New York production decided to take the show internationally, so we are remounting the production for Tokyo audiences. We'll be there a little over two months. At the end of the run, we'll return to our regular jobs in the Broadway show." "Oh, how wonderful for you," chirped Bernice. "I always knew you'd be a dancer when you grew up. I remember you used to put on shows for us when you visited." Mally smiled, remembering times she'd corral the family following dinner. Uncle Harry would put the 78 rpm recording of Die Fleidermaus on the record player, roll back the carpet and announce his niece, the prima ballerina. Mally quickly put on her toe shoes, fastidiously securing the ribbons in place. The family watched her dance the entire recording, delighted by her effort to perform. The conversation continued until Griff and Mally heard their flight being called. "Oh, that's us," said Griff, noting the announcement. "We have to go," Mally said, reaching for her uncle. "Thank you for meeting us! And the leis are so thoughtful, not to mention fragrant!" "They should last another few hours if you sprinkle them with water occasionally," advised Bernice. Another round of hugs and they were off, heading across the tarmac to their JAL flight, standing ready. Tokyo, Japan was eight and a half hours away.

Chapter 8

Wanted, Unwanted Advances

It was mid Sunday morning. The phone rang several times in succession. Julie stood at the sink, her face full of soap. The constant ringing was annoying but persuasive. Grabbing a towel, she hurried toward the relentless sound. Wiping off suds as she reached for the receiver, she paused to catch her breath. The voice on the other end was soft, familiar.

"Julie?" "Yes." "This is Nicholas." Her breath caught as she tried to stay calm. After what seemed an awkward pause, she responded with enthusiasm. "Hi. This is a pleasant surprise!" Another moment passed until he continued. "It was great to see you the other night at Allen's. How are you?" "I'm good, couldn't be better," she purred. "What are you doing right now?" Julie glanced at the clock. It was 10:00 am and she was readying herself for laundry and weekly grocery shopping. "We're dark, it's my day off." "Do you have plans?" Julie's breath slowed as she tried to process this sudden development. Working to regain her composure she replied, "Actually, no, nothing special." "Well then, may I take you to lunch followed by a walk in Central Park? It's a beautiful day." Staring at the pile of laundry and the grocery list on counter, she caved. "Great, where should we meet?" "Say in front of the Russian Tea Room, about 1:00?" "Oh, that sounds lovely. Where is the Russian Tea Room? I've never been." "It's on West 57th Street next to Carnegie Hall, between 7th and 6th Avenues on the south side of the street. You can't miss it. See you soon and wear comfortable shoes. Bye!" There was a click. 'Oh my God, he actually called!' Redialing, she waited breathlessly. Catherine picked up on the third ring, her voice groggy with sleep.

"Cath, you'll never believe this. That gorgeous waiter from the Greek place just called and asked me out! Can you believe it?" Slowly Catherine gained her equilibrium as she settled back against the headboard. "Julie, do you have any idea what time it is? This is our day off, for crying out loud!" "Yes, I know, but I just had to tell you, my wish came true!"

"Well, be careful what you wish for, if you get my drift!" "Seriously, Cath, he asked me to lunch today!" "You accepted, right?" "Well, what do you think? He's been on my mind since I first saw him!" "Well, take it easy and for heaven's sake, play a little hard to get, okay?" "Oh for crying out loud, I'm not that easy. I'll wait to have sex with him." "Good grief, I'm going back to sleep. Bye, Julie, have fun," she muttered, abruptly hanging up. Julie replaced the receiver, contemplating the day ahead. 'This is so great. I wonder if it's true that Greek men are good? Time to find out,' she thought, as she headed to the shower.

It was nearly 1:00 pm as she hurried to the Russian Tea Room. After the call that morning she took great pains to make herself as attractive as possible for him. Her normally long, wavy dark hair was pulled back in a ponytail, her make-up subdued. The outfit, flattering to her slender body, included a tea length skirt, with a slight slit, accenting her lithe legs. She added her favorite boots, turtleneck sweater and decorative vest. She looked ethnic and purposely so. Adding a touch of her favorite perfume, she grabbed a light coat and left in haste. Arriving at the restaurant, she glanced up and down 57th Street, hoping to spot him. That way, she could prepare herself before he showed up. Just looking at him quickened her pulse. A few seconds passed and she heard her name. "Julie!" Turning, she watched him approach, smiling with warmth enough to melt her toes. "Oh Nicholas, hi," she responded enthusiastically. He bent down and kissed her gently on her cheek, causing her to blush. "It's good to see you. I made a reservation. Shall we?"

The two entered and were shown a table to the side. Nicholas offered a chair and sat down next to her. Taking her hand, he squeezed gently. "I'm so glad you came. You look lovely!" Julie's breath caught as she tried to stay in the reality zone. "Thank you! You look very good yourself." He smiled and continued. "I have wanted to call you for some time, every since you first came to Mulfetta's." A waiter approached. "Good afternoon. My name is Boris and I will be your server today. May I start you with a cocktail?" Nicholas glanced at Julie. "I would love a Dubonnet on the rocks with a twist." "Very good, Miss. And you, Sir?" "Do you have Ouzo?" "Yes, of course." "I'll have Ouzo on the rocks, please." "I'll be back in a moment." When he was gone, Nicholas moved closer. The heat between them was overwhelming. Those deep brown eyes never left hers; the touch of his hand stirred her beyond reason, his soft, mellifluous voice held her rapt. He could read the Manhattan directory to her, pure poetry! Yes, Julie had it bad, captivated totally by this young Greek. She hoped he would take her beyond just a friendly lunch. Following drinks, they ate, attempting small talk. 'Our meeting is only social foreplay,' she mused.

Across town, Pat waited for Blaine's call. He'd been gone only a few days but it felt like a lifetime. How she missed him and all the little things; the way he played with her hair in the morning, gently brushing strands off her face, kissing and arousing her. Or his constant reminder that she was number one in his life. He always listened, discussed and appreciated her. Even the most minor question or simple request was considered. The time he took in bed; exploring new possibilities, creating, their love making constantly exciting. Beyond the bedroom his standards and values; dedication, drive and integrity were traits she cherished in him. Yes, they had reconciled and were now committed to each other after a rocky ending and new beginning.

Thinking back, Pat recalled her journey with Owen Matthews. She shuddered recalling the distance he kept between them, beckoning her to his bed when it suited him. He kept up the pretense of being exclusive to her. Adding insult to injury, Owen's touting her for the lead in *Centipede*, brought her little peace. She was deeply in love with him and he betrayed and played her. He met Stephanie McNeil, a reporter he considered prime, a sexual challenge, one he took on aggressively. He carried on with her to quell his rampant libido. All the while he kept Pat on a string. When the truth erupted, the hurt and pain nearly destroyed her. Clearly, it took time to free herself from him emotionally and soon, artistically. What started as an occasional dalliance with Blaine Courtman the previous year, during the *Bravo Business* tour, left Pat with fierce conflict and guilt over seeing him behind Owen's back. In truth, she wanted only Owen. His occasional calls and visits on the road led her to believe there was a future, but it also left her wanting, desperate and lonely for him as time wore on. Her wealthy suitor filled the gap, stroked her ego and gave her the attention she felt entitled to. She never for a moment thought she could or would fall in love with the entrepreneur.

Blaine, on the other hand, fell hard for Pat. His largess offered him independence to show up in places en route; wining and dining her, declaring his affection, undivided attention and indulgence, suiting her needs and his. It was exciting and helpful for Pat to have a focus and distraction with a man wealthy beyond compare. Blaine was handsome, impeccable with every detail of his lifestyle; a prince charming of sorts, one found only in romance novels. But, in spite of all, Blaine wasn't enough for Pat. When he proposed, after courting her over the months, she flatly refused, ending their affair.

Blaine never fell out of love with Pat. When they met again during *Centipede's* opening night party at Sardi's, his feelings were as strong as the night she broke it off in Salt Lake City. She, on the other hand, was distant and distracted that night, more interested in what Owen was doing. Annoyed to find him conversing intimately with another woman, she cut short her conversation with Blaine, but accepted his business card. He was in New York indefinitely, working a deal for his company. When Owen and Pat were over, Pat found the forgotten card and contacted Blaine. Reluctant at first, he steered carefully, the memory of her hurtful and sudden ending of their affair still cutting deep. However, his love for her was true until he was unable to stay away. They decided to try again, more slowly, more realistically, but firmly resolved to reconcile. These and many other thoughts vanished as the phone in Blaine's suite rang. Picking up, he heard the voice of the woman he hoped to marry.

"Patricia, my beautiful girl, I miss you. "Oh Blaine, I'm missing you, too. When will you be back? It's been a long week." "I'm leaving Montreal tomorrow. I'll be waiting for you after the show." They continued to speak sweetly to one another, the growing love between them so rich and respectful. Blaine continued. "How are the newcomers doing?" "They are superb additions and blend right in. Mally's replacement, Catherine Andrews is a peach. I'm kind of looking out for her." "Oh?" "Well, she's young and tender and reminds me of me when I first started out." "She's lucky to have such a stunning role model, my lovely. So, you aren't missing Mally too much?" "Well, it's only been a few days. Let's just say that Catherine is keeping me focused and feeling like a big sister. It's fun." "I'm glad. Well my angel, have a good day off. I can't wait to hold you." "I love you, Blaine." "And I love you more than you will ever know. Goodbye for now." Pat put down the phone and smiled. "It doesn't get any better than this," she thought, tears welling.

Following Monday night's show, the girls were removing their make-up when Catherine leaned toward Pat. "Pat, do you have a minute?" "Of course, what's up?" "I'll tell you when the others have left. A few minutes passed, the room now emptied. Catherine looked around cautiously then walked to the door, closing it.

"I may have a problem here." "What is it? Something to do with the show?" Catherine sat before the mirror, taking down her hair, her eyes fastened to Pat. "Catherine, for heaven's sake, your hands are shaking! What's going on?" Catherine let her hair fall to her shoulders. As she picked up a brush, tears began. Alarmed, Pat moved closer, putting her arms around her in an attempt to calm. "Catherine, please, what's bothering you?" Slowly the tears stopped.

"Pat, I may be overreacting, but there's someone in the company who gives me the creeps. Every time I look up or over, he's locked on me. It's as though he's undressing me with his eyes!" "Who is it? You can tell me, please!" "It's that Tim Bartel. What do you know about him?" Pat sighed and sat back. "Oh God, I could have guessed," she said, her voice now edged with contempt. "Has he said anything to you, made advances?" "Yes, he has. Opening night he made a suggestive comment to me during the performance that threw me off. Later, when everyone had cleared out, he waited for me in the shadows backstage. I tried to avoid him, but he edged me up against a wall in a sexual way. If Danny Bartlett hadn't come along and pretended to be my date, I don't know what I would have done." "Catherine, Bartel's a snake. You're not the first he's approached. Rumor has it he dallied and dropped Cynthia and Fran. He's bad to the bone, but the problem is, he's an exceptional performer and technician. For all intents and purposes, Owen favors him and management considers him an asset to *Centipede*." "Then, what you're saying is I have to grin and bear him, right?" "The only way he could get the ax is being caught compromising a female company member on site." Catherine relaxed. Pat took her hand, patting it gently. "Tell you what. Let me keep tabs on him for awhile. You tell me if he bothers you again. Ok?" "Thanks, Pat. I appreciate your feedback. I don't want to feel uncomfortable here at work." "No one does!" Changing the subject she added, "How does a drink at Allen's sound?" "That sounds perfect!" The two girls finished dressing, grabbed their coats and headed out. 'Time to put that creep Bartel in his place,' Pat pondered, a delicious idea forming.

Chapter 9

Land of the Rising Sun

Centipede would arrive at Haneda International Airport, Tokyo, after a journey of 4,062 miles. The departure from Honolulu was on time, the take-off smooth and eye-catching as the plane banked and turned toward Japan. From the plane's windows the group could see azure blue ocean, the majestic Pacific brushed with sunlight, millions of diamonds reflecting back from the waves rolling toward the beach at Waikiki. In the distance the familiar Diamond Head stood impressively, seen in travel brochures world-wide. Anticipating a long night, a few of the cast slept off and on, some quietly chatting and getting acquainted, others reading or playing cards. Griff's studied his Japanese, which would soon be necessary and useful. Mally could sleep anywhere under any conditions. The hum of the aircraft's engines lulled her into a delicious space, there to remain for most of the flight. Jeff and Nora cuddled, held hands and dozed, Nora resting on Jeff's chest. They were committed to each other and considering an engagement after the first of the year. They were inseparable after the show had opened in New York.

Chad sat with new recruit, Neely Sorenson, Jim Sorenson's sister. They were close siblings. Jim, who had been in *Bravo Business* and an original member of *Centipede,* had encouraged his baby sister to audition. Neely was a superb ballet-trained dancer, with extraordinary jazz technique as well. Jim instinctively knew she had a good chance of catching Owen and Jonas' eye. When she was cast, he sent her off with his blessing, knowing Jonas and Phillipe would look after her. Chad was very interested in looking out for her. She was adorable.

Forty-five minutes later, at cruising altitude, Japanese hospitality and service took over once more; warm scented towels, an assortment of beverages and meals of stir fried beef or chicken with vegetables and rice filled the cabin with delightful aromas. Dessert was served separately, a choice of warm apple pie or fresh fruit. Coffee, Tea, Cognac and many other cordial choices were offered. Cabin lights dimmed, naps quickly followed, it was becoming a long day.

The trip seemed endless as the hours passed. Two hours away from Tokyo, cabin lights were bright again, with an announcement: "Ladies and Gentlemen, if you would like to refresh yourself, please do so now, we will be serving a light meal shortly." How they did it, no one knows for sure; juice, coffee, tea and fluffy asparagus omelets topped off the long, long day.

As the flight drew closer to the islands of Japan, the descent was magical. Lights twinkled here and there; outlines of pagodas, temples, lakes and unusual looking trees created a fantasy setting in the dim light of evening. En route, they had crossed the International Date Line west of the Hawaiian Islands, leaving the daytime of yesterday for the next in the Far East. Suddenly the voice of a stewardess came through the cabin. "Konbanwa! Genki desu ka? Ladies and gentleman, we are now making our final approach into Haneda International Airport.

Please make sure your seatbelts are securely fastened, your seatbacks are in the upright position and tray tables securely locked. Replace all personal belongings taken out during the flight and see that they are stowed under your seats or in the overhead for landing. We will be on the ground in 20 minutes. Domo Arigato Gozaimasu."

The approach was smooth, the descent flawless and, when the giant tires squealed on contact with the runway, the *Centipede* troupe burst into spontaneous applause. Taxiing to the terminal, JAL ground workers guided the plane to position on the tarmac where they would disembark. When the plane came to a stop, Griff rose to make an announcement.

"Company, we will be passing through Japanese immigration and customs. Please have your passports and immunization cards out and ready for officials. Once you've been cleared, you will proceed to baggage, collect your luggage and go to customs. Stay together and we'll get through this as quickly as possible." A Japanese voice was next.

"Ladies and gentleman, welcome to Tokyo, the local time is now 7:30 pm. Be sure to take all personal belongings with you. Thank you for flying with us today. We sincerely hope your stay is pleasant here in Japan or wherever your travel plans may take you. Sayonara!"

"Oh Griff, we're here," exclaimed Mally, barely able to contain her excitement as she hugged him. He retrieved their hand luggage in the overhead. The others chatted as they grabbed dance bags, hand items and other paraphernalia from above and under seats. Slowly the line moved through the cabin, passing by the open cockpit. The captain, first officer, flight engineer and three flight attendants bowed repeatedly and enthusiastically as the gypsies exited.

"I love all this politeness," murmured Jonas, giving a wave to the crew. "This is the best!"

Phillipe smiled. "I couldn't agree more, Cheri! I was told they are gracious and from all indications, it's true." Descending the stairway, the group headed to the terminal. A light breeze caught them, a slight chill in the air.

"I can't believe we're in Japan, Jeff," said Nora with enthusiasm. "I'm in love already!" Jeff grinned and reached for her carry on, planting a kiss on her cheek. "Well, I'm in love with you! And the rest is a bonus," he murmured. They caught up to the group waiting in line at immigration.

The whole process took over an hour before the gypsies boarded a bus for central Tokyo. The route to town was picturesque; landscape dotted with miniscule, unpretentious Japanese houses, architecture so unlike home. A feast for the eyes, each prefecture, or district was unique in layout and topography, a blend of quaint and modernity. Sculptured gardens and trees, perfect in detail and execution, looked like giant Ikebana displays. Even in the shadows of evening, the panorama was enticing.

It was late when the bus pulled up in front of the Nikkatsu, a modern structure that housed business offices and a hotel. It was the accommodation selected for the *Centipede* cast by the Watanabe group. As the gypsies made their way through the lobby, they were advised that the hotel began on the 7th floor and directed to a row of elevators, taking them from lobby to check-in. Griff led the group, splitting them up in order to get everyone transported as quickly as possible. The interior of the hotel was modern, but lacking pretention. The décor was simple, the ambience welcoming. The manner with which the gracious staff handled arriving guests was already familiar to the gypsies having experienced the courtesy of the JAL airline crew. As everyone lined up, Griff took over, greeting the manager-on-duty.

"Konbanwa. Ogenki desu ka?" "Hai, okagesama de," replied the affable gentleman behind the front desk, bowing. Griff returned a bow. A smile spread on the manager's face as he glanced at the group. "Welcome to the Nikkatsu Hoteru! I'm Ishide-san. How may I help you?" Griff smiled, thinking, 'This gentleman has class and impeccable English.' "I'm Edwards-san, production stage manager of *Centipede*. Our group reservation should be under the names Kaplan-Maggli or Watanabe." The manager looked through the file and pulled a card, nodding.

"Hai, here it is! I believe Mr. Watanabe-san ordered this. We have reserved a block of 20 rooms for your group. Three rooms are doubles, is that correct?" "Yes, there are three couples and the rest will require single rooms." "Chotto matte kudasai," he replied, placing forms on the counter and retrieving keys from the message center cubby holes, collecting and placing them in a pile.

"We require that each occupant of your party sign the registration and submit his or her passport. The Nikkatsu will keep your passports secured for your protection and ours. Now, if you will kindly make two lines, we will have you checked in as soon as possible." The gypsies began lining up, each given a registration form to fill out. Ishide-san continued. "We have selected rooms on floors 7 and 8. Each registration card shows a room number, so as soon as you have completed and returned the forms, I will give you the corresponding keys to the rooms."

Griff and Mally waited for the others to register. Jonas and Phillipe would share as well as Jeff and Nora. In less than an hour everyone was checked in. Before their departure to assigned rooms, Ishide made a quick announcement.

"There is a full service restaurant on the 8th floor, which opens for breakfast at 7:00 am and closes at 10:00 pm. The cocktail lounge is next door, open from 5pm to 1am. We hope you enjoy your stay with us," he enthused, bowing once more. "Domo arigato gozaimasu!" By now the gypsies were exhausted and feeling the effects of 24 hours traveling and the time change.

Standing in line at immigration and customs for over an hour, riding from Haneda Airport to central Tokyo and the wait to check in wiped them out. The need for sleep was first and foremost. Griff made an announcement before they dispersed. "Company, our first meeting will be the day after tomorrow, Friday, at 2:00 pm with Mr. Watanabe, the producer and staff. Please meet in the lobby here at 1:30 and we will be taken by bus to the Nissei Gekijo. We are giving you an extra day and a half to get used to the time change. Please get some rest, you'll need it! Thanks!"

Groans and sighs filled the air as the group shuffled off, in need of relief only a good night's sleep could bring. 'So this is jet lag,' Chad mused, as he shouldered his bag, the weight reminding him that it was time to find a bed. Jonas started for the bags. "Cheri, let me," insisted Phillipe, handing over the key to their room. "I'll make two trips. You check out our room and I'll follow." He smiled and patted Jonas' ass, before following him down the hall. From all indication, Jonas' body language showed extreme fatigue. He was known to make the smallest occurrence major drama at the slightest opportunity. It was one of many things Phillipe loved about him.

The remount of *Centipede* was about to take place on the other side of the world. The gypsies would soon experience Japan's reverence toward American performing artists.

Mally and Griff didn't wait to unpack. However, a shower sounded just right before climbing into bed. They had departed New York the day before and now had lost an additional day, upon arrival in the land of the rising sun. It was inevitable that the time change would catch up with them in a day or so. Undressing, Mally was the first to step into an inviting spray. Her muscles ached and she felt off. Griff was brushing his teeth, when she peeked out. "Griff, I'm getting a cold. My throat is sore and I'm stuffy in the head! I felt great when we got to Honolulu." "Darling, you're tired and you might have a delayed reaction to the inoculations." Turning off the shower, she stepped into a large towel, he held for her. "Let's dry you and bundle you off to bed. You need a good night's sleep." The towel felt warm and soft next to her skin. He dried her gently, blotting her wet hair. "Come on, Mrs. Edwards, time to sleep. Fooling around comes later." Mally looked through her bag and found flannel pajamas. As she slipped them on, she remembered. "Did you pack the electrical adapter? My hairdryer is in the suitcase, side pocket." "Yes, Darling, but you can take care of that later. Let's tuck you in," he insisted, taking her hand. Walking her to bed, he pulled back the covers and helped her in. Leaning over, he kissed her gently. Mally caved in to his kiss and added comfort of clean sheets and soft blanket. Perfection! "Sweet dreams, Mrs. Edwards," he whispered. Heading toward the bathroom, he glanced back. Mally was already asleep. 'I'm not far behind you, my angel,' he mused, as a wave of fatigue suddenly engulfed him.

The company's day off began with the discovery of a sunny restaurant and pleasant wait staff.

As cast members took tables in close proximity to each other, a tall, young waiter, with a coat hanger smile approached the group. "Ohayo Gozaimasu! Ogenki desu ka?" Jeff couldn't resist as he blurted out, "Hai, okagesama de!" Heads turned, the gypsies clearly impressed with one of their own. Nora's mouth dropped open. "Jeff, what did he say and what did you say back?" Everyone was all ears. The affable waiter picked up the cue, repeating in broken English, "Good morning, how are you?" Jeff followed. "Fine, thank you!" "God, Jenkins, you are on top of it," said Chad, chuckling. The others applauded. The waiter continued.

"I am Mori-san. Welcome to breakfast at Nikkatsu!" "What is your desire?" There was a resounding response, "Coffee!" He nodded, adding, "Chotto matte kudasai," as he hurried off.

"I can't get over how polite the Japanese are," said Nora, fidgeting with a napkin. "Americans could learn a thing or two from them." Jeff agreed. "Their culture is so far-removed from the U.S. and yet the arts and advancing technology go hand in hand in this country. Chad jumped in.

"Hey, Jenkins, how come you know so damn much?" Jeff turned toward his buddy. "I've been doing some research ever since we got this gig. I'm pretty excited to get the max out of the time here." Maddy Nichols, one of the newcomers, spoke up. "Let's assign Jeff our official tour guide!" "Hey, I'd like that, gang. I'll look into some day tours once we've settled and we're in the swing of things, ok?"

Mori-san returned with a tray of several Thermo-Serve pots, small pitchers of cream and tiny bowels of sugar cubes. "Coffee here," he announced, placing the tray on a stand. He passed out the pots to each adjoining table. "Does anyone prefer tea?" Nora, Neely, and Maddy raised their hands. "Back in a moment," he announced, hurrying off. The gypsies eagerly poured coffee into cups already placed on the tables. "Do you think they know how to cook eggs?" "Oh, for crying out loud, Chad," said Jeff. "This is post war Japan. Of course they do!" Mori-san was delighted with the collective large order. He enjoyed his work and was happy to accommodate the Americans. Each dancer chose one of two daily specials. Some ordered eggs, cooked to their liking, with bacon, potatoes, toast and juice. Others settled on a choice of French toast, pancakes or waffles. Two of the girls wanted oatmeal with fresh fruit on the side. Maddy Nichols, always dieting, asked for shredded wheat and a banana.

The men ate heartily, having not eaten since the day before. The women were more conservative, although Nora and Neely were starved, wolfing down their orders of eggs and bacon and every smidgen of potatoes and toast! The food was tasty and similar to American cooking. Following breakfast, Jeff waved to Mori-san. The happy waiter approached, bringing their checks. "Would you like to sign to your room?" Nora was surprised. "Can you do that? Seeing Mori-san's quizzical look, she changed gears. "I mean sure, that's great!" Having signed, the gypsies began to disperse. Jeff waved to get attention. "Hey, anyone want to do some exploring? There's a lot to see around the hotel area." Some declined, but a few thought it a great idea. "I want to stop by my room and change shoes," Maddy insisted. Some of the other girls agreed. "Fine, let's meet in the lobby, about 15 minutes," suggested Jeff. The group broke up. As Jeff and Nora started to leave, Mori-san stopped them. "If you need any assistance locating points of interest, please call on me. I am here from 7 to 12 every day," he said, his enthusiasm obvious. Jeff smiled. "That's great, thank you! I mean Domo Arigato!" They headed to their room, eager to freshen up and start exploring. A surprising adventure lay ahead.

Chapter 10

Meanwhile

The newcomers had proven their worth in the Broadway Company. *Centipede* continued to play to capacity houses, with no sign of a let-up in ticket sales. Kaplan and Maggli were ecstatic, having gambled on an unknown, a concept that had proven a risk well-taken. The integrity and quality of the work remained, satisfying Owen's artistic sensibility.

On a personal level, Catherine Andrews was satisfying his more base sensibility, in the bedroom. She was exceptional in all ways; beautiful, talented and young. She was also relatively naive and very cooperative. Getting into that body was pure delight for Owen, stirring his relentless libido, while she, head-over-heels in love, submitted to his demands. Her worship of him was unrequited, as with all of his former women. Artistically he had conscience, but emotionally, he was a taker without restraint. Former lovers would attest to his flagrant, irresponsible behavior. He was a clever seducer; persistent, as he played them along.

During the week, Owen would occasionally stop by *Centipede* unannounced. His purpose was to keep an eye on Catherine's progress and watch the show. Anticipating Pat's resignation at the end of her contract, he plotted his course, biding his time until he could move Catherine into the lead. By then, Jonas would be back from Japan and partnering her. The timing was perfect.

Catherine was at his beck and call. All it took was a spontaneous invitation and she was at his door. She willingly submitted to all nuances of his sexual proclivities; his clever come-ons, his deft technique. Occasionally he would insist on kinkier sex, where domination was the game. Being bound was a turn-on to insatiable Owen. Oral sex followed, whether giving or getting. All-night marathons were not uncommon. He simply couldn't get enough. Catherine took it all in stride, naively believing she was indispensible. She was rapt by his fatally glamorous persona and power in the business. Owen had it all and Catherine wanted to be part of it. Ironically, both the former and present lover of Owen had bonded, without knowledge of either's involvement with him. Pat and Catherine were becoming close friends. Catherine looked to Pat as a mentor, someone to confide in. Pat loved being needed, respected by a colleague. She considered Catherine someone who could potentially fill her shoes when her contract was up. She was that promising. Ever since Catherine mentioned trouble with Tim Bartel, Pat chafed at the thought of that low life. The notches on his ego were obvious and he needed a lesson! How could she make it happen without putting herself or Catherine at risk? No, she needed more evidence to somehow get him canned. The very thought brought a smile.

As discussions of a national tour continued, Owen considered a potential company. The cast could include dancers currently in the Broadway production, wishing a change. They would be given that option. Another consideration was using those gypsies returning from Japan the first of January. So much to consider and Universal Pictures was definitely interested in a project with the irrepressible Owen, later in the year.

It was Friday afternoon, two days since the gypsies had arrived in Tokyo. As they gathered in the lobby of the Nikkatsu Hotel, the air was electric with anticipation. Today they would tour the Nissei, their theatre home for the next two months lead by Hiro Watanabe and staff. Details of the rehearsal schedule and other pertinent information would be given.

Griff and Mally arrived, followed by Jonas and Phillipe. "Good afternoon, Company! Let's head downstairs." The gypsies filled the elevators, assembling on the street. A bus stood ready to transport them to the theatre. Boarding, they selected seats, chattering, a cacophony of animation and enthusiasm. It was a ten minute ride, passing through a canyon of buildings; colorful signage bearing calligraphy, streets filled with Japanese both in modern and traditional dress. The bright fall sunshine paved the way through the unfamiliar scene.

The Nissei was massive, a state-of-art design. It rose impressively before them as they exited the bus and entered the foyer, where a gentleman was waiting. He extended his hand to Griff, bowing. "Mr. Edwards-san, I am Uki, your escort. You and your group follow please." The group ascended the staircase of the impressive lobby. They were ushered into a large conference room by an attractive Japanese woman in modern dress. She bowed and gestured as they passed, her manner formal and pleasant. "Konnicha Wa! Dozo!" Murmurs followed, as the group settled. Suddenly a middle aged Japanese gentleman, impeccably attired and groomed, entered followed by several others. He was formal and distinguished in manner. Griff brightened and approached. "Konnichiwa Mr. Watanabe," said Griff, extending his hand. "Yorokonde," responded Watanabe, returning a handshake. A slight bow followed between the two. Griff continued. "Mr. Watanabe, may I present my wife and our *Centipede* lead, Mally Edwards, our director-choreographer Jonas Martin and assistant choreographer, Phillipe Danier?" "It is good to meet you. Welcome to Tokyo, welcome to all of you," Watanabe said, looking around the room. Some of the gypsies waved, while others sat quietly enjoying the exchange of formality and greetings. Watanabe beamed as he called the meeting to order.

"Today marks a special occasion as we begin a journey together, bringing your production to Japanese audiences. I had the pleasure of seeing your *Centipede* opening night on Broadway last January, convincing me that the concept would attract our public. Yours is unprecedented in its artistry and execution. And now I would like you to meet staff, who will assist you making this a reality." A group of Japanese stood by, waiting to be introduced. "First, your personal interpreter, Mr. Haruhiko Kubota. He will assist in finding points of interest, arranging day trips or group tours. He will answer questions like, "Where is nearest pharmacy?" Kubota grinned and bowed. Watanabe continued. "This is my personal assistant and chief of stage management, here at Nissei Theatre, Mr. Keisuke Suzuki. Suzuki-san will assist you, Mr. Edwards with any of your needs." Griff extended his hand to Suzuki, who returned the gesture enthusiastically. "I will now introduce the rest of my staff. This is Mr. Sumio Yoshii, director of technical dept; Mr. Akira Suzuki, director of stage policy; Mr. Hisanori Fujimoto, vice director of technical department; Mr. Kaori Kanamori, chief of design; and Miki Abe, our costume designer and wardrobe coordinator. The group bowed to enthusiastic applause from the gypsies, which the Nissei staff enjoyed, judging from their wide smiles. "We will now tour the facility, followed by tea break. At that time we will take questions." The tour took the better part of an hour. Every detail and design of the theatre was impressive. The stage area and scene shop were mammoth, dressing rooms and green room equipped with closed-circuit TV. The orchestral area had a lounge for musicians and the costume department contained a work and storage area, beyond anything imagined. Curiously, there was no rehearsal hall. Returning to the conference area, two women wheeled in a cart of green tea and rice snacks. The company settled and Watanabe encouraged questions. Jonas was the first to raise his hand.

"Mr. Watanabe, where will the company rehearse?" Some exchanged looks of concern. "Good question. We are in the process of building a new space here at the theatre, which regretfully will not be complete during your stay. However, you will rehearse at a school not far from here. We have arranged a bus to take you daily to and from the Nikkatsu. The school custodian, Mr. Kamata-san, lives on site and will assist you whenever necessary. You will have the gymnasium for rehearsal." Griff spoke next. "Mr. Watanabe, will Mr. Kubota be with our company?" "Oh yes, he will translate. Many Japanese do not speak English. He will accompany you wherever you go and assist in all matters concerning your group for the duration." "Thank you; we appreciate every effort on *Centipede's* behalf." Watanabe grew serious.

"The school building is without heat. We will provide you with hot tea as needed." Chad grimaced. "Great! I can't wait for muscle knots and leg spasms," he whispered to Jeff. Jeff took no notice as he listened, intrigued. "Once the technical is set-up, you will be able to rehearse on stage, in about two weeks," added Watanabe. Griff spoke. "Company, you will need to layer your rehearsal clothes accordingly. We will all make do. The schedule is the same as back home; 5 minute breaks on the hour, lunch from 12:00-1:00 pm and finish at 6:00 daily. We start at 10:00 sharp on Monday. You have two weeks to learn the show before we tech, so work diligently. Jonas and Phillipe are here to set the show, so listen and learn as quickly as you can. Are there any further questions?" Maddy Nichols raised her hand. "Yes, Maddy?" "Why do we have two days off before we start?" Mr. Watanabe interceded. "You will have costume fittings to complete this weekend. A list of times will be given to your manager. Mr. Edwards-san, you and your associate, Mr. Martin-san will have an opportunity to visit school to check conditions of gymnasium and floor. At that time you will meet resident custodian, Kamata-san. You may measure and tape floor for rehearsal start. Also, you will be involved in technical meetings for the rest of the weekend as well," explained Watanabe. "Company, you have two additional days to get settled and then our tight schedule begins. I suggest you take advantage of this time off to rest and take care of essentials," added Griff.

Applause filled the room as the gypsies got up and were escorted back to the bus. Griff stopped Mally as she started from the room. "Darling, I will be detained for awhile with Mr. Watanabe. Why don't you ride back to the hotel with Jonas and Phillipe?" "Yes, I will. I'm going to go back and rest before dinner. This cold has gotten the better of me and I'm really tired." "I'll see you soon. Take it easy, Darling." "Hey guys, wait for me," Mally croaked, hurrying to catch up. "Oh good gravy, you have a nasty one, Miss Mal. Come with us," ordered Jonas. "Thanks, guys," my head feels like it's stuffed with bubblegum!" They boarded and found seats just before the bus pulled out into Tokyo rush hour.

It was well after six when Griff returned to the room, finding Mally asleep. The sound of the door opening caused her to stir. Slowly opening her eyes, she glanced over the coverlet. "Oh Griff, I've been asleep since I got back. What time is it?" "It's about 6:30 and time to think about some dinner. Can you manage it?" "I think so. I guess a hot shower might revive me." "I'll get it started for you, my darling." Mally slowly made her way out of bed and headed toward the bathroom, the sound of running water drawing her. Griff had set towels aside and was already undressed. Helping her slip out of her pajamas, he took her hand and guided her into the bathtub. The heat and steam was soothing as he eased her under the spray. He began to massage her neck, shoulders and scalp. "Oh, Griff, this feels like heaven," she murmured. "You need some tender loving care, my darling. If you felt better, this could lead to something even more heavenly," he whispered. "Don't let an old virus stop you," she giggled.

The hint taken, Griff's hands began running down her back and around her waist. She sighed. "Oh more, keep going." She gasped as his hands reached her mound, his fingers playfully twisting wet pubic hair. Breathing heavier now she opened her legs wider, giving him entrance. He entered and probed, his fingers reaching deep inside. Mally's sighs became urgent as she moaned her approval. "Oh yes, yes, make me come!" Griff had full access as he held her, accelerating his moves in and out. The water ran cooler as she cried out. He moved with her through waves of orgasm, holding her firmly. Gently turning her to face him, he caressed her wet hair and kissed her deeply. Prolonging the moment he then pulled away, winking. "Better than a cold tablet?" Reaching for the faucet he turned off the shower, now running cold. Let's get you a towel and some nourishment." "I feel better all ready," she smiled, following his lead.

The dining room was quiet as Jonas and Phillipe enjoyed dinner. They had returned following the meeting, made love, grabbed a short nap and headed to dinner. The food was delightful and they ate with relish. As they were finishing, Mally and Griff entered and spotted them. "May we join you two?" "Of course, we'd love it," remarked Jonas, rising and hugging Mally. "How's our girl? Feeling any better?" "Getting there. Griff's an excellent nurse," she giggled, the wink not lost on him. As they sat, a waiter approached. "Konbanwa! I am Kurisan. May I offer you a drink?" Griff glanced at Mally and back at him. "Could you fix a hot brandy and tea, by any chance?" The waiter looked perplexed. "I do not know this, but I will ask. And for you sir?" "I will have a vodka martini straight up with a twist." "Hai, this I know," he replied with enthusiasm, hurrying off." "I can't get over the courtesy here. It's just the best," said Jonas. "Did you enjoy the tour today?" Griff nodded as he unfolded his napkin.

"Yes, I believe we're in good hands with Watanabe and staff. The Nissei is impressive, but will take getting used to." "Dancing in that cold school will take getting used to," added Mally, shivering slightly. "Darling, would you like me to get your cardigan?" "No, I'm fine, but the thought of cold muscles with all the work ahead gives me pause." "Agreed," said Phillipe. We'll have to layer, move constantly and drink lots of warm tea!" "Maybe I'll be able to sweat this bug out." "Another couple of days of rest and you'll be your usual fireball, Mal," said Jonas, smiling. The waiter returned with drinks. "Time for a toast, friends," said Griff, raising his glass. Mally followed, lifting her teacup. Jonas and Phillipe joined in with the remainder of their drinks. "To a first class *Centipede!*" They all sipped and reflected, aware the adventure was just beginning, in a place unlike any experienced before.

Chapter 11

Back Home

Julie Jensen was in love! She and Nicholas had spent a full afternoon together. Lunch followed by a sunny walk in Central Park, made it perfect! The stroll had been relaxing, allowing time to get acquainted. Toward late afternoon, they stopped for a Cappuccino and more conversation. The attraction was mutual. Nicholas was a perfect gentleman. The most aggressive move he made was taking her hand to cross a street. His touch was comforting and promising. Every time he looked into her eyes she felt herself drowning in his gaze and did little to look away. She hoped to take it to a more intimate level later. As the sun began to set over the Hudson River, he suggested seeing her home. 'The best is yet to come,' she mused. He signaled a cab and they got in. Riding along Central Park West was pleasant but uneventful, as Julie's expectations were high and he had yet to make a move. "Which building is it?" "The brownstone with the dark green awning, number

61," she said, fishing in her bag. "No, this is my fare," he insisted, stopping her. "Thank you so much. Do you want to come up?" "I'd love to, but my sister Calista and her fiancé have invited me to stop by for a drink. Perhaps another time," he said, helping her out of the cab. She stood expectantly, waiting. He didn't make a move. By now, Julie's impatience had the best of her. Without hesitation she kissed him squarely on the mouth, pressing deeply. He stayed put for the moment, then pulled away. "You are lovely, Julie. I want to see you again, but I want to move slowly, all right?" There it was! 'He's old school, courtship before sex. Damn it,' she thought. "I had a great time. I'll call you soon." He reached for her hand, kissing it gently. "Bye, Julie." Without further hesitation he turned and walked along 86th toward Central Park West.

She was already turned-on, horny as hell. Watching him walk away was frustrating. He had the chance to make a move and he passed. She wanted him the first time she laid eyes on him at Mulfetta's. Now laundry and grocery shopping was waiting. Slowly she climbed the outside stairs to her apartment entrance. Using her outside key, she opened the door, closing it behind her. Reaching her apartment on the second floor, she paused as she realized her phone was ringing. Quickly unlocking, she dropped her purse on a chair and grabbed the receiver.

"Julie, it's me, Cath." "Oh, hi, what's up?" "You sound pensive. How was your date with the Greek?" "Well, let's put it this way, he wasn't up!" "What? You were expecting sex?" "Well, he's got that Mediterranean blood. I thought he might show a little heat!" "Maybe he's just a respectful guy. There must be a few out there!" "He said he'd call, so maybe that's promising."

Catherine changed the subject. "Are you hungry? I'm starved and thought I'd grab a burger at Allen's. You want to join me?" "When?" Well, it's about 6:30 now. Can you meet me at say, 7:30?" Julie stared at the pile of dirty clothes and linens, deciding that dining with her best friend was preferable to the drudgery of laundry. "I'll see you at 7:30. Whoever gets there first, grab a table, okay?" "Okay!"

Catherine headed to the bathroom. A sudden ringing of the phone changed her direction, as she reached for it. "Hello?" There was a pause. Then a voice whispered. "Hi, Red, how are you?" Catherine's stomach clenched, realizing the caller was Tim Bartel! "What's the matter? Cat got your tongue, beautiful?" Ire rose quickly as Catherine navigated carefully. "What do you want? How did you get my number?" "Never mind, I have connections. What are you doing right now?" Heat rising, she found courage through her fear. "None of your business and don't call me again!" Slamming the phone down, tears sprang to her eyes as she tried to calm herself. She redialed, Julie. It rang repeatedly, but no pick up. "Damn it, Julie, please answer. Julie had left.

The wind had come up, as darkness moved across the city. Julie felt the first rain drop splash on her nose as she hurried to Joe Allen's. She had needed a few things at the drugstore, so she quickly changed into jeans, sweatshirt, sneakers and a trench coat and headed there first. Now she was late and Catherine was a stickler for punctuality. As she headed to the subway station at the 86th Street entrance, she pulled a single bill from her coin purse and hurried to the ticket booth. Buying two tokens, she approached the turnstile and deposited her fare. Pushing through, she noted a train pulling in and hurried, gauging which door to enter. She crossed the gap and found a corner seat.

Thoughts of the previous afternoon kept intruding. Nicholas had spurned her. 'How could he? I know he's attracted to me, what's he waiting for?' Her thoughts were a jumble as she gazed around the car, looking at various men seated and standing. She was horny, lonely, in need of male company. She rode to 42nd Street exited the train and walked three blocks to Allen's on 45th. Entering, the place was not crowded. A friendly host seated her at a corner table. She had clear view of the door, as she waited for Catherine. A waiter approached. "Would you care for a beverage?" "Yes, please. I'm waiting for my friend, she should be along soon." "Very good. What would you like?" "Do you have a house white?" "Yes of course. We have two choices, Chardonnay or a nice Riesling. Which would you prefer?" "Chardonnay, hands down! I like my wine dry." "Coming right up! Would you care to start a tab?" Julie winked. "Why not?"

As she gazed around the restaurant, she spotted a familiar figure entering. The body language spoke of a guy clearly sure of himself. He sat down at the bar. 'Why is he so familiar? I know him.' Then it hit her. 'Tim, Tim Bartel!' She had admired him from afar. He was easily the best male dancer in *Centipede* and from all indications, straight! 'I wonder if he's noticed me around the theater.' Her thought was interrupted by the sound of Catherine's voice.

"Julie, you got here so fast!" Julie stood and hugged Catherine warmly. "How are you?" "So so, I guess." "What do you mean?" Catherine took of her coat and settled. "I had an unexpected call just before I left. It kind of threw me." "Oh, who was it?" "No one special, a distant cousin from Michigan," she lied. The waiter returned and placed Julie's wine glass on a napkin. Turning to Catherine, he brightened at the sight of her. "What would you like?" "A house red if you have it." "Is Merlot all right?" "Perfect." He smiled, attracted by her beauty. "I'll have that for you in a moment." "Thank you!" He managed to pull himself away, but not without a furtive look back as he headed to the bar. Julie studied her friend closely.

"Cath, you seem off tonight. What's going on?" "I'm just a little edgy. I got my period last night and it is heavy." "Well, that explains a lot. I get grumpy when the old curse comes around." "Julie, you're never grumpy, always cheery." "Not at the moment. Nicholas made absolutely no move on me today." "Oh, so you fantasized that he'd get you into bed right away?" "Well, I thought since he's Greek, but I guess that's a cliché." "No kidding!" The waiter brought Catherine's wine. "Would you ladies like to order?" "Yes, we're here for your burgers, what else? I'll take mine medium with grilled onions, extra pickles and does it come with a side of fries?" "Yes, but you can substitute a salad if you like." "No, I'll take the fries, thanks!" He turned to Catherine. "What can I get you?" "I will have a California burger, medium and a side salad with French, please." "I'll get those for you right away," he said, smiling at her. Julie noticed, as he hurried away. "I think you've enticed the lad." "Don't be ridiculous. And besides, I could care less. He's too young and probably gay." "Oh, oh, tough room," she teased.

"I need to use the ladies room. I'll be right back," Julie said, getting up. "So, while I'm relieving my bladder, behave yourself with the waiter," she giggled. She couldn't miss the roll of Catherine's eyes.

Heading in the direction of the ladies room, she glanced toward the bar. Tim was sitting alone, nursing a beer. Feeling bold, she walked toward him. He looked up, surprised to see her. "Hi, Tim, how are you?" He looked her over slowly, his eyes taking all of her in. "It's Julie, right?"

"Yes, I'm the female swing, remember?" "Yes, vaguely. Have you covered yet?" "No, not yet, but I hope to soon." "Have a seat." "Thanks,

I'd love to, but I'm here with a friend." "Oh, not a male friend, I hope." Julie grinned, enjoying the exchange, encouraged by his interest. "No, a girlfriend, actually," she said, pointing across the room. Tim glanced over the restaurant, spotting Catherine. His pulse quickened, but he remained nonchalant. "Catherine from the show? She's your friend?" "My best friend in New York." "Well, why don't you ask her to join us? I love the company of beautiful women." His flattering was cheap, but in spite of the cheesy approach, Julie was riveted.

"We've ordered, so I have to go," she said, feeling his heat. His coming on to her was heady, but something inside resisted. "Good to see you, Tim," she said, starting to leave. He caught her wrist and pulled her to him. His grip was strong, persuasive. "Perhaps we should meet up another time," he insisted. By now he was close to her, his mouth almost touching hers. She felt wetness in her panties, an irresistible pull as she responded. "Yes, I'd like that," she stammered. Tim released his grip. "Your dinner is getting cold. You better get back to your girl-friend. See you later and that's a promise." He watched her go, his eyes fastened to her ass. 'A bird in the hand,' he thought, a grin growing. Julie had almost forgotten the ladies room. Suddenly the urge to pee was intense as she entered. Pulling down her jeans, she sat down. She was wet and turned on. 'What is it about him? Could I be that horny that I'd settle for him?' She shivered as she finished relieving herself. Hastily pulling up her jeans, she washed her hands and hurried back to Catherine. Back at the table, her burger sat, getting cold.

"Where have you been? I thought you fell in," Catherine said, with a tone of admonishment. Hers was almost gone as she sipped between bites. "Oh, I just took my time." "Let's finish up, it's getting late and we have a show tomorrow." The girls ate and paid the check. Outside the rain had taken over, coming down hard on 45th Street. The girls waved a cab down and shared it all the way uptown. Back at the bar, Tim ordered another beer and thought about the cute brunette, who had approached him. He would check her out at the first opportunity. She was probably ready for a good roll. 'I can loosen her glue,' he thought, smugly.

Monday evening came quickly. The company arrived and checked in at the call board. Friendly banter and enthusiastic greetings filled the air at half hour. The narrow back hall of the Royal stage door area filled quickly. After a day off, the first performance of the week was always energizing. The women's dressing room resounded with snatches of gossip and pre-show prep. As Pat did her hair, she noticed Catherine, sullen and quiet. Pat approached, her manner, gentle.

"Catherine, you okay?" Mally's replacement eyed Pat in the mirror, her eyes filling. Alarm washed over Pat as she moved closer. Taking Catherine's hand, she took the eye pencil from her. "Okay, let's have it," she whispered. "What in hell is going on with you?" Catherine motioned toward the hall. Standing she headed toward the open door, Pat following closely.

They rounded a corner and entered the woman's room. Locking the door, Pat turned to face her distraught friend. "All right, come on, spill!" Catherine reached for Pat, trembling. "It's that Tim Bartel. Somehow he got my phone number and called yesterday." "Shit," mumbled Pat. "How did he get it?" "He claims to have connections. He was intrusive, suggestive." Pat grimaced. "That oily son-of-a-bitch doesn't give up!" "Oh Pat, what am I going to do?" Pat paused, trying to think. "There must be a way to get the creep fired. The problem is, he's an excellent dancer and delivers. That's all management cares about. His personal business is his own." "I think he borders on dangerous." "Agreed, but nowhere on his bio does it read he's a rampant womanizer!" Catherine had to giggle. "So how do we get rid of this sniffing cur?" Pat's smile was apparent. "Well, that's more like it. That guy can smell fear, so don't show him any! In the meantime, let me work on this." They hugged and hurried back to ready themselves for curtain.

Chapter 12

Tokyo Rehearsals

Time off included fittings, errands and rest, but now the hiatus had ended. The *Centipede* troupe boarded a bus taking them to Suntori Shougakkou, a primary school in the Roppongi section of Tokyo. It was their first rehearsal week. Spirits were high; gypsies chatting, anticipating their new adventure, in a place far removed from Broadway and 45th Street. The drive took fifteen minutes, the bus moving down narrow streets lined with industrial and residential buildings. At last they pulled up to the school. Chill in the morning air hadn't abated. The troupe entered the unheated building and directed to a large gymnasium on the first floor. The building was similar in design to older public schools in the U.S. A small stage stood at one end of the spacious room. The ceiling was high and along one wall, windows were visible, allowing daylight in. On the far side, racks were placed for the cast's belongings. A production table was set-up next to an upright piano, fully tuned for rehearsal. The gypsies moved about, finding spots to settle. At 10:00, Griff called order and requested Jonas and Phillipe join him up front.

"Ladies and Gentleman, welcome to your first day. Once again, I would like to introduce Mr. Haruhuko Kubota, your guide and interpreter for the duration. Kubota-san bowed and smiled. Griff continued. "If you have any questions, Mr. Kubota-san will be happy to assist. I would like you to meet Ted Benedict, your accompanist and associate conductor. I will be in and out during rehearsals, dealing with our tech elements back at the Nissei. Jonas is in charge with Phillipe assisting. Are there any questions?" Chad was the first to raise his hand. "Yes,

Chad?" "How will Equity breaks be handled?" "We are out of Equity jurisdiction here in Tokyo. However, we will stand by the rules and regulations of the union. There will be a 5-minute break on the hour, or if preferred, a 10-minute every hour and a half, determined by your chorus deputy, who should be appointed during lunch today.

"Yes, Jeff?" "Otearai wa, doko desu ka. Where are the toilets?" Impressed with Jeff's homework, Griff turned to Kubota-san, who quickly responded. "Otearai is located on main floor, through that door and down the back hall," he stated, pointing. Maddy raised her hand. "How will we tell which is for women and which for men?" All eyes were on her. "Usage is for all," Kubota answered. "Good grief," Neely gasped. Uncomfortable sighs mixed with giggles were heard, the first indication of a definite cultural difference. "Here at Shougakkou, Otearai is large room with tiled floor with troughs along center, toilets and urinals along walls." Looks were exchanged amongst the gypsies. Griff took over. "Thank you Mr. Kubota-san. Let's take a 10-minute and check out the area. I believe there are drinking fountains back there as well." Some dispersed, clearly surprised, some in shock. Kubota approached. "Mr. Edwards-san, arrangements have been made to provide a catered lunch each day for your cast. The hostesses will arrive at 1:00. There will be hot green tea provided throughout the day." "Domo Arigato, Mr. Kubota-san. We appreciate your consideration and look forward to our association with you and the Nissei." The two bowed.

After ten minutes, the company returned. Ted was seated at the piano, ready to go. "Gang, find a space of your own and spread out. Let's begin a warm-up," said Jonas, taking position at the front of the group, with Phillipe at his side. Each dancer found a spot, as Ted began a Gershwin piece, *Someone To Watch Over Me*. Music filled the space as their perfect gypsy bodies came alive; reaching, stretching, euphoric to be moving. Mally and Chad worked together, holding each other as they stretched, feeling their power, happy to be partnering again. The company was an amoebic mass; facile, moving and sweating and grateful for the work. The first week together would build strength and unity.

Following the warm-up, Jonas matched couples to begin blocking the Cole Porter piece. Mally and Chad took the lead as planned. Nora and Jeff were paired, followed by Georgia Kemper and Tom Sutton, Neely Sorenson and Andy Wendt, Candy Roth with Jim Jaris,

Betsy Allan and Kent Freeman, Daria Douglas and Jeff Boyd. The two assigned swings, Maddy Nichols and Terry Becker would learn each position in the show. Theirs was the most challenging assignment in the company, as it had been for Nora and Jeff in New York. It took a special performer to cover everyone in an ensemble, ready to go on at a moment's notice. Owen had recognized their strength, technique and willingness under pressure at the audition. Plus they had a generic look, demographically, fitting in anywhere. Attention was paid to every nuance of Owen's style and his demanding movements. They both kept notebooks to make the necessary notations, committing the choreography to memory. Detail-oriented, quick and fearless individuals made the best swings.

Jonas worked without notes, the entire show in his head; every shoulder, head, torso, arm and leg movement, permanently etched in his psyche. He was a wonder. Phillipe aped him as each section was taught and blocked. The two had spent weeks going over the grid of the show, talking through each number. Upon arrival it was just a matter of teaching the material. Mally and Chad were already deft as partners, having been paired not only in the New York *Centipede*, but both were former swings in *Bravo Business,* their previous tour. Nora and Jeff were given new placements, but they already knew the entire show from months of covering in New York. Now in permanent spots, they enjoyed the freedom of not having to learn each number from scratch. After the first hour, layers of clothing were discarded, the troupe sweating through each section of the Porter number. At noon, lunch was called. A group of young Japanese women entered the gym, carrying lunch and beverages. The spread was placed on a table which included a variety of sandwiches, accompaniments and hot tea served in tiny cups.

The gypsies toweled off and put layers back on, feeling the cool air suddenly tightening muscles. Dampness of fabrics made some cringe, while others welcomed more covering. The lack of heat would take getting used to. "God, I'm parched and starved," mumbled Jeff to Nora, who was shivering at the thought of drinking anything warm. The others finished layering and headed to the food.

"Konnichiwa! Dozo," one woman said, pointing to the repast. Mr. Kubota-san took over. "Please, help yourselves, courtesy of the

Nissei. There is hot green tea and water." "The tea sounds heaven," said Jonas, his arm around Mally, as they neared the table. "How do you feel, Sweetheart?" Shrugging Mally reached for a plate, loading it with food. "My head's clearer this morning, so maybe I'm sweating this damn bug out!" "I hate colds," agreed Phillipe. "Jonas, remember the one we shared last season? I didn't think I'd ever get over it or Detroit!" "Ah, *Centipede* in Detroit," interrupted Jeff, "Wasn't that fun?" "Has anyone heard how Jerry Thompson is?" "He's had a good year since the accident, but decided to hang up his jazz shoes. He's gone into business with his partner, Ray, running the bar," said Jonas, knowingly. "No shit, I hadn't heard that," remarked Chad. "He was a hell of a dancer until his knee gave out in Motor City." "A nemesis for us all," added Nora, grabbing a sandwich, adding pickles and chips to her plate. The green tea went down quickly. Grateful for warm liquid, perspiration lost in rehearsal was replaced.

When lunch was finished Jonas called a short meeting. "Griff has requested that we appoint an Equity deputy. Since we're out of New York's jurisdiction I think we can dispense with formality. Anyone care to volunteer? Jeff raised his hand. "I'd be glad to!" Applause broke out. "Okay, done! Now you're not only our official tour director, but our protector as well. Congrats," said Jonas, patting Jeff on the back. "I'll inform Griff. Now let's get back to work. Take a five, use the Otearai while you have a chance," he said, with a grin. Some rolled their eyes, deciding to take turns in the unisex potty. The rest of the day flew by, dancers putting out to the maximum as six o'clock drew near. Mr. Kubota-san appeared. "The transport is at the door to take you back to the Nikkatsu." Discarded clothing was picked up as the gypsies exited.

Jonas took a head count as the group gathered, then joined them on the bus. There was silence all the way to the hotel. Nora laid her head on Jeff's shoulder. Tenderly he took her hand and kissed it as they rode through the backstreets of the neighborhood. "Good job today, Honey. You're amazing. Your strength is beyond incredible." Nora smiled faintly and dozed off, safe with the man who was her friend and protector through her ordeal the previous year. 'Had it only been a year since the abortion?' Jeff thought back to the whole business and shuddered. 'I could have lost her.'

At the Nikkatsu, the gypsies exited the bus and made their way slowly to the elevators. It had been a long, intense day, but satisfying from Jonas' perspective. They were an exceptional bunch, not one weak link in the group. Reaching the lobby of the hotel, the group separated, making their way to rooms and rest. "Hey Mal, catch you later. Get some sleep, Sweetheart," insisted Jonas, who grabbed Phillipe's hand as they walked to their room. "Time for a shower, hot meal and sleep," said Phillipe, clearly tired and ready for respite. "You got it, Babe. I'm too wiped for a roll," he winked. "That will be a first," whispered Phillipe, patting his ass. "Let me know if you feel the same later." "You know me well," giggled Jonas, following him into the room and closing the door.

The rest of the week went quickly. Numbers were blocked, the company grew stronger and the choreography maintained brilliance. Jonas was more than pleased with his charges. "Gang, you're incredible. Keep up the good work. We have another two weeks until tech, so we'll be on the home stretch before you know it. Monday, we'll run and clean all the numbers we've blocked so far. Half the show is already learned, amazing!" There was applause as the group exited. He turned to Phillipe as they gathered their bags. "We'll start with the sailor number on Monday. It's the toughest in the show. They might need a few days to get that one. The Latin piece went smoothly. What do you think?" "Seriously, this troupe is as good as any, Cheri. They pick up quickly and understand the subtext well." Jonas agreed, "Well, with Owen, subtext is everything. It is the soul of his staging. It makes his work superior to any other." "Come on, Cheri, let's not miss the bus. I'm in dire need of alcohol and your derriere!" 'No argument there,' thought Jonas.

On Saturday, some of the girls woke up in pain. The intense workout all week coupled with cold conditions at the school had tightened muscles, now protesting! Relief was a must. But where would an American, unfamiliar with Tokyo, go for such remedy like a massage? Mally worked her way out of bed gingerly and entered the shower, her body aching intensely from head to toe. Griff had left for the Nissei and she was on her own to figure out her dilemma. The heat of the spray temporarily relaxed her as she shampooed and scrubbed, gently. 'God, I've never been this sore,' she mused, finishing and turning off the water. The towel felt rough against her skin as she gingerly tried drying. Bending over was an effort. 'How ironic; my head is clear, the bug is gone, my body has turned to shit!' Wincing, she dressed with painstaking effort, dried her hair and pulled it back in a ponytail, each moment a challenge. Even her scalp hurt. No make-up today! Hunger pangs reminded her it was time for breakfast. She headed to the dining room.

Spotting Maddy, Nora and Neely, she joined them, groaning as she sat down. "Hi, girls, anyone sore?" "Does a duck have lips?" Neely, always ready with a quip added, "I feel like a truck ran over me, backed up and did it again! Shit! This is miserable!" "Whoever thought of the unheated rehearsal space is a sadist creep," Maddy complained. Nora glanced up from her coffee, chuckling. "What a bunch of wimps! Work in Europe! It's like being in boot camp. This place is a walk-in-the-park!" "Tough-as-nails Nora, do tell," tossed Neely. "I'm just saying, I've danced under worse conditions than this," returned Nora. A waiter approached and took breakfast orders. He served Mally much-needed tea to get her started. While waiting for their food to arrive, the gypsies sipped beverages, rampant complaints continuing. "This calls for necessary action. After we eat, let's talk to the front desk and find out where to get a massage," suggested Mally. "Good idea, some body work would help," added Neely. Breakfast arrived and the girls ate with relish.

The day clerk was busy working the front desk when the girls approached. He looked up and smiled at the attractive group. "Ohayo gozaimasu! How may I serve you?" Mally was their spokeswoman. "Can you advise us? We're dancers from New York opening at the Nissei Theatre next month. We're interested in a massage. Do you know where we can get one?" The clerk blushed for a moment, giggled, and took out a street map. With a pen, he drew a line to a spot a few blocks from the hotel. "This is Tokyo Onsen," he carefully pointed out. "It is club for tired business men!" "Yeah, well, we're tired American women," Neely replied with a cheeky tone. Again, he blushed. "You will find massage here. Only 1800 yen for hour. About $5.00 dollars, American." Nora interrupted. "Do we have to make an appointment?" "Iie." "What does that mean?" She was becoming annoyed. Jeff had taken off with Chad for the day, with their Japanese/English diction-ary. "I think he said, 'no.' You don't need an appointment," said Maddy, trying to reassure. "Then what are we waiting for? Let's go!" The girls returned to their rooms, grabbed purses and put on walking shoes.

The trek to the Onsen took less than 20 minutes on foot, following the street map given them by the hotel clerk. Each step off a curb was dis-tressing, as butts, calves and thighs protested each change in elevation. In spite of their discomfort, it was a fascinating stroll through lots of eye candy. The beautiful late autumn day was sunny, with a cloudless blue sky over the city. Pachinko parlors, similar to American slot machines, were in full swing, as sounds of clinking bells and money dropping in trays provided a cacophony of sound, reminiscent of Las Vegas. Shops and restaurants overflowed with customers. Japanese couples with chil-dren scurried by, some dressed in traditional attire. Colorful kimonos were everywhere. The children looked adorable, like little dolls, wear-ing wooden sandals with ankle-length booties on their feet. After a few minutes the girls arrived at a modest building skirting the Ginza.

The Onsen reception room was sparse with few chairs and some pillows about. Tatami mats and rice paper screens added a touch of local ambience. Large goldfish were evident as they swished through a small pond in the room. The air, fragrant with Eucalyptus, held a pleasant and welcoming aroma. Two women in traditional dress stared at the American women approaching.

"Konnichiwa, how may we serve?" Mally explained their dilemma and need for massages. The women listened, clearly surprised by the request. "This is spa for men. We do not cater to ladies." Nora spoke up. "We are American women and would like to speak with your manager!" Intimidated, one woman hurried away. The gypsies looked around, spotting only men. In moments, a well-dressed gentleman walked over. "Ladies, I am Shinji-san. How may I help?" Mally was forthright and pleasant, careful not to insult the establishment. "We are American dancers opening soon at the Nissei Theatre. We desire massages. Is it possible to accommodate our group?" After listening, the gentleman promptly presented a sheet of paper, a list of services and prices. "For one hour, you have hot tub, wash and full body mas-sage for 1800 yen." "Sold," said Nora, opening her purse. The others followed. After paying, they were issued receipts and asked to sit. Mally looked around the room, scrutinizing the place. "What happens now, I wonder?" "I don't know, but it'll sure be interesting," whispered Maddy.

Suddenly a side door opened and four young barefoot women in halters and shorts appeared. Taking each dancer by the hand, they were led back through the door. Mally was taken to the first room in the hall, others continuing on. "Hope to see you again," tossed Neely, apprehensive, but curious. "I hope this isn't white slavery," added Maddy. Mally was brought into a tiled room with a wooden tub in the corner, a small adjoining area with a cot and shelves holding towels, bottles of oil and lotions. The young girl couldn't have been more than 18. She was shy and sweet. "Dozo, please remove your clothes!" Mally nodded and began slipping off her things, placing her shoes and clothing in a pile in a small wicker basket provided. "Now, step in here," she said, opening the wooden box. Mally slipped in, finding a small stool to sit on. She suddenly felt small and vulnerable. "You will soak for a few minutes and then I will wash." Heat began to build around Mally, her body relaxing into the moisture and warmth. Only her head was free. A sense of helplessness mixed with curiosity came and went, as she sat, feeling sweat running down her face. Minutes went by until a small bell rang. The young woman came to Mally, lifting the lid and opening the box.

"Dozo, please stand. Take this bucket. Please rinse off completely. I will soap and cleanse you. You will rinse and I will dry you." As odd as it was, Mally cooperated. Turning the bucket over on herself brought a gasp, the contrast in temperature, startling. When she had rinsed, the young woman began with a soft sponge, soaping her completely. Surprised, she enjoyed being attended to. "Please rinse yourself." The warmer water felt good as it cascaded over her, a towel liberally applied by the girl, following. Once completed, she was led to a small cot. "Please lie face down." Mally, still tender, eased her way. The girl's hands began working over Mally's shoulders, arms, back, buttocks, thighs and calves. Mally winced at the first touch, then the next. More strokes followed, with each rub and pressure more intense than the first. She squirmed and called out to no avail. The girl appeared to hear nothing and continued her routine. Mally felt her feet being pressed deeply, causing her to gasp. Each toe was now being twisted and pulled, her instep pressed so hard she yelped. She was completely immobilized, held captive by the strength and determination of the masseuse.

"Dozo, turn over now," she said. But Mally had quite enough. "No thank you. That's fine. I want my clothes and I will be going." The girl seemed puzzled, shrugged and handed Mally the basket containing her belongings and left. It took effort to get dressed after the pummeling, but she managed carefully. Her eyes filled with tears as she made her way to the reception area. 'So this is what the tired business man gets? No thank you,' she thought, clearly disappointed. Waiting patiently, she fought the need to cave in and cry. 'They save face in this country, I'm told,' she thought feeling miserable. Minutes seemed like hours, the time moving slowly. As each gypsy emerged, it was obvious how worn and annoyed they were. "Well, let's get out of this joint," Neely remarked, wincing with pain, her dissatisfaction obvious. "I think we'd been better off and 1800 yen to the good if we had soaked in our hotel room tubs." "No shit, kiddo, this was the pits," muttered Maddy, walking with effort to the door.

Mally was noticeably quiet as they exited. "Mal, are you okay?" Just outside, the floodgates opened and she sobbed. Nora, concerned, grabbed and held her until she calmed down. "Mal, what's wrong? Please, tell me!" In moments, Mally found her voice. "That was the worst experience I've ever had, just horrible. That girl beat me black and blue!" "Well, if you ask me, if that's what the tired Japanese businessman does to relax, he's a fucking masochist," agreed Neely. "Shit, it'll take me days to get over this," added Maddy. "They can't be trained properly and aren't that attractive physically, so what's the big deal?" "Come on, let's go find a place to sit and calm down." "Is it too early for a drink?" Neely chuckled, "I'm afraid so, damn it!" The gypsies headed back toward the Nikkatsu. So much for a relaxing massage on their day off.

Monday's rehearsal was intense, as Jonas blocked the sailor's-on-leave number, the second act opener. While on a mid afternoon break, Mally noticed two young girls watching them from the hallway. Glancing at Nora, she indicated their presence. Catching the eye of one, she gently waved and smiled. Two bright smiles returned with waves. In an instant they hurried off. "That's curious," remarked Nora. "I wonder who they are." "Let's ask Kubota-san," suggested Mally, approaching him. "Mr. Kubota-san, do you know the children I just spotted?"

"Hai, they are children of Hiro Kamata-san. How you say in English? He is caretaker of school. He lives here with his family. They have small quarters on the premises." "Really, how interesting," said Nora. "Why haven't we seen children before? Isn't this a grade school?" "Hai, but it has been closed by prefecture, temporarily. Repairs are in place for next year." Mally was fascinated. "I will ask Mr. Martin-san if they are welcome at our rehearsals." "Domo Arigato," said Kubota-san, bowing. The afternoon continued until the sailor number was completely blocked and rehearsed. Two days passed. The company was on a break, as some of the girls headed to the toilet. As Mally entered the hall, a young girl approached. "Konnichiwa," she said, sweetly. "Hello!" Mally was enchanted with the youngster; polite, shy. "Do you speak English?" "Hai," replied the girl. "I am Yuriko, I live here." "Oh, do you have sisters? I saw you the other day." "Hai! My father takes care of school. My mother takes care of us," she said, pleasantly. "Would you like to come and watch us dance?" "Hai! May I bring my sisters?" Mally hadn't approached Jonas, but felt it would be okay. "Yes, of course. We are here from 10 to 6 every weekday." Yuriko smiled and bowed. "Domo Arigato! Sayonara."

After lunch, the sailor number was reviewed and cleaned. The group was strong, willing to work it as long as necessary to perfect Owen's concept. At 6:00, the gypsies gathered their belongings and headed to the exit. Mally approached Jonas. "I met someone who lives here at the school, a family member whose father is custodian. Can the children watch rehearsal?" Jonas thought for a second. "Sure, Mal. If they're quiet, I see no problem." "Quiet is an understatement, Jonas. The young girl I spoke is so shy and sweet, I doubt she would know how to raise a ruckus!" "The next time you see her, encourage her to come in." "Thanks!"

Centipede continued to rehearse, as the company familiarized themselves with Tokyo. There was so much to offer, so many points of interest. Jeff and some of the boys had discovered a few local shrines, the inner city transit system, the Imperial Palace grounds and a great Tuna salad sandwich at a cafe near the Nikkatsu. Their interpreter, Kubota-san had suggested a day trip to Kamakura, By-The-Sea on their upcoming day off. The picturesque fishing village, about an hour by train, was home to many shrines including the famous 700 year-old giant bronze Buddha, Daibutsu. A few gypsies decided to make the trip on Sunday.

At the theatre, the technical staff was busy constructing *Centipede*. Though the show was minimalist in design, there were levels, ramps, a complex lighting plot and a huge cyclorama to install. Griff worked well with the Nissei group; advising, guiding and developing rapport. These men were his core crew, those who would work directly with him every performance. Many were proficient in English, but appreciated Griff's attempt at Japanese, which often brought smiles from those hearing him speak. Griff made friends and respected colleagues wherever he was and the Japanese tech crew was no exception. The wardrobe department, headed by Mariko Ugachi, was busy; cutting, fitting and sewing, following the original costume design plot of Nira Fontaine. Corrections and adjustments would be made as needed. Depending on availability of particular fabrics and experienced workers to construct, the process would move at a reasonable pace, without pressure or time constraint. In general, the Japanese were serene by nature, able to work focused and relaxed, to accomplish whatever needed to be done. Griff quickly learned their serenity was a definite plus; no egos, no confrontations, just productivity, creating a pleasant working environment.

The time was growing close. The cast would move into the theatre in a week. Griff checked in periodically to get updates from Jonas and to check on company welfare. He and Mally had had little time together since their arrival. Between her daily rehearsals and his tech meetings, there had been no quality down time. He decided that at the first opportunity they would steal away to a Ryokan, a Japanese inn, on their day off. At the school, rehearsals were intense. Jonas pulled out all the stops, taking on Owen's proclivity for demanding excellence, perfection at the highest level. The old pros took it in stride, the newer cast members, sagging. A ten-minute was called. Some gypsies headed to the drinking fountain. "God, he's Mephistopheles," muttered Neely to Maddy, noting the change in Jonas' tone. "Where did Mr. Nice and Easy go?" Nora overheard. "You're lucky you're not in the same room with Owen." "Do tell," said Maddy, a tinge of sarcasm in her tone. "If he heard you gripe like that, you'd be on the next plane back." "Really?

How do you know?" "He despises complainers and slackers, pure and simple. Believe me, I've seen it. He's tough, that's why his work is the best." "Shit, Neely, you better watch your mouth," giggled Maddy, giving her a playful poke.

Back on the floor, Jonas' ran the entire show, number after number. At one point he stopped, noticing four curious faces peering from the hallway. Mally noticed too, raising her hand. Irritated, Jonas groused, "What is it Mal?" "Jonas, these young ladies are family members of Mr. Kamata-san, the custodian here. Jonas' tone changed instantly. "Dozo, come here," he said, gently. The girls walked in. Curious eyes followed them. "Gang, these young ladies live here. Please introduce yourselves." The girls giggled and bowed. The tallest stepped forward. I am Yuriko and these are my sisters; Haruko, Mirako and Sachiko. "We live here. Our father is Kamata-san, the caretaker." "Guys, would you get folding chairs for our guests?" "Smart move for international relations," whispered Neely. The rehearsal continued, as the Kamata girls sat, enthralled. At the end of day, Yuriko thanked Jonas for his kindness on behalf of her sisters. "You're welcome," beamed Jonas. "Please come back to see us. We will be here one more week." The girls nodded eagerly and hurried away. Mally winked at Jonas, clearly pleased with his hospitality. The rest of the week continued intensely; reviewing and fine tuning *Centipede.*

Griff called a company meeting for 10:00 on Saturday, a week before the company was set to move to the Nissei. Hiro Watanabe provided a tasty lunch in the theatre's conference room. When all had assembled he greeted them warmly. "Ohayo gozaimasu! We are happy to see you. Please enjoy," he said, pointing to the repast that included American and Japanese cuisine.

Following lunch, Griff called the group to order. Eager faces were glued to their PSM as he presented details of the next phase of their stay.

"Company, I understand from Jonas, that rehearsals have gone very well. We are a week away from the first rehearsal on stage. You will have tomorrow off and resume at the school on Monday at 10:00. Next weekend, you will be provided with a day off on Saturday, a complete run with a full orchestra on Sunday afternoon, followed by three days of tech, a preview on Thursday and opening on Friday. Be prepared to adapt to an unfamiliar physical set-up. Our technical elements will be in place and we will most likely run a dry tech without you, Sunday night, prior to opening week. Jonas, I will need you and Phillipe at that run. I will post a complete schedule on the callboard as well as copies for each of you to reference. Are there any questions? Yes, Jeff?" "Griff, how many dress runs will we have?" "We plan to do Sunday's orchestra and Monday's run without costumes. Tuesday and Wednesday will be full costume and make-up run-throughs, taking us to preview and opening nights. Thank you! Enjoy your days off." Dispersing, the group headed for a few hours of respite. Performing for the Japanese public would soon be a reality.

Chapter 13

Advantage and Dilemma

For Catherine, being the second lead in a smash Broadway hit was a plus, though she would be more content if Tim Bartel's constant intrusion and his base insinuations would cease. Coupled with the Bartel problem was nagging insecurity over her sometime relationship with Owen Matthews. They had seen less of each other since she joined the New York company, leaving her on shaky emotional ground. It had been weeks since he had made love to her with his usual ferocity and ingenuity. In fact, he hadn't approached her at all. She was becoming desperate for his company, for reassurance that he still wanted her. Her mind swarmed with constant thoughts of him. She had missed him at the theatre, not knowing when or if he would show up. In truth, Owen Matthews was commuting to Los Angeles in recent weeks, causing rampant rumors to circulate that he had signed with Universal Pictures. He had been approached by Shel Friedman, Vice President of Project Development at that studio months before. He was now set to direct his first film next year, based on his Broadway hit, *Bravo Business*. Universal was looking for major investors, as the studio was not known for musicals. Hiring Matthews involved a new direction for them. That new direction didn't include Catherine.

During Owen's first commute to Universal, he was introduced to Karen Eliot, Shel Friedman's secretary. Their mutual attraction was instantaneous and a sizzling affair began. It started with simple flirtation and then a casual lunch, followed by Owen's inviting her to dinner at an upscale French bistro in Malibu. When he wasn't at the studio talking shop, he was with Karen, wining and dining, engaging in randy all-nighters.

She was not his usual type. Her tawny-skin, dark hair and fuller figure was new and enticing. Karen was challenging, not an easy lay by any means. Bright, coltish and sexy, she reminded him of his late wife, Vera Daniels. Karen knew what she was doing when handling men. Owen, the reputed womanizer, was no exception. He definitely suited her fancy with his exceptional looks, fit physique and generous equipment, which he shamelessly packaged in tight jeans. He was perfect and she aimed to have some fun.

Shel Friedman had offered her the good life early on. Hired as his secretary, then his mistress, they had an understanding that either could end the affair at any time. Karen learned the ropes, wheeling and dealing within the Hollywood machine, acquiring an insider's knowledge of the industry boy's club. Shel saw to her personal needs generously; providing a new Mercedes convertible, top-of-the-line wardrobe and make-over and luxury apartment on Sunset Blvd. In exchange, she was at his beck and call, furnishing him with sexual servitude and a listening ear.

The affair with Shel passed, but Karen kept a respected position and permanent place in Friedman's infrastructure at Universal. In truth, she wielded almost as much power as her mentor. Owen's proclivity for beautiful woman and his rampant libido and attraction to Karen, made his set-up at the studio perfect. Nothing like working creatively and getting his sexual needs met at the same time! He had that history and was ready to take her on.

Owen was back in New York for the time being. He got settled at his apartment on the west side and decided to check in. After two rings, Dick Landry picked up. "Royal Theatre, backstage, this is Landry." "Good evening, Dick, Matthews here." "Owen! How are things on the coast?" "Fine Dick, just got in this afternoon. I was thinking of coming by, checking the show tonight." "Do you want me to make an announcement to the cast?" "No, let it be a surprise, it's been a while." "Sounds good. How about following intermission?" "That works. I'll meet you and the gang in the green room." "Great, see you then." The call finished, Owen settled back, reached for a smoke and poured his favorite scotch, Glenfiddich. He'd check the show and focus on Catherine. After all, Karen was on the coast and he was hornier than hell.

At half hour, the company prepared for the show, their usual energy and enthusiasm in high gear. Pat and Catherine chatted as they worked their hair and applied make-up. Theirs had become a solid friendship in recent weeks. Pat felt like Catherine's big sister, a listening ear, willing to advise and liked socializing with her outside the theatre. Besides being fellow artists, they had an unknown in common, Owen Matthews! Pat's former lover was also Catherine's, present, though neither knew of the other's former or current involvement. They also shared a deep disgust with Tim Bartel. Back in high school, six years before, Tim was Pat's first lover. He cleverly courted, used her for sex and dropped her abruptly, causing deep humiliation and hurt. That betrayal created Pat's low self esteem and insecurity where men were concerned. When Owen approached her during *Bravo Business* the previous year, she was star struck by the re known director. Hooked by his attention, she became an easy mark for an affair. He was fatally glamorous to the naïve Pat, who hopefully clung to the relationship, such as it was. Though Owen fell in love with her, a fact that surprised him, he had no intention of claiming her publically or making a permanent commitment. He used her to his advantage both artistically and sexually, leaving Pat totally besotted with him.

When the show opened to smash reviews, Owen began an affair with a *New York Times* reporter, Stephanie McNeil, who did a featured article on him and *Centipede* for the paper's variety section, prior to the Broadway opening. She was all business in the beginning, but though she was professional, Owen found her incredibly attractive, a challenge and a turn-on. In time her reserve and resistance waivered, moving her toward a potential affair. At the time, Pat was on leave from the show, tending to her father, Alan, who had suffered a near fatal heart attack and was being cared for by the Byrne family. One evening, Owen and Stephanie happened upon each other in a bar, as she and some newspaper pals were celebrating her birthday. Owen moved in with his usual approach, taking full advantage of the inebriated reporter. Offering to see her home, she did nothing to resist him. Seduction turned to mutual need, the two engaging in sex whenever possible. She became wild, once unleashed sexually, creating an entrée for his kinkier side. Just the thought of her made him horny, that only taking her would abate. Then, a slip-up! Following a period of doubt and suspicion over Owen's elusive behavior and lack of attention, Pat stayed over, making up for lost time with rampant and continual sex. As they sat eating breakfast the next morning, the phone rang. The female voice on the other end was hard to miss. Stephanie! Owen tried to cover the unexpected call, hanging up abruptly. But Pat knew, convinced of an affair. Following a major confrontation, she fled. It was over, breaking her heart. In time, the pain wore off, but doing his show was a challenge. Blaine Courtman, multimillionaire and major financial backer of *Centipede* showed up opening night, much to Pat's surprise. A former dalliance on tour, he fell madly in love with Pat. Though she abruptly ended the affair, Blaine never gave up the notion they might one day renew their friendship. Once she was emotionally free of Owen, Blaine moved into her heart. A bright future lay ahead.

Catherine became Owen's next interest, following his break-up with Pat and Stephanie ending their affair. He found Catherine, sitting alone in a bar and approached her with his glamorous allure and artistic reputation. She was a dancer; new in town, star struck, ambitious and ripe for taking. He was immediately attracted to her beauty and charmed by her obvious naiveté. Getting into that body, her dance skill was secondary at first, but then he realized, it was to his advantage to make Catherine his exclusive lover and hire her as a replacement in *Centipede*. Encouraging her to audition was easy. She'd do anything for him and so, she showed up and was cast! His plan was perfect! She would dance for him, fulfilling her ambition, as she satisfied his insatiable libido. Everyone had a price and that's how Owen rolled.

The cast heard Dick's voice over speakers at intermission. "Company, please report to the green room at the 5-minute call." Upstairs, the gypsies dried off, redid soggy face paint, straggling hair, in preparation for the sailors-on-leave opener. It was almost time for the second act, as they made their way to the change area. When all were ready they assembled in the green room. Dick took a head count and waited for them to quiet down. "Ladies and gentlemen, we like to surprise you on occasion. Owen?" An audible gasp escaped from Catherine. Pat nudged her, whispering, "He's just full of surprises, isn't he?" Others took his appearance in stride, as he sauntered into the room. He was tan, a healthy glow on his face. His cropped hair was lighter than usual, highlighted by the California sun. As always, his mustache was neatly trimmed, his body fit and his manner, smooth. "Well, gang, the first act looked great; tight and clean. You haven't lost your finesse and timing. Thank you for keeping the numbers from unraveling." His charges hung on every word. Joe, who never minced words, spoke up. "Hey boss, where have you been keeping yourself lately?" Murmurs were heard throughout the group.

"Well, you'll hear this sooner or later, so I'll make it sooner. I've signed with Universal Pictures to direct the movie version of *Bravo Business* next year. A deafening cheer went up amongst the group. Joe's voice cut through the noise. "That's great, Owen, ever direct a film?" "It will be a different application to go from stage to screen. But, as you well know, Joe, I never back off from a challenge," he said, smiling. "Right now the studio is looking for investment partners. The brass insists on a financial guarantee to back a huge gamble. Producing a movie musical is an unknown, a major risk for them."

Pat was barely listening to Owen's spiel until she heard 'investment partners.' Suddenly perking up, she couldn't wait to tell Blaine about this development, which might hold interest. "Places, please," said Dick, checking his watch. Excusing himself, Owen left the green room and headed to the back of the house. Catherine, feeling bent and moody, started toward her position. Suddenly, Dick handed her a note, surprising her. She found a bit of stage light to illuminate the paper, quickly unfolding it. The message was written in Owen's hand:

"Baby, meet me at my place after the show tonight. We have catching up to do." Catherine felt a rush of warmth through her body, her mind beginning to whirl. 'He wants me, he really does. God, I can't wait!' The sailor number took off. Following the show, she hurried through her change, gave Pat a hug and left the theatre.

It was late when the buzzer rang. Owen went to the door and glanced through the peep hole.

Catherine stood, red hair cascading over her shoulders, green eyes bright with excitement. Without delay, she was in his arms. His kiss burned through her, his tongue exploring her lips and mouth. She sighed, as he continued, his hands caressing her face. Gently, he pulled away, a penetrating gaze fixed on her. "Baby, I've missed you so much," he whispered, taking her hand and kissing it gently. "How does champagne sound?" Catherine eagerly dropped her bag on a chair and followed him to the bar. "Let me look at you. You're so beautiful. I love your hair down," he soothed, as he popped the cork. "I could come in my pants, when I look at you!" She normally blushed at his flattery, but tonight it felt empty and much too practiced. "I've waited for you to stop by or call for weeks," she said with an edge. Owen poured her a glassful and one for himself.

"Now Baby, I've been on the coast, you know that," he explained carefully. "No, I didn't know, not until your announcement tonight." "I had to keep it under wraps until the project was official." "Couldn't you at least have called?" Owen set his glass down abruptly. "What is this, the third degree? Baby, don't push me," he said, his voice rising. "Never question me!" Owen was forceful and in that moment, Catherine backed down. She was weak with longing, hooked on him, in spite of her mood. Owen tried a different tact.

"Baby, come on, you're here now with me. Let's drink to our reunion." Raising his glass he nudged hers and together they downed the bubbly. "Would you like another?" She nodded and handed him her glass. Together, they finished the bottle. Catherine was completely buzzed and eager, anticipating what was to come. Without a word, he swept her in his arms and carried her to his bed. Her body ached in anticipation. No time was wasted undressing her. No words were spoken as he began his masterful work. His tongue found hers, his hands coveting her completely. Forcing her hands behind her back, Catherine felt a silken tie being wrapped around her wrists. Surprised but excited, she waited for his next move. Owen forcefully pushed her down, a wild look on his face. She watched as he stood before her, slipping off his t-shirt and unzipping his fly. The jeans came off seamlessly, his large erection in full view. Breathlessly, she lay bound, wet with want. He approached, fondling himself, a smirk on his face. Though fascinated, Catherine found this randy approach intimidating. He knelt and with little effort his hands plied her as his tongue penetrated. Gasping, she felt his hot breath, the wetness of his tongue deep inside her. His rhythm varied, like perfect choreography, while she writhed and moaned. "Come Baby, come for me," he whispered, his voice hoarse. Catherine felt her orgasm near the brink. Then a rush, her body exploding in ripples. As waves of pleasure subsided, Owen stood, with a look of satisfaction on his face. "Good girl, you did well. This calls for more champagne."

He left the room, leaving her tied and spent. Minutes passed before he returned with two glasses and a bottle of Moet. Helping her sit up, he released her wrists. Pouring a glassful, he joined her, handing her the drink. The cool bubbles and wetness of the champagne relieved her dry mouth and throat. Owen sat nearby and drank, silently gloating at his handiwork. "Did you like being tied, Baby?" "You never did that before, how come?" He shrugged. "I thought a change would be fun, something a little different for my girl. Bondage is a turn on, don't you agree?" Catherine was silent for a moment. Tears welled as she tried to form her words carefully. "I don't know, I like sex when it's mutual." He noticed her tears. "Hey, what's this?" Catherine looked away, wiping her eyes. "I've missed you, that's all." "Well, I'm back for now." Catherine put down her glass. "Yes, I know. I just thought you might have missed me a little." "For crying out loud, you're in my bed aren't you?" She took a different tact.

"You know, there's a guy interested in seeing me," she toyed. Owen perked up. "Oh, who's that?" "I don't know his name, but he keeps showing up, coming on to me and he's very attractive," she teased. "Well, Baby, if that's what you want, go ahead. Fuck this guy and we're through, get it?" Surprised, she backed down. "I don't want him, I want you," she said, her voice cracking. Owen smiled. "Well, as long as we understand each other, Baby. Come on, stay the night?" She reached for him, hugging him close. "I love you Owen, only you!" "Let's go again he said, taking her glass. Smiling weakly, she handed him the silk scarf. "This time, can I tie you?" He chuckled wickedly, turned around and positioned his wrists, waiting to be bound. "Whatever you say, Baby. Have at it!" Catherine stayed.

Across town, Pat arrived at the Plaza. She was eager to see Blaine, who had been on another business trip to Canada. The Long Island venture was a go, with Courtman Enterprises building a facility there. The Canadians had shown interest as well adding to the company's potential expansion in Montreal and now, Vancouver. This acquisition would further the company's holdings and triple the investment. Using her key, Pat walked into the penthouse at the Plaza she now shared with Blaine. He had surprised her, following their commitment, by leasing a larger suite for them, one that included all the amenities of a luxury apartment; two bedrooms with walk-in wardrobe closets, a fully-equipped kitchen, dining room, den and living room. Each bedroom had a luxury bath with sunken tub, Jacuzzi, bidet, and shower.

For a moment she listened, the air still. Not being sure if Blaine was in, she put down her things and went from room to room. As she rounded the corner she gazed into the den, spotting Blaine in front of the fireplace, sipping a snifter of Courvoisier. He looked delicious, newly showered, in his luxurious robe, his hair falling carelessly on his forehead. "Blaine!" He turned and smiled. Holding his arms out to her, she hurried to him. Enfolding her, their lips met. A tiny essence of brandy made the moment even more sensuous, as he kissed her deeply. She sighed, staying put, his embrace meaning everything. She was deeply in love. Returning his love, he made a promise that their future together was assured. She was his princess and he, her knight, who returned after her heartbreaking breakup with Owen Matthews. Pat never revealed to Blaine her former relationship with the director, ancient history now. All she knew or cared about was her second chance at true love, with a man who was everything to her. "Join me, Patricia," he murmured, patting a spot on the settee next to him. "Would you care for a brandy?" Pat slipped off her jacket and cuddled up to him. "Yes, I'd love one and hear about your trip." "No business right now. I just want to hold you. I've missed you so much. Let's sit for awhile. The fire is so pleasant." He poured her a snifter and handed it to her. "Do you know how much I love you? When I travel for business, all I can think about is returning home. You make me so happy, my Patricia." She smiled, tears welling, as she gently caressed his face, playfully brushing the lock of hair off his forehead. They sat, sipping cognac, enjoying the fire and each other. After a long silence he put down the snifter. "How is the show going, Darling?" "It's good and tight, no worse for the wear, eight shows a week." Then Pat remembered.

"Owen Matthews stopped by the theatre tonight. He hasn't been around for awhile. Rumors were confirmed when he told the company he's been in L.A., signing a contract with Universal Pictures. He's going to direct a film version of *Bravo Business*, to be produced next year."

"Really, how interesting!" "There's more, Blaine. He let it slip that the studio is looking for investment partners as a guarantee for the picture. Apparently they are charting a new direction and they need additional finance to cover a gamble like this one." Blaine was silent for a moment.

"I like this development, Patricia. I might be interested." "Investing?" "Absolutely, you know my love for the theatre!" "But, this is film. Have you ever been involved before?" "No, but my pal in Houston, Gregory Morgan has. He's invested in several projects with his old fraternity brother from his undergrad days at Dartmouth, Shel Friedman." "Who's Shel Friedman, for heaven's sake?" "He's Vice President of Project Development for Universal, a real character and a close pal of Gregory's." "Really? What a coincidence!" Blaine picked up his drink. "Let's drink to this potential and to us!" They finished the cognac. Putting both snifters aside, he pulled her close, running his hands through her hair. "Let's not waste a moment more, my beautiful Patricia," he whispered. "I'm going to make love to you all night long," he murmured, pulling her to her feet. "You've showered and I need one," she giggled, as they headed down the hall toward the master suite. "Don't keep me waiting," he teased. "I'll be with you in a heartbeat," she assured, pulling her sweater off, tossing it with the finesse of a stripper. Blaine could feel his erection growing as he watched her remove all her clothing and pull back her hair. Her ridiculously long legs, tight, round ass and small breasts were like a smorgasbord of visual delights. Her mound was shaven, adding to his desire to explore that tantalizing region, framed by milky skin and a neat strip of red pubic hair.

Drawing back the covers, he waited for her to complete her shower. In minutes his Venus stood before him, a flash of flaming tresses cascading over her tiny shoulders. Blaine had disrobed and was lying on top of the coverlet, a heavenly sight for Pat, who quickly joined him. And so their night of lovemaking began; deliciously languid, torridly intense and all consuming.

Julie Jensen couldn't get Tim Bartel off of her mind. Something about him intrigued her, but what was it? She could sense his transparency in matters of sex, sport fucking with no complications. She found it intriguing, knowing nothing of the danger. Her Greek, Nicholas, hadn't pounced, though she was willing to let him. Not even a call since their brunch date! She had overestimated his attraction. Though Greek, he was no sexual Adonis! How wrong she was to waste her time, time better spent with someone more attentive to her. Horny and out of sorts she pondered her next move. The selection of date possibilities in *Centipede* was sparse. The straight newcomers seemed a little too career-minded and the gay boys were fun socially, but offered no sexual potential.

'Damn it, I need relief,' she thought, her mind in a whirl. She was becoming convinced that Tim Bartel was the one she'd zero in on. Picking up the phone, she dialed Catherine and waited. Two rings later, she heard her best friend's voice. "Hi Cath, it's me. Do you have time to meet for a bite at noon? I have something to run by you. "I guess so. Let's meet at 1:00 at Allen's, okay?" "Perfect, see you then." Catherine found Julie at a table near the bar and joined her. They hugged and settled. A waiter took their orders, Cokes and the house burger special. Julie appeared agitated as she sat immersed in thought. Catherine noticed and finally got her chatting.

"Ok, Toots, what's going on? You seem preoccupied. Is it your Greek friend?" Julie shot her a pinched look, followed by a caustic reply, "For crying out loud, Cath, I haven't heard from him at all, the fucking loser!" Catherine sat back, out of firing range. "Whoa, Julie, how'd you get that burr up your ass?" "Well, he hasn't bothered to call after the nice afternoon we spent. I don't know what his deal is, honestly!" "Maybe he found you too direct. You're not exactly the shrinking violet type, now are you?" "Well, thanks for nothing! What kind of pal are you?" "An honest one, Julie. I saw how you came on to him at Mulfetta's, not once, but twice." "Well, he did call, now didn't he?" "Yes and invited you to brunch, which doesn't constitute a roll in the sheets." "Damn it, Cath, I thought we had potential, but if I wait for him to call, I'll be too old and dried up, if you get my drift." "Perfectly! You are a crazy, horny broad!" Julie ignored the remark, pressing on. "So where do I go from here? Where do I find a guy who's interested in sex without complication? For Christ's sake, I'm available, healthy and horny!"

Lunch arrived and as they ate, the silence between them deafening. Wolfing down her burger, Julie paused and sipped her Coke. She watched Catherine with interest. "Are you seeing anyone? Are you getting some?" Catherine put down her burger and wiped her fingers on a napkin. She proceeded carefully, not wanting anyone to know about Owen, especially her best friend. "Believe me, Julie, I see someone away from the show, but it's really no one's business," she said with a defensive edge. "I'm not just anyone. Who is it? Come on, fess up!" "No one you know and certainly not a chorus boy. He's a business man, who has nothing to do with show biz," she lied. "Wow, how did you meet someone that stable?" Catherine continued her lie. "Pat Byrne introduced us. He's a friend of her boyfriend and he's all class." "Has he pounced? I mean, have you gotten laid?" "Julie! Is that all you think about? He's a gentleman through and through. We see each other as often as possible." Julie couldn't resist. "Is he good in the sack? I mean, are you getting your needs met?" There was a faint blush on Catherine's face. "I really don't think that's anyone's business," she snapped. "Easy, Cath, I meant no offense, just curious that's all. It's nice to know someone I consider my best friend is getting taken care of!" "Quite well, thank you," said Catherine, though in her mind, she felt sad and incomplete." Julie perked up.

"Well, I'm available, no doubt about it! Say, what do you know about Tim Bartel? I'm kind of attracted to him. He sure is sexy!" Catherine almost choked on the rest of her burger. Gathering her thoughts, she took Julie's hand and squeezed it. "Julie, you can't be

serious. Tim has one of the worst reputations around *Centipede!* Julie
was suddenly all ears. "How in hell do you know so much, on whose
authority?" Catherine continued. "I heard that he was seeing Cynthia,
going hot and heavy, then dumped her flat. He moved on to Fran and
practically raped her. There's no telling his history, but I bet there's a
long line of women he's used for sex and discarded!" "It's probably gossip from disgruntled women who wanted him and didn't get a tumble."
"Don't be so naïve, Jules. He's a predator, through and through." "I still
would like to know who told you this shit." "The truth is he's tried to
come on to me several times. He's creepy, I mean really nasty and oily.
He tried to score a date during the show, affecting my performance. I
confided in Pat Byrne and she filled me in about him." "Well, it's probably all malicious gossip and sour grapes. The guy is fabulous looking
and can he dance! And, to put it bluntly, did you ever get a load of the
package in his dance pants? Heaven sent!" Catherine had enough.

"Julie, you're riding for a fall. Don't say you weren't warned! Please
don't invite trouble, this guy will hurt you!" Julie abruptly reached for
the check. "This one's on me! No thanks for the crummy advice. I've
got to go. See you at half hour." Julie paid the waiter and was out the
door, leaving Catherine deeply concerned. 'Oh Lord, what now? What
a fool!' Trouble was on the horizon for Julie Jensen.

Chapter 14

Tokyo Environs

Rehearsals at the primary school had ended and the company was
ready to work at the theatre. The Kamata girls stopped to watch
rehearsals the final week, introducing their parents to the company.
Through conversation, Mally learned the family planned to attend the
show sometime during the run.

On the last day off before tech week, Jeff organized a group to Kamakura and back. The ancient village was only an hour by train and featured points of interest not to be missed. Mr. Kubota-san offered to escort them as they would require assistance with directions and language. Following breakfast, Jeff waited in the lobby for those going, including Nora, Chad, Maddy, Neely and Terry, the male swing. Mally decided to stay behind and relax before the final push to opening, but encouraged her fellows to take photos and bring back details. Other company members declined, wishing to use the day off for personal business. The six intrepid ones and Kubota-san set off for Tokyo station, eager to begin their adventure. Their guide and interpreter created a sense of comfort, knowing they were in good hands.

Arriving at Tokyo central station, Kubota-san purchased seven round-trip tickets. Soon, they were on board, finding seats nearby, while Kubota sat at the front of the car. As the vast city of Tokyo gradually disappeared into a rural setting, all eyes watched the countryside fly by. Japanese commuter trains were modern, high speed transits with plush interiors, a variety of refreshments for purchase, comfortable high back reclining seats and tinted windows. "Look at the tiny villages. They're so quaint!" Clearly intrigued, Nora pressed her nose to the window, not wanting to miss a detail. "How fast do you think we're going?" "Faster than New York transit, I'd wager," said Chad. Jeff paged through his guide book noting the speed. "This baby will travel up to 95 mph!" "You're joking, what's the hurry?" Neely was feeling the motion, closing her eyes to ward off growing nausea. "Fuck me, I'm a dancer and I'm motion sick," she murmured to no one.

An hour passed and the train gradually slowed, moving into the station at Kamakura. Kubota-san was first off and stood on the platform waiting. "Stay together and we will go on foot through Kamakura. There is much to see." As they walked down narrow streets past tiny houses of paper and wood, the gypsies got an eyeful. The crisp day was a delight, a display of grey blue sky and inviting sun. Some had appropriate outer wear for the cool day. Nora wore a heavy sweater and knitted cap, being a freeze baby. The long walkway ended at an open plaza just ahead. Maddy spoke up.

"Mr. Kubota-san, where is the giant Buddha, the one you see in travel brochures?" She only had to wait a moment. As the gypsies rounded a corner, there stood the colossus Buddha, Daibutsu. "Oh my God, he's for real," shouted Neely. "I've seen this on posters for years!" As Kubota and the gypsies approached, a small crowd of Japanese and foreign tourists stood, transfixed by the majesty of the statue. Only clicking cameras could be heard. "It's almost like being in church, an unmistakable silence here," observed Jeff, thrilled to be at the foot of the giant. Minutes passed before Kubota spoke. "We can walk to the sea from here. The fishing is abundant this time of year. You will see the fisherman's nets for miles." Joining him, they walked past tea shops, small businesses and tiny houses. Nora was enthralled. "This is such an amazing opportunity, being here, Jeff! I'm so glad we're doing this together." He hugged her close. Suddenly the seashore came into view, a vast panorama of cloudless sky, etched by choppy waves. Rows and rows of fishing nets, as far as one could see, were suspended on wooden pillars. Waving gently in the breeze, the moving nets looked like slow motion dance, framed by distant hills beyond. Stopping along the shore, the gypsies took in fresh salt air and aroma of sea life dotting the wet sand. Some snapped photos, lasting images to take back to the States, a treasure trove of new memories just beginning.

Later, Kubota-san suggested a teahouse for refreshments before returning to Tokyo. As they ventured down a back street, a charming place appeared. The modest wooden store front held flower boxes of withered and pale plants. A sign in Japanese, hung over the front door. "The owners are friends of mine. They have been expecting us. Dozo," he added, gesturing for them to enter. The tiny store was without heat, but warm compared to the seashore. The gypsies found chairs as a kimono-clad older woman entered from the back room, carrying a tray of tea and tiny cups. "Konnichiwa!" A toothy grin, followed by a bow, she proceeded to place pots and cups on tables. "Dozo," she said, pointing. "Please have some tea," motioned Kubota, sitting down. The gypsies joined him, passing pots to each other. Steam rose as green tea was poured, the warmth taking the chill off. The woman returned with small bowls of snacks, unfamiliar to them. "Rice crackers dipped in tamari, very popular and tasty," said Kubota, noting quizzical looks. The offering was welcome, as they had missed lunch. Time passed quickly. Returning to the station, the group boarded a train back to Tokyo. It had been a pleasant day of firsts, observing a culture vastly different from theirs. As the train sped through the countryside, Nora dozed against Jeff's shoulder, while he perused his guide book. The others chatted quietly, sharing impressions of their visit, an adventure, thankfully not missed.

On Monday it all began, the call beginning at noon. The gypsies entered the massive theatre and were shown to dressing rooms. Spacious, immaculate and equipped with the latest furnishings, they selected places to sit along shiny Formica dressing tables. The mirrors were impressive, lined with light bars, the illumination flattering to any face. Closed circuit TV was suspended above a seating area, filled with comfortable furniture. Those off stage during a performance could watch the action, hear audience response and note a coming cue. The entire Nissei theatre was latest state-of-art down to every detail. *Centipede* was selected to commemorate the first anniversary of the venue, the close of its present season.

As the company settled, Griff's voice was heard through speakers in each area. "Ladies and Gentleman, please report to the house in five minutes. Thank you!" There was general activity and haste as dancers finished setting up their places along mirrors. It was tradition that once you chose a spot, it remained yours throughout the run. The dressing rooms were conveniently located on the stage level, with easy access to the wings. No more running down several flights to make an entrance! Gathering in the 1500 seat house, some gypsies chatted, while the curious stared at the surroundings until Griff appeared with Mr. Watanabe-san and staff. The group quieted, waiting for an announcement.

"Good morning, company! Welcome to the Nissei Theatre. Before we begin a work through today, Mr. Watanabe would like to say a few words. Mr. Watanabe?" The producer took the mic from Griff and began. "We are pleased to have you with us for this engagement. We have a few house rules to follow. There will be no smoking anywhere on the theatre premises. At the stage door exit there is an area with an overhang, protective during inclement weather. Ashtrays are provided for convenience. Please deposit the remainder of your cigarettes when finished. No food or drink in the dressing rooms. Our green room provides you with vending machines and places to sit, eat, read, or whatever activity you choose. Our dressers are fluent in English, so you will want to introduce yourselves at the first dress rehearsal. Discount tickets are offered to cast members during the run. You may invite four guests to our final dress next week, if you wish. Looks were exchanged amongst the gypsies. "Who does he think we know here to invite?" "Shush Neely, it's a courtesy, that's all," whispered Maddy. "Maybe some of the Kamata family will come," said Nora, overhearing. "Well, we are acquainted, sort of," cracked Neely. Griff took over.

"We will do a run-through of the show this afternoon with our tech elements in place, minus orchestra. Ted Benedict will play from the pit. Your musical director, George Eliot will conduct a full run with the orchestra on Wednesday afternoon. I've posted a schedule in the green and dressing rooms. Chad raised his hand. "When will we work in costume?" "You will have costumes tomorrow to try and on Wednesday, we will run the complete show including make-up." "Yes, Neely?" "Will the run today be start and stop?" "Yes, as we have to. I suggest you acquaint yourselves with the layout. This venue is vast backstage and the difference in distance from the change areas to stage right and left entrances may require you to adjust your timing. The change areas are on the lower level adjacent to the orchestra pit. Please walk your route before our start today. Are there any other questions? Yes, Maddy?" "Can Terry and I watch from the house this afternoon?" "Absolutely, feel free to sit anywhere you have the best overall view of the show. Also, please walk the backstage area, so in the event you have to swing the show you will already know your timing to and from the stage." "When is half hour today?" "Nora, half hour is at 1:30. We will run at 2:00 sharp, so please stay in the theatre. Are there any other questions?" Griff noticed a hand go up. "Will we run the show twice today?" "Yes, you will be given a break between 5:00 and 7:30. We will treat 7:30 as half hour throughout the run. On matinee days, half hour will be 1:30. It is now close to 1:00. Please take some time to familiarize yourselves with the backstage area. Thank you!"

As the group dispersed, Jonas and Phillipe approached. "Griff, do you want us with you at the production table this afternoon?" "Yes, I will need you within ear shot to address any concerns. Phillipe, please take notes while Jonas and I confer. If you see any potential problems adapting our choreography to this space, let me know." "Done," said Phillipe. "Why don't you guys take a few minutes while I do the pre-set? I'll see you back here at 2:00." "Thanks, Boss, we'll be here," said Jonas, grabbing Phillipe by the arm. The two walked the stairs to the stage and disappeared behind the show drop.

On the lower level, the gypsies made their way through the cavernous space. "Wow, this feels like a jaunt," muttered Neely, as she walked the route from changing area to her first entrance stage right. "I get Griff's point." "No shit," added Chad. "This feels mammoth after the Royal!" "Going from swing in New York to a regular 8 times a week will be different," said Nora. "It's weird, but I kind of miss being swing. I hope I don't get complacent and sloppy with a regular spot," said Jeff. Nora added a thought. "Who's going to serve as dance captain once Jonas and Phillipe go back to New York? I hope one of us can keep an eye on things. The newcomers have enough to think about just learning and keeping up." "Yeah, we had six weeks back at the beginning. They've had three here," observed Chad. "I'm sure Jonas will have this covered. He'll assign during the first week run, guaranteed." "Hope so," said Nora. "Come on, Jeff. Let's do a warm-up," grabbing his hand. Jeff grinned as he was pulled toward the stairs. "You're such a stickler, Babe!" "That's why you're crazy about me, right?" Jeff grew serious. "Just one of the many reasons, Honey," he murmured softly. Stopping briefly, he took her in his arms and kissed her deeply. "Hey, you two, save it for the hotel," Chad tossed, passing them on the stairwell.

Always ready with a quip, Chad covered whatever was bothering him with humor. In truth, he longed for a lover. He missed his former fiancée, Mary Jane, who ended their engagement, preferring life in Detroit and earning a PhD. The bright lights of New York held no allure and Chad's potential earning power was dubious at best in show biz. No, she needed someone financially stable, someone willing to reside in Michigan. The break-up cut deeply. Following the break-up, of the women in *Centipede,* he was most attracted to Pat. When he showed the slightest interest, she made it clear he was a friend, nothing more. He wasn't interested in a backstage affair, a liaison beginning with fierce sexual attraction, followed by a torrid tryst, burning out at a show's closing. No, Chad Chapman wasn't interested in short term, or becoming a swinger. He was a constant, committed sort of guy.

At 1:30, Griff called half hour. Anticipating a long afternoon, the first tech could be painstaking. However, Griff was impressed and pleased with Watanabe's crew. They were disciplined, respectful and seasoned, making his job potentially facile at the helm. At the very least, it might move quickly. The dressing rooms were buzz with chatter. Though no one was bothering with make-up for the afternoon tech run, some of the girls tied their hair back or anchored it to the top of their heads for convenience and safety sake. Nora and Maddy, both having short hair, were the envy of the other women. After two hours of executing Owen's staging, even the tightest bound tresses became soaked and straggly. However, having short hair limited one's versatility for different looks and styles. Some shows provided wigs, regardless of an individual's hair length. *Centipede* was an exception, focusing on body line, execution and subtext, taking precedence over fashion. The choreography was the only star, the gypsies, facilitators of Owen's concept. They were hired to execute and carry out the context of his intention, nothing more.

At 2:00 PM sharp, Griff called places. The cast took their opening position, a freeze, aloft a 3-foot platform unit with a visible staircase at the front and escape stairs down the back. The amoebic vision stood motionless, as with the Broadway production. The only visible movement was obvious breathing, chests rising up and down in anticipation of the output it would take to dance the show from beginning to end. *Centipede* was not typical of Broadway shows with librettos, running 2 to 3 hours including intermission. Each act was 45 minutes of constant motion, nonstop with no breaks until intermission, allowing respite for 20 minutes, including changes. If Owen had his way, there would be no intermission; no break in the momentum of his staging, no interruptions of audience focus. Actor's Equity would not allow such a lengthy running time, given the physical demand on the performers. Well-being was paramount!

Ted Benedict was ready, seated at an exquisite baby grand, his fingers poised to start. On Griff's cue, he began the overture. Watanabe's sound crew had placed speakers in locations that best served to send sound throughout the house and backstage area. The orchestra pit needed no additional amplifying, save for one mic for the musicians, placed near the podium, next to conductor, George Eliot. On Wednesday's run, the cast would experience a first! No less than forty musicians would be in the pit, including musicians brought from New York: Ted Benedict, pianist and associate conductor; Andre Crenshaw, first violin; Fred

Granger, bassist and Jimmy Grey, percussion, all hand-picked, all excellent! Until then, Ted would solo, providing music. At overture's finish, the massive show drop rose slowly, revealing a wash of pastels on the cyclorama, while downstage, dimly lighted, an amoebic mass of bodies stood frozen. Moving slowly at first, one couple began to break out, then another. Following in tandem until the entire stage filled with whirling, writhing entities, each couple worked the position and spacing they were assigned. As the music intensified, so did the choreography, until every gypsy in the ensemble danced to his or her maximum. The bright stage lights, something not experienced in rehearsal by the newcomers, visually brought out every form, line and nuance of Owen's creation; blatantly erotic and unmistakably suggestive.

Out in the house, Maddy and Terry watched transfixed. The show swings had worked upstage of the regulars during rehearsals and had no idea what the total picture looked like. "The work is a turn-on, right in-your-face," whispered Terry," glancing over at Maddy. "Do you like it?" A blush returned. "Yes, but I'm wondering how I'll feel with hands besides yours all over me the first time I go on!" "Hell, we've rehearsed the choreography together for weeks, partnering with some other guy shouldn't be a big deal." "I know, but I'm comfortable with you," she said, reaching for his hand. "Well, thanks, I guess," flattered by her admission. Technically, there were no glitches in act one. The dancers found the stage floor top notch; no rough spots, imperfections, predictably safe. Many were familiar with less than desirable conditions in theaters across the country on tour, but the Nissei had everything! Griff called a 20-minute break, the length of intermission. Some of the gypsies gathered in the greenroom to grab a snack or hydrate. The Nissei provided filtered water through a dispensing unit for the convenience of cast, crew and orchestra. Mally was the first in line.

Her head cold was long gone, but she continued to drink copious amounts of fluid to keep hydrated, hopefully flushing out any lurking microbes. At sixteen, she developed a strep infection treated too late, compromising her immune system. A functional heart murmur was diagnosed which fortunately never limited her activity, but kept her keenly aware of her health. Taking a cool drink, she felt a sense of relief. "Places for act two," announced Griff, sending the gypsies to the preset. Many in the cast found the sailors-on-leave number their favorite.

Owen created movement suited to each couple's particular strengths. Based loosely on Jerome Robbins' ballet, *Fancy Free,* originally presented by Ballet Theatre in the late 40's, three sailors on a 24-hour leave see three women who attract them, culminating in love affairs, represented through the staging. At the start, the movements were buoyant, flirtatious and innocent. But soon the couples' time together was growing short, bringing a sense of urgency. The choreography became blatantly erotic and sensuous. Owen was masterful at creating symbolic consummation through dance, fulfilling audience fantasy.

Mally and Chad took the leads, followed by Nora and Jeff. Neely and her partner, Andy Wendt were the third couple featured. The remainder of the company represented city folk against a backdrop of buildings through lighting effects. In the event that either Mally or Chad missed a performance, Nora or Jeff would assume their roles, the swings Maddy and Terry filling in for them.

Remounting the original *Centipede* was an exact science, the replication imperative. Jonas was excellent teaching Owen's staging. Detail-oriented and infallibly accurate at making sure nothing was overlooked, he never missed a style nuance or failed to communicate Owen's intention in the subtext. He earned his place in Owen's creative infrastructure though dedication, exceptional technique and performing in his mentor's countless hit shows. Having Phillipe to assist was an added bonus. At first, their chance meeting in Atlanta was all about sex. Jonas was on the *Bravo Business* tour with fellow gypsy and his partner of ten years, Gary Hanson. When Gary was critically injured by a hit and run driver and unable to continue the rest of the tour, Phillipe replaced him. As time went on lust developed into commitment, as they fell deeply in love, becoming committed partners. Working as a team, putting together Owen's work in Japan, was an opportunity they cherished. At the end of afternoon tech, cast members headed back to the hotel. The need for a nap and shower was intense. The evening half hour call was for 7:30, allowing them time for a quick bite as well.

Mally, Jeff and Nora walked together to the Nikkatsu, a short stroll from the Nissei. In the past months Nora had blossomed with Jeff, following the company's return from the road. As they entered the elevator, Jeff had a tight hold on Nora's hand. Mally couldn't help notice. "So, when are you going to make it official?" Jeff gazed down at Nora, who returned a smile. "We've talked about it, but for now the show is first and foremost. If we get engaged, you and Griff will be the first to know, okay?" "Wonderful! Think about doing it here in Japan! What could be more romantic?" Reaching the hotel lobby, they headed to their rooms. Half hour call would come soon enough.

On Wednesday, the orchestra was added. Forty musicians filled the pit. The massive group was quite a sight to behold and larger than any orchestra on Broadway. On the downbeat, the gypsies couldn't believe the sound, so irresistible and inspiring! As the massive show drop rose, the richness of the music was like a transfusion of inspiration and transformation. *Centipede*, as though unearthed from a hidden place, was a forceful entity, beyond brilliant and inspiring.

Opening night was fast approaching as the show tightened. It was obvious to everyone: the company, Griff, Jonas, Phillipe and crew and Watanabe and staff, that something truly unique was about to transpire in the city of Tokyo. Watanabe had played a hunch and doubtless it was a right decision! Owen was contacted, but declined to come all the way across the continent and Pacific to attend the opening, choosing instead to trust those he hired to bring it. His confidence in Griff and Jonas was absolute, his faith in his veteran dancers was earned and after all, he had chosen the remaining dancers from the audition. He regarded his decision-making as fool proof. Also on his mind was his fast approaching Hollywood project. Bringing his Broadway hit, *Bravo Business* to the screen would take months of preparation. He now had to deal with higher echelon of the movie business, their egos and the task of transcribing a stage concept to film, a totally new animal to the Broadway veteran. He would be returning to Los Angeles in a few weeks, eager to clear any obstacles of finance, his creative process and seeing Karen Eliot, a perfect distraction and relief for his persistent libido. In the meantime, the New York production was a hit, continually sold out and Catherine was his sometime interest and recreation. Life was terrific!

Chapter 15

The Nissei Opening

Friday night arrived with a readied company, crew and orchestra. The house had been sold out for weeks including the Japanese general public, cultural and political dignitaries, press and local celebrities. More floral arrangements than one could count arrived! The dressing rooms were alive with pre-show activity. The lobby was filled to capacity with eager patrons filing into the house. Like Broadway tradition, celebratory activity would take place following the show.

Watanabe arrived with his devoted wife, a noted physician, Uriko; two sons, Mori and Shegeki, both esteemed teachers; and his lovely daughter, Myoshi, newly graduated from college. Currently interning for her father, she hoped to work full time as an accountant in his organization. The Watanabe Family was shown to their private box, house right.

"Fifteen minutes," announced Griff. "Please come to the green room for a short meeting at five minutes. Thank you!" The gypsies hurried through last minute prep, some quickly heading to the change area for costumes, while others put final touches on hair and make-up. "Oh God, this is nerve wracking," said Neely, checking herself in the mirror. Mally and Nora exchanged looks, remembering *Centipede*'s opening on Broadway.

Griff and his crew were immersed in pre-show preparation, a well-organized machine; light, sound, tracks and rigging checks in full swing. At five minutes he called the company together.

Eager faces greeted him as Jonas and Phillipe joined him in the green room. When all had assembled, he began. "Company, tonight we are about to embark on what could be a plus for international relations. The Japanese public is eager to see what we've brought here. The audience is ready and we are as ready as we will ever be. Please note glow tape marking set piece positions and the closest safe exit. During blackouts, proceed with caution. There is greater distance to cover here, so find the most expedient and safe route to take as noted in rehearsal. You are a remarkable group and management is grateful for your dedication and hard work. Turning to Jonas, he smiled. "Anything to add?" Jonas stepped forward and glanced over the group.

"Gang, both Phillipe and I are impressed with the caliber of your work, your attention to each detail of Owen's staging. You are to be congratulated for replicating *Centipede* in the truest sense. Thank you! Break a leg!" Applause broke out as a hand went up. "Neely?" "Griff, will there be an opening night gathering of some kind?" "Yes, the tradition here calls for an on-stage ceremony following the performance and then a party. The party will be held on the third floor. There will be signs posted by show's end. Following the bows, please remain on stage. Thank you! Places, please!" After that, it was a blur.

When the overture ended and the show curtain rose, the sound was deafening. The cavernous house was filled to capacity. As the show unfolded, cheering from ecstatic patrons was thunderous. *Centipede,* a uniquely crafted pastiche; eclectic, exquisitely staged and performed, had immediate impact, grabbing the aesthetic sense of the audience. Owen Matthews' work was a masterpiece, uniquely American, profoundly brilliant. Two acts flew by. As the show came down, the audience rose up en mass, like a tidal wave spilling over the gypsies, now spent and breathless. As bow after bow continued, containment in the house was impossible. The roar from patrons grew stronger as Hiro Watanabe appeared with an entourage following him. The group, dressed in traditional attire, snaked through the house, up the stairs to the stage, where they formed a circle, enclosing the cast. The women carried garlands of red and white flowers and began passing one to each gypsy. When all were assembled, the orchestra began playing *Kimi Ga Yo*, the national anthem of Japan, as the Japanese flag was lowered from above. Glorious voices filled the air, as the entire audience joined in. At the conclusion, the crowd heard *The Star-Spangled Banner* erupt, as the U.S. flag descended slowly. Goose bumps dominated, the gypsies wiping tears away as they sung in full voice. Enthusiastic applause followed as Hiri Watanabe stepped forward. His voice was filled with emotion as he spoke into a mic, provided by an assistant.

"Tonight, we acknowledge these fine artists for their contribution to the culture of our land and to greater world culture. We are privileged to receive one of the finest representations of American Musical Theatre, *Centipede*. It is our honor to welcome you to our shore. Please accept our admiration, blessings and humble thanks for a successful run here at the Nissei."

As he spoke, a group of six men arrived, drums attached to their torsos. As percussive sounds issued forth, six kimono-clad women carrying large fans moved into position next to each drummer. On cue, each dancer moved consecutively to the beats, using the fan to enhance their movements. Breathtakingly beautiful, their precision was flawless as they performed for the throng. The gypsies stood, riveted and moved by the demonstration, the Japanese dancers beautiful, with their doll-like make-up and traditional wigs. At the conclusion of their dance, Watanabe spoke again. "Please join us for a party on level three." The crowd dispersed and the company, still in the glow of their triumphant beginning, headed to dressing rooms. "Jeez, this is so thrilling," cooed Nora, giving Jeff's hand a squeeze. "I'll meet you on level three in a half hour, okay?" "I'll be there, Honey," he whispered, stealing a kiss. Chad was right behind him. "Oh, give it a rest, will you?" "Hey Chad, are you dateless?" "Come now, Jenkins, pretty slim pickings in this group, wouldn't you say?" "What about some of our gals? That's a fairly good selection!" "I don't like to date dancers. Most of them are too into themselves." "Not Nora." "No, you lucked out with her. You're a lucky man!" "Yes, I am," said Jeff, growing serious. "I never planned on this. It was just meant to be." "Kismet?" "Yeah and sheer luck! See you upstairs."

The party was bustling as the gypsies gathered amongst the crowd. A large buffet table was a welcome sight with an array of Japanese specialties and American choices as well. At one end of the room musicians played various string instruments, soft and gentle under scoring as attendees conversed. Waiters moved through the throng, offering champagne. A fully stocked bar was available with an array of Japanese and American beer, wine and mixed drinks. Some gypsies had discovered Asahi, Kirin and Sapporo brands, enjoying a different beer taste from U.S. favorites.

Griff, Mally, Jonas and Phillipe arrived together, elegantly dressed. The handsome quartet was greeted by Watanabe, who introduced his family. Gracious charm was in evidence as they were welcomed. Mally took to Mrs. Watanabe and daughter, Myoshi immediately, admiring their deportment, dressed in traditional kimono attire. They in turn couldn't take their eyes from her. Mally wore a tea-length lavender sheath, her upsweep encircled by a crown of delicate pink tea roses. The Watanabe sons were too well brought up to stare at *Centipede's* leading lady, but a hint of blush was visible. "Mr. Watanabe, thank you for hosting us. We appreciate your generous hospitality and welcome presence tonight," said Griff. Watanabe bowed in return, his pleasure obvious. "We are pleased you are here. Please, help yourselves to food and drink," pointing to the repast. Jonas and Phillipe headed to the bar, a sudden thirst taking over. Griff and Mally circulated, chatting with dignitaries and various press throughout the room. Chad and others arrived and worked their way to the buffet line. The selection of foods was extraordinary.

Neely noticed the choice of utensils; forks or chopsticks. Picking up a pair of wooden sticks she whispered, "What do you call these?" "Hashi," replied Jeff, as he helped himself to Sashimi. "Smart ass," she giggled. "Seriously, get used to them, they're the national utensil." "Once you have the hang of it, no problem," added Nora, selecting Tempura shrimp and vegetables, spearing a few pieces carefully. Maddy perused the table, spotting some unidentifiable items. "I wonder what that is." "Try it," encouraged Jeff, "Nothing ventured, I always say." "Ok, I will," she said, reluctantly, taking a small portion. Taking a bite, a strange facial expression formed. Jeff pointed to the dish, inquiring of a passing waiter, "Nan desu ka? Dozo!" "Hai, Tako, Unagi, Ika," he replied affably. Maddy swallowed reluctantly. "Well, what is it?" "You don't want to know, Maddy," he chuckled. "Come on Jeff, what?" "It's a combo of Sautéed eel, octopus and squid!" "I think I'm going to be sick," she whispered, putting the dish aside.

Across the room Chad stopped, mesmerized by the lilting, hypnotic music. As he listened to the haunting sound of the Koto, he felt a presence next to him. Turning, his breath caught as he looked into the face of a Dresden-doll. She was Japanese; petite, flawless in a blue silk kimono. Her long black hair was tied back, held in place by a single, fresh Gardenia. Her exquisite face framed dark, wide eyes, etched by long lashes. "You are a dancer, yes?" "Yes, I am! You speak English," said Chad, surprised by her lack of timidity. "Yes, I am fluent." Chad immediately felt comfortable. "*Centipede* is masterful, intriguing. I love the movement," she continued. "I'm Chad Chapman and you are?" "Myoshi." "Would you like some Sake?" "Yes, please!" "Wait here, I'll be right back."

Hurrying to the bar, Chad had slipped into another reality, completely captivated by the exquisite girl. Ordering Sake for two, he waited impatiently as the barman warmed the bottle, setting two small cups on a tray. Looking back, he studied her. She was unlike any woman he had ever seen. When the warmed rice wine was ready, he hurried back to her. She had made herself at home in a small alcove, smiling when he returned. He thought his heart would cease. Pouring for them was difficult, as he tried to steady his shaking hands. Handing hers, he raised his. "To *Centipede*," he said, self-consciously. "Thank you, Chad." They drank in silence, occasionally glancing at each other. For Chad, the attraction was intense. He felt like a school boy, a country rube, unable to form a clear sentence. Finally, he spoke.

"Tell me about yourself, Myoshi." "There is not so much. I finished college and I'm interning now." She took a sip of Saki, never taking her eyes from his. "I haven't met many Americans. You're the first I've been alone with." "You're kidding! How old are you?" "My birthday is next week. I'll be 20." "How old are you, Chad?" He hesitated, but decided to come clean. "I'm 25. I've been dancing professionally for four years." "Oh please, tell me everything!" He was struck by her candor, her refreshing approach. "Not a lot to tell, actually. I'm from Detroit, Michigan. Ever hear of Ford?" She nodded. "Our family has built cars for three generations." She sat riveted, focusing on every word. He continued. "I have three brothers in Detroit." "Do they make cars too?" Chad chuckled. "My two older are at Ford, my younger is a mathematician." "You have no sisters?" "No, it's just the four boys." "I, too, have only brothers. They are both older and are esteemed teachers." By now repeated cups of Sake had loosened Chad.

"Do you have a boyfriend?" "Oh no, I'm not old enough." Chad put down his cup. "You're kidding! You haven't dated?" "No, no, you must understand, it is proper for parents to select a potential husband. We are then allowed chaperoned exchanges." He felt like he'd been hit by a two-by-four.

"What if you fall in love with someone else, what then?" He reached for her, touching her face. "You are so sweet, Myoshi, I want to see you again." "Oh, I don't think so. It would make trouble for us." "Why?" Tears welled in her eyes as she looked away. "I can't, I'm so sorry." "Just my luck, I meet you, but it's not all right to see you. Well, I guess it's sayonara," he said, tinged with sarcasm, his disappointment obvious. "Oh please, Chad, don't be upset," she said, pleading softly. Without a word, he stood and walked away. Myoshi watched him disappear into the crowd. Her heart was bursting as she realized she, too, was attracted to the American.

The evening was triumphant. Jonas and Phillipe made the rounds, visiting with guests and press alike. Two attractive Japanese men approached. "Konbanwa!" "Good evening," echoed Phillipe in return. "I am Hukio Yoshii and my friend, Kori Fugata. We enjoyed your show." "Well, thank you," acknowledged Jonas. "We are delighted you came." There was something in their manner beyond a simple exchange of pleasantries. "You are dancers, yes?" "Yes, but not here. We staged *Centipede* for our director Owen Matthews, who is in New York." "I see," said Hukio. "Have you been out? We know places," he said, eyeing them up and down. "We have had no time to socialize. It's been constant work since we arrived." "We would be honored to show you around. Would you care to join us tonight?" Jonas and Phillipe exchanged looks. "Perhaps another evening," said Jonas. "It's a bit late and we've had a long week." The two bowed and walked away. "Cheri, are you thinking what I'm thinking?" A grin was visible on Jonas. "Two horny natives looking for action!" "Mais oui," whispered Phillipe, patting his ass. "Shall we?" "Hai, Dozo!" In moments, they were off to the Nikkatsu. Private party time!

The reviews were sensational. It was clear that *Centipede* had taken the Japanese public by storm! Box office reports indicated a sold-out run with only a smattering of single seats available for matinees. The weekends were completely gone. The cast achieved what it was here to do, if ticket sales were any indication!

With the show open and a hit, it was time for Jonas and Phillipe to return to New York. Owen had called to wish them well opening day and phoned Griff for a report following the reviews. He was extremely pleased his concept had wowed the Japanese, that Watanabe's hunch had proven correct; the show was innovative enough to achieve success overseas. He would now focus on his directorial film debut next year as well as a national company of *Centipede* in spring. He was at a pinnacle, career-wise, proving his work best of the genre.

Jeff Jenkins was notified that he was officially dance captain following Jonas' departure. No one else was considered as Jeff was swing on Broadway. Next to Joe Pinto, Owen's assistant during Jonas' absence, Jeff was technically adept and a natural leader. The gypsies respected his affable personality and skill. Yes, he was the right choice. Jeff was pleased with his new assignment and even happier being in love. Nora was the light of his life and he planned to propose. Mally's suggestion of making it happen in Japan was a romantic notion, but one that made sense.

He would find the appropriate time and place. Jeff knew with certainty he was ready for marriage and Nora was too.

Ever since their fateful meeting, Chad couldn't get Myoshi out of his mind. He had fallen hard. He phoned his best pal, Jeff. After two rings he heard, "Hey Chad, what's doing?" "I'm in a situation and need advice." "What's going on?" Chad took a moment, his thoughts whirling. "I've fallen in love." "Are you serious? I thought you weren't interested in our girls." "I'm not!" "Who is she?" "Her name is Myoshi." "She's Japanese? Whoa, buddy, this has complication written all over it!" "Yes, I know, but I have to see her." "And get your heart broken?" "She's worth the risk, Jeff." "I've read the Japanese are conservative about dating before marriage and especially racial mixing. You don't want a samurai sword up your ass!" "Thanks for the vote of confidence. I'll take my chances." The conversation ended.

Jonas and Phillipe would leave for the States soon. With the understanding that Owen would give them vacation time before returning to the Broadway production, Jonas phoned his father, Charles Martin in San Francisco. They would fly to California and spend a few days with him. Jonas was at peace ever since he came out to his father, the weekend of his mother's funeral two years before. All his life he'd struggled with his true identity, unable to be close to the elder Martin. His mother, Elizabeth, ironically reunited them through her passage. When he brought up his relationship with

Phillipe, Charles was accepting and encouraged the two to come for a visit. The timing was perfect!

With the show open, Mally and Griff finally had some down time. On days off, they would make forays in and out of the city, lapping up the culture and enjoying adventure in an unfamiliar setting. They planned to visit Kyoto soon, booking a night in a Ryokan, a Japanese inn. The lodging was all-inclusive with private suite, mineral springs, attendants and catered meals. The rest of the company enjoyed Tokyo environs; shopping, sightseeing, checking out Pachinko parlors near the Ginza and catching a performance of Kabuki. In the meantime, Jeff set up a private tutor, through the company interpreter, Kubota-san. Fumiko Mori came to the hotel to provide lessons in Japanese. She was a language major at Tokyo University, tutoring Japanese students in English. A perfect choice! Only a few showed up, convening in Jeff and Nora's room. Those who sensed the advantage of knowing basic Japanese enjoyed the experience. Miss Mori was an excellent tutor; very upbeat and patient with her American charges. Nora took to the lessons with a vengeance, hoping to keep up with Jeff's aptitude and interest in all things Japanese. She was told by her tutor that if she closed her eyes, she would think Nora Japanese when she spoke! Nora was thrilled and continued to work at it, purchasing a guide book of her own, *Japanese at a Glance.*

The gypsies of *Centipede* were treated to many firsts. A day trip at Nikko, a sacred destination for the Japanese, was financed by the Nissei Theatre. The venture proved astonishing. The bullet train sped through stunning country vistas when Mount Fuji was spotted in the distance, snow-capped and majestic. At one stop, the famous Wise Monkeys of "*Hear no evil, See no evil, Speak no evil*" fame were spotted, carved into the giant gates of the world-famous Nikko shrine. Building after building stood silent, solid, a feast to western eyes. After completing the shrine tour, the gypsies were bused through a rocky interior of narrow roads with winding switchbacks, along waterfalls spilling over crevices and other breathtaking sights. At the base of the mountain, a vast ice blue lake dotted by snow-capped peaks in the distance appeared like a painting! A forest of pine trees provided a scenic entrance to a magnificent pagoda-roofed building, with large picture windows and winding walkways leading to a massive front entrance. The gypsies exited the bus and were led into the inn's dining room, where a breathtaking view of the lake and mountain backdrop was visible. A small staff of servers stood at attention until the group was seated, then proceeded through the tables, serving a choice of hot green tea or Saki. Warmth of the beverages took any remaining chill away, as the dancers chatted amongst themselves.

Suddenly Kubota-san stood to address them. "Today's luncheon is courtesy of your host, Watanabe-san and will now be served. There is a choice of shrimp, squid, or eel tempura and vegetables or roasted duckling with citrus and steamed rice. Please indicate which you would prefer when your server arrives. Jeff spotted Maddy, rolling her eyes. "Here we go again," she whispered. "I think the shrimp tempura is probably okay, but pass on the slithery guys," he chuckled. Following lunch, the group was ushered back to the bus. Climbing aboard and finding seats, many fell asleep during the ride back to the train station. Jeff and Nora cuddled and conversed quietly. "This would be a perfect setting for an overnight sometime," he murmured, playing with her hair. Nora sighed and moved closer, taking his arm and wrapping it around her torso. "I bet Kubota-san could recommend any number of places for us. Let's check with him and do an overnight soon." They kissed.

The following week, the *Centipede* men were invited to play baseball against the Nissei tech team, the date to be announced. Baseball was the most popular team sport in Japan, taken very seriously. The gypsies received a formal challenge by the Japanese crew and were issued uniforms for the game. The women loved the idea and formed a cheerleading squad, creating American style chants to add to the fun. On the day of the game, a bus provided everyone transportation to a site on the outskirts of Tokyo. A large chain link fence surrounded the property with a wooden enclosure around the field. As the teams formed and lined up, spectators found seats in the stand, including Nissei staff, orchestra, crew and curious onlookers. Before the game began, prerecorded Japanese and American national anthems were heard through speakers, as the throng sang along.

The gypsies worked hard trying to take the game, but the Japanese were tough! Their obvious skill was matched by intense determination and enthusiasm. At the top of the 9th inning it was clear the Nissei boys were out to win and they did, 12 to 6! Camaraderie broke out as the victors graciously accepted the Americans' applause. Two cultures coming together in respectful cohesion was in contrast to the site of the game; a former prisoner-of-war camp during World War 11. As the gypsies filed toward the bus, Chad heard his name. Turning, he spotted Myoshi approaching. His stomach pulled at the sight of her. "Myoshi!" "Hello, Chad." "What are you doing here?" "I am interning at the Nissei. I was given permission to watch the game. You play well," she said, a blush evident. "In the States I'm not a jock, but thank you!" She looked puzzled. "What is jock?" Chad smiled. "It's someone who is avidly involved and good at sports." Spotting the bus, he stopped and took her hand. "It was good to see you, thanks for coming!" Her grip startled him. "Please Chad. I want to see you!" He melted. Leaning toward her ear he whispered, "It might be trouble for us." "I don't care, please!" He was moved by her change of heart. "I guess the best way is to call. I'm at the Nikkatsu Hotel, room 720." "Yes, yes, I will," she said eagerly. Turning, she hurried away. Chad stood for a moment puzzled, his mind in a whirl. 'This has to be kismet,' he reasoned, all the while fighting his conscience. 'Is it wise to get involved with her?' It was risky; one Chad Chapman from Detroit was willing to take.

Chapter 16

Manhattan Happenings

The Broadway production of *Centipede* continued to pack houses. If one could choose only one show to see in New York, the obvious choice was Owen's brainchild. Box office lines, running the entire length of 45th Street, were a daily occurrence. Scalpers were getting four times the value of tickets. House seats were non-existent as a wave of celebrities wheeling and dealing in town continued to seek favors from the Kaplan-Maggli organization. West Coast big shots, doing high-stake business during daytime hours, would look to Broadway shows to dazzle, distract and impress clients. Movie stars considered *Centipede* a status topic during cocktail conversations. Sports figures, politicians and foreign dignitaries depended on managers and assistants to acquire the 'gold' of choice seats, making their attendance a sure thing. The originals, who opened the show, worked diligently to keep the integrity of Owen's concept. Joe Pinto held brush-up rehearsals at least bi-weekly. Owen would stop in unexpectedly, which to some newcomers was nerve-wracking. He had an overwhelming presence both inspiring and intimidating.

Pat was counting the weeks until her contract was up. She and Blaine were making long-range plans, which included finding other avenues for her to satisfy her creativity. She was still relatively young and had a few more shows in her, but she was beginning to find the work tedious, without growth potential. She had already been a star in her first Broadway show. Exploring other possibilities for Pat was intriguing. Since their discussion regarding Owen's coming movie venture, Blaine had his eye on investing in the project. He loved to gamble and had a knack for courting and nurturing a winner. He would prevail on his pal Greg Morgan in Houston to come aboard when the time was right. Morgan had been a classmate of Shel Friedman, who was Universal Pictures' go-to-guy on the project, responsible for bringing the film to fruition. Blaine would work out the logistics before pitching the idea to Morgan, an investment he couldn't refuse. In his head an idea was forming that would give Pat an opportunity to play a new role, one where she could leave performing and become an integral part of his empire.

Julie was restless. Her recent conversation with Catherine had only produced frustration regarding Tim Bartel. 'He just can't be that big a cad. If it's true, he'd be out of the show. Management wouldn't condone such behavior' she reasoned. She checked in at half hour and was told to cover Marcy White's show, as she was out with a stubborn case of bronchitis. Julie welcomed the opportunity to swing Marcy's spot. She was breathless after each number, realizing that it took performing eight shows a week to build one's cardio strength. At intermission, she changed and headed to the green room. 'One act to go,' she thought as she entered the actor's lounge. Finding a chair to sink into, she relished a few minutes of rest before the second act. Closing her eyes felt great as she began to relax. Suddenly, a hand on her cheek caused her to lurch. Looking up she couldn't believe her eyes! Tim! He knelt before her caressing her face. His intention was obvious, as he murmured, "You busy tonight?" His hand traced along her neck, his touch promising and sensual. Barely able to respond she nodded and whispered, "Yes!" "Meet me at Allen's, I'll buy you a drink, maybe two," he said, winking. The second act was a blur as Julie, preoccupied with Tim, did what was necessary in Marcy's place. Following the bows, she hurried to the change area, then to the dressing room to repair her make-up and hair. She appeared in a hurry. Catherine and Pat noticed. "Nice job, Jules! You did great," said Catherine as she undid her hair and brushed through knots. "Nora's shoes are hard to fill kiddo, but you did beautifully," added Pat. "Thanks, girls," she purred, accepting the compliment.

"How about joining us for a drink at Allen's?" Julie had to think fast. "Gee, I'd love to, but I promised a cousin of mine from Detroit I'd spend time after the show," she lied. "Maybe another time, okay?" "Yeah, sure," she mumbled quickly toweling off. Changing into a spare pair of panties, she finished dressing, slipping on her jeans and top. One last look in the mirror and she was satisfied, although she needed to reapply her lipstick. "Good night, ladies," she tossed as she hurried out the door. Catherine, puzzled looked at Pat through the mirror. "That's odd!" "What do you mean?" "Julie would never turn down a free drink or two. She was in an awful hurry, don't you think?" "I don't know her as well as you, Cath, but she did seem very preoccupied." "Must be an important relative, this cousin," added Catherine. "Do you want to toddle over to Allen's anyway? Blaine is out of town and I would love some company." "I'd love to, Pat. Give me a minute and I'll be ready."

Allen's was jammed. Saturday night on Broadway meant area restaurants were filled to capacity with locals, tourists and gypsies. Sunday, they were off. Julie hurried down the short flight of stairs from the street and into the place, her eyes scanning for him through the smoke-filled room. She didn't have to wait. A hand reached out as she passed through the door, stopping her in her tracks. "Hi, Baby!" She melted at the sight of him, his direct manner compelling, drawing her in. "I found a spot over there. Come on," he insisted, taking her arm and leading her to the bar. He indicated a stool for her to sit on and stood next to her. "What are you having?" "I'd love a beer please!" "Great, I'll join you," he said signaling the barman. "Two Heineken's for now, but start a tab, got it?" He was forceful, sexy. She liked the way he handled himself and her. The beers arrived. "Do you want a glass?" "Don't need one, thanks." They drank in silence. He appeared to be a man of few words, but his presence was overpowering. Pulling out a smoke, he offered her one. "I don't smoke, thanks!" He scowled. "Every fucking dancer smokes," he scoffed, lighting his. "You ever watch Owen Matthews? Man I hear he's a five-pack-a-day man. I'll bet he smokes while he fucks," he chuckled. Inhaling deeply, he flicked an ash, as he studied her carefully. "You're a sexy girl, Judy!" "Julie, my name is Julie!" "Sorry, I never remember names," he smiled, brushing it off. "Close enough, I guess," she said, ignoring his mistake. "Want another? Your bottle is empty." "Sure, I'm still thirsty." Tim ordered two more as he moved closer, putting his arm around her. "I want to fuck you Judy, I mean Julie!" Julie could scarcely breathe as he leaned into her ear, his warm breath holding her rapt. "I'd like that," she stammered, the wet in her crotch building. "Let's chug these and get started." As Julie sat under Tim's spell, she didn't notice Pat and Catherine enter Allen's. The girls were shown a table across the room, with an open view. They made themselves at home, removing their coats and placing them on the backs of chairs. Pat ordered her favorite, a glass of Merlot, while Catherine settled on a Bloody Mary. As they drank, Pat glanced across the room. A sip suddenly went down wrong, causing her to cough violently. "Pat, what is it?" For a few moments she couldn't find her voice as she tried to clear her throat. "Oh my God, look over at the bar!" Through the smoky haze, Catherine looked across the room. Gasping, her eyes hadn't deceived.

"Oh my God, it's Julie with that snake, Bartel! What do we do?" Pat gained her ground and stopped Catherine when she started to rise. "We do nothing Cath, absolutely nothing!" "Are you crazy? Julie may be in trouble!" "She's over 21 and an adult." "That's really a horrible attitude, Pat!" "Look, she was warned about him and since she persists on getting involved with the creep, let the karma play out for God's sake." Pat's mind was in a whirl. Catherine was shaking. "I'm worried,

Pat. What if . . . .?" "We just have to wait it out. Finish your drink and let's get out of here."

Following the second beer, Tim paid the check and helped Julie with her coat. "Come on, Baby, let's vamoose!" As they exited Allens a misty rain was falling, hurrying them along toward Ninth Avenue. Tim held firm Julie's hand, moving quickly through the soft rain. He was commanding, exciting to be with. "Here it is," he said, pointing to a renovated brownstone. "Come on!" They entered a first floor studio, small, but clean. Julie eyed the bed in the center of the room, unmade and tossed. "Come here, let me help you out of these," he said, removing her coat. The rest of her clothes came off easily. Before she could speak, his tongue was at the back of her throat, his hands all over her. She was turning on, loving his aggression. Pushing her down on the bed, he quickly peeled off her panties. Julie moaned her approval as his fingers explored. She writhed and begged as he increased his moves. Then, abruptly he stood and walked to the dresser. Julie lay back waiting. Returning, he held a long silk scarf. "This is for you, roll over!" "Why, Tim?" "Just do as you're told, roll over now!" She reluctantly turned over, her chin in the tangled sheets. Then she realized as he pulled her wrists together, what he was up to. He was binding her tightly, getting off on it. "So now I can do what I want and you'll dig it! Ready?" Rolling her on her back, Julie couldn't miss the smirk. Reaching down, he aggressively played with her most private self. "Wow, are you wet! Good girl! Now you're going to get what old Timmy's got!" Julie quivered feeling a mix of emotions; desire, excitement and underlying fear.

Tim slipped off his shirt and jeans, his hard on ready for the plunge, but first, some teasing was in order. Straddling her, his fingers playfully pinched her nipples, moved down her torso to her mound, teasing as he twisted her pubic hair and suddenly plunged deep inside. Julie writhed, begging for more. "Yes, Tim, oh yes, do me!" Grinning, he climbed on, ready to give her his all. He felt her take him easily, tightening around him as her orgasm erupted. Tim followed rocking and twisting. "Fuck, yes! Oh yeah," he screamed. Their mutual explosion left them spent. Lying motionless the minutes passed. There was no intimate afterglow, no sweet words or soft caresses. Julie lay there feeling conflicted. Was the sex worth it? She felt cheap, used. Finally he spoke. "Wow, you were horny! Like a well-oiled engine! When's the last time you had it this good, huh? Tell me," he demanded. Julie faked a smile and murmured, "Never like this, Tim! You sure know how to fuck!" Instinct told her she was safe as long as she fed his ego. He'd never know how disgusted she was. "How about a drink and another go? I can keep going indefinitely!" Julie's heart sank, realizing her mistake. "Sorry, I have to get going. I'm meeting my cousin from Detroit early in the morning." "Oh, I don't think so, I'm not through with you," he said, grinning.

Without a word he got up and sauntered to the kitchenette, opening the small fridge and reaching for two chilled bottles. Julie watched him with dread, his egoist swagger suddenly unappealing. He returned and noticed she was still tied. Loosening her, he handed her a cold one. "Hurry and drink up, I want to go again," he insisted. Julie felt her pulse quicken as she took a sip. Tim's eyes never left hers. "You're going to suck my dick." She blinked at his uncouth directive, but readied herself by playing along. "Oh good, I like yours, impressive," she teased. Tim grinned and chugged his beer. 'He likes this kind of talk,' she thought, continuing her charade. "Why don't you come here and I'll show you?" "Finish up, Judy, let's go!"

Setting the bottle aside he didn't wait for her to finish. He moved toward her, his eyes fastened to her. He began stroking his erection, as though performing a ritual dance. He waggled his tongue as he continued, his erection now throbbing. Julie waited, feeling nauseous as he stood at eye level. "Ok, give it to me," he demanded, grabbing her hair and pulling her to him. Julie cooperated in spite of her fear. Closing her mouth around him she sucked and stroked. "Oh yeah, that's good. Come on, harder, faster!" She continued using all her strength, hoping he would come and it would be over. 'I have to get out of here,' she thought, desperation building. Finally, he was bursting and let go! "Oh fuck, yes, yes, it's good!" He shook as he held on to her shoulders, while Julie nearly gagged. Slowly he calmed down. Stepping back he studied her. "Good job, Judy! Give me a few minutes to take a leak, clean-up and we'll go again!" He left her and closed the bathroom door.

Julie had enough. Quickly she found her clothes and hastily dressed. She could hear the water running and knew there was little time to get out of there. Grabbing her shoes, she stumbled slipping them on. Finding her coat and purse she slipped out. She never stopped running; out the front door, down 9th Avenue, and over to 8th, a hard rain washing over her. She could barely see the cab light in the downpour, but once it was closer, she signaled the driver. He stopped at the corner. "West 73rd Street between Broadway and West End, driver," she said, climbing into the back seat. Like the downpour outside, the memory of being at the hands of Tim Bartel washed over her, causing her shame. She'd not used discernment, not in the least. Even with a stern warning from friends, she went ahead determined to mine him and ended up humiliated and used. Shivering, she wept quietly all the way home to her flat on the upper west side.

The gypsies day off flew by and it was another Monday night at half hour. Julie checked in, wary of running into Bartel. She noticed that Marcy was still out with bronchitis, so she reluctantly headed for the dressing room. Walking in, she noticed Pat and Catherine glance her way. Pat kept applying her make-up, but Catherine was loaded for bear. "So, how are you? How was your date?" Julie, stone-faced, stared straight ahead, eyes welling. Catherine continued, not letting up. "Jules, I asked you, how was it?" Throwing down her sponge, Julie began to cry. The other girls noticed but stayed out of it. "Come on, Jules, you're coming with us," said Pat, tugging on her arm. Catherine joined her, as they walked Julie down the hall to the restroom. Locking the door, they sat her on a nearby settee. Julie became unglued as she grabbed Catherine. Clinging to her she sobbed. Pat, not visibly concerned, cut in. "Ok, let's have it. What happened?" Julie looked up, her face stained with tears. "You were right! I'm such an idiot. The excitement of the moment got the better of me! He was vile!" Pat didn't blink. "Did he hurt you in any way?" "No, he just wants to get off. He tied me, fucked me and forced me to do fellatio on him! It was the most degrading thing I've ever been subjected to! I almost threw up. I slipped out when he took a shower." Again, Julie dissolved into sobs. Pat paced. "Enough is enough. He's got to be stopped, end of story." Catherine perked up. "How is that possible?" "I don't know, but there must be a way." In the meantime Julie, stay clear of him. He's dangerous." "Oh believe me, I will!" "Now we have a show to do. Let's go!" The three returned to the dressing room. Julie had major repair work to do on her face. The rest of the evening continued without incident.

Later, following the show, Pat caught up to Dick Landry. "Do you
have a minute, Dick? I need to talk." "Sure Pat, let's go in here," he
said, indicating his office. Closing the door behind them he offered
her a chair. "What's up?" "I'll give you the short version, Dick. As stage
manager I hope you can help." "I'll try." Pat took a deep breath and
began. "We have a sexual deviant amongst us. He's stalking, making
unwelcome advances on some of the girls." Dick looked impassive.
"Seriously, Dick, it's becoming a problem. They're afraid to come to
work." "Who is it?" "Tim Bartel!" "You're serious?" "I couldn't be more.
From the day he came in to replace Jerry Thompson, he's been trouble." "What can I do? They're over 21!" "That's not the point, Dick. He's
not just a sleaze, he's potentially dangerous!" "I see." "No, you don't! I
wouldn't be bothering you with this if it wasn't a major concern." "Do
you want me to phone Owen?" "No, leave him out of it. Talk to Griff,
he may know how to handle this," Pat said, irritated. Dick sat silently,
processing Pat's news. "For God's sake, Dick, if he was bothering Dana,
you wouldn't hesitate!" "I see your point, Pat. I'll see what I can do, but
without proof it'll be difficult. He's one hell of a dancer, a great asset
to the production." "And he's a real threat to our well being. He needs
to be stopped!" She was now shouting. "Calm down, Pat, I'll speak to
Griff." "Well, do it soon, before rape is legal! Thanks for your time,"
she tossed, clearly annoyed. 'Tim Bartel needs to go away,' she thought
derisively, as she walked out of the office in a huff.

It was afternoon in Tokyo. The production phone rang several times
before Griff picked up. Dick Landry's voice came through loud and
clear, a good connection considering the distance.

"Hey Dick, how goes it?" "We're fine here, Griff. The show continues to sell out. The cast is solid and the show is clean. How are the
Japanese?" "Incredible people, Dick and do they love our *Centipede!*"
"That's great. Say, I'm calling regarding another matter." "Oh, and what's
that?" "What do you know about Tim Bartel, other than his dance
ability?" There was a long pause. "We've had some trouble with him
in the past. Why?" "Pat spoke to me. She's convinced he's a threat to
the women in our show. She claims he's a sexual predator, but without
proof, it's impossible to pin him." "Yes, I know. He's a solid and consistent performer. However, I caught him in a compromising position

with one of the girls during previews. He received a warning then. I haven't kept tabs on him lately." "Do you want me to alert Owen?" "No Dick, let me handle this. I have first-hand experience with Mr. Bartel. I'll talk to Owen." "Thanks, Griff. I appreciate this! Take care and my best to Mally, Nora, Jeff and the others." Griff put down the phone and thought about the next step. He decided to call the boss.

Owen was in great spirits. His first directorial assignment for Universal Pictures was the film version of *Bravo Business*. It was due to start shooting in the fall. His two companies of *Centipede* were major hits and his relationship with Catherine Andrews was still going strong. He was still heavily infatuated with her. She was beautiful, sexually compatible and a strong asset to the Broadway production. He would have her take over Pat's starring role when Pat's contract was up. This was his intention when he hired her from day one. He couldn't afford to lose her, so he kept her on a short leash. He would insist she come to him whenever his libido was in high gear or loneliness set in. Being the most successful director-choreographer on Broadway had its advantages.

His phone rang suddenly. Picking up, he recognized Griff's voice immediately. "Hey Griff, what's doing?" "We're doing well. The show's sold out over here. The Japanese public can't get enough!" 'Like some of my exes,' he mused to himself. "That's great news, Griff. It's the same in New York. People are ready to knock off relatives to ace tickets!" "On another note Owen, I just spoke to Dick Landry. It appears we have a problem." "Oh?" "A male company member is preying on our ladies." "No shit, who?" "Tim Bartel. We had an incident involving him last winter. He got off with a warning." "Hell, I've never faulted a guy for having his dick in overdrive as long as he delivers on stage!" "Yes, but if he borders on dangerous, the matter should be looked into." "Well, do what you need to do, Griff. Anything else?" "No, but I thought this worth a mention." "You got it, thanks for calling." The conversation ended. Owen sat back, pulled out a cigarette and sipped his scotch. 'Bartel sounds like a brother under the skin,' he mused.

Tuesday's show was in high gear, audience response deafening number after number. Following the performance, Catherine hurried to change, tidy her make-up and head to Owen's. Grabbing a cab on 8th, she mentally prepared for the night to come. It would unfold as usual, starting with a couple of drinks, then Owen's insistence on jumping in bed. Catherine had grown weary of his constant preoccupation and absorption in carnal activity, longing instead for more meaningful interaction. She was no fool; highly educated and well-versed on many subjects, she wanted to share ideas and thought-provoking conversation. Mostly she found herself undressed, under his spell and repeatedly a sex toy. 'Tonight will be no exception,' she thought wistfully, as she pressed the elevator button.

Owen opened the door, his face lighting up. "Baby, I'm so glad you're here!" Pulling her close he tongued her while his hands traced her breasts. Closing the door, he walked her into the living room, helping her off with her coat, tossing her bag in a nearby chair. "It seems like a long time," he murmured, playing with her hair. "How about a drink?" "Sure, what do you have handy?" I have Vouvray chilling or would you prefer Moet?" "The wine is fine, thanks." Owen sensed Catherine's mood while uncorking the wine. He poured her glass. "Give me a second while I fix a scotch." "Of course," she said stiffly. "Are you okay, Baby? You seem distracted." Without waiting for him, she sipped, lost in thought. "I wouldn't expect you to be interested," she mumbled. Joining her, he took a long sip and swallowed. "What's this? Is something wrong, Baby?" "Yes!" "Well?" Taking a drag on his smoke, he leaned on the counter waiting. "I have a friend who's being bothered by a guy who's stalking her. I don't know what to do to help." "Why is he stalking her?" "He wants sex and though she's repeatedly told him to back off, he won't let up. He's becoming a bother and she's frightened." "Who is it?" "I'd rather not say, but I could use some advice." "Oh for God's sake, Baby, if she's over 21, why not? She might like it!" "I don't think you understand, he's a creep, not someone she wants to get involved with in any way!" "Why so interested?" "Because she's a close friend and they work together." "Well, it's pretty basic, I'd say. Either she wants to fuck the guy or she doesn't," he said with nonchalance. "Come on, drink up. We have some serious catching up to do. You look gorgeous and I want every inch of you." Catherine put down her glass and moved closer. "Can we ever just have a meaningful conversation, an exchange of ideas?" Owen put out his cigarette, eyeing her quizzically. "What's this? Are you playing the intellectual card now? Don't pull that shit, Baby, it bores the crap out of me. Now come on," he insisted, his voice compelling. Catherine glanced toward the bedroom. "Are you asking or commanding me, Owen?" "Jesus, what's come over you?" She felt a flush as she observed his face drawn into a scowl, his voice darkening. "Now you listen to me. There are any number of women in this town who want to fuck me just for one night and you're complaining?" "I'm not complaining I just want more!" "Well Baby, this is it! I'm about work, good booze and sex! Now are you coming?" She felt herself weaken as he led her down the hall. "I'm going to make you glad you stayed."

Tim Bartel was livid. That Judy broad had skipped out! He'd show her a thing or two. She'd be sorry she took off. He'd make sure of that. She was currently covering someone. 'Easy access,' he mused. Ever since that horrific night at Tim's, Julie had stuck close to Catherine and Pat. She felt vulnerable and nervous. She was right under his nose and likely to run into him at some point in the theater. The week passed without incident until Saturday night. Marcy was still out with bronchitis, ordered to take additional days off. Julie had to swing her show. As she ran through each number, several trips from stage to changing area and back again were necessary. At the end of the first act, rounding a corner, she saw Tim hurrying to make a change. 'Oh, shit, it's him,' she thought, nausea suddenly rising. He didn't appear to notice her, luckily. What she failed to see was a sinister grin. Following the show, Julie was distracted. Pat and Catherine were aware of her mindset as they changed and readied themselves to take off. "Hey Jules, want to join us for a drink?" "I think I'll pass. I'm tired and just want to go home," she sighed, as she continued changing. "We'll walk you out if you like," Pat suggested. "It's okay, see you Monday." She gathered her things and left.

The backstage area was empty and quiet as Julie descended the stairs. Everyone appeared to have cleared out immediately after the show. Saturday night meant the next day off for Broadway. Orchestra, cast and crew tended to hurry through post show activity in order to get to watering holes around the theatre district, the most popular being Joe Allen's. She had barely reached the stage level when she heard a noise. Her pulse quickened as she peered through the darkness. "Is someone there?" Taking a few steps, she heard it again.

Suddenly a strong arm grabbed around her shoulders. Julie screamed before a hand covered her mouth, her pulse throbbing in her ears. Kicking and thrashing, she felt herself dragged across the stage. "Bitch, scream all you want, but I've got you!" The voice belonged to him! Behind a large unit Tim pushed her down, banging her head against the floor. Tears sprang as she was rolled on her stomach, her hands tied behind her. Grappling a side zipper, Tim pulled her jeans down, as he pinned her with his body weight. "So you thought you could walk out on me? No one does that, Judy!" Julie struggled, but it was no use. He had her. Crying out, she felt a violent slap across her mouth. "Shut up, bitch!" Julie realized the worst was about to come, as she mentally prepared. Then, suddenly voices, a scuffle and he was pulled off her. "Hold the son-of-a-bitch," yelled Dick Landry as two others assisted. Tim struggled as Joe Pinto and Hal Royce took control of him. "Take this scumbag to my office and hold him there," ordered Landry.

Pat and Catherine rushed in. "Ladies, please give Julie a hand!" Untying her hands, they looked for her discarded jeans. Julie grabbed on to Catherine, her body shaking uncontrollably. "Oh my God, don't leave me, Cath!" Pat took over, assisting Julie to her feet. Catherine spotted her shoes and grabbed them on the way to the green room. "Come on Jules, in here," Pat pointed out, finding her a comfortable chair. Both women knelt in front of her, trying to calm. "Easy, Jules, it's over!" Catherine found a box of tissues nearby and wiped Julie's face, as she wept. When she had calmed down, Pat handed her a cup of water. Julie's eyes were wild, as she anxiously looked around. "Where is he?"

"Jules he's through, the boys have him under control. "He's out of *Centipede.* Equity will suspend the bastard! When this gets out, I doubt he'll ever work again!" Julie was numb, but able to speak. "Thank God, you were here!" "Well, we happened to leave last, heard screaming and came running. By the time we got downstairs, Dick had the situation under control," said Catherine. "I had a feeling Bartel might try something. The important thing is he didn't get away with it!" "Ah come on, Pat! He got away with far too much," said Catherine, anger rising.

Another scene was playing out in Dick's office. Joe had forced Tim into a chair with Hal's help, removing his scarf to tie Tim's wrists behind him. Tim looked straight ahead. He was flushed and angry, refusing to acknowledge them. Dick arrived and wasted no time. "All right, Bartel, let's have it." Dick, normally easy-going, had all he could do not to punch Tim out, he was so upset. "Your behavior is disgusting, unacceptable and against the law. Explain your actions, now!" Tim shot him a look. "I was giving the bitch what she deserved, Landry. She's a fucking prick tease and needed a lesson!" Joe stepped forward, ready to hit him, but Hal held him back. "Easy Joe, don't lose your head. Let Dick handle this, he's in charge." Dick pulled up a chair and sat directly across from Tim. "You broke the law. Terrorizing and assaulting anyone is cause for termination of your contract and suspension by Actor's Equity. As far as I'm concerned you're a disgrace to this production and profession. "You can't fire me over trying to fuck a consenting bitch!" "Didn't look consensual to me, you bastard," yelled Joe, lunging at him. Hal made a grab, pulling him back. "Joe, that's enough! Bartel will get his due," he said with satisfaction.

Dick stood and withdrew the chair. "Here's what's going to happen, Mr. Bartel. Griff Edwards will be notified. You will receive two week's pay and let go immediately. Under the circumstances, you will not remain in this production. Your final check will be mailed. Are there questions?" Tim remained silent for a moment. When he finally spoke, venom etched his voice. "I was sick of this fucking show anyway, so good riddance!" Joe piped up. "You might change your tune Bartel when Actor's Equity says, good riddance. They'll suspend your ass!" "Untie him and get him out of here," demanded Dick, who had had enough. "Go collect your personal gear and clear out! Joe, Hal, stay with him and see that he leaves this theater without further incident." "With pleasure," said Joe, untying Tim. Without a word they left Dick's office, Tim in tow. There was silence as they led him to the men's dressing room and waited. He picked up his make-up, towel and dance belt and was shown the door. Dick planned to phone Griff in the morning, but at the moment he needed to check on Julie. She had calmed down and was able to converse. Pat and Catherine sat nearby, waiting for word. Pat stood when she saw him. "Dick, what's happened?" "Mr. Bartel has been served his two-week, effective now and is being escorted from the theatre. I will update Griff in the morning. My question is do you want to press charges, Julie? Assault is a felony and you have a legitimate complaint against him." All eyes were on her. "I just want him gone so he can't bother or hurt anyone else," she whimpered. "Julie, are you sure? You were practically raped!" "Calm down, Catherine, its Jules' decision," Pat cautioned. "At the very least, he will be boycotted from this theater and receive a year's suspension from Equity," added Dick. "Does this work for you?" "Yes, yes it does, Dick. Thank you so much for your support." He studied her closely. "Say, that's quite an egg on your head! I think you should be examined by a doctor to make sure you're all right." "It's only a bump to my pride, Dick. I'll get it over it." "Well, if you change your mind, the exam is covered by our insurance. Now I think it best if the girls see you home. I will take care of the remaining details, okay? Mr. Bartel's firing will be announced to the company on Monday night." The girls walked Julie out the stage door and hailed a cab. It had been a nightmarish end of a week for Julie Jensen. For Tim Bartel, it proved nightmarish, ending his employment on Broadway and possibly his career.

Dick phoned Tokyo the next day. He reported the assault on Julie Jensen and the firing of Tim Bartel to Griff, who approved Dick's decision unquestionably. "Please inform Equity so they can proceed with Bartel's suspension." "You'll have to replace him as soon as possible, Dick. Hal will be on swing overload should another guy need coverage." "When are Jonas and Phillipe due back?" "They will be leaving Tokyo the day after tomorrow. Phillipe is the right replacement for Bartel. I'll inform him he'll be going in as soon as they return. Owen will be updated." " Joe Pinto could put Phillipe in. It's an easy spot to set, he'll just need placements." "Good call, Dick. As soon as possible, call a replacement rehearsal with the entire company. Let's aim for a week from Monday." "I'll take care of details from this end," said Dick, already mentally charting his course. "Thanks Dick, I'll be in touch. Bye for now."

The sleepers were awakened by repetitious rings. Jonas managed to find the receiver as he fumbled for the switch on a small lamp next to the bed. Picking up he struggled to wake up. "Hey Griff, why so early? It's practically the middle of the night!" "Sorry to disturb, Jonas but something's come up in New York. Tim Bartel was given his two-week and we need to replace him fast. Jonas was now fully awake.

"What happened?" "Bartel was caught trying to assault one of the girls on theater property! He's out, done!" "Holy shit, I had a feeling this would happen one day! That guy was trouble from the get-go." "How fast can you and Phillipe get back to New York?" "We're ticketed to leave the day after tomorrow. We were going to visit my father in San Francisco on the way back." "I'm afraid you'll have to forego your visit for now. We have to get Bartel replaced and Phillipe is the best choice. He already knows the show and will just need placements. Hal Royce will be on overload until then." "Damn, I was looking forward to San Francisco." "Not this time Jonas, we need Phillipe back as soon as possible." "Okay, got it! We'll be back on Wednesday." "Good, he'll have to start rehearsing on Thursday, jet lag be damned," said Griff, with a chuckle. "No rest for the weary and that's show biz," sighed Jonas. "No rest for now. Joe Pinto is prepared to put Phillipe in. I'm going to insist you take some time off. You've earned it!" "Thanks, I guess," he laughed. The call concluded.

On Wednesday morning, Jonas and Phillipe took off from Haneda International airport, anticipating the 20 hour of flight back to New York. Looking out over a vast sea of blue, they held hands and thought about the next step. Jonas planned to call his father when they landed in San Francisco and explain the situation. As much as he wanted Charles and Phillipe to meet, it would have to wait. "I hope I can pick the spot up quickly, Cheri!" "Piece of cake, Babe, you'll hit the stage running." "Truthfully, I've missed performing since we left New York." "I know you have, so the timing couldn't be better!" "Don't you miss it?" "Not so much anymore. I like assisting Owen. I hope he'll consider me to remount the proposed national company of *Centipede* in spring and there's the film version of *Bravo Business,* coming up next fall." "What will you do in the meantime, Cheri?" "I'll let you support me, Babe. I'll be the housewife and you, the breadwinner!" "Keeping the home fires burning?" "Yeah, every night when you come home tired and horny, I'll have to sort you out. "I like the sound of that." Slipping down in their seats, they kissed and fondled, as the whirr of engines provided a pleasant cover.

Chapter 17

Passion and Pledges

As the Tim Bartel debacle back in New York was being sorted out, Chad waited for his phone to ring at the Nikkatsu Hotel in Tokyo. It had only been a few days since the baseball game, during which the Nissei tech team beat *Centipede's* finest. His hours and days were filled with thoughts of Myoshi, beautiful Myoshi. She had stolen his heart and he could think of nothing else. He was on automatic pilot during the show, scanning the audience for any sign of her. Then, it happened. Her call early one morning aroused his senses at the sound of her soft voice. After a few awkward seconds, they conversed for nearly an hour. The plan was to meet for lunch the next afternoon at the Ginger Blossom, a small, out-of-the-way café in the Marunouchi section of Tokyo, not far from the Ginza. She explained it was her day off and on the pretense that she was meeting her girlfriend, Fumiko Narada, drew no suspicion. With their plan in place, Chad found it difficult to concentrate on anything else. Mally had noticed his distraction and approached.

"Chad, are you all right? You seem so far away, are you homesick?" "A little, I guess. I miss New York." "I understand, Chad. It's very different here and takes getting used to." "The show is great and I am honored to be part of this company, but it's lonely when you aren't with someone. You know what I mean?" "I do. Do you still think about Mary Jane?" "It still stings sometimes, Mal. I was certain it would work out, her moving to New York and all, but I was wrong." "Have you been interested in dating at all?" "Yeah, I've tried, but I'm not a short term kind of guy. Most of the girls are only interested in brief affairs. Do you know what I mean?" "Yes, I guess so. Well, don't be a stranger. Have

134

dinner with Griff and me soon, okay?" "Thanks, Mal. You're always so kind." They hugged.

The Ginger Blossom was a tiny, tucked-away kind of establishment. It was noon as Chad hurried along a narrow street, looking for a sign that would lead him to her. When at last he arrived, his heart was in overdrive. Entering the tiny room, his eyes scanned and widened when he saw her. Myoshi! She was dressed in western attire; a pretty wool dress in soft yellow, her hair pulled up under a beret. Smiling, she waved in his direction as he hurried to her side. "Konnichiwa, Chad!" He took her hand in his and patted tenderly. "It is so good to see you, Myoshi!" "Yes, please sit down. I have ordered tea to start. Do you like green tea?" "It takes getting used to, but I'm trying, thank you!" Their first moments were awkward, unsure. He felt he'd been put under a spell. She was the loveliest girl he'd ever met. "How have you been?" "I have been fine, working many hours at the theatre. I hope to be hired full time. I will soon know." "How are the performances?" "Good, actually great. I love our audiences. They're so responsive to the concept. It was a gamble that proved a good one!" "I am glad you came today," she said, touching his sleeve. He blushed, feeling like a hapless school boy.

Myoshi ordered lunch for them and sipped her tea. Her eyes never left his. "What are your plans when *Centipede* ends?" "I haven't thought that far ahead, but I'll return with the company to the States. Have you ever been?" "Oh no, but my father has. He travels quite a bit." "Maybe someday you'll come to New York," he said, hopefully. "Perhaps, but right now I need to be employed full time." Lunch arrived in lacquer bowls, a set of hashi for each. "I hope you like tempura. Do you enjoy seafood?" "Yes, I do," said Chad, attempting to grab a piece of slippery mystery with the chopsticks. Succeeding, he popped the morsel in his mouth and chewed. The piece was rubbery, unyielding no matter how aggressive his chewing. After awkwardly giving in, he glanced at Myoshi, smiling at his attempt. "Have you ever eaten unagi and tako?" "What?" "It's a specialty here, deep fried eel and octopus!" Chad carefully put his napkin to his mouth and spit out the half-chewed piece. He felt clumsy, foolish. "Oh, you don't like! So sorry, it's not typically American," she said. He was flushed as he tried to hide embarrassment. "Oh Chad, it's all right. I should have asked first." She took his hand and held it to her face. Suddenly he lost all need to eat. Waving to the waitperson, he held his wallet up. "Let me take care of this!" After paying the bill he took her hand and led her out. It was surprisingly quiet for lunch hour, the area less-congested than some. "There is a beautiful park close by. Would you care to take a walk?" "He smiled and squeezed her hand. "Hai, Dozo!"

The day was bright, the sun ruling across a cloudless sky. Chad put his arm around Myoshi as they walked, caught in the moment. Occasionally she glanced at him and snuggled closer. He didn't know where to put all his feelings. He hungered for her, to be with her. Her touch put his senses in overdrive. 'What am I going to do? I'm falling in love,' he thought. They arrived at a beautifully manicured area, filled with Ming trees, tiny bridges over man-made ponds. A small pagoda stood at the center, the sides open to the outside. Myoshi took the lead and crossed the bridge holding Chad's hand. "Come with me, I want to show you something," she insisted. Arriving at the center of the small structure, Chad observed a large marble pond. Bright Koi swished through the water adding ambience to the quaint scene. "This is where dreams come true, if you believe enough. It is customary to take coin and toss into well. Your wish must be strong for it to come true."

Chad reached into his pocket and found a coin to share. Closing his eyes, he reached for her hand, while he readied the other to toss. "Make a wish, Myoshi!" She closed her eyes. His pulse quickened as he silently wished she were his. Tossing the coin, he opened his eyes quickly to see a tiny ripple widen as the coin hit the water surface and gently sank. "Did you make a strong wish?" Her dark eyes held hope as she looked into his. "Yes, the strongest one possible!" He took her face in his hands and kissed her gently, lingering. She stayed, the soft certainty of his lips holding her rapt. Pulling away his eyes stayed fastened on hers. "I'm falling in love with you, Myoshi. Please be mine!" "Yes, yes," she whispered returning the kiss. Her sweetness was unlike any woman he'd known; so dear, so innocent. They stayed together the rest of the afternoon, not realizing the complications they had set in motion.

Later that week, Mally received a letter addressed to the Edwards at the Nikkatsu. The handwriting was child-like, but legible. Hurrying to their room, she hastily found an opener and sliced the envelope. Once open, she read the brief note:

Dear Mr. and Mrs. Griffen Edwards-san!

We are happy to ask you please to come to Shougakku Oteari on nichiyobi no, juichigatsu hatsuka, to dinner prepared for you and ni others at go ji han. Please respond to Tokyo 222-5050.

Kazoku Kamata.

As she finished the door opened and Griff appeared. Before she could speak he tucked her in his arms and kissed her longingly. "I need time away with you. How does an overnight somewhere next weekend sound?" "Darling, have a look at this first, please. What does it mean?" From his constant interaction with the Nissei crew, Griff picked up basic Japanese. His natural aptitude for language had served him well, making it easier to work with crew and call the show. "I need a translator," Mally said, tickling him. Chuckling, he snatched the letter from her and sat on the bed, reading. "It appears we have been invited to dine at the school where *Centipede* rehearsed, in the Kamata family apartment, on Sunday next at 5:30! We may bring two others from the show." "Oh how fun, Griff! Who should we ask to join us?" "Let's invite Jeff and Nora. He has such an affinity for the Japanese culture and people. We must call the Kamata Family to confirm right away." The Edwards night away would have to wait.

A gentle snow fell on Sunday at dusk. Griff, Mally, Jeff and Nora shared a cab to the school. As they rode through winding streets and narrow roadways, the four chatted with enthusiasm, anticipating the evening ahead. Pulling up to the front door, they were greeted by Kamata's oldest daughter. "Konbanwa! Hajimemashite! Dozo, yoroshiku," she exclaimed excitedly, bowing. "Konbanwa! Domo arigato gozaimasu," said Griff, bowing in return. "Please follow," said Yuriko, leading them to the rear of the building. Tucked away was the family quarters consisting of several modest rooms.

"Please come in," she said, sliding back the sukurin, a screen made entirely of paper and wood that served as the entrance to the apartment. Before entering they followed her lead by removing shoes. Shown into the largest room, Yuriko hastened, "Dozo, please, be seated!" The four found soft pillows on tatami-covered floor. "This is very special," remarked Jeff, looking around. Mr. and Mrs. Kamata entered and bowed, followed by Haruko, Mirako and Sachiko. Haruko carried a tray, on which a pile of neatly rolled towels had been placed and handed it to Griff. "Domo Arigato," he said, passing to Mally, Jeff and Nora. The warmth and moisture of the towels carried a sense of welcome, typically Japanese. They were then collected and taken away.

Mr. Kamata sat nearby as food was prepared table side by his wife and served by his daughters; Sukiyaki and cooked vegetables in a savory sauce served with rice was offered. The Kamata family watched Griff and companions partake with relish. 'This is so curious, they're not joining us,' Mally mused, while Mirako poured green tea. Nora, too, was puzzled. "I wonder why they're not eating with us." "I'll explain later," said Jeff, quietly. The food was satisfying and plentiful. Throughout, the family served their guests with cordial enthusiasm. As the meal concluded and dishes removed, Haruko came into the room carrying a small recorder, plugging it into an outlet. Yuriko entered, dressed in an exquisite silk kimono, make-up and hair worn like a traditional geisha. She carried an enormous fan. Waiting for Haruko to press the recorder, she stood motionless. As the sound of ancient music filled the air, Yuriko began her dance. She was doll-like, captivating, waving the fan in sync with her body, the two becoming one. The delicacy and grace of her simple dance was spellbinding. The gypsies were moved by the joy of her performance. They were witnesses to a private world so culturally unique and simplistic, one few Americans were ever privileged to experience. At the end of her dance, they applauded. Yuriko simply bowed her head and left. Dessert followed including tiny rice cakes in almond and ginger sauce, fresh fruit and hot Saki.

The evening soon drew to a close as Griff and party were shown to their shoes. Mr. and Mrs. Kamata bowed and smiled, shaking everyone's hand. Yuriko led the way to the front door. "Thank you for coming to our home. It has been our honor to serve the first Americans to cross our door!" She bowed and pointed in the direction of the main road. "You will find taxi service one block further. Sayonara!" The light snow that began earlier was heavier now, as the foursome walked together, recounting the evening. Mally and Nora's high heels were no match for the snowy street. Griff reached for Mally, wrapping his arms around her as they hurried along. Nora kept pace with Jeff, eager to get an answer to an earlier question.

"Jeff, you promised to explain why the family didn't join us for dinner," said Nora. "Well, I believe it's customary to be hospitable to invited guests by providing the meal and not joining in. But also, I think the Kamata family saved a great deal to provide for us. What do you think, Griff?" "Yes, I agree. It's not only typical of Japanese to provide for others, but these are modest people. For that reason I think we should invite them to our show as a way to thank them for their kindness tonight. I will take care of the arrangements by asking Mr. Watanabe to provide a VIP box for the family." "What a wonderful idea, Griff," enthused Mally. "Come on, let's grab a cab," suggested Jeff, cuddling Nora, who was shivering. They weren't dressed for the unexpected conditions and hurried to the main road. The evening had been unique, one not soon forgotten. They had been welcomed into a Japanese family's inner sanctum, something exceedingly rare for Americans.

The afternoon Chad and Myoshi had spent together increased his desire. He was hopelessly in love and not sure what to do. For now it was a waiting game. When would they meet again? Though his heart was bursting, how would he handle her innocence? She was no doubt a virgin. Holding hands and chaste kissing was deliberate and restrained, considering his intense longing for her. Distracted, he pondered the situation. How was it possible to be with her? Where would they go? In the past, he had experienced girlfriends, but only Mary Jane Douglas had wanted to marry. She was a hometown girl from Detroit; dependable, predictable, stable. They got engaged and planned to marry when she finished her degree. Time and distance changed all that. She ended the engagement, hurting him deeply, but eventually he let her go. Myoshi was different, their chance meeting life changing. He would give anything to have her, whatever the risk.

As he lay in his room, the phone rang, startling him. Picking up, a soft, gentle voice greeted him. "Konnichiwa, Chad, it's me!" He smiled, hearing her voice. "Myoshi, where are you?" "I'm at work." His stomach clenched as he pictured her. "Can we meet?" He hadn't expected her to be so eager. "Yes, can we meet for lunch tomorrow at the same place?" "You mean Ginger Blossom?" "Yes, tomorrow is good at noon."

"Yes, I will see you then." There was a click. As he put down the phone his hands shook. 'My God, this is too good to be true,' he reasoned. Maybe it was possible to have her. Maybe she would love him back, the memory of their first conversation regarding arranged marriages, forgotten. Chad felt renewed, hopeful. Counting the hours until their next meeting was agony.

It was noon the following day. Chad paced in front of the Ginger Blossom, checking his watch every so often. 'Where is she?' He was anxious, consumed with her. Suddenly, a hand touched his sleeve. Startled he turned seeing a warm smile directed to him. Chad reached for her hand, kissing it with the formality of a courtier. "I'm so glad you're here, Myoshi," he murmured. "I cannot stay long. There is much to do at the theatre this afternoon." They entered and sat at a table near the window. He ordered green tea for two. He was intoxicated as he gazed at her simplicity, her natural beauty. "I've missed you so much, Myoshi," he murmured, self consciously. "I wasn't sure I'd see you again." "Why, Chad?" "I don't know, maybe because I'm an American." "Oh no, you thought that?" She reached for his hand," a smile growing. "I'm here, is this proof?" "I guess so. It's just that I'm just an American hoofer from New York and you're a very traditional girl!" "Please Chad, let's be together and forget our differences," she said, tears welling. "Oh Myoshi, I'm sorry! Please forgive me! Are you hungry?" "Not so much, I just wanted to see you." For a few minutes they were silent, sipping tea. "Want to go to our wishing well?" "Yes, please!" Chad paid the check, failing to notice a Japanese man watching them from across the room. As they left, he stood and followed at a discreet distance.

The day had turned cloudy, a slight chill in the air. "It looks like it might rain," he remarked, hugging her close, as they walked. It was a short distance to the park, the single pagoda visible through the trees and bushes, tidily manicured. Crossing a foot bridge, they stepped inside the sheltered area, the wishing well within view. With no visible presence of others nearby, Chad kissed her tenderly. She stayed briefly, feeling the warmth of his lips, but pulled away. She appeared nervous, her eyes darting here and there. "Chad, I must go back to work," she said, anxiously. "Please, Myoshi, stay awhile." "I cannot be late," she said emphatically. "I'm in love with you," he whispered, trying to prolong the moment. "When will I see you again?" "I don't know." "Can you we meet on a day off?" "Oh, no, my family spends time together, it would be difficult," she said, a tinge of regret in her voice. "Please try, I will miss you," he said, voice trembling. "Yes," she said, hopefully. "Now, I must return to Nissei!" Chad walked her back to the main street, hailing a taxi to share. No words were exchanged as they rode through the afternoon traffic crush. Pulling up to the theatre, he assisted her out of the backseat. "Call me soon, please. I'm free except for Wednesday and Saturdays at 2:00." "Yes, yes," she said, hurriedly turning and rushing off. As he stood near the entrance, he didn't see the same Japanese man watching. Heart heavy he walked back to the hotel. He was getting in deeper with each meeting, a dicey place to be.

Chapter 18

Solutions

For Jonas and Phillipe, it was good to be home! Their building in the West 60's never looked better, as the cab pulled up. It had been a long flight home, with stops in Honolulu and San Francisco. Jonas had called his father, Charles, regretfully begging off their visit under the circumstances. It had been a warm conversation and far too long since they had spoken. Charles mentioned he would be coming to New York in the next couple of months and would pay them a visit.

In the meantime, they had settling-in to do. Phillipe unpacked, sorting clothes; a pile for the downstairs laundry and one for the dry cleaners, while Jonas looked through mail, collected by a neighbor during their absence. "Hey Babe, we've got rent, Con Ed and Ma Bell coming up." "We've got a couple of week's grace, Cheri." "I know, but my OCD kicks in at every turn! Phillipe looked in cupboards and the fridge. "We have to market, Cheri!" The two continued; Jonas sorting mail and making a grocery list, while Phillipe changed the bed linens and put fresh towels out. Toiletries were unpacked, put away and suits hung up. The afternoon hours passed quickly. "Are you hungry, Babe? I could eat the ass out of a dinosaur!" "Mon Dieu," gasped Phillipe, feigning distress. "How about hitting Joe Allen's for a juicy burger and a beer?" "You have excellent ideas, Cheri, let's go!" Forgetting the pile of chores, they headed out to midtown.

Centipede had just come down and some of the gypsies had also decided it was an Allen's night. Hal Royce and Joe Pinto were now seeing each other and dropped by to relax. As they sat at the bar, they noticed Jonas and Phillipe walk in. Waving to get their attention, Jonas perked up when he saw them and the two hurried over.

"Welcome back, you Marys," said Joe, embracing his pals. "When did you hit town?" "We got in this morning. It was an 18 hour haul!" "Jeez, you must be wiped out," said Hal, working on a beer. "Hey, let's take that table over there," said Joe, pointing to a place for four. "Le Roy, start a tab, okay?" The bartender looked up, "Sure thing, Joe. What do you guys want?" "I'll have what you have on tap," said Jonas. "Babe, what're you drinking?" "I'll have a brandy and water, thanks." The four settled near the back of the room. "You got back in the nick man, what a caper," said Joe. "What happened exactly, with Bartel?" "The guy couldn't keep it in his pants. He finally got caught trying to nail Julie Jensen backstage." "We caught him at it," added Hal, with a twisted grin. "We literally had to pull him off of the poor kid. She was pretty shook!" "How is Julie doing now? Is she able to work?" "Landry gave her a couple days off as soon as Marcy, out with bronchitis, came back. "Where's Bartel now?" "He got his two week notice on the spot and Equity has undoubtedly started the process of suspending him." "Landry had us assist in removing him," crooned Hal. "I had a feeling it would come to this. He was trouble the minute he arrived in Detroit to replace Jerry Thompson. Good riddance," added Jonas. The boys drank in silence. Jonas and Phillipe ordered the Allen's burger special and two more drinks. Joe and Hal had a second round.

"So what else is new around here?" "Hal and I are having a thing," Joe said, nonchalantly. "Ah, the new kid on the block getting some from the old man," said Jonas, chuckling. "I like older men," said Hal, defensively giving Joe a reassuring squeeze. "Well, I have no doubt Pinto has little trouble getting it up, right Joe?" "You could have found out, but you preferred French pastry," said Joe, with an edge. Phillipe, clearly bored with trash talk changed the subject. "So what time do we rehearse tomorrow?" "I think we'll start at 10:00 and get all your placements in and quit at 6:00," said Joe. Friday, the same deal. Landry is calling for your put-in on Monday at 1:00. Jonas, feel free to stay clear until then if you want." "I could use a couple of days off," Jonas admitted. "Would you like me to come in tomorrow, Joe? After all I'm covering Bartel's spot until Phillipe takes over," said Hal. "Good idea," said Joe, glancing at the clock. "Guess we should head out, guys." Jonas paid the bill, adding Joe and Hal's drinks in. "Thanks, Jonas. Good to have you guys back." They wrapped it at Allen's. For Jonas and Phillipe, it had been a long, long day.

Phillipe's rehearsals went exceptionally well. He had a keen eye and was a quick study. Many of the show's combinations were known, as he was one of the originals in *Centipede*. It was a matter of reversing choreography depending on what side of center stage Tim danced. Phillipe's technique was matched by his drive and performance experience. And his eye appeal was known; easily the most stunning man in the company. Women were always in hot pursuit until they learned his preference. His dark hair and eyes, long legs, tight ass and bountiful package always drew attention when he walked into a room or on a stage. Over the years he had few lovers, save for older, wealthy men, who lavished him with luxury in exchange for sexual servitude. A chance meeting in Atlanta ended the 'kept man' pattern as he fell in love for the first time with Jonas.

Phillipe was returning to eight shows a week, starting Monday. Jonas was content taking a leave of absence, having worked constantly for the past 15 years, racking up a record five original Broadway shows and three national tours. He would eventually phase out of performing and work as a choreographer and hopefully, direct like his mentor, Owen Matthews. Two projects were looming ahead and he hoped Owen would want his assistance; a national tour of *Centipede* and the film version of *Broadway Business*. For Jonas, the future was unfolding as he had hoped and worked so diligently for.

On Monday, the entire cast arrived a little before 1:00. Settling in the house, the gypsies waited, chatting quietly until Dick Landry took over. "Company, we've replaced Tim Bartel with Phillipe Danier, who most of you know. For those of you new to the show, be sure to introduce yourselves. We will run the show in start-stop fashion as we work number to number. Danny Bartlett raised his hand. "Yes, Danny?" "What happened to Tim?" There was general murmuring as the group speculated. Pat, Catherine, Joe and Hal exchanged looks, but remained silent. Julie wasn't present, still keeping her distance until the show settled in with Phillipe. "Due to unfortunate and unaccept-able behavior, Mr. Bartel was given his two-week and is no longer in the company. If you need clarification, see me privately." Several of the women exchanged glances.

Jonas suddenly appeared upstage and joined Dick and Joe along the pit. Dick smiled as Jonas approached. "Welcome back, Jonas!" Spontaneous applause broke out amongst the old timers, as the two old pals hugged. "You're a sight for sore eyes," said Dick, resuming announcements. "For those of you not acquainted with Mr. Martin, he's Owen's right hand just returning from Japan, where he remounted *Centipede* with Phillipe's assistance. You auditioned for him last fall. You want to add anything, Jonas?" "I just stopped in to watch. Mr. Pinto has the situation well in hand." Hal applauded, earning him an annoyed glance from Joe. "Now if there's nothing further, let's go," shouted Joe. The gypsies rose like a wave in the house and joined him on stage. "Dick, will you be adding tech elements?" "No, Joe, only work lights. I figured that's all we would need this afternoon." "That's fine. Let's get started!" Phillipe joined the group for the opening freeze and rehearsal was off and running. Frank Dugan, rehearsal pianist, was back. Phillipe was ready and eager to begin. He had missed danc-ing and was psyched to be back on the boards.

As the afternoon unfolded, he didn't miss a detail or step in the staging. At rehearsal's end, the company broke into applause. Excused until half hour, the group dispersed, leaving Phillipe sitting on the edge of the stage, drying off and catching his breath. Suddenly, a pair of arms encircled him, a wet kiss planted on his cheek! "Ah, Mon Cher Patricia, merci beaucoup," he murmured, returning a kiss. "Oh, Phillipe, I've missed you and Jonas so much! How are Griff, Mal and Chad?" "They're wonderful and send their love. They'll be home the first of the year." "Where's Jonas? Did he leave during rehearsal?" "Yes, he ducked out after the sailor number. He's just exhausted!" "How is Blaine?" "Never better! We're more in love than ever!" "Fabulous, Cherie, I'm so happy for you!" Pat suddenly grew serious. "You've missed a lot of drama. Tim Bartel is history, thank God!" "I'm so sorry the young lady had such an ordeal. What's her name, Julie?" "Yes, Julie. She sure found out about Bartel the hard way!" "What do you mean?" "She was warned about the creep and got together with him anyway. Something must have gone horribly wrong. He turned on her! Awful! God knows how many others he's hurt!" "Let's forget him," insisted Phillipe, changing the subject. "Would you join me for a drink tonight, following the show?" "I'd love to!" The two friends walked to the stage door arm in arm. 45th Street was alive with rush hour, a cacophony of sound and furious activity. As they parted, Phillipe glanced at his watch. 'Mon Dieu, not long until half hour! I need rest and food,' he mused, hailing a nearby cab.

Following the show, Pat, Phillipe, Joe and Hal got together at Allen's. Tim's replacement had brought renewed enthusiasm and spirit to *Centipede*. Joe insisted on buying a round when they settled at a large table. Hal was happy to pass the torch to Phillipe. Though covering Bartel's spot had been a great opportunity to perform Owen's work, he was ready for a break. Jonas begged off joining them, remaining at home to sleep off jet lag. He had yet to experience culture shock, though he'd heard other gypsies talk about the difficulty of returning to the U.S. after time spent in a vastly different culture. So far Jonas had ventured out very little, preferring to relax at home for the time being. The change was hardly noticeable. The group chatted quietly, enjoying liquid libation. After a second round, Pat felt the need to get some sleep before Blaine's return from Texas in the morning. With each return, she looked forward to sharing with him all that happened during his absence. The love between them had grown and matured during the past months. Blaine had purposely held off proposing, waiting for the right moment to ask Pat to become his wife. The boys continued a third round at Allen's. Pat excused herself and found a cab on 8th Avenue.

Returning to the Plaza, she was ready for a shower and a good night's sleep. The night clerk handed her a note. She opened it eagerly in the elevator, carefully reading the contents. 'Oh no, I missed Blaine's call,' she thought, as she fumbled for her key. Opening the double door, she slipped in and bolted it behind her. The sound of a ringing phone caused her to drop her dance bag quickly and pick up. "Patricia, it's me. I know it's late, but I was worried. I called about an hour ago." "Oh Blaine, I'm sorry, I went to Allen's with Phillipe, celebrating his return to the show tonight." "Oh, that's right, they've returned. Who did he replace?" "Tim Bartel was served his notice and they needed a replacement fast. Phillipe was the perfect choice." "How's Jonas?" "Suffering jet lag and ordered to take some time off, otherwise no worse for the wear."

Blaine changed gears. "I'll be flying in a bit later tomorrow." "Oh, did something unforeseen come up in Houston?" "Well, something excellent I think. Greg spoke to his old friend and frat brother, Shel Friedman at Universal. It looks like we'll be financing the new Matthews' film. Our investment offer is the best on the table. Greg is backing me a hundred percent as chief investor. The picture is now a definite go!" "Oh God, how exciting!" "Yes, it's another way to support *Bravo Business,* a project dear to my heart! After all, that's the show where I met and fell hopelessly in love with this stunning redhead," he said, chuckling. "Now get to sleep, we have much to catch up on. I'll see you tomorrow night following the show. We're going to celebrate, my beautiful girl." "I love you, Blaine. Hurry home safely!" "I will my love." Pat put down the phone, her mind in a whirl. 'Blaine's making the picture possible,' she thought, suddenly too excited to sleep. Attempting to calm down, she undressed and indulged in a soothing shower. The warmth of the spray relaxed her, slowing her mind. And with only one sleep to go, she'd be in his arms again.

Blaine's private jet arrived at TEB, Teterboro, New Jersey the next evening. Earlier in the day, he had taken the liberty to speak with Louis Lambert, the Plaza's general manager with a special request. He wanted private use of the hotel's dining room, following regular business hours. The Plaza management regarded Blaine as an indispensible guest, resulting in privileges not afforded others. It was the perfect setting for Blaine's plan and Lambert set about ordering the finest meal to be prepared upon their arrival. Weeks before he had called Tiffany & Company to consult with Hans Meertens, an old friend and general manager of the renowned jewelry store. Blaine wanted the best for Pat and Hans would ably guide him. The choice could be nothing ostentatious, so size wasn't a consideration as much as quality. After much deliberation, he chose a one and a half carat yellow diamond in a simple gold setting.

The next night following the show, Pat spotted the familiar limo as she excited the stage door. Blaine's driver, Keith Noonan came around the car. Tipping his hat, he opened the back door. "Good evening, Miss Byrne!" "Good to see you Keith, how have you been?" "Very well, thank you. Mr. Courtman has asked me to drive you to the Plaza. He will meet you in the dining room." "There must be some mistake, the dining room closes at 10:00!" "Normally yes, but Mr. Courtman has been given an extension for tonight." "How intriguing! Let's go," she giggled. Keith's attention to detail was top notch. At the Plaza, Keith opened the door for Pat. "Good night, Keith, thank you!" A faint flicker of a smile was visible as he nodded to her. As she entered the hotel, she took in the lush setting. At that moment she was about to find out her lover had been busy making plans. As she entered the quiet dining room, Blaine rose when he saw her. Hurrying to him, his waiting arms wrapped around her. He leaned down, kissed her longingly and lingered a few moments. Holding her, he felt immense pleasure. "My beautiful girl, you're radiant tonight!" Pat stayed put, immersed in his attention. "I've missed you, Blaine." "Come, sit," he said, offering her a chair.

The table was set with the Plaza's finest; exquisite Ulster white linen, Limoges china, Waterford crystal, and Reed and Barton silver service. Long white tapers flickered, highlighting an arrangement of roses in various shades, lilies and graceful greens at the center. The head waiter stood by holding a bottle of chilled champagne. "Will the "Dom Perignon be satisfactory, Sir? "Indeed, Randolph. Thank you!" The cork popped and the contents poured into two flutes given to Pat first, then to Blaine. The remainder was placed in a silver bucket table side. "Will there be anything else, Mr. Courtman?" "Not at the moment. Please give us a few minutes." Randolph hurried off to oversee the menu. Raising his glass, Blaine's eyes never left Pat's. "My beautiful girl, let's drink to us!" Looping arms they sipped lost in each other. Finishing, he took their glasses, placing them to the side. Slipping out of his chair, he crossed to her, bending to one knee. Reaching into his pocket, he produced a small velveteen box and opened it. Glistening in the candlelight was an exquisite diamond, causing Pat to gasp! Taking the ring he gently placed it on her left hand. "My darling Patricia, will you do me the honor of becoming my wife forever? It would make me so very happy!" Pat began to cry. "Oh Blaine, of course I will, forever and ever!" "My beautiful girl, don't cry," he softened, gently brushing tears away until he couldn't hold back. Tears erupted as they kissed, repeatedly. Dinner followed, brilliantly planned and prepared by executive chef, Marcel Du Bois. The repast was astonishing, but compared to Blaine's proposal, anti climactic!

Chapter 19

Complication and Consequences

For Chad and Myoshi, infatuation had turned to love. From their chance meeting opening night of *Centipede*, the two were fixated on each other, sharing a meal or taking long walks. They hadn't considered the consequences if discovered. Chad struggled, fighting his intense desire for her, frustrated by the cultural differences and her obvious virginity. His need increased with each contact. But, to what end? There was no opportunity to be intimate. The thought of making love in a hotel room felt cheap and not worthy of her. For now he would have to accept the limitations. What he wanted most was to bring her back to the U.S. and marry her. Feeling alone and unsure of the next step, he asked his best friend, Jeff to join him for a drink. Following the show, they met at the Nikkatsu bar. Settling, an ice cold Japanese beer sounded great. Dancing *Centipede* for two solid hours brought intense thirst.

Chad was quiet, leaning on his elbows, his beer untouched. Jeff broke the silence. "What's going on? You seem off!" "Is it that obvious?" "Yes!" "Well, remember when I mentioned I met someone?" "Yeah, if memory serves, but that was weeks ago. Who is she?" "She's Japanese. Her name is Myoshi." "Holy shit, Chad, what are you playing at?" "What do you mean?" "She's Japanese and my guess, very traditional and only allowed to date a prospective husband!" "How do you know so much about it?" "I've been doing a lot of reading about the culture and customs of Japan. Marital matches are still made by parents here. A young woman's never a free agent unless she's disgraced in some way, then she's disowned by the family!" "That's harsh and completely unreasonable, Jeff!" "It apparently works here and has for thousands of years." "It's bullshit, that's what it is! I'm crazy in love with this girl. I want to bring her back to the U.S. and marry her, if she'll have me!" "Are you nuts? You can't do that!" "Then what? Just leave her when the run is over?" "You'll have to, end of story!" The exchange ended with the two not speaking. Jeff finally broke the ice.

"Chad, please listen to me carefully. End this infatuation before there's trouble. You're walking on shaky ground and it stands to get worse. If the family finds out, you'll be in deep shit!" But Chad wasn't listening. He was lost in her, the only place he cared to be. Jeff paid the check and patted Chad on the back. "Be careful, my friend, there's rough sea ahead. Quit before you drown," his last words before he left.

A few days later Chad met Myoshi across town from the theatre, in a small park. The day was blustery and wet. Sharing a large umbrella, he held it over them, cuddling her against the cold. In spite of the conditions, they were happy to be together. "I'm so glad you're here, Myoshi. I have something important to ask you." 'What is it?" Her eyes were wide with curiosity as she sat gazing at him. "I'm in love with you. Will you marry me?" He didn't expect the fallen face or the sudden tears. She began to weep, holding him tighter with each sob. "Oh Chad, I cannot! My parents will never allow it. You are an American, not Japanese. They will select a husband for me." "But you love me, don't you?" "Oh yes, yes, Chad. I love you!" "Then be mine, Myoshi, say you will," he urged. His sudden move caught her by surprise, as he kissed her longingly. Dropping the umbrella, he held her face repeatedly kissing her, as the soft rain fell on them. How long they embraced wasn't certain, but unnoticed stood a Japanese man, taking photos of them from across the street. Feeling the dampness engulfing them, Chad pulled away, scooping up the umbrella. "I have to get back, I will be missed," she murmured sadly. "When will I see you again?" "Soon, but now I must go!" "Please let me walk you," he insisted. "Chad, I must go alone." As she hurried away, he felt a pull of sadness, his chest tightening. 'I can't stand this,' he thought, tears welling up. Across the street the man continued taking photos. Little did Chad know, an earthquake of conflict was about to erupt.

The following day, Griff's phone rang in his office. Hearing it repeatedly from the hall, he hurried to pick up. A Japanese voice greeted him. "Konnichiwa, Mr. Edwards, this is Uki Ishide, from Mr. Watanabe's office. He has requested a meeting with you at your earliest convenience. When are you available?" Griff glanced at his desk calendar. "I'm open tomorrow morning, say about 10:00?" "Chotto matte kudasai." Griff held, waiting with curiosity. "Hai, Dozo, come to office, third floor." "Domo Arigato, Mr. Ishide!" Griff put down the phone, finished his paper work and headed to the Nikkatsu.

'Watanabe has something on his mind,' he mused, entering their room. Mally looked up from her crocheting, noting the puzzled expression. "Darling, are you all right?" "Yes, I guess so. I just had a phone call from Watanabe's office. He has requested a meeting." "That's curious. I wonder what he wants." "Well, I'll see him at 10:00 tomorrow and find out. In the meantime, come here, Mrs. Edwards." In moments she was in his arms, his heat pressing against her. "We need a getaway soon, maybe Kyoto." "Oh Griff, I hear it's so romantic! Can we stay in one of those little inns?" "They're called Ryokans and yes, anything for you, my love." "I can't wait, Griff. I've always thought they only existed in Hollywood films!" "My love, your enthusiasm would charm a brick wall," he chuckled. With half hour a few hours away, they lay down and snuggled. Soon, they were making love, followed by a mid afternoon nap.

At 10:00 the next morning, Griff walked into Watanabe's office. A warm smile greeted him. "Ohayo gozaimasu! Mr. Watanabe will be with you shortly, Mr. Edwards." Griff nodded, removing his outer jacket and sitting down. He reached for the *Asahi Shinbun*, Tokyo's daily newspaper, glancing at the front page. Watanabe emerged, a sober look on his face. "Good morning, Mr. Edwards," he said, formally extending his hand and bowing. "Please come in." Griff preceded the producer into an elegantly simple office, the décor pure Japanese. The furniture was modern, including framed posters of past productions at the Nissei, liberally displayed. "Please sit down, Mr. Edwards, would you care for tea?" "I would, thank you!" Watanabe pressed the intercom. "Uki, please bring Mr. Edwards tea." A minute or two passed without conversation. Griff settled in observing Watanabe who stood staring out the window. There was a soft knock at the door. Uki appeared, carrying a pot of tea and two cups. Placing the pot on the desk, he proceeded to pour the traditional brew. Handing Griff a cup he glanced at Watanabe, who nodded and took a second cup as offered. Without another word, Uki turned and left, closing the door carefully.

The two men sipped, the silence engulfing them. Watanabe finished his tea, placing the cup on the tray. He turned to Griff, face stern, voice low. "Mr. Edwards, I have asked you here because there is a situation that must not continue." Griff looked up, surprised. "What is it?" "I have reason to believe, one in your cast is seeing my daughter, Myoshi! This cannot be! My eldest son, Mori saw them together a few weeks ago, then again this past week. He followed her when she took lunch and this is what he discovered." Watanabe handed Griff a manila envelope. Opening the flap, Griff pulled out several black and white photos. Each shot showed a couple conversing, embracing and kissing. He didn't recognize the young woman, but it was clear who the man was. "Mr. Watanabe, the gentleman is Chad Chapman, our dancing lead!" "He appears not to be a gentleman," said Watanabe, clearly upset. "On the contrary, Chad is one of our most valued performers and of good character."

Watanabe began to pace. "What is he doing with my only daughter, taking unacceptable liberties?" "I have no idea, this is news to me." Watanabe grew more serious. "In our country, a young woman may be allowed the company of her intended only, one chosen by her parents. She is not allowed alone without a chaperone present. Mr. Chapman doesn't understand our ways. What he is doing is forbidden and therefore must be stopped. I cannot have this!" Griff took a large breath, feeling the weight of Watanabe's concern and position. "What would you have me do?" "I want you to explain why he must stop seeing my daughter!" Griff stood. Extending his hand across the desk, he gazed directly at the producer. "It will be taken care of, Mr. Watanabe. You have my word." "Thank you! I trust that you will handle it immediately."

"Yes, I will," said Griff. "Thank you for bringing the matter to my attention." Again, they shook hands and bowed. Griff excused himself and left, sifting through the unexpected development.

Myoshi Watanabe was preoccupied. Every moment away from Chad was an impediment to their growing love. But how could she explain to her parents her love for an American, a performing artist? Worse, he lived in the U.S., returning there at the end of *Centipede's* engagement. How could she live without him? She was well aware of her culture's tradition of matches with one of her own. It was just a matter of time, although up until now her parents were unaware of her forbidden new love. As she sat typing, the intercom buzzed. Startled for a moment, she picked up her phone. "Ohayo gozaimasu, Myoshi." "Chi Chi! Ogenki desu ka?" "Hai, okagesamade!" "Daughter, let us speak English. It is important for you to practice." "Hai, Chi Chi!" Her father's voice was tight, filled with concern. "I want you to join me for lunch in my office today." "Of course, Chi Chi! Itsu desu ka?" "Come at noon," replied Watanabe. "Hai, Chi Chi!" She put down the phone, puzzled. Her father usually didn't eat lunch during a work day. Happily she would see him, a rare occurrence for he was usually away on business or arrived late from the office most evenings.

At noon she hurried to her father's office and was greeted by Uki, who showed her in. Watanabe rose from behind his desk, a smile on his face. She was radiant, her beauty moving him as always. Embracing her, he didn't want to let go, considering his purpose. "Please join me for lunch, Myoshi." She followed her father into the adjoining room where a repast was waiting, Uki standing ready. Seating her first he sat next, nodding to his assistant, who began serving. "I ordered your favorite, nori and ika!" "Domo arigato, Chi Chi," she giggled, her delight spilling over him. Having been served, father and daughter delighted in a dish of squid, seaweed and rice. Green tea followed, served with fresh fruit. As they finished, Watanabe seemed preoccupied as Uki removed dishes and exited the room. She could see concern on his face.

"What is it, Chi Chi?" "My beautiful child, it has been brought to my attention that you have been in the company of a Caucasian man, an American. Your brother spotted you on numerous occasions and without a chaperone. Do me the courtesy of explaining, please!" Myoshi's eyes conveyed utter shock at her Chi Chi's words. Forming them carefully her eyes filled with tears. "Oh Chi Chi, I am in love. He is Chad and lead dancer of *Centipede*." "How did this happen? You know this is not our way! It will have to end!" She began to sob, alarming Watanabe. He reached for her, cradling her head, attempting to sooth. "My child, this is unfortunate. I have no doubt that your feelings for this man are sincere and strong, but you may not continue this infatuation!" "But Chi Chi, this man I wish to be with forever!" Watanabe pulled away from Myoshi and stood, his voice trembling. "I see now that I must forbid you to see him! If you continue to do so, there will be serious consequences, my child!" "But Chi Chi, how can I? I'm in love with him and he will be hurt!" Watanabe calmed down and faced her.

"I have taken certain measures to end this unfortunate situation. I have spoken to this man's superior, and he will advise the young man, as I now must you." Myoshi weeping intensified, inconsolably. Attempting to calm her, Watanabe changed the subject to try and appease. "Your mother and I have good news, my child. We have found a suitable match, a young man of our own, who comes from a revered family in the community, Dr. Senji Ono, an esteemed physician in Osaka," he said, smiling. But Myoshi was not smiling. "I will love Chad until my dying day, Chi Chi. No matter how you plan my future; it will be dark without him!" Rising she looked intently at her father. "I must return to work now, Chi Chi! Sayonara," she murmured as she departed. Watanabe sat in silence, his heart aching as he ruminated the enormity of this impossible situation, one in which his beloved daughter was mired.

At the theatre, Chad sat silently at the mirror. He could only think of beautiful Myoshi. Every minute away from her was agony. As he applied pan stick, Griff's voice came through the men's speaker. "Chad Chapman, please stop by my office at intermission. Thank you!" As though under water, he slowly continued his prep for the show. At pre curtain, he slipped into place at Mally's side. She could tell he was off. "Chad, are you all right?" He smiled and gave her a little peck. "I couldn't be better, Mal." "You seem distracted, or something." "Nope, I'm fine. Do you have any idea what Griff wants?" "I don't." "I guess I'll find out soon enough." The first act flew by. As preoccupied as he was with Myoshi, he danced an exceptional show, partnering Mally with consistent energy and verve. No other man in the company could hold a candle to him. At intermission he hurried to change for act two. Following, he hastily went to Griff's office. "Come in, Chad," said Griff, without looking up. "Hi, you wanted to see me?" "Yes, I'm wondering if you have time to join me for a drink, after the show." "Sure thing, Griff. Where?" "The bar in the Nikkatsu will do, say about 11:00?" "I'll be there!" Griff called places and the second act took off.

Later, Chad arrived at the hotel lounge and looked around for Griff, spotting him at the bar. Noting his arrival, Griff suggested a booth in the corner. "What are you having?" "Anything on tap will be great." "Make yourself comfortable, I'll order for us." Smiling affably, Kazu, the barman, greeted Griff. "Konbanwa, Mr. Edwards-san, Ogenki desu ka?" "Hai, Okagesamade! A Sapporo on tap, and a vodka martini, extra dry, with a twist, Dozo." "Chotto made kudasai," replied the barman. In a moment, drinks in hand, he joined Chad. Handing him a beer, he settled. Raising his glass, he didn't miss the irony as he murmured, "Cheers!" They sipped for a minute, until Chad spoke, a serious tone tingeing his voice. "This isn't a social meeting. What's on your mind, Griff?"

"I have to talk to you regarding something personal, something that directly affects our relationship with the Japanese. As you know, we are guests of this country and as such, it is important we respect the culture and maintain a good relationship with our hosts while here." "Oh, oh, this sounds serious, Griff. What gives and why me?" Griff paused long enough to take a large sip of his martini. "It has been brought to my attention that you are seeing a Japanese girl." "Who told you this, Jeff Jenkins?" "No, Chad, I was informed by her father, Hiri Watanabe, the producer of our venture. Myoshi is his only daughter." Chad sat frozen.

"I don't believe it! How is this possible?" Griff pulled out the envelope containing the photos. "You were spotted by her brother at a cafe first, followed several times afterward. These are proof." Chad looked through the photos, his face a mask of shock. "Christ, Griff, this is madness!" "Yes, it is unfortunate. Culturally, this cannot happen. Japanese parents arrange marriages for their children. You must honor this tradition as a gentleman and let her go." "I'm in love with Myoshi and she with me! I want to take her back to the States and marry her!" Griff's concern was building. "You cannot! Chad, you must break it off, for your sake, hers and *Centipede.*" "This is fucked, Griff!" "I am free and over 21 and love this girl. I want to be with her for the rest of my life!" "I regret to say you must end it as soon as possible. You will only bring heartbreak to her and lose your credibility as an artist and a man."

There was silence, awkward and heartbreaking. Chad put his head in his hands and wept. Griff sat, unable to cajole or ease the pain his best dancer was feeling. "Chad, I am so sorry. I wish I could offer a solution. Unfortunately there is none. The sooner you can take care of this the better. From what I understood, Mr. Watanabe was going to inform his daughter that your relationship must end. Out of respect for the gentleman and his decision, I must insist that you carry through his request. I hope you can understand how difficult this is for me. You are an artist and person I respect immensely. Under normal circumstances, I would not interfere in your personal life, but there is far too much at stake here for everyone concerned." Chad rose and reached out his hand. "I'm sorry you had to be the one to break this to me, Griff. You know I respect you as my boss and friend." "And I know you to be a man of your word, Chad. I wish you well." The two parted without another word. Chad went to his room immediately. 'So this is what it feels like having your heart cut out,' he thought. Undressing, he stepped into the shower, allowing the warmth to sooth his aching body. His heart was another matter. No amount of warm water could ease the pain inside. As the spray ran cold, he sobbed repeatedly, realizing what he had to do.

The next evening, the performance brought another standing ovation. Positive response was a nightly occurrence, the Japanese showing their enthusiasm, show after show. Chad did his usual top-notch performance, but his heart was dry, his emotions on automatic pilot. Finishing, he changed and headed to the stage door. Several cast members had already left for the night, leaving him one to leave. Stepping outside, a cool, soft rain permeated the night, causing him to shiver. The alley was dark, an occasional street lamp lighting the walkway. Suddenly, he heard his name called. She was there. Myoshi! She looked so small, so fragile. His instinct was to rush to her, take her in his arms and hold her close. Instead, he had to be strong, consciously changing his approach. "Myoshi, what are you doing here so late?" He was fighting not to take her in his arms." "I came to the show tonight to see you!" "Myoshi, I need to tell you something." His voice wavered, caught in his throat. She reached for his hand, cupping it with hers. Looking deep into his eyes she forced a smile. "Chad, it will be better if you just say what I know you must." Looking around carefully, he took her face in his hands. Tears welled, her innocence and purity piercing his soul.

"Oh, my dearest Myoshi, we cannot see each other anymore. To do so would be to dishonor you, your family and the artistic agreement we have with your father. The only reason I'm here is by the grace of those who hired me." Seconds flew by as she formed her words carefully. "Chad, I didn't think about my family. I only know I love you and want to be with you until my dying day. Now, it is not possible." With a cry, she clung to him, his resistance falling away, as he held her close. "Oh Myoshi, I am so in love with you. You're all I care about. I can't live without you!" She became alarmed, his words literal in her mind. "Please, Chad, don't say that! Maybe we could be friends at least." "I doubt it! Your future has already been decided," he said bitterly. "I can't fight tradition and neither can you. That's the way it is." "Chad, please don't be angry with me," she pleaded. "All I know is I love you!" "I'm not angry with you, I love you!" Caught up in the moment, they kissed passionately, hunger and desperation displacing reason. Then moments later, realizing they must stop, Chad was the first to let go. "We can't do this, Myoshi! Please, just go away," he demanded, his voice distant and firm. He looked at her, fighting back tears as she bowed her head. "Sayonara, Chad, I will love you forever!" Hurrying away, she never looked back.

Chad leaned up against the building and let go, sobbing uncontrollably. He didn't notice the Japanese man standing in the shadows a few feet away. He approached. Chad, startled, stepped back, his paranoia building, as he observed the man. "Who are you, what do you want?" The man extended his hand. "Konbanwa, I am Shegeki. I believe you know why I am here." Chad looked puzzled, as he wiped tears away. "No, not really," he said, trying to be cordial. I brought my sister here tonight, at our father's request." "You are Myoshi's brother?" "Hai!" Chad lifted his arms in mock surrender. "Well, Mr. Watanabe can stop worrying. I will not see Myoshi again," he sputtered, an edge obvious. "You have done the honorable thing, Chad. It is Chad, yes?" "Yes, I've let her go." "Domo arigato gozaimasu, Chad, for your understanding." He bowed and walked away. Chad watched him disappear in the rain. 'Understanding, my ass,' he thought angrily.

In the morning, the phone rang in Edwards' room. Mally picked up, noting a strained voice. "Chad, is that you?" "Mal, is Griff in?" Griff was pouring over a day old copy of the *New York Herald Tribune*. Looking up, he noted the puzzled look and her mouthing, "Chad." She decided to give him privacy and went to the restaurant for more coffee. Only awkward silence until Chad spoke. "I won't beat around the bush, Griff. I took care of your request." "Chad, there was no other choice. You did the right thing." "I met Myoshi's brother last night. He thanked me for ending it." "He was there?" "Yes, he brought her to say "Sayonara." There was another pause. "Griff, I wasn't thinking clearly, never realizing how complicated things are." "The human heart doesn't always use logic. I'm glad you did." "Well, I guess I'm destined to be a bachelor in Japan!" Griff chuckled. "Well, you haven't lost your sense of humor, my boy. Good on you!" "Have a great day, Griff. Again, thanks for helping me." As Chad put down the phone, he realized he'd slowly find his way back. In time, he would return to New York, to his life as a dancer and a much wiser man.

Chapter 20

Hooray for Hollywood

At noon Owen received a call from Shel Friedman's office at Universal Pictures. By evening he was on a late flight out of JFK, heading to the coast. Sitting back, he enjoyed his usual, Glenfiddich on the rocks. An attractive stewardess in first class with a stunning ass and pleasant manner caught his eye. When the aircraft was at cruising altitude, she went about her business, seeing to the passengers. Owen was at cruising speed as well, ordering a second and admiring the landscape. He was relaxed, in charge. When she stopped by to offer a pillow, he made his play. "What's your name, beautiful?" "I'm Terri, how's your drink?" "Great!" "Would you like a pillow?" "If you share it with me," he said, adding a wink. "Not possible sir." "Are you based in L.A.?" "Yes, our entire crew is out of LAX." Owen brightened. The thought of possibly laying her was a delicious notion. "I'll be in town for a week. May I call you?" "Let me think about it," she said, welcoming his attention. "What's your name, again?" "Terri, Terri Shelton. And you are?" "Owen Matthews." Her mouth gaped with recognition. "Owen Matthews, the celebrated director from Broadway?" "The same," he replied, encouraged by her interest. "When we land, Miss Shelton, I'd like to buy you a cocktail. Is that a possibility?" "Very," she tossed, hurrying to the in-flight intercom. 'That broad is as good as mine,' he mused. The flight would take over four hours, during which Owen, perpetually horny, imagined Miss Shelton out of uniform!

The night before hadn't gone as well. Catherine had been summoned to stop by his place for a nightcap and sleepover after the show. She was moody, distracted, while he was eager for sex. From the minute she arrived, he sensed her preoccupation. Offered a glass of Vouvray, she drank it quickly and requested a second. "Baby, slow down, I want you to feel what I plan to do to you." Downing his scotch, he reached for her, kissing her hard, his tongue in overdrive. She struggled away from him, her mind elsewhere. Owen poured another scotch and lit a cigarette. Taking a deep drag he carefully let the smoke trail from his nostrils. He studied her intently. "Okay, Baby, what's going on? You're cold tonight." "First another," she said, pointing to the Vouvray bottle. "Baby, you're becoming a lush," he mused. "No, I'm upset." "Oh, must be something important, to break away from me." Leaning on the bar, he gave her full attention, his scotch and ashtray nearby. "Ok, shoot!"

"Were you notified of Tim Bartel's firing?" "Of course, Dick Landry informed me that Danier replaced him. Good timing considering they just got back from Tokyo. How's it going?" Catherine sat, stunned. "Owen, that's not the point! Were you told why he was fired?" "If memory serves, he nearly raped one of the girls." "Well?" "Well, what?" "How do you feel about one of your dancers being assaulted by a cast mate?" "Take it easy, Baby! He acted on his own!" "Do you recall a previous conversation regarding a friend of mine being bothered by a guy, who was stalking her? Remember what you said?" "Jesus Christ, Baby, what is this, a cross examination?" "No, it's a reminder! You seemed very indifferent at the time, like it was no big deal!" "Catherine, what a guy does with his dick off stage is his business!" "But this didn't happen off stage, it was in your theatre!" Her voice was rising as she continued pouring another glass. "What the fuck? Is there a point to this?" "Yes, there is, Owen. The point is that Bartel was bothering me for a while before he turned on Julie Jensen. I was afraid to tell you, but now it's clear had the girl assaulted been me, you would hardly have broken a sweat! You don't give a shit about me! All you care about is getting laid!" Owen took a last drag on his cigarette, put it out and rose. "I think we need a break," he said, his voice low, his anger tempered. Catherine faced him squarely. "Owen, have you ever loved me?" He didn't respond as he lit another cigarette and poured another scotch. Without a pause, she picked up her coat and bag and walked out. No tears for Catherine Andrews, just cold, hard reality and a firm choice.

Landing in L.A., Owen was ready for another drink. Terri Shelton suggested meeting him at the Tiki Hut, a bar along the concourse.

Settling in a booth, he waited, enjoying his smoke while planning his next move. He didn't have to wait long. She appeared, jacket and hat removed, the front of her uniform blouse strategically unbuttoned and revealing. "You look beautiful, Miss Shelton. What would you like?" Setting her flight bag down, slipped in next to him. "I'd love a Bacardi, crushed ice, please!" A waiter appeared. "A Bacardi for the lady and I'll have Glenfiddich, neat, rocks." "Very good sir!" When he'd left, Owen pulled out his Chesterfields and offered one to Terri. "Thank you, Mr. Matthews; I'm dying for a cigarette. We can't smoke while on duty!" "Owen, please," he soothed, lighting one for her. Taking a long drag, he studied her closely, admiring the view. "You know, you're very pretty. Have you ever considered modeling?" "Oh no, you must be joking," she giggled. "I'm serious," he said, moving closer. "You could do very well with your great bone structure and lovely figure. How tall are you?" "I'm 5′ 8″ in my stocking feet." "Well, they like them tall in that business. If you ever decide to look into it, I have contacts." "I appreciate the suggestion, Mr. Matthews, but I love flying, I really do!"

The drinks arrived. They sipped and talked. Conversation turned to innuendo. "I'm at the Beverly Wilshire this week, care to join me?" "Gee, I don't know if I can. I'm flying to JFK again the day after tomorrow. We have a lay-over in New York for 24 hours and then fly home." Small talk was wasting valuable time. "Why don't you come to the hotel tonight?" "What do you have in mind, Owen?" "I'm going to pleasure you up one side and down the other!" "I'd like that," she murmured, breathless. "Come on then," he insisted. Owen paid the check and took her bag, leading her out of the bar. A sudden announcement caught their attention. "Terri Shelton, please report to United Airlines information kiosk on the main concourse." Puzzled, she paused, considering the page. "I wonder what's going on." Again, the voice repeated the message. "Terri Shelton, please report to United Airlines kiosk on the main concourse." "Looks like someone's paging you, Terri," said, Owen, slightly annoyed. "I'll have to check in. Please come with me, okay?" Reluctantly, Owen followed her down the concourse and over to the United desk. An affable young lady was waiting as Terri approached. "I'm Terri Shelton," she said, her business-like persona kicking in. "You have a call," she said, handing the phone. "This is Terri Shelton." "Baby, my flight got cancelled. I'm here. Thought I'd wait for your flight and take you home." She turned pale, looking around anxiously. "Where are you, Brad?" "I'm at door 4! Meet me there, Honey." "I'll just be a couple of minutes, Brad." Handing the phone back, she looked at Owen," a sheepish look growing. "Gosh, Owen, I can't go with you. That was my husband, Brad. His flight to Denver got cancelled, probably due to weather." "What the fuck? You're married?" "Yes, to a TWA pilot. I'm sorry, maybe next time," she mumbled, hurrying off. Disappointment didn't come close to describing Owen Matthews' demeanor.

Owen woke up grumpy and horny. The throbbing from his hardened anatomy was an obvious reminder he hadn't laid Terri Shelton. Wiped out and hung over from the long flight, he ordered coffee and stepped into the shower. As the warm spray gently pelted his body his hands would have to do. 'Fuck, this is annoying,' he thought, stroking his shaft aggressively until he felt the build-up and release. Rinsing, he stepped out and reached for a towel. Slipping into a complimentary hotel robe, he heard a tapping at the door. A bellman brought coffee, Bromo Seltzer and the *Los Angeles Times,* setting the tray on a table. Pouring coffee he handed Owen a cup, smiling. "Will there be anything else, Mr. Matthews?" "No, thanks," he muttered, as he gave the fellow a tip and closed the door. The headache continued as he lit a cigarette. The phone suddenly rang, the voice not a familiar one.

"Mr. Matthews, this is Lois Campion calling for Mr. Shel Friedman. He would like to move today's meeting to 10:00 tomorrow. Will this be satisfactory?" 'A small fucking miracle,' thought Owen. He'd have time to get rid of the hangover and catch some sleep. "Yes, that will be fine." "Very good, Mr. Matthews, I will let Mr. Friedman know." Owen hung up and lit another smoke. His thoughts moved to Karen Eliot, Friedman's assistant. There had been many raucous nights together during his first trip. She'd take care of his needs as soon as he could arrange it, guaranteed! Karen was Hollywood-sophisticated, a maverick persona that attracted him and was decidedly feisty in bed. In truth, she was a bonus coinciding with his upcoming film project. With time to kill he picked up the phone. Checking the directory of services he decided to book a massage. High time for the ex-hoofer turned movie director to be pampered in style.

At 9:30 the following morning, the Beverly doorman hailed a cab for Owen and he was off to Universal. At the studio gate, he was welcomed and the driver was given directions to the executive offices. Entering the building, he was greeted by Lois Campion and shown to the meeting room where Karen Eliot was setting up the conference table. Glancing up, her face remained placid when she saw him. "Hello, Owen," she said, with little enthusiasm. 'Cool as ever,' he mused and took a seat. "May I offer you coffee, tea or would you prefer a Bloody Mary or Screwdriver?" 'I'd prefer a screw,' he thought, dryly. "Coffee, cream and one sugar, please." She walked to a side table, poured coffee, adding cream and a sugar packet. Taking a napkin and spoon she placed them on the table, handing him the cup. "How have you been, Karen?" "I've been busy traveling. Shel sent me to Tahiti for a little vacation." "Nice that your boss is so generous," he said, his voice hardly masking his mood. "Owen, nice is hardly descriptive. It's paradise, pure heaven," she purred. "Have you been?" "I can't say I have, but your time away certainly agrees with you. You're glowing," he continued, trying to evoke some warmth. "I was on my honeymoon. It's the perfect place, so romantic!" Owen's cigarette dropped from his lips. His coffee tipped over, spilling into his lap. Struggling to his feet, he reached for several napkins, trying to mop up the burning liquid and locating the cigarette on the carpet. When he recovered he stared at her, incredulously. "Honeymoon? You're married?" "Why, yes, to Jean Benoit. He's head cinematographer here at the studio and lead camera on your film." Owen suddenly didn't feel well. Re-lighting his cigarette he sat back, trying to recover from shock. "Aren't you going to wish me every happiness, Owen?" He could feel her goading him into a response. "Good luck, Karen," he said flatly.

An awkward moment was abated as Shel Friedman arrived with two associates. Extending his hand, his greeting was warm and enthusiastic, unlike that of his newlywed assistant. "Welcome to L.A. Owen, great to see you! May I present, Nick Silverman and Sid Rose, my associate producing partners." Owen returned handshakes, feeling slightly out of his depth in that celluloid world. He'd have to watch his step around these power players. Karen stood by, eyes locked on Owen, a slight smirk on her face. Pleasantries over, Friedman turned to her. "This calls for champagne. Karen baby, please bring us four Mimosas.

Gentlemen, be seated." Karen dutifully left the room. When everyone had settled, Friedman began. "We're here today to discuss our coming venture, *Bravo Business*. We're all looking forward to this project, Owen and need to clarify some details before shooting begins, next summer. It was touch and go for awhile acquiring a guaranteed investment to make it fly. Fortunately, we have two solid, top-of-the-line investors who will bring the picture in." Karen returned with Mimosas, handing them to each." "Thank you, Karen, baby." She smiled and took a seat next to Friedman, pulling out a steno pad and pencil.

Owen sat across from her, fighting his supreme horniness; the voluminous hair, piled up in a tidy do, hazel eyes and perfect teeth. The memory of those long legs wrapped tightly around him during those randy nights. 'Shit, all I want is to fuck her! Now, there isn't a chance in hell,' he mulled ruefully. His intense need for nicotine kicked in. Lighting up, he sipped his drink, quickly, in an attempt to get his mind on the meeting. "If you open the project outline in front of you gentlemen, we'll get started." Owen opened the cover and began perusing the contents. Crushing out his cigarette, he reached for another, lighting it. "Karen baby, Owen's glass is empty, would you mind?" She stood, took his glass and prepared another Mimosa across the room. Handing it back, she stared right through him, causing him distraction. Friedman's voice pulled him back.

"As you can see, the budget breakdown for *Bravo Business* is itemized parallel to the project sequence and timeline. The budget at this time totals $25 million. Since this figure was beyond our corporate resources, we were fortunate to acquire backers, Messrs Courtman and Morgan who are familiar with and admire your work, Owen." Owen choked, hearing the name Courtman. In the deep recesses of his mind, he hadn't anticipated dealing with an old foe.

Friedman noticed immediately. "Owen, are you all right?" Recovering with some difficulty, Owen ceased coughing, took a swallow of his drink and resumed smoking with care. "Fine, just fine, Shel." Continuing, Friedman laid out the order of activity over the next six months. "In June of 1966, we will begin casting the picture. I would like you to address the numbers immediately including a complete breakdown of principal roles, chorus personnel, your personnel, assistants, rehearsal requirements, accompanists and locations to rehearse.

We'll need summary costs of royalties, wardrobe, scenery, crew and musicians. The original producer, Vincent Lehrman, still owns a large piece of the pie and must be privy to all decisions made regarding his property, the original production." Karen raised her hand. "Yes, Karen, baby?" "Will all casting be done here at Universal?" Owen interrupted, clearly annoyed with her. "I will be looking primarily L.A. talent." "Who do you have in mind for the two leads?" "I'd like to test several with musical capabilities. Diana Lee and Mack Morris come to mind. They closely match the original in type and talent." "Well, your potential principals will have to be seen through agents and managers. We'll put out a casting call in all the trades for chorus dancers and singers, but I imagine if you're considering top notch talent, they will have first refusal." "As will I," said Owen, adamant, as he glanced at Karen. "Let's set the casting call for the month of June and go from there. Do you want to set a call in New York as well, or will our auspices be satisfactory?" "Let's do it out here. I'll bring my assistant Jonas Martin in. There is no one in our business more suitable or familiar with my work. Once we've seen everyone, I'll make the final casting decisions." "Keep in mind, Owen, that budget will be the governing factor in final decisions." "Yes, I get that. God forbid, you don't want to inflame the bean counters!" Friedman let out a belly laugh. "You're catching on my boy, very quickly!" "I may be new to pictures Shel, but I do know my away around musicals." "Touché, Owen!" "Let's meet again after the first of the year. I'll arrange a meeting in New York with our investors, my associates, and your people. Nick, Sid, any questions?" "No Shel, we're good," replied Sid, clearly satisfied. "Great meeting you, Owen," said Nick putting out a handshake, followed by Sid. "Karen, baby, have you anything to add?" "Nothing, Shel, sounds like Mr. Matthews is catching on," she replied, the put down not missed by Owen. "Thanks for your hospitality, Miss Eliot." "Actually, it's Mrs. Benoit, Mr. Matthews. Have a nice trip." The meeting broke up, the room cleared and Owen was ready for a scotch. 'Things are different here, I'll have to watch my step with these people,' he thought, finding his way out.

Chapter 21

Ryokan Retreat

With a day and night off, Mally and Griff decided to head south-west to Kyoto. As they sat formulating a plan over breakfast, Jeff and Nora walked into the dining room. Griff caught Jeff's attention with a wave. "Good morning, you two! What are your plans for the day off?" "We haven't decided, what do you suggest? We're up for a break from the city." "Ah, great minds at work! How about joining us for a trip to Kyoto, by rail? Mally and I are considering an overnight in Kyoto at a Ryokan." Nora beamed, "Oh Jeff, could we?" "This sounds like a plan," said Jeff, always game for exploring. "I'll speak with our translator, Kubota-san. He'll be able to recommend an inn to suit our needs and help with arrangements for the four of us. We can travel down together," added Griff. "This sounds fantastic, I can hardly wait," cooed Nora, holding Jeff's hand. Mally and Griff exchanged a knowing glance, having observed the growing love between them. "I think we should try to get the earliest train possible. It's about a three-hour trip. We'll want to have enough time to explore and enjoy the ambience of the inn." Following breakfast, they all departed for their *Centipede* two-show day. A change of scene would do them good.

On Sunday bright and early, the four left for Kyoto on the Hakone Line out of Tokyo Central Station. Kubota-san, had made all arrange-ments, including booking them for one night at Osumi Ryokan, nestled in the heart of Kyoto. Within walking distance of many beauti-ful shrines and parks, the cost of the inn was 8,500 yen, about $23.61 per person, a rate Griff and party considered reasonable. After being advised the inn would provide traditional bedding, clothing and food during their stay, they packed mostly toiletries, a change of clothes and reading matter. All American customs were to be put on hold for 24 hours! Arriving in Kyoto, Griff spotted a Japanese gentleman holding a sign that read *Edwards Party*. Approaching him, the man's smile widened. "Konnichiwa and welcome to Kyoto! Dozo, please, to follow me," he said in broken English. Jeff busied himself looking through his English/Japanese dictionary, as the four crowded into a Nissan van, parked adjacent to the station. "We go now to Osumi, not far from here," said the guide.

The day was bright and sunny, the air crisp and clean, as the group took in the charming scene. The narrow roads twisted and turned revealing doll-sized houses of paper and wood, many with pagoda-style roofs. Ming trees dotted the landscape along with rustic fences and, in some cases, open spaces through which ponds with archaic tiny bridges spanning could be seen. "Oh Jeff, this is heaven," sighed Nora, already transported to a different world from her roots in Muncie, Indiana. Jeff was buried in his guidebook, learning facts. Kyoto was considered to be the true repository of traditional Japanese culture. The main attractions were century-old temples, shrines and gardens. "Hey kids, did you know that there are approximately 400 Shinto shrines and 1,650 Buddhist temples located along the thousand-year-old streets and paths here?" "Well, Jeff, we only have 24-hours so we better get a move on," replied Griff, chuckling. Mally, whose eyes darted everywhere, was clearly in a trance, taking in every detail. Within minutes they pulled up to an immaculate compound, a circular driveway bringing them to a gated entrance. On either side of the main walkway beautifully manicured foliage was on display, while at a short distance a man-made pond could be seen, a brightly colored bridge across it.

When they approached the front door, a kimono-clad woman bowed and gestured for them to enter. "Konnichiwa, please come in," she said. Once inside, the group observed a simply-furnished lobby. Griff approached a man, who stood waiting at a small counter. "Konnichiwa," said Griff, cordially. "We are the Edward's group from Tokyo, here for one night." "Hai, Dozo," said the man, indicating the guest register. "Your rooms have been taken care of by the Nissei Theatre, Mr. Edwards-san." Griff, not often surprised, was taken aback. "How is this possible?" "Compliments of Hiri Watanabe-san, who desires you and your party to enjoy the comfort and serenity of Osumi for a night." Mally and Nora hugged as Jeff bowed. "Domo arigato gozaimasu," said Griff, signing the register for himself and Mally. Nora and Jeff followed suit, adding their signatures. When the check-in concluded, they were escorted to a remote part of the compound, through a maze of hallways, ending at a suite. Advised to remove their shoes outside, they were shown into quarters; two separate sleeping rooms, a sliding wooden door in between. On either side of the door, folding screens served as additional enclosures for privacy sake. Adjacent to the suite was a tiled spa, a common area with a large tub and whirlpool, two steam cabinets, commodes, troughs and a wash basin. Wooden benches around the tub were for the use of bathers, a large stack of folded towels nearby.

Griff and Mally were the first to be taken to the sleeping area, which matched Jeff and Nora's in detail. There were no beds visible, only rolled up bedding on large straw matting, covering the entire floor of the room. A small table, low to the ground, sat center with lush, thick pillows carefully placed around it. They were shown small cabinets in which to place their western clothes, once they were ready to settle. Traditional attire would include kimonos in appropriate sizes, tabbies to be worn on their feet while inside the inn. The unusual ankle-high socks were stitched like cloth boots, an obvious split between the big toe and the rest. It was inappropriate for Americans to dress as Japanese in public, so attire was strictly worn within the compound.

"Lunch will be served here in 30 minutes. Make yourselves comfortable! Dozo," said the Japanese woman, departing quickly. "This is beyond my imagination," said Jeff, cuddling Nora. "Mal, can you believe this place?" "No, it's something you see in a movie!" "Well, my darling, this is for real," added Griff, sitting down on the nearest pillow and pulling her onto his lap. When she settled he kissed her playfully on the nose. "Jeff, Nora, try these pillows out, he added, wiggling his toes. "Come on, Honey, when in Rome," Jeff hastened, helping her to the floor.

As the group got comfortable, another Japanese woman entered with a tray holding small carafes of Saki and tiny cups. "Oh, oh, if that's what I think it is, we'll never get up," said Jeff pulling Nora close. Handing out cups, the hostess poured Saki in each, bowed and left the room. Raising his, Griff made the toast, "To our adventure in Kyoto!"

"Here, here," echoed Jeff as he took a first sip, followed by the girls. "Wow, this is delightful tasting," said Nora, her enthusiasm growing. "Careful, Honey, Saki's pretty potent stuff. Sip slowly!" "Oh, I will, Jeff, I don't want to overdo and miss everything!"

Following lunch comprised of a delightful selection of tempura, vegetables and rice, the group decided to explore the area. As the couples strolled hand in hand, they discovered Kyoto was definitely a place to walk. The late November day continued beautiful, cloudless with a temperature of 50 degrees. Temples of every size and description dominated the landscape. Entering one, they removed their shoes, found a spot and sat on the stone floor. The sound of chanting was heard, the voices of Shinto worshipers rising above them. The smell of incense filled the air, causing Mally to sneeze. Covering her nose, she reached for a hankie offered by Griff. Recovering briefly, she excused herself and headed outdoors. The others weren't long and joined her sitting on a rustic bench. It was pure pleasure to soak up sunshine and fresh air. The backdrop of the shrine added ambience of a more ancient time. "Hey Mal, you're not alone, that incense was too much for me," said Nora, wiping her eyes with a Kleenex. "I guess I'm not cut out for monastic life," said Mally, a half-grin on her face. "Not possible," said Griff, kissing her gently. Jeff caught up to the group. "Come on, it's still early, let's take in some more shrines." He didn't catch a roll of eyes from Nora, as she reached for another Kleenex in her bag. "As long as we don't go inside, I'm fine," she said firmly.

As the afternoon continued the group visited several Shinto temples, a few curio shops, a museum and a stroll along a stream, a tributary to Lake Otsu, on the outskirts of Kyoto. Around 5:00 they returned to the inn and arrived at their suite. Once inside they discovered kimonos and accessories laid out for their use. A tray of hot tea for their pleasure was placed on the table in the center of the room. "This is civilized living," remarked Jeff. "Culturally, the Japanese invented the word '*gracious*' for my money!" "There is certainly a lot of attention to detail and presented with such charm," added Mally. A soft knock brought their attention. "Come in, Dozo!" A different Japanese woman from earlier in the day appeared. "Konbanwa! We will serve dinner in one hour. The spa is ready for your enjoyment. Please to disrobe and join together for bathing. You may leave your clothing here and put on kimonos. Spa room is adjacent. When it is time to return, a bell will sound. Please come back to the rooms, change for your evening meal." Nora turned to Jeff. "She's kidding, right?" "No, Honey, in Japan, it's customary for groups to bath together." "Jeff's correct. Other cultures aren't uptight like ours regarding nudity. Come on," urged Griff. Jeff took Nora's hand, leading her to their sleeping quarters. "I assume we have kimonos waiting there," he tossed, excited to try communal bathing. "Jeff, this is kind of embarrassing, I mean bathing with Griff and Mally!" "Oh Honey, it'll be fun. Remember, when in Rome," he chuckled.

In minutes the two couples met in the spa. The steam created a fog of modesty for the girls, as they ventured into the large whirlpool, having deposited provided kimonos on wooden benches. Griff and Jeff joined them, fearless and enjoying the novelty. The warmth of the water and gentle steam quickly dispelled any embarrassment the girls had.

"This is so relaxing! I had no idea we could have this after our ill-fated experience at the Tokyo Onsen," admitted Mally. "What a misadventure!" Jeff's curiosity was peaked. "What happened, Mal?" Nora jumped in. "Well, some of us were extremely sore from rehearsing, so we decided to check out a spa-massage establishment. We were put in wooden cabinets and hand-bathed, which was kind of strange, then pummeled within an inch of our lives. Those massage girls had no idea what they were doing! We ended up more miserable than when we started!" "You never told me, Darling!" "You were off at the theatre. By the time you got back to the hotel, I was out of my misery, fast asleep!" "Jeez, Nora, why didn't you tell me?" "I didn't want you to think I was such a baby! Besides, you were so buried in that guidebook of yours, I didn't think you'd be interested!" "Oh, Honey, I'm sorry, you should have said something!" "I just did, Jeff," she added, chuckling. He pulled her close and whispered in her ear. "I'll make it up to you, Honey. Count on it." They kissed deeply. Mally, covering the awkward moment, added, "Well, if the Tokyo Onsen was established for tired Japanese businessmen, then they are a bunch of masochists!" A bell sounded, indicating dinner. Griff climbed out and reached for Mally. Before he dried himself, he took her in hand and toweled her dry. She in turn, dried him. Jeff and Nora, still in the pool, watched closely. "Those two are still on a honeymoon," he whispered. He then did the same for Nora.

Dinner was served in the common room. The meal was typically Japanese: an onion, mushroom- laced broth, greens with ginger dressing, Sukiyaki with bean curd and vegetables, served with steamed rice, table-side. For dessert, a fresh selection of mango, papaya and pineapple bits concluded the lovely meal. Throughout dinner generous servings of hot Saki added to the ambience of the evening and at the finish, green tea. Jeff was feeling no pain. Following true to his mantra, "When in Rome," he indulged and was feeling the effects. "I think it's time to find a pillow, Nora!" "Yes, time to put you to bed," she agreed, adding a wink. A trio of servers arrived to remove the remnants of dinner and soon the area was cleared. "Good night you two lovebirds," muttered Jeff, Nora leading him next door. "Good night kids, pleasant dreams!"

Retiring to their soft, unrolled bedding, Mally and Griff disrobed and lay together. It felt so good to be away from the show for one night, to bask in the serenity and peaceful surroundings of the Ryokan. With only a soft lantern for light, they made love slowly and, entwined in each other's arms, fell into a pleasing sleep. The gentle breeze outside moved through wind chimes just outside their quarters, making a heavenly sound for their comfort and rest.

In the next room, Jeff removed Nora's kimono and laid her gently on the bedding. The fabric was soft to touch, but no more so than the woman he had fallen deeply in love. Now he was holding his soul mate, the woman he hoped would be his forever. His fingers traced along her exquisite form, causing her to shiver. His mouth found hers, the kiss long and fulfilling. Nora sighed and pulled closer, giving him full access to her most feminine self. Fingers tracing her mound, he played and teased momentarily, slipping in and out. "Oh Jeff, be mine," she whispered. Her moisture drew him in, his hardened shaft finding entrance. Together they rocked gently, consumed completely. Hearts beating quickly, they peaked together, their mutual explosion leaving them breathless. For a few minutes they lay quietly, filled with the joy of each other. Bodies wrapped securely around each other, Jeff stroked Nora's face, whispering softly, "I'm so in love with you. You're the best part of my life!" He felt warm tears against his neck, as he held her close. "Jeff, I never want to be without you, ever!" He smiled and murmured the words he had planned to say for months. "Honey, will you marry me?" Nora's eyes widened as she gasped, "Oh Jeff, of course I will!" "Wait, just a minute!" Sitting up quickly, he slipped off the bedding and hurried to the cabinet, fishing around until he found his toiletry case. There, in a tiny box, was the ring he acquired at Mikimoto's on the Ginza. Returning, he knelt and placed it on her tiny hand. By the lantern's light, Nora saw four perfect pearls, set in a swirl of silver. "Oh Jeff, how did you know I love pearls?" "The pearl is synonymous with Japanese culture, so when in Rome! Do you like it?" "I love it and most of all I love you, my darling Jeffrey!" Crying and laughing and making love again, they finally fell asleep, just as dawn was breaking over Kyoto.

In the morning, the group enjoyed a small breakfast, packed personal items they had brought and checked out. After being driven to the train depot, they boarded and got comfortable. Jeff waited for the right moment as they got underway. During a lull in the conversation, he reached for Nora's hand. "Griff, Mal, we wanted you to be the first to know, Nora and I have made it official. We're engaged!" "This is great news," said Griff, his enthusiasm obvious. Mally reached for Nora's hand. "Oh, it's a beautiful ring, dainty like you, Nora. Congratulations!" They hugged each other as the train sped toward Tokyo. It had been a perfect getaway, Japanese-style. Now it was time to hit the boards again.

Chapter 21

Byrnes and Blaine

Following Blaine's proposal, Pat called home to share the news with her parents. They had yet to meet him. Pat was always one who kept her personal business to herself. The Byrnes never knew how entrenched their only daughter had been with Owen Matthews, who they met the previous Christmas. In time, when she was better able to handle her feelings following their break-up, she mentioned the bare bone details of her ended relationship to Maureen. Later, her parents found her enthusiasm infectious when she shared her news regarding Blaine Courtman. It had been a few months since her recovery and subsequent move from Jonas and Phillipe's place. Now situated at the Plaza with Blaine, it was time to bring him around to meet her family. A phone call home announced their coming to the Bronx.

On Pat's day off, rain pelted Manhattan with persistence. They grabbed a cab for the Bronx, pulling up in front of the Blarney 30 minutes later. Exiting quickly, Blaine and Pat dodged the driving rain as they headed to the door. Before they entered, Blaine leaned down and kissed Pat gently. "I hope I pass inspection, Patricia!" She giggled and took his hand, pushing the door open with the other. The pub was practically empty, the rain keeping the regulars away. Slowly their eyes adjusted to the dim lighting as they made their way to the bar. Alan was humming, wiping glasses dry and placing them under the counter. Glancing up, he noticed the handsome couple. "Saints be, Patricia!" Coming around the end of the counter, he threw his arms around her and hugged tightly. "Darling girl, it's good to see you!" "Dad, I want you to meet Blaine," said Pat, easing away. "Blaine, this is my father, Alan Byrne. Dad, this is Blaine!" The two shook hands, Alan sizing up the new man with interest. "Well, I'll be, Mr. Courtman, great to meet you, sir!" "The pleasure is mine, Mr. Byrne," said Blaine, his deportment obvious. "Alan, please!"

As the three chatted, Maureen came out of the kitchen carrying a tray of mugs. Spotting Pat, she set the tray down on a nearby table and ran over. "Oh Pat, how wonderful to see you," she shouted. Warm tears meandered down her cheeks as they embraced. "It's been much too long! I've missed you, darling girl!" "Mom, this is Blaine," said Pat, slightly distracted and feeling somewhat embarrassed by her parent's attention. Maureen broke the embrace and extended her hand. "Blaine, welcome! Please sit with us," she insisted. "What are you drinking, lad?" Blaine smiled and winked. "Have you Guiness stout on tap?" It was Alan's turn to smile, which widened at Blaine's request. "Well, I'll be! Coming right up, Blaine!" He chortled happily reaching for 4 pints.

Pat, Maureen and Blaine sat at a nearby table, their conversation animated and warm. Maureen was fascinated by the stunning ring on Pat's left hand. "Oh Pat, your ring is beautiful," she said lifting her hand. "Blaine, I must say, you have an eye for beauty." "Patricia inspires me, Mrs. Byrne." "Maureen, please!" "I understand congratulations are in order," shouted Alan, approaching with a tray of Guiness. Placing a glass in front of each, he raised his excitedly. "May you know nothing but happiness from this day forward!" The others raised glasses and began to drink.

"Tell us about your prospects, Blaine," inquired Alan with interest. "Dad, for heaven's sake," said Pat, a tinge of reprimand in her voice. Blaine took Pat's hand, squeezing it gently.

"I'm in shoes," he replied. Alan's eyes widened. "Shoes?" "Yes, my family has manufactured shoes for four generations, starting with my great grandfather, who started the business. He trained his son, my grandfather, to take over. When Grandpa Courtman passed, my father became head of the company for years. He died three years ago." "Oh, lad, I'm sorry to hear that." "Thank you, Alan, you're very kind. So now I'm the guy in charge of what people wear on their feet," he said, with a chuckle. "Fascinating, to be sure," remarked Maureen. Pat interrupted. "Dad, Blaine was the chief investor of *Centipede!* "Really? Is that how you two met?" "Well, not exactly. I saw Patricia's show, *Bravo Business* last year; first in Jacksonville, Florida, then in Houston, Texas, followed by Vancouver, B.C. I was taken with her from the very beginning. We re-met at Sardi's, opening night of *Centipede.*" "I think this union was meant to be," said Alan, smiling. "Its fate," said Blaine, winking at Pat. "Must you travel a great deal?" "Yes, my business has me on the road frequently. However, once we're married, I plan to stay put. Wallace, my younger brother, will take over the travel portion of our business. I find it difficult to be away from Patricia for very long." "Have you set a date, my boy?" "Sometime next year," said Pat, wanting into the conversation. "We've discussed it and both agree that a quiet, low key affair is what we want." "Really, this is a surprise! Then, why wait?" "I guess you might as well know, Dad." I'm not renewing my contract with *Centipede*," said Pat, casually. "What? You aren't going to continue dancing?" The news caught Maureen off guard. Blaine could see the surprise and stepped in.

"Patricia can choose whatever she wants to do. I'm encouraging her to follow her heart and do what pleases her most." "Is this your idea to have her quit?" "Ma, for heaven's sake," said Pat, her voice rising.

"This is strictly my decision. I want to try other avenues of the business. I just don't know as yet," she replied with an edge. Blaine could see tension building. "It's too early to tell the direction Patricia will take, but whatever it is, she will put a lot of thought into it," he said, trying to reassure. "I will back her 100%," he added, taking her hand. "Well, no matter what your wedding plans, please allow us to hold a reception here, to include family and friends!" Blaine and Pat looked at each other and smiled. "That's a lovely idea, Dad. Thank you!" "It would be our pleasure," added Maureen, as she hugged them both.

Glancing at his watch Blaine saw it was getting late. "We should let you folks go about your day," he hastened, helping Pat on with her jacket. Slipping on his coat, he extended his hand. "It's been a pleasure meeting you, Mrs. Byrne. I assure you that Patricia is and always will be my number one priority." "Thank you, Blaine. I'm happy to know that," Maureen replied, more formal now. "Please let us know the date of your wedding, so we can firm plans." The moment was awkward. Not wishing to prolong any further discussion, Alan walked them to the door, opening it carefully. The rain swept by in torrents, the wind blowing fiercely. "May I call you a cab? Oh, here comes one," he shouted, waving the driver over. Pat was anxious to get going. "I love you, Dad." "I love you too, darling girl. Come back soon. Take care of her, Blaine!" "Rest assured, I will, Mr. Byrne!" Slipping in the backseat Pat settled, as Blaine followed, closing the door. Waving, she smiled and blew a kiss to her father, as the cab pulled away. Going back to the Blarney felt odd. In her heart, she had left ages ago.

Catherine Andrews hadn't heard from Owen Matthews in weeks, nor did she expect to. Their last meeting had been strained to say the least. She had grown tired of their limited relationship. It was more than obvious that all she did was provide temporary relief for his inexhaustible libido. At their first encounter she was impressed by his artistic reputation. Quickly she became wildly attracted by his sophisticated, worldly approach. An additional benefit to their on-going affair was a spot in *Centipede*, cast over hundreds of others. But in time, she grew tired of the limitations, involvement with him created. She wanted more, far more. So, she walked, thus ending it. Though she missed Owen's attention, she didn't miss spending most of their time in bed, his dismissing her when she was inconvenient.

Following Saturday night's show, she asked Julie to join her for a drink. She was hungry for some girl time and felt that enough time had passed since Julie's near assault at the hands of Tim Bartel. Julie grabbed at the invitation and the two set out for Joe Allen's. Saturday night, post performance brought gypsies to the various watering holes, Allen's the most popular. Standing in line waiting for the first available table, they spotted Danny Bartlett, one of *Centipede's,* waving in their direction. As they joined him, they noticed a fourth chair, unoccupied. "He'll be along in a few minutes," said Danny, working on a beer. "What would you ladies like?" "I'd love a house red," said Julie. "Make mine any white that's on the sweet side," added Catherine. Danny ordered from a passing waiter and settled in with the girls.

"How's it going, Danny?" "Ok, I guess. My girlfriend gave me the boot a couple of weeks ago. We were talking about getting married in a couple of years, as soon as I saved enough money. She apparently took up with someone she liked better." "You're certainly taking it well, Danny." "Well, I don't like playing second fiddle, if you know what I mean. I think the distance between us was more than geographic." The waiter returned, bringing a glass of Cabernet for Julie and Chablis for Catherine. "I'll have another tap, please." The waiter nodded and took off. Danny raised his glass, "Here's to us," he said, downing the remainder of his beer. He set down the empty and gazed at Catherine. "You look especially pretty tonight, Catherine." Her blush was noticeable as she continued sipping. Julie looked around through the smoke-filled room, trying not to notice. "So, who's joining us?" "A friend of mine from Queens. He's not in the business, but a really nice guy." He scarcely finished speaking when the nice guy from Queens showed up. "Hey, Nick, how's it going?" 'Oh Lord, Nicholas, the waiter,' Julie thought, nudging Catherine's foot under the table.

"Hi Dan, sorry I'm a little late. I had to lock up tonight." "No problem, have a seat. Nick I'd like you to meet two gals from the show. Catherine, Julie, this is Nick Pappas." Julie was squirming. "Yes, I believe we've met before at Mulfetta's, twice, "said Catherine, barely able to keep a straight face. Julie smiled weakly and mumbled, "Hello, Nicholas." "Wow, what a coincidence! I had no idea you had met before," said Danny, suddenly enthusiastic. "I invited Nick for a beer and you two happened to walk into Allen's practically at the same time!" "Yes, quite a coincidence," mumbled Julie, slightly embarrassed.

"What are you having, Nick?" "I'll take a beer on tap, Dan. Thanks!" A waiter stopped by and Danny ordered two more wines and another beer for Nick. Conversation was awkward at first. The liquid libation was comforting. Nick attempted to break the ice.

"How have you been, Julie? I've meant to get in touch, but we had a family situation back home. "Oh, what situation was that, Nicholas?" The edge in Julie's voice was hard to miss. "My father was taken ill in Greece. I had to go to Athens for a couple of months to help my mother while he recovered." Suddenly Julie felt the sharp toe of a boot bump her shin, a stern look from Catherine across the table. Julie now caught, softened. "I'm sorry to hear that. Is your father all right now?" "Yes, my uncle Darius took over the shop to help my mother until my father was able to return full time. I just got back a week ago." "Are you still working at Mulfetta's?" "Oh yes, they have me on overtime. I'm putting in about 12 hours a day." "I'm happy to see you, again," said Julie, feeling like a fool. Nick changed gears.

"So, what's new in your life?" "Oh, not much, just eight shows a week." By now Catherine and Danny had broken away, lost in a conversation of their own. Nick's soft brown eyes were once again, pulling Julie in, as he moved closer. "I enjoyed our date that Sunday. Would you consider having dinner with me sometime?" Julie could feel her cheeks grow warm. "Yes, I would like that very much. Sundays are best." "I still have your phone number. May I call you soon?" Julie's breath grew shallow. "Yes, I'd like that very much." The second round arrived, the group's mood overall light and pleasant. Noticing the time, Catherine suggested they pay the bill. "Nope, this is on me," insisted Danny. "No Dan, this is my tab," said Nick, grabbing the check away.

The four exited the restaurant, discovering a driving rain. "Can I buy you a cab, Catherine?" Danny had taken her hand, as they stood under the bar's awning. "That's sweet of you, Danny." "Let's share one. Aren't you on the west side?" "Yes, thank you!" Hailing a cab that had stopped at the corner, the two waved to Julie and Nick, dashing away. Nick watched for a moment then turned to Julie. "Well, I would be remiss not offering you a ride" he said, smiling. "May I see you home?" Julie's stomach tightened as Nick took her hand in his. "Yes," she whispered softly, as a cab came near. Opening the back door, he let Julie slide in first, following behind. When they were settled, he put his arm around her shoulders. She could feel his warmth envelop her. As the cab pulled away, one thought was crossing her mind, 'God, this may be my second chance!'

Owen was back in New York. Restless, the trip to L.A. hadn't gone well. Karen Eliot's former interest in him was a wash. He was horny, out-of-sorts. Succumbing to his mood, he reached for the phone. Lighting a smoke, he waited for the nicotine calm. The sound of ringing repeated. Finally, a sleepy female voice! "Hello?" Owen waited for a moment; "Baby, it's me," he announced. "I've missed you! Come on over, I'll be waiting." A pause, a click and Owen held only a receiver in his hand. Smashing it down, he stood and paced. Taking a drag, he walked to the bar and poured a double. Drinking it quickly, he worked on the rest of his smoke. His mind was in a whirl, his thoughts tumbling. 'The fucking, ungrateful bitch! How dare she pass on me?' Slowly he calmed down, consuming several more shots, lighting, but not finishing cigarettes. There was no one available to bed! More than pissed, the thought of firing Catherine Andrews came to mind.

Blaine and Pat sat enjoying a quiet dinner at the Plaza. Pausing between bites, he took her hand and kissed gently. "My lovely Patricia, how does a simple wedding ceremony with just our families present sound?" "I would love that, the simpler the better!" "We should set a date. What's your pleasure?" "It should definitely happen after I leave *Centipede*. I've always loved Valentine's Day!" "Then Valentine's it is. The honorable mayor of this fair city, newly elected John Lindsay, is an old friend of the Courtman clan. I'll ask him if he would officiate." "Oh, Blaine, do you honestly think he would?" "I'm sure he would. I'll give him a call in the morning to make sure he's available that day. He will likely perform the service in his private chamber." "I'd like to limit this to my parents, Mal and Griff. I'll ask Mal to be my matron-of-honor." "Done, my beautiful girl!" "Blaine, I haven't met any of your people, who will you invite?" "I'll ask Greg Morgan to be my best man. My two brothers Wallace and Stuart will attend. You haven't met my elder sister Yvonne, but you will someday. She lives in Paris with her husband, Pierre Bouchet, of Bouchet Patisserie chain, one of the finest in France. They may not be able to make it over, due to their schedule." Pat grew serious. "Blaine, do you think they'll like me? I'm a barkeep's daughter from the Bronx!" "They'll fall in love with you!" "But I'm not from the same social level!" "All the more reason! Our family is well-off, but not pretentious, you'll see." "That's an understatement, Blaine, well-off indeed," she chuckled, returning to her salad. Blaine resumed eating a serving of fois gras. Moments passed before he spoke. "I want to take you on a honeymoon of your choosing. Where would you like to go, my beautiful girl?" "Oh Blaine, I've never been out of the U.S.! I've always imagined Paris in spring!" "Then Paris it is! We can delay a trip until then. Remember, your parents would like to host a reception at their place." "Yes, it's very generous of them, but predictable. Dad loves to entertain. The Byrne's have a tradition of hosting Christmas Day every year at the Blarney. If he offers, we have to accept." "I agree. Perhaps they would have the gathering on the Sunday following. That way your fellow cast mates can attend." Perfect! I'll let them know." Dinner ended with cuddling, then to the bedroom. Lost in each other, they fell into a delicious sleep, immersed in wedding thoughts.

Chapter 23

The Last Weeks

It was hard to believe that *Centipede* was already winding down and in the final month at the Nissei Gekijo. The American production, sold out from opening night, had tripled the grosses estimated before the show had arrived in Japan. A delighted Hiro Watanabe had reported each week to Joseph Kaplan in New York. The show's original producers, Kaplan and Maggli, were ecstatic. They had gambled on an unknown and the risk paid off. Everyone concerned, including chief investors Blaine Courtman and Gregory Morgan were pleased they had taken a chance financing the project. It had paid off. Owen Matthews was also pleased, owning a piece of the pie.

The New York production was nearing its second year and ticket sales were stronger than ever. He was relaxed now that the film version of his hit show, *Bravo Business,* was on tap. In addition, a national tour of *Centipede* was a surety, with the remount taking place the first of March, 1966. He was sitting pretty financially, but personally not having a present lover galled him. His incessant craving for sexual satisfaction was far from fulfilled. He needed to acquire a regular fix, a woman who would accept the limitations he would insist on. Pat was gone forever, Stephanie had moved on and Catherine Andrews was dead in the water. He'd bide his time until someone struck his fancy. Unfortunately he had to! Hookers simply didn't appeal to him.

On Monday night, following their overnight in Kyoto, the company quickly learned of Nora and Jeff's engagement. Nora was thrilled with her ring and excited to show the girls at half hour.

Neely was the first to notice, letting out a loud whoop when she spotted it. Having drawn attention, the other women got up and clustered around Nora. Enthusiasm was in high gear. "Nora! Oh my God, you're engaged," said Neely, grasping Nora's hand, in order to get a closer look. Maddy was next, examining every detail of the swirl of silver and pearls. "This is exquisite! Leave it to Jeff to choose pearls. It's so Japanese!" Mally sat back, enjoying the excitement, as she'd been privy to the news early on. Georgia, Candy, Betsy and Daria each took a turn, as compliments and congratulations were offered. Then, they were back to business as Griff's voice cut through. "Half hour, half hour, please!" The group gave hugs before returning to pre-show prep. Suddenly Nora began to cry softly. Mally noticed immediately and reached over, giving her a gentle squeeze. "Nora, what's wrong?" "Oh Mal, I can't believe this! I never thought I would ever have someone as wonderful as Jeff!" "You're both pretty special, Nora. Griff and I are so happy for you two!" "Thanks, Mal, I hope we have as successful a marriage as you two have." "The hard part is over, Nora. It's obvious you two were friends first and your love grew over time. That's how it happened for us." "Really? Well then, we can't miss!" "Places please for act one!" Griff's announcement brought them back to the moment at hand, to dance!

With Christmas just weeks away, the Americans found the lack of holiday décor and spirit strange and unique, as they roamed public venues and streets. In the U.S., commercialism hoopla and events brought in the Yule, always in evidence from Thanksgiving to New Year's. The cast of *Centipede* needed an outlet to remind them of New York. Some were homesick in spite of the successful run in Tokyo. Others grabbed any opportunity to experience Japanese culture. Jeff was certainly one most interested and vocal when it came to local custom and flavor. An idea struck him following the Monday night show. Spotting Griff, who was wrapping up post show details with two of his running crew, he approached. Griff looked up in mid conversation and saw Jeff patiently waiting for an entrée. "Chotto matte kudasai," he said, concluding his business with his tech guys.

Jeff now held his attention. "What can I do for you, Mr. Jenkins?" "Now that Nora and I are officially engaged, I thought it would be special to be married here. Is that at all possible, Griff?" Crew member Soto-san overheard and perked up. "Edwards-san, this could be arranged by the Nissei and Watanabe-san, who would assist with details. It would be an honor to celebrate with your cast." "Are you sure you want to do this here? Your families won't be included, unless of course you have another ceremony state-side later on." "No, Griff, this is for Nora and me. We're both only children and consider you our family." "I see, well let me see what I can do. You'll have to do it on our day off, before our departure at the end of December. Then of course we'll need a location, an official who can perform the wedding and a place for a small reception. Lots of details, Mr. Jenkins, but let me get started working it out." "Thanks, Griff! Domo, arigato gozaimasu!" "Do itashimashite," he returned, as Soto-san stood by, grinning profusely. Jeff left in a daze, thrilled with the prospect of marrying Nora in his adopted country.

The following morning, Griff phoned Watanabe's office. He was immediately put through to the producer, who greeted him cheerfully. "Ohayo gozaimasu, Edwards-san!" "Hai, ohayo gozaimasu," Griff returned. "What can I do for you this morning?" "First of all we wish to thank you for your generous gift of our overnight stay in Kyoto!" "Edwards-san, it is my pleasure. You carried out my wishes to end the situation with my daughter. For that courtesy, my family and I thank you. We are pleased with the outcome. Our Myoshi is already promised to a young man of our country and will be wed next year." Griff remained silent for a moment, forming his words carefully.

"Watanabe-san, two of our dancers became engaged on our recent visit to Kyoto. Jeff Jenkins and his fiancée, Nora Blake would consider it an honor to be married here. Is there a possibility we could arrange a small ceremony and reception within your auspices at the Nissei Theatre?" After a brief pause, the producer responded with enthusiasm. "It would be our pleasure to host such an event, especially since the betrothal has taken place here! Please choose a date and we will begin arrangements!" "Domo arigato gozaimasu, Watanabe-san," said Griff, clearly pleased. "I will inform them straight away and get back to you as soon as possible." "Iie, doitashimashite, Edwards-san!" The call concluded. Sunday, December 21st was chosen for Jeff and Nora's big day! The wedding was to be simple, with a touch of Japanese, something Jeff insisted upon. He asked Griff to be best man, while Mally was chosen as Nora's matron of honor. In addition, Griff would assist with details and act as liaison between the couple and Watanabe's office. The wedding would take place at 4:00 PM, followed by a simple reception with only the company and Nissei personnel in attendance. *Centipede* would end its run the following Saturday, December 27th.

The remaining weeks of *Centipede* were playing out. As the production wound down, the Japanese public continued to acquire tickets, making sell-out performances. Each audience clamored for more as *Centipede's* sheer artistry won hearts and respect. It was hard to believe the troupe would soon be leaving to return home. The show would pack up and load out on Sunday, the company flying back to the States on Monday, at 10:00 AM, Tokyo time.

One Wednesday afternoon, the Kamata girls stopped by, following the matinee. They were dressed in school uniforms, bearing gifts of some of their best Origami and other paper treasures. The young women, from high school to elementary school-age, were thrilled to see the show after observing early rehearsals at the school. Waiting patiently for the gypsies to emerge, they spotted Mally first, as she stepped into the corridor. Rushing forward they giggled nervously, presenting her with a lei of paper cranes, all in rainbow hues. The other cast women heard the commotion outside and quickly exited the dressing room, finding the Kamata sisters waiting with gifts for them as well. The girls had fashioned colorful papers rolled into tiny beads, threaded to form necklaces. More hugging and laughter continued, as the group chatted, the girls complimenting the dancers' performance. After a lengthy conversation, the gypsies excused themselves, needing time between shows to rest and fuel up. The rest of the week was usual, with packed houses and post-show greetings from the public.

Sunday, December 21st arrived as Jeff and Nora prepared for their wedding. The ceremony would include Reverend George Campbell, a local Christian minister officiating with Nubi Shinzo, a shinpu, performing a portion of the Shinto no gishiki, a Shinto ceremony. On their special day, the couple wanted a mix of east and west to usher in their marriage. Only Griff and Mally would be present. Cast, crew, orchestra and Watanabe's staff would attend a reception immediately following in the theater's lobby. At 4:00 PM, the smell of incense filled the air. Jeff, Griff and Mally took their places at an altar of teak, with fragrant blooms woven into a bamboo arch above the group. Candles flickered nearby as a quartet of musicians from *Centipede* played. The simplicity of the scene was breathtaking. Jeff wore a dark suit with a mid thigh-length coat, a small orchid on his lapel. Mally and Griff wore their finest dress clothes for the occasion. Griff wore a similar orchid on his lapel, while Mally carried a single white rose.

Into that quiet scene, the bride entered in a white silk gown, similar to a kimono, her short dark hair, encircled by a halo of jasmine blossoms. In her hands she carried a small bouquet of jasmine and tiny purple orchids. On her ears, tiny pearls matched a small, pearl choker around her neck. Jeff's breath caught as he saw his bride. Eyes welling, he held on for dear life, waiting for her to be at his side. When all were present, George Campbell spoke first, greeting the group with sweet words. In his homily, he spoke about Jeff and Nora's journey, how they had found commitment through friendship and love to carry them into marriage. Nora choked back tears, holding fast to Jeff's hand. When he concluded his portion, the reverend stepped back allowing Nubi Shinzo to share traditional words of marriage in the Shinto faith. When he concluded, the vows, written by the couple followed, each taking a turn. Jeff spoke first, "I Jeff, take you, Nora, my best friend and soul mate for my wife. I will cherish you forever. You will never want for anything as I comfort, honor, love and protect you, holding you above all others." Nora followed with, "I Nora, take you, Jeff, my best friend, lover, partner, and soul mate for my husband. I will cherish you forever. You will never want for anything as I comfort, honor, love and protect you, holding you above all others."

Upon their words, Griff handed Reverend Campbell the rings, which he gave to the couple. "Jeff, please repeat," With this ring, I thee wed," which Jeff did excitedly. "Nora, please repeat, "With this ring, I thee wed," as she repeated softly, choking back tears. Nubi Shinzo spoke a few words in Japanese, followed by George Campbell who concluded in traditional fashion, "We now pronounce you man and wife. You may now kiss!" Jeff bent down and kissed Nora gently, through applause. The couple hugged Griff and Mally and thanked the officiates. What joy! Immediately following the vows, the group went to a reception hall. Applause rang out as they entered, those waiting expectantly, cheering. The gypsies threw rice, through which Griff and Mally followed, enjoying the excitement. A receiving line formed as cast, crew and orchestra waited. As well-wishes continued, music filled the room with the same wedding quartet of musicians playing in the background. To one side, a catered buffet was displayed, filled with American and Japanese food choices. Jeff and Nora, surrounded by their fellow dancers beamed and graciously accepted their congratulations.

Hiro Watanabe arrived with his family. Through the hubbub, Chad, who had been talking to Jeff, suddenly noticed Myoshi, his heart tightening at the sight of her. She was so stunning and tiny as she stood next to a mature Japanese man, her arm looped in his. As he observed, the group approached Jeff and Nora. Chad tried to find a way to disappear. Griff saw the awkward moment and intervened. "Watanabe-san, may I present Jeff and Nora Jenkins, our new couple!" Watanabe bowed, shaking Jeff and Nora's hands and motioning to his party. My family wishes to congratulate you both." All bowed their heads. Watanabe continued. "May I present my daughter Myoshi and her fiancé, Dr. Yubo Amori." The moment passed as Chad's anonymity was protected by Griff, who handled the delicacy of the situation with his usual aplomb. But Chad felt a deepening pain as he gazed at Myoshi, whose eyes didn't give away her true feelings. He walked away, fighting back tears.

Heading to the bar, he felt the need to anesthetize. Ordering a carafe of Saki, he waited for a warm plunge into ambivalence. Suddenly he saw Maddy and Neely heading his way. "Hey Chad, you want company?" Without invitation, they cornered him, one on either side. "What're you drinking, big boy?" "Saki, hot Saki," he mumbled, without enthusiasm. "Well, Saki to me," giggled Neely, enjoying the play on words. "Say, you look down in the dumps," noted Maddy, putting her arm around him. "Aren't you happy for Jeff and Nora?" Chad remained silent as he downed the first carafe. He ordered a second. The girls sipped quietly, feeling his sulk. "Come on, kiddo, what's going on?" Chad gestured toward Myoshi, across the room. "See that Japanese girl over there?" Neely and Maddy spotted the exquisite young woman in a scarlet kimono, hair caught in a cluster of matching roses. "Wow, she's beautiful!" "Well, it so happens I'm fucking in love with her! I want to marry her," he said, beginning to cry. Neely, clearly surprised, huddled. "What are you talking about? Chad, shush, who is she?" "A girl I met opening night. We saw each other a few times and fell in love." Neely pressed him further. "Did you have sex?" "God, are you fucking kidding me? She's Japanese for crying out loud! She's saving it for marriage and unfortunately, not for this American," he murmured, bitterly. "Oh Chad, I'm so sorry. Anyway thing we can do?" Maddy was all ears. "No, but I'd like to be alone, ok?" "We get it, friend. Hang in kiddo, promise?" "Fuck, yes. I'll survive," he said with half-hearted smile. The girls left. Moments later, he felt a hand on his shoulder.

"Konbanwa, Chad-san." Glancing up, he looked into her eyes. A moment passed, until he was able to speak. "Hello, Myoshi," he said, sadly. "May I sit down?" "Gee, I don't know, what would your fiancé say?" "Oh please, Chad, don't be upset. Yubo is a fine man. My parents have known him for years." "He looks old!" "He is 40, a physician and well-respected!" "Are you in love with him?" "I belong to him, Chad." Chad put down his drink and stared longingly at her. "Answer me, Myoshi. Are you in love with him?" "Chad, please don't. It only makes it more difficult sitting here next to you, knowing my true feelings." "Oh, and?" "I love you! I will always love you!" "But you can't be mine," he said, tightly. "Oh Chad, please, let's not part like this. Must we end this bitterly?" Chad calmed down and took her hands in his. "I'm sorry, Myoshi, but this hurts more than you can imagine. I don't think I'll ever get over you." "I must leave now, I will be missed," she whispered. "Yes, I know. Good bye, Myoshi." He closed his eyes, trying to make it easier not to watch her walk away. Moments later, as his eyes blinked open, he saw her walk to her intended, bow her head and follow him out. Catching the barman's attention, he gestured to him. "Dozo, hit me again!"

Christmas in Tokyo was unique. Some of the boys found a fake tree and set it up in the green room. The girls got together and shopped the Ginza for lights and ornaments. The company drew names for a gift exchange, setting the amount of $5.00 or 1800 yen per gift. As Christmas Eve fell on Thursday, a performance night, the cast agreed to gather following the show. The gypsies were in a holiday frame of mind as they took their final bows. Entering the green room the group, in highs spirits, put gifts under the tree. Griff got everyone to contribute to snacks and beer, Sapporo and Kirin, being the favorites among the Japanese labels. Dressed casually, the group sat around the tree, conversing and singing favorite carols led by Mally and Nora. Griff acted as Santa, handing out anonymous gifts. As paper ripped from gifts, both tasteful and raunchy, each item revealed caused comments and applause, adding to the festive nature of the evening.

In the midst of celebration, a strange, unfamiliar sensation began. The room started to tremble, then shake! The tree swayed causing several ornaments to fall. Those standing lost their footing, falling on fellow dancers in a heap. For several seconds it felt like the room was coming apart! Several gypsies screamed, trying to hold onto each other as the floor continued to shake. The company was in the midst of an earth tremor, a minor earthquake, indigenous to Japan. The guys, some trying their best to stay calm, tried to hold on to something solid as the room swayed. "Oh my God, I don't want to die here," cried Maddy, sobbing and grabbing on to fellow swing, Terry. During the ruckus, Jeff pushed Nora to the carpet, covering her with his body. Mally hugged Neely, trying to calm her while she screamed obscenities. "No, shit no, this is fucking crazy!" Chad, unusually calm, took over. "Hey, hit the floor and cover your heads! Curl up in a ball, now!" The dancers dropped to the floor, lying fetal-like through the commotion. Then, as quickly as the tremor came, it stopped, leaving dishevelment and shock.

When all was calm again, several got up from the floor, some hugging, others crying. What had seemed like an eternity was only a minute in real time, but the effect was clear enough. Griff did his best to bring order. "All right everyone, the fun is over. Let's calm down. We've had our first earth tremor, nothing serious. Is everyone ok?" "I think it's time to go home," yelled Jeff as he helped Nora to her feet. Others got up, shaken, but uninjured. The gathering ended abruptly, the gypsies hurriedly gathering their belongings, gifts and other holiday paraphernalia. "Company, those of you who set up for the holiday please return tomorrow to take down the tree, clean up and leave the green room intact. I'll make sure the stage door man is aware that you will be coming by at noon. Thank you." When the last company member had left, Mally took her husband's hand as they headed to the stage door. Outside, a few yards ahead Maddy and Neely huddled. "I won't forget this night anytime soon," said Neely, her hands still shaking, as she zipped her jacket. Maddy wound a long scarf around her neck as they started to walk back to the Nikkatsu. "How does anyone tolerate living in California?"

Centipede's last week at the Nissei Gekijo arrived. Griff called the New York production office. He was immediately put through to Joe Kaplan. "Griff, you must be in your final week in the land of the rising sun." "Yes, Joe, we'll be back a week from today." "Wonderful! We'll welcome you with open arms. Say, the numbers are exceptional. We tripled our gross estimate of ticket sales. I need to send you overseas more often, my friend." "Anytime, Joe, Mally and I really enjoyed this one." "Say, speaking of your lovely wife, do you remember my offer on your wedding day last year? I think it's time to collect on it, Griff. I'm sending you two on a long-overdue honeymoon vacation to my villa in Bermuda, commencing on your return." "Joe, I don't know what to say!" "You deserve some respite and relaxation. You've worked non-stop for us well over a year. Take some time off, I insist." "Well, if you put it that way, Joe!" "When you get back from Tokyo next week, take a couple days to unwind. We'll follow up with a post production meeting." "Thanks Joe, see you soon."

As he hung up, Mally came into the room. "Darling, I have a surprise for you!" "Oh?" "I'll give you three guesses," he teased, pulling her onto his lap and kissing her nose. Mally giggled, ruffling his hair, creating an explosion of strands every which way. "Let's see, we're staying at the Nikkatsu forever!" "Nope!" "You've secretly mastered the art of origami and will redecorate our New York flat!" Mada desu!" "Smart ass, what does that mean?" "It means 'not yet'! Come on, Darling, one more guess!" "You're growing a mustache!" "Nein!" Mally threw her arms up. "What? I'm dying of curiosity!" Joe Kaplan is making good his wedding gift and sending us to Bermuda for ten days when we get back." Mally let out a squeal. "Really?" "Yes, it's time for a little rest and you having my undivided attention!" They kissed deeply. "I'm giving you a preview of what to expect in the tropics, Mrs. Edwards," he whispered, lifting her off his lap and laying her gently on the bed.

Saturday night, December 27th brought the closing in Tokyo. The performance was sold out, an overflow of patrons relegated to standing room only at the back of the house. The gypsies were in top form from the opening tableau through the second act, the sailors-on-leave number receiving the biggest response of the evening. Some of the ensemble became emotional, realizing this would be their last performance in Japan. As the show came down, the massive audience stood, the applause intensifying with each passing minute. Bow after bow continued, the gypsies smiling and waving. Then, the unexpected, the entire orchestra rose and applauded the troupe, joining the audience in a colossal ovation. When at last the show curtain came down, a massive cheer went up, the group embracing each other and thanking the running crew. Griff gathered everyone on stage, including the orchestra and wardrobe people. Hiro Watanabe arrived with his dutiful staff following behind. When everyone had settled Griff began.

"Ladies and gentlemen of the Nissei Theatre, we of *Centipede* take this opportunity to express our gratitude to all for your cooperation, courtesy and support. I believe I speak for the entire company when I say we consider this experience an honor and privilege, one we deeply appreciate and will never forget. We take many fond memories back to the U.S. of our time here. Thank you for hosting our production and for the generosity and respect you have shown us these past two months."

Watanabe spoke next. "We have enjoyed your visit and your great contribution to the culture and enjoyment of our people. We wish you well in your future endeavors and consider you all our friends always. Please return one day! Sayonara!" Applause rang out as the Nissei group dispersed. Watanabe shook hands with Griff and graciously departed, his staff keeping up. Griff took a moment while the stage quieted down. "Company, may I have your attention? The crew and I will strike tonight and continue the pack up and load out tomorrow, Sunday. You will have a personal day to prepare for our flight to New York. For now, make sure you return all costumes and shoes to wardrobe. Go over the dressing rooms thoroughly and check for personal items. Be sure to take them with you this evening. Have your bags tagged and marked with your name and home address and place them outside your hotel door no later than 2:00 AM, Monday morning. The call is 8:00 AM. Please take care of your hotel bill and be checked out by then. A bus will transport us to Haneda International Airport, leaving in front of the Nikkatsu at 8:30. Our flight on JAL is number 1280, departing at 11:00 AM. Thank you!" In moments, the gypsies went about their business, readying themselves for departure.

Monday morning came soon enough. The cast climbed aboard the bus in front of the Nikkatsu. Dance bags were secured in the overhead as they all took seats, settling in for the trip to Haneda. As the bus pulled away, everyone cheered and waved. The ride would take them past the Nissei Theatre and along the Imperial Palace Grounds, the walls hiding the royal compound for two miles. The crowded streets, overflowed with workers heading to jobs, reminding the gypsies that *Centipede* was already just a memory in the day to day scheme of things. As the ride continued, many settled back for an extra few minutes of snooze. Chad sat, lost in thought, steeped in memory of his beautiful Myoshi. Her face and continence were forever etched in his psyche. At the moment, conversation with anyone was impossible. He ruminated over his loss; a future without her, half a world separating them forever. He felt a sudden tap on the shoulder. "Are you glad to be leaving?" Only silence. Jeff caught on immediately. "It's that girl, isn't it? You haven't been able to let go!" "Mind your own fucking business Jenkins," he snapped back. "Chad, take it easy," urged Jeff, feeling a tug on his arm. "Honey, lay off. He's got to feel like this until he doesn't," coaxed Nora." Others heard the exchange and grew silent.

The rest of the ride was tense as the miles flew by. Griff was waiting at the main door to the terminal for the *Centipede* cast and key associates. Once everyone had exited the bus, tickets were handed out, the group instructed to head toward passport control. With passports ready for inspection and custom declaration forms in hand, the group lined up. The process went quickly. Griff, who had preceded them, stood ready to lead them to the JAL waiting area at gate 13. Maddy noted the number and elbowed Neely, following in tandem. "I hope number 13 means an event-free trip!" "Relax, the flight over was smooth as silk!" "I know, I know, but I detest flying, period!" "Well, my advice is to have as many cocktails as possible and go to sleep!" "Thanks, a lot!"

As they approached the gate, Mally spotted familiar faces, the Kamata girls, expressions of joy and sadness etched on their faces. Yuriko, Haruko, Mirako and Sachiko waved as they approached. Yuriko, the oldest and most fluent, stepped forward. "Ohayo gozaimasu, Mally-san, we have come to say goodbye to *Centipede*." It's wonderful for you to do so, Yuriko, how did you manage to get here? Chichi arranged our transportation with a friend who has a car she replied, we will return by public bus. As she spoke the others began passing out origami paper necklaces to the entire cast. Jeff became teary when approached, his fondness for the Japanese, obvious. Each gypsy received a colorfully-crafted string of paper beads in vibrant colors. Some were caught off guard by the gesture, the customary courtesy and sweetness of the Kamata daughters. Much bowing, many tears and thanks continued until it was time to board. Mally hugged each girl, feeling the last precious minutes tick away. "Sayonara, our friends, we will never forget you!"

Once on board, the gypsies settled in for the long journey. Departing right on schedule, the route from Tokyo would again take them over the International Dateline to Honolulu where they would land Sunday evening, the day before they left Japan. It was a brief chance to re-live time by the clock and, a unique experience for some to talk about. Along the way, the cabin service and meals were delightful, a point Terry Becker would remember to mention to his dad. After a brief stop for Hawaii bound passengers and refueling, it was on to San Francisco. A two hour layover and change of airlines they would continue to New York. Although the shortest leg of the trip, the four and a half hours seemed like forever. In all, they would be in the air over 18 hours.

As the plane lifted off, an eerie quiet settled over the cabin. Ten weeks of work was now a memory to the gypsies of *Centipede*. It was time to regroup, get back into the swing of Manhattan. Some would rejoin the Broadway cast, while others would be offered a spot in the forthcoming national tour of the show. Some would audition for the film version of *Bravo Business,* directed by Owen and slated for production the following summer. They were young and an optimistic group. Plenty of opportunities for everyone!

Chapter 24

Homecoming

It seemed like a shorter trip home. Their United flight landing at JFK 20 minutes early due to favorable westerly winds. Deplaning, the gypsies proceeded to baggage claim, collecting luggage, making the obligatory passage through customs and immigration and boarding a bus to The Royal Theater, from there they were on their own. Hugs and kisses, exchange of phone numbers and strong assurances to stay in touch filled their last moments as the Japanese *Centipede!*

Mally and Griff grabbed a cab to their place in Chelsea. Nora and Jeff headed to the upper west side to begin married life at a friend's sublet, until they could find a new place of their own.

Maddy and Neely, roommates before their Tokyo stint, grabbed the train to the west Village and their fourth floor walk-up. Chad, alone once more, headed to his studio apartment in the theatre district. The others scattered to various parts of Manhattan. A post production meeting at the offices of Kaplan-Maggli would include everyone involved in Tokyo the following week. For now, it was time to reconnect with their New York lives. Jet lag was expected, but for some culture shock would be more daunting.

New Years 1966 passed quietly, uneventfully, for the returning *Centipede*. The post production gathering was set for Monday, January 5th in the producer's offices, including a catered lunch for all. Jonas and Phillipe hurried from their apartment in the west 60's to join the group. "Joe hasn't lost his touch! His power lunches are legend," remarked Jonas as they hopped on the IRT, Broadway line, for mid-town. Lunch was slated for 12:00 followed by a meeting. The day was cold and windy, creating a need for additional warmth added to their winter outerwear. Jonas wore a long, soft muffler in deep blue, his favorite shade that Mally had crocheted for him in Tokyo. The need became obvious, following their first drafty week of rehearsal in the unheated Tokyo school. He treasured her handiwork and wore it often, especially when westerly winds blew across the Hudson River from Jersey. Phillipe favored wool skull caps, owning several in earth tone shades. The habit began during his youth in the French Quarter, New Orleans. Winters there were predictably damp, creating his prefer-ence. If his head was covered, he didn't feel chilled. His dark French features and curly hair, which he wore long, would fit a movie scene filmed on a Marseille waterfront. The two climbed the subway stairs and out onto the street, catching a gust of wind. Rounding the corner they headed down Broadway to the Kaplan-Maggli offices. Friendly banter and pleasant conversation filled the conference room as the gypsies gathered. Griff and Dick were engaged in shop talk as the oth-ers entered. Jonas and Phillipe joined the group, who cheered their arrival. Animated chat and hugs all around were in evidence as the Kaplan's secretary collected coats and bags from the gypsies.

After everyone had arrived, Joe Kaplan and Leonard Maggli entered, followed by Gary Hanson, Maggli's personal assistant. "Good afternoon and welcome back! At the far end of the room we've set up a buffet. Please help yourself and make yourselves at home. Enjoy!" The dancers, traditional chow hounds, lined up to choose a variety of offerings. The producers had thought of everything; sandwiches from the kitchen at the Stage, one of New York's most famous and revered delicatessens. Everything from cole slaw, potato salad, sauer-kraut, pickled beets, giant dills and tossed salads to Matzo ball soup and Borscht were available for the taking. Coffee, tea and sodas were included with platters of desserts; three kinds of cheesecake, éclairs, cream puffs, brownies and cookies!

"I better dance soon or I'll get fat as a pig," whispered Maddy, pil-ing a giant scoop of potato salad on her plate. "This beats the hell out of squid, eel, and octopus," sighed Neely, purposely selecting a corn beef and sauerkraut on pumpernickel. "What do you call that?" Neely rolled her eyes. "Where have you been all your life? You've never had a Reuben?" "Nope, can't say I have," tossed Maddy, eyeing a giant dill and adding it to her pile. "An old maid's dream," she whispered, indicating the pickle. "You horny little thing," added Neely, with mock disgust.

As the company enjoyed lunch, Owen suddenly walked into the room. Dead silence followed until Jonas began applause, followed by the group joining in. "Welcome back, gang! I hear you're a big hit in Japan!" "Owen, please enjoy lunch," Kaplan insisted extending his hand. "Good to see you Joe. It's been a while." "How is it going on the coast?" "Coming together," said Owen, as he gazed around the room, noting the female scenery. A male voice pulled his focus temporar-ily from the assortment of potentials. "Good afternoon, Owen." "Griff, glad to have you back on our shore! We need to discuss business and soon. I have work for you!" Joe overheard and interrupted. "It will have to wait, Owen." "Oh? How so?" "This indispensible gentleman and his lovely lady have earned some needed time away. I insist they collect on my wedding gift offering of last year!" Owen smiled, reaching for them both with a hug. "Yes, you've earned it, but come back soon. I need you both here."

With lunch complete, Kaplan called the company's attention. Dishes we're cleared as the group settled around the room, all eyes on the producers. Joe spoke first. "Company, you are to be congratu-lated for an impressive and successful run of *Centipede*. I spoke with Hiro Watanabe weekly and the show exceeded all expectations. The Japanese public embraced our show, breaking all previous estimates and topped the number of ticket sales in the Nissei Theater's history. In eight weeks, the gross number of sales came to over two million dol-lars, truly unprecedented!" Applause rang out as the gypsies whooped and cheered. "Because of your commitment, you will all be given a one week's salary bonus for your care and dedication to our engagement overseas. Thank you!" Joe gestured to Owen. "Gang, I'm pleased. Not only is the remount a creative and critical success, but a financial one! That's hard to beat! You've done our team proud and have pleased me totally. For that reason, you will have first dibs on my two forthcoming projects." Jonas raised a hand. "Yes, Jonas?" "Owen, you've already told me what's ahead, but I think our cast would appreciate being informed." "Fair enough," said Owen, lighting a cigarette. "Some of you are wondering what the future holds, so here it is. We are planning a remount of *Centipede,* our first national tour, which will begin rehearsals in February and will hit the road in late March. All those interested in the road company should give their names to Griff. We need to recast by the end of January. It is a six-month commitment. Some of you may prefer to stay in town, take a chance on getting cast in another Broadway show, or act as replacements on Broadway. However, touring allows you to make more bread and a chance to travel. It's a good time, gang! Ask any of our seasoned travelers and they will fill you in."

"Secondly, I am making my film debut directing my previous hit, *Bravo Business* for the screen. If interested filming begins next summer, but auditions for ensemble will take place on the coast in June. It's at least a three-month commitment and a screen credit. Can't beat it! Those hired will have to join SAG, Screen Actors' Guild. Your first week's pay will cover initiation and membership fees. Nothing would please me more than to see some of you have this opportunity. You don't necessarily have to be familiar with or have danced in a company of *Bravo Business* to make the grade. I'm always looking for attractive dancers with outstanding technique and a desire to work. You will be notified for all these auditions."

General murmuring was heard throughout the room. Griff took over. "Are there any questions for either Mr. Kaplan or Mr. Matthews?" Jeff's hand shot up. "Yes, Jeff?" "Does being in either the Broadway or the Japan production give us an advantage for the national tour?" "I can't comment at the moment until I confer with Mr. Matthews," replied Griff. "I can answer your very direct and honest question," stated Owen. "Yes! You will all have first refusal if you are notified directly of an open spot. Auditioning will be a mere formality. I'm certain Mr. Martin and Mr. Danier are well-aware of your capabilities!" The murmurs continued. It was Kaplan's turn. "We are pleased with your work. You have the advantage of future work with the Kaplan-Maggli organization. I believe that takes care of business for now. Thank you all for making our production in Japan such an overwhelming success." The group began to disperse as Kaplan called his team together. "Owen, Jonas, Phillipe and Griff, please stay for a few minutes. Mr. Hanson, will you take notes? You're aware that Lenny had to leave for a dental appointment and Janice has her prenatal doctor's check-up." "Yes of course, Joe," said Gary, taking a seat. After a second round of coffee was offered, Kaplan began the confab.

"I am pleased to inform you that Blaine Courtman and Gregory Morgan are now on board to fully finance the national tour. They are both extremely enthusiastic and pleased with the grosses garnered during the Japanese run. With that said, we now have a financial guarantee to make it happen. We now need to talk logistics. Owen, the floor is yours." "It's simple, really. Jonas, I'd like you to remount the road production, directing and staging with assistance from Phillipe. Griff, I insist you to take this company out. There is no one I trust or rely on more than you. I could easily place your lovely lady in the lead and insist on Chad Chapman in Jonas' original spot. "I think we could be persuaded, Owen. Mally and I have discovered a mutual love of travel." "Great! Jonas, how do you feel about working full time on the production side?" "You're serious?" "Yes, I am, my friend. You've earned this step up, but are you willing to stop performing? It's a major career change. It was for me back in my day." "It's a dream come true, Owen. Thank you!" "Good, that's settled. "Phillipe, do you want to do the same or do you still have performing in your belly?" "I go wherever I'm sent, Owen, preferably alongside Jonas." "Great! Then that's done. Expect to be involved six-weeks in rehearsal here, a week on the road, setting up for the opening late March in Cleveland. We can send you out for brush-ups in each city." "Merveilleux! Merci, Owen!" "We have the route in place already, a six-month commitment," said Joe, referring to a file in front of him. "After Cleveland it's on to Toronto, Philadelphia, Washington, D.C., Detroit, Los Angeles, San Diego and a wrap up in San Francisco!" "Great itinerary," tossed Gary, his pencil flying. "We'll have a six week run in D.C. and open-ended in San Francisco." Jonas had a suggestion.

"Owen, you may want to offer the second leads to Jeff Jenkins and his bride, Nora Blake, now a package deal. They have a strong working knowledge of the show, having been our original swings." "Great idea, I need veterans on the road." "The Tokyo group was excellent, with invaluable working knowledge of the staging. "Some of our troupe will be precast to save time," allowed Owen. "Yes, but be advised, you must have an Equity call to hold to union rules if replacements from outside our personnel are necessary," said Griff, who always played by the book. "I'll leave the details to you, my friend," Owen said, giving Griff a shoulder pat. "I'll work out a schedule of audition dates and rehearsals based on Joe's time frame." "Good," said Joe. "Then are we all up to date?" "Yes, but Owen tell us about your film plans," said Jonas, eagerly. Owen grinned, lighting another cigarette.

"My friend, you will continue into the next phase, following the remounting of the road *Centipede.* I will also need your irreplaceable assistance on the film version of *Bravo Business.* There's not another who can top your experience or eye, Jonas." "I could do that show in my sleep, but I imagine adapting it to the screen will be new and different." "Absolutely different, but a good time," said Owen, knowingly. The whole deal from casting to completing the film will take about six months!" "Wow, I could get used to this, boss!" "Well, get used to it. These Hollywood people have a lot to learn from us. We'll include your pal as well. Phillipe, ever been to Lotus Land?" "Never, but I've heard enough about the lifestyle out there." "You'll be too busy working your ass off to work on a tan!" The others laughed, knowing how easily Phillipe could darken with little exposure. "We will meet again to discuss the upcoming Hollywood project once the audition and casting for the national tour is complete." "Have we covered the preliminaries?" "We're set for now," said Joe. "Great!" "Thank you, gentleman! It's good to have our whole team back in the same room!" The meeting ended. Jonas and Phillipe headed to Allen's for a celebratory drink. Griff hurried home so he and Mally could plan their Bermuda trip. And Owen, ready for scotch and hopefully sex, headed to the Taft. He just might get lucky. He was more than ready.

Julie was excited as she showered and chose her prettiest underwear. Nick had been a continual mindset since they happened to run into each other at Allen's weeks ago. He had seen her home, but still hesitated to come on to her. 'What was he waiting for?' They had yet to make love. She was more than ready since the day she first laid eyes on him, months before. There had been a lot of water-under-the- bridge since and frankly he was the first man she dared to date following the Tim Bartel debacle and near assault. She'd soured on men and had lost hope of ever trusting one again. But Nick was different, rather old school. He chose to court her slowly. Tonight he was taking her out to dinner, a surprise location. She explored her closet, trying to select an appropriate outfit, one not too revealing but tantalizing enough to encourage some advance. She spotted a favorite, a soft peach Jersey, with long sleeves, high neck and backless, revealing to the waist. Slipping it on, she zipped over her bottom and stood admiring her profile, trying to catch her backside in the mirror. Deciding it was just flirtatious enough; she slipped on some pumps and brushed through her short curly bob. She'd let her hair grow a bit, deciding that men liked longer hair, even though short was better on her as a rule. A touch of powder, rouge and mascara and she was ready for him. The buzzer sounded.

Nick stood on the other side of the threshold, breathtaking in a dark green tweed sport coat, brown slacks and pale yellow shirt. He held a bouquet of pink sweetheart roses. Julie almost forgot to speak, staring up into deep chocolate pools, etched in dark lashes. "Nick, hi! Please come in!" As he entered he bent down and kissed her gently on the cheek. Handing her the bouquet, she blushed as she accepted them. "How sweet, thank you!" "They are almost as lovely as you, Julie." Going to her kitchen, she reached high in the cupboard and pro- duced a small vase, filled it at the tap and slipped the flowers into the water. "These are so pretty, where do you think I should put them?" "Over there," he said, pointing to her coffee table. You can see them from every part of the room that way." "Good idea!" When she turned she noticed he had sat down.

"Would you care for something to drink?" "Yes, what do you have?" "A surprise," she giggled. Returning to the kitchen she took two small glasses and a mystery bottle. Pouring the contents for both, she returned and handed him his. "Oomph Pa!" Nick took a sip of Ouzo and smiled. She followed, her eyes never leaving his. Before she could finish, he took her glass and set it down. Setting his nearby, he took her face in his hands and kissed her tenderly. She sighed as the longing rose up, causing her to shiver. "I want to make love to you, Julie. I've wanted to since we first met, but I was afraid." "Why, for heaven's sake?" "Because you are a worldly woman and I am very inexperienced." "No, I don't believe you," she murmured incredulously. "It is true. I want to be with you in that way." Julie couldn't breathe as she tried to process Nick's words. Finding it difficult to speak, she trembled, "What about dinner?" "It can wait," he whispered, moving closer. Unable to resist, she stood and took his hand. "Are you sure, Nick?" "Yes!" Without another word, she led him to her bed. This was not the outcome she expected, not by a long shot, but why not? She was more than ready to explore Greece.

Catherine was dating Danny regularly. They had always hit it off as cast mates, but she had been so blinded by her obsession with Owen, she couldn't see beyond the director. Ever since that night he was cavalier about Tim's attempted assault on Julie, she was put off and somehow the realization hit her and hit her hard. He didn't give a damn, not really. They were together because he called the shots. She was a convenience, sexually and now, she was through with him. Danny, on the other hand, was adorable, kind and straight, a real plus in a business where men were typically gay, bi-sexual, womanizing, off limits, married, divorced or terrified. She had only one lover before Owen, a fellow student she met at the University of Wisconsin, Madison. They had dated all through college while in the BFA acting program. She gave up her virginity to him and when they graduated, they vowed to stay friends but drifted apart. He went on to UCLA for a Masters in direction, while she had a dream to get to the Great White Way. Both had succeeded.

As Catherine hurried along 8th Avenue, thoughts of Danny held her rapt, as she stopped for a red light on the corner of 45th Street. As she glanced across the intersection, she spotted a familiar figure waiting to cross. Closer inspection brought terror to her heart. Tim Bartel! 'Has he seen me?' She trembled at the thought. Her mind raced as she tried to think what to do. Any encounter with him, however brief, scared the daylights out of her. As the light changed she pulled her scarf over her nose and mouth. With her head down and looking the other way, she rushed past him. She couldn't be sure he hadn't seen her. As she reached the curb, she quickly glanced back. He had stopped and was staring in her direction! 'Oh my God, what am I going to do?' Should she make a run for it or casually keep walking? The latter seemed the better choice until, out of the corner of her eye, she saw him retrace his steps toward her. Heart beating wildly, she felt tears begin to pool in her eyes, as she picked up her pace. Just as she reached the stairs at Allen's she felt a tug on her sleeve. "Hey, how are you Red?" She stiffened, trying to ignore his greeting. Remaining silent, she thought he would walk away. His hold became tighter as he leaned into her. "You passed on me once, now you have to make it up," he snarled. Catherine squirmed and tried to yank away, but his grasp was firm as he pulled her down the street. Feigning to pass out, she went limp until she had a chance. Lifting her foot suddenly, she brought her heel down along his shin violently, scraping until Tim yelled and let go. Catherine screamed too, at the top of her lungs. From the corner, Danny heard her screams and came running. Tim tried to lunge again, but she ended his attempt. Kneeing him directly in his equipment with lethal precision, he doubled over, fell to his knees on the pavement and grabbed his crotch. Danny reached Catherine just as he saw Tim go down. "You bitch, you'll be sorry," Tim croaked, through dry heaves. Triumphant and fearless at last, she leaned down, facing him nose to nose. "No, Tim, you're the one who's sorry, a sorry ass!" "Come on, Cath," said Danny, pulling her away. A police officer approached.

"What's going on here?" Tim, still on the sidewalk in a heap, started to shout, "That bitch attacked me! I was minding my own business!" The officer turned to Catherine, a half smile on his face. "Care to tell your side of it, Miss?" Two female bystanders, who had witnessed the whole encounter, stepped up. "Officer, we saw what happened," said one, pointing at Tim. "That guy tried to force himself on her. She simply defended herself from the creep!" "I see." Turning to Danny, he continued. "Will you verify this?" "I was planning to meet Catherine here when I heard her screaming and saw him roughing her up," he said contemptuously, pointing to Tim. "She did what any savvy woman in her situation would do and defended herself." "Very well, be on your way. You on the ground, get up!" Tim slowly got up with great difficulty. "If I ever see you on my beat or catch you bothering another woman, I'll throw your ass in the slammer! Got it? Now, get lost," he demanded, leaving no room for further discussion. Tim Bartel wasn't listening. He was thinking this was the last straw. He was washed up in New York. 'Time to move to a friendlier place,' he sulked. He would decide what to do, but for now he was going home, have a few beers and ice a particular part of his precious anatomy.

Catherine and Danny continued with their plans. First they each ordered the house burger at Joe Allen's, the best hamburger in the city and, later, took in a movie they both wanted to see, *Nights of Cabiria*, held over by popular demand at the Third Avenue Cinema on the east side. It was still early when they got on a cross town bus and returned to Catherine's apartment. Entering, she reached for a wall switch, but before she could turn on the light, Danny's mouth covered hers. His lips, so sensuously soft, continued to explore her neck stopping at her ear, his warm breath stirring her, causing her to cooperate fully. Up until now, she had resisted going further than necking and petting, but tonight she was ready. Something had shifted and she wanted Danny in the worst way, hungry for intimacy with a new man. Their kissing continued as she removed his jacket and scarf. She followed his lead as he backed her over to the sofa and slipped off her coat, never breaking from her mouth. Reaching up, he pulled the combs from her long, red tresses, now falling over her shoulders. He unbuttoned her blouse, awkwardly at first, but as his ardor built his hands found facility to unfasten faster. Fingers brushing gently against her bare breasts caused a shiver, as she allowed him complete access. Sliding her blouse from her shoulders, he continued, unzipping her jeans. As they opened he slipped his hand inside, exploring eagerly. She gasped, feeling pressure of his finger tips against the fabric of her crotch. "Cath, be mine tonight." She sighed, eager for more. He continued, sliding her jeans to the floor, her panties following. "Lie down," he whispered, guiding her to the sofa. Now on her back, Catherine spread her legs. She felt the first warm caress of his tongue along her lips and the nub of her femininity. Her moans caused him to move more quickly. Now his fingers probed deeper, encouraging her to let go. No longer able to hold back, she rocked through her explosion. He held her steady, continuing to kiss and caress until she calmed down.

Catherine lay prone, reveling in Danny's handiwork. Her eyes were closed as she breathed slowly and deeply. Moments later, she opened them finding him naked and erect. Reaching down, he pulled her gently to him. Following his lead, as if they were dancing an erotic adagio, Catherine lifted to his torso, wrapping her legs around him. His voice was gentle, soothing, not brusque or demanding. "Where is your bed?" As she nodded toward the hall, he smiled, turned and carried her to the bedroom. Catherine felt safe and content. Danny's gentility and sweetness, irresistible! But, mostly she felt a growing sense of peace. This was where she longed to be from now on.

Chapter 25

Plans

With the Edwards return from Tokyo, management called Pat to request an extension of two weeks on her contract. Pat originally planned to leave *Centipede* at her contract's end, January 15th, but was persuaded to stay the extension in order to allow her best friend time away on their delayed honeymoon. A phone call from Kaplan's assistant, Janice, convinced her to do two more weeks, time enough for Mally and Griff to vacation and return for a brush-up rehearsal, preparing her to take over Pat's spot at the end of the month. Janice continued. "Mrs. Edwards is the perfect choice to replace you since she knows the show better than anyone we have at the moment," remarked Janice, her nasal business tone intact. "Yes, of course. I hear she was marvelous in Tokyo." "Yes, I believe she will be partnered by your counterpart, Joe Pinto. Joe wants to stay on indefinitely and we're pleased he is willing." "Good news, an easy fix," added Pat, slightly annoyed by Janice's know-it-all approach. "Well, I think that covers it, Miss Byrne. I'll have an amendment to your contract drawn up today. We'd appreciate your coming in to sign all copies at your earliest convenience." 'Don't let the door hit you in the ass, Miss Byrne,' Pat thought, derisively.

Meanwhile, down in Chelsea, Griff and Mally packed a week's worth of warm-weather clothing, into two bags, no easy task. Before leaving for Japan, they'd created ways to store summer-wear in nooks and crannies, challenging in their small, one-bedroom apartment. Their flight was to depart from Kennedy International in the morning. "Griff, have you ever been to Bermuda?" "No my darling, this will be a first! My guess, knowing Joe's penchant for generosity and quality, it will be carte blanche." "What hotel will we be staying at?" "Oh, oh, a detail I forgot to mention. He's invited us to stay at his seaside villa, managed by a year 'round staff." "You're kidding, really?" "Absolutely! I've seen photos of the property and believe me this is a spectacular place." "Griff, I've never stayed in a villa! This is thrilling!" He smiled and took her in his arms, kissing her gently. "You know one of things I love most about you, why I married you?" "No, what's that?" "Your infectious enthusiasm and unspoiled Midwest character!" "Oh drat, I thought it was my Wiley ways and irresistibly sexy ass!" "Well, that too," he chuckled, as he swept her up. "Mrs. Edwards, I think we need a little warm-up before we hit the cabana," he murmured, kissing her deeply. "Take me to your bed, sir," Mally insisted. "That's exactly what I intend my sweet!" That's exactly what he did.

Pat was on the home stretch of her dance career with Owen Matthews. What was her next move? Where would she end up? She didn't consider herself an actor or singer, other than how it served the ensemble, but a longing was taking hold. Blaine could see how restless she had become, how fierce her desire was for a change. As much as she loved performing and being featured on Broadway, that big break had lost impact, given Owen's betrayal. As she pondered the end of her contract, Blaine walked in. Opening his arms she ran to him, her ardor in high gear. They held each other for a few moments. The kiss that followed was sweet, tender.

"My Beautiful Patricia, I have a surprise. We are dining with Greg Morgan, who is in town. He wants to talk a little business and celebrate our coming wedding! "Blaine, that's wonderful. You know how I feel about Greg!" "Yes, well it's mutual. And, he's made it quite clear that if I don't treat you like a queen at all times, he'll chastise, disown or worse, separate me from my equipment!" "Well. I'd heed his advice. He's a serious man!" "And the best friend I've ever known. When my father died, he stepped in and became my advisor and father figure." "Have you asked him to be your best man?" "Not yet, I thought I'd spring it on him tonight." "What should I wear?" "Whatever you choose will be perfection. We're to meet him at 8:00 at Sardi's. Keith will be downstairs at 7:45." "I'll be ready," hastened Pat, heading to the shower. "Keep the water running, I'll join you shortly." The evening ahead would prove surprising.

Owen was restless. His mindset was getting a national tour of *Centipede* readied in two months. Preplanning his film schedule, details and meetings with the Hollywood big shots and casting the screen version of *Bravo Business* also lay ahead. Contemplation was a bitch without the help of good scotch and a bed partner. His sexual needs had not been satisfied in some time, requiring frequent masturbation to satisfy his beastly libido.

He wasn't particularly interested in doing escorts. He'd had his share in the days of his first Broadway success, a time when achievement meant carte blanche. Any need could be met by simply being Owen Matthews. His celebrity, brilliant talent and desirable looks made for a complete and irresistible package to most women, men, too! More than once he'd been approached by other men, flattering, but not his scene. No, he was ready for a broad, pure and simple. As he showered and shaved, he decided on a stop in midtown, perhaps meeting up with someone he'd consider bringing home. The idea made him move through his grooming ritual with more haste than usual. He was horny and eager to check out the landscape. Getting dressed, he retrieved his smokes, money clip and keys and headed downstairs to a cab.

Blaine's driver, Keith Noonan, pulled up to Sardi's, a minute to eight. Opening the door for his boss and lady, he was asked to return at 10:00. Blaine took Pat's hand and led her through the front door. As they checked their coats, they spotted Greg waving from the cocktail lounge.

"Blaine, over here!" As they entered the room, Greg approached, a smile growing when he saw Pat. "Good evening, Patricia, how good to see you," he soothed, bending down and kissing her cheek. With a chuckle he turned to Blaine. "Some guys have all the luck! How are you, my friend?" "Good, Greg, welcome to New York!" "Join me for a cocktail? There's room at the bar. Our dinner reservation is for 8:30. Is the lady starved?" "Not at all, Greg, I'll be fine," reassured Pat. "Peanuts or pretzels will suffice for now, thanks." "See that, Blaine? A beautiful fiancée and a good sport!" "Yes, she is. You got off easy this time. She requires fuel frequently with her metabolism!" "Yes, you burn off calories and carbohydrates fast so fat doesn't have a chance to settle. But, you're hungry all the time," added Pat with a giggle. "Well, on you, it's evident," said Greg, with a grin. "Easy, Greg, she's mine!" "Like I said, some guys have all the luck!" "What would you two like?" "Patricia?" "I'd love a house red, Blaine." "Good enough. I'll take a Rob Roy, rocks, please." Greg signaled the barman, gave their order, and continued sipping his Martini. When the other drinks arrived, Greg raised his glass. "Here's to my favorite couple, congratulations on your coming wedding." They all took a sip. "Well, as long as you've mentioned it, I need a favor." "Oh, what is it?" "Patricia and I would be honored if you would serve as my best man."

Greg put down his drink, his voice catching. For a moment he didn't speak, tears welling in his eyes. "My boy, I would like nothing better. Thank you so much." They continued enjoying their drinks. "You have set a date?" "Yes! We've chosen Valentine's Day," said Pat, excitement in her voice. "Ah, the most romantic day of the year. Good choice, dear girl." "We're going to keep it simple. We want to marry at City Hall, in the mayor's office." "In Lindsay's chambers? Good choice, Blaine. John's an old friend and a class act. This city is fortunate to have him at the helm." "He agreed to clear his schedule." "What about a reception for this lovely lady?" "My folks have that covered, Greg. They have asked to host a party that weekend at the Blarney, my family's bar in the Bronx." "Well, now that sounds perfectly delightful! I hope I can get Guiness on tap!" "Are you kidding? I'm from a long line of Mick's. We'll take care of you, Greg!" "Well in that case then, I will consider myself invited."

They ordered another round of drinks, delighting in each other's company. As they sipped the second, Greg eyed Blaine slyly. "Where are you taking your bride to honeymoon, Blaine? I trust something less mundane than Niagara Falls!" "What a kidder you are. I asked Patricia to choose and she suggested Paris." "How I envy you both!" The second glass of wine had loosened Pat a bit. "Have you ever been married, Greg?" He smiled, thoughtfully. "Yes, I have been married. My lovely wife, Lydia passed away a few years ago. I remarried, Celeste, twenty years my junior. She enjoyed the lifestyle I offered, but in truth, she never loved me, just what I could give her. Many considered her my trophy wife and to be honest, she was. She had everything to turn an older man's head; beauty, charm, a drop dead gorgeous figure and a gift for gab. I was lonely, out-of-sorts and naturally, succumbed. We lasted three years until I found out she was having an affair with a much younger man who was well-heeled and hung. That did it! Thank God, I had a pre nuptial agreement in place. We have since gone our separate ways." "I'm so sorry, Greg." "What for? Live and learn. Looking at you two gives me hope to perhaps try again one day!" As they conversed, they were suddenly called to their table. Escorted into the main dining room, they settled at the back of the room, a choice spot for observing activity.

Owen was in the mood for a pleasant evening. Sardi's food was to his liking. He was always treated like a king by the staff and single women were known to patronize the bar. He might get lucky! Exiting a cab, he strolled into the vestibule, gave the coat check girl the once-over and removed his overcoat. She was a cute blonde, with plump breasts peaking out of her top. "What's your name, sweetheart?" She blushed, took his coat and handed him a claim check. "My name is Mimi. I know who you are." "Oh, how can you be so sure?" He was in a contrite mood, enjoying the game, as he moved in closer. She had a curvaceous body, one he would like to explore. "You're Owen Matthews. My cousin described you." "Really, who's your cousin?" He was becoming more curious with each passing second. "Marcy White. She's one of your dancers." "I'll be damned! Now this is a coincidence!" Abruptly changing the subject, he grew serious.

"How old are you, sweetheart?" "I just turned 18. I'm old enough to work here now. The tips are amazing," she said with enthusiasm. 'This child would make me a pedophile,' he thought, backing off. "Well good luck, Mimi, I hope you make lots of tips tonight!" 'Wow, that was a close one," he thought, hurrying to the bar. Ordering his favorite, Glenfiddich on the rocks neat, he lighted the familiar cigarette, taking a drag, inhaling deeply. He enjoyed the smoke as it left his nose, curling around him. Glancing around, noting the environment, his eyes fell on a knockout seated alone at a nearby table.

She was tall, lean, with small, perky breasts, legs to get wrapped in and short, cropped hair. Her cheekbones were model gorgeous and her manner, sophisticated. He couldn't take his eyes from her. She suddenly noticed him, indicating interest as she gestured for him to approach. Picking up his drink, he proceeded to saunter over, his eyes never leaving hers. "Hi!" "Hi, yourself, care to join me?" He cared to all right, pulling out a chair and sitting as close to her as he could get, without appearing too easy. "What are you drinking?" "A perfect Manhattan. Care to buy me another?" Her gaze cooked his toes. "Yes, of course. Be right back," he said, rising and heading to the barman. "Yes sir, Mr. Matthews. Would you care for another scotch? Glenfiddich, is it?" "Yes, please and another perfect Manhattan for the lady." "I'll have that for you in a moment. Care to start a tab?" "Yes, we'll be here awhile," he said, hopefully. When the drinks were ready, he carried them back to the table. Handing hers, he sat down and reached for his smokes. "Care for a cigarette?" "Yes, thanks, I could use it." Taking the cigarette she placed it to lips, waiting for a light. Her eyes stayed glued to his, causing his shorts to tighten.

With the ice broken, they settled into conversation. She was a looker and she knew it. He liked the way she approached him. He was attracted to a woman sure of herself and this gal was a turn on. "Whose company am I sharing?" "I'm Diana Corliss." "Owen Matthews." "The name is familiar, how come?" "Do you attend musicals? When I'm in New York, I try to catch one, occasionally. "But you're not a connoisseur?" "Well no, not really. I live on the other end of the country, Seattle. Grew up there." "What brings you to Manhattan?" "I'm visiting my older brother. He's at Young and Rubicam advertising, a partner there." The conversation continued, as the two engaged in small talk. Diana was beginning to feel the effects of her perfect Manhattan. "Would you care for another drink?" "Why not? I'm not working at the moment," she said, winking. "Hold on, let me order another round," said Owen, entranced with her. 'I wonder if she fucks like a jack rabbit.' He mused at the possibility, approaching the barman. "Two more of the same, please." "Certainly! Be right up." He glanced back at Diana, who had him in her scope. 'She's interested. The rest will be a snap,' he thought smugly.

Returning, with drinks in hand, he pulled his chair closer. "What do you do for work?" "I'm an actress, Seattle Repertory," she said without conceit. "I'm between plays at the moment, so it seemed as good a time as any to visit Art." "Art?" "My brother." "Are you staying with him?" "No, he has a lover. It would be a little crowded not to mention awkward." "How so?" "He and Larry are kind of new and very private. They're at the honeymoon stage of it." "So where does that leave you?" "I'm at the Abbey Hotel on 7th and 51st Street. My brother is generous, covering my stay." "Nice guy. How long are you in town?" "A couple more days, then I have to fly back. The Rep is mounting a production of *Cat on a Hot Tin Roof.* I will be playing Maggie. Are you familiar with the play?" "Vaguely, but I'm not really a fan of Tennessee Williams." "Really?" She appeared disappointed. "Not in the least," said Owen, a little intimidated. "It's one of my favorites. The show has such sensitivity and it's downright sexy." Owen perked up. "Sexy, how so?" "Well, my character is horny as hell; her husband's an alcoholic, bi-sexual and impotent! She spends most of the play in a slip, trying to get laid. "Does that turn you on?" "Well, I'd be lying if I didn't find it a turn-on. The subtext is obvious. Maggie's only desire is to get her husband Brick to want her, to take her. I've got some research to do to make it work. She's wickedly hot and hasn't been laid in a while." Owen sipped his scotch, contemplating his next move.

"Have you eaten?" "No, I'm starved!" "May I buy you dinner, Miss Corliss?" "Oh, certainly, I haven't eaten in hours. Thanks so much!" Owen stood and walked to the host's desk. He glanced up, saw that it was Owen and smiled. "Mr. Matthews, how good to see you here at Sardi's. "Hello, George!" "How may we accommodate you?" "Would you happen to have a table for two available?" "Mr. Matthews, for you, I'll do what I can. Give me a moment." George quickly scanned the table chart, checking around the room. "Ah yes, I see we have a table for two in the center of the room. Will this be satisfactory?" "How soon, George?" "Oh, right away Mr. Matthews." "Terrific! I'll get the young lady. She's in the lounge." "Very good, sir." Owen quickly returned to the bar. "Miss Corliss, I scored a table. It's ready for us." Diana rose and grabbed her hand bag, cocktail and winked. "You work fast, Mr. Matthews!" 'Oh babe, you have no idea,' he thought wickedly. The two entered the dining room and were seated at center.

Across the room, Greg and his dining companions were deep in conversation. Finishing their appetizers, they sipped an early Vouvray as they waited for their meals. Pat gazed around Sardi's dining room, enjoying the ambience, a long standing tradition on the Great White Way. Caricatures of anyone who had made their mark in show business, adorned the walls. Sketches of notables like Ethel Merman, Helen Hayes, Julie Harris, Lunt-Fontaine, Marlon Brando, Karl Malden and Ray Bolger among many others were recognizable and viewed from every location.

"This is such fun, Greg. Thank you for inviting us. "The pleasure is mine," he said, raising his glass. "To my adopted son and his soon-to-be wife! Blessings to you both!" Another sip and dinner arrived. "You'll enjoy the steaks. They're the best in the city," said Greg, knowingly. As the waiter moved to the side, Pat gasped. "What is it, Patricia?" She nodded toward the center of the room. There sat Owen, deep in conversation with an attractive companion. He was so close in proximity, he looked pasted to her. "Well, well, Owen Matthews, the celebrated director-choreographer!" "With an attractive dinner date," said Greg stretching for a glimpse. Blaine changed the subject.

"Patricia's contract with *Centipede* ends the 15th," said Blaine, taking her hand. "I haven't had a chance to tell you the latest, Blaine. The producers have requested I stay on until the end of the month. They've agreed to an amendment on my contract," explained Pat. "Why, darling girl?" "I found out that Griff and Mally are finally going on a well-deserved break, a delayed honeymoon and gift from Joe Kaplan." "How generous and well-timed," said Greg. "From what I've observed of him, Kaplan is magnanimous as well as a shrewd individual." "Mal will take over my spot when I leave the show. There's little she has to do to get up to speed. She did the lead in Japan and was fabulous from all reports." "How fortunate for management, a seamless transition." 'Far more than Owen deserves,' thought Pat, cutting her filet. "I honestly thought Catherine Andrews would be in the running as my replacement, but I think Mal is the better choice, from her experience and wonderful stage presence. Cath is still growing and will be a great stand-in for Mal." "Sounds like you've worked it all out, Patricia," mused Greg. "What's next for you?" Pat and Blaine exchanged looks.

"I want to branch out, take a different path in the business." Greg put his fork down. "But you are such a gifted and smashing presence on the stage. I picked you out from the rest right away in Houston.

The other female dancers paled by comparison." "Well, I'm flattered, but as I've explained to Blaine, a dancer's body doesn't last forever. I could go on being a gypsy until I'm 30, then what? Injuries are a reality and show business is highly competitive. Greg thought for a moment. "What are your options?" "I'd like to do something on the production side, but not stage management. That's the toughest and most thankless job in the theatre. Few women can cut it. Ask anyone!" Greg replied, "What then?" Blaine continued.

"I think Patricia would be marvelous staying in show business since she understands it better than most, but apply her expertise to another area. Darling, I think you'd make a savvy producer!" "I never thought of that. Could I?" "Of course you could. You're mature; you've been around and can relate to talent." "Blaine can teach you the financial aspect of it. He's the best guy I know, other than myself for garnering financial gains." "Well, thanks, Greg. Coming from you, a most successful entrepreneur, that's high praise." "You're worthy of it, my friend." "We have to find Patricia a project to get involved with. Any ideas?" "Well, we're the principal backers of the first national tour of *Centipede.* "That's a possibility, but Patricia needs time to learn the functionality of a producer." "Yes, of course. Patricia, what do you think?" "Well, Blaine tells me you're both going to back the film version of *Bravo Business.*" Now there's a notion we can work with and develop!" "Yes, I like that, especially since we all met Patricia on that tour!" "It's perhaps one of my all-time favorites." I think we should groom her as production associate with final approval on all casting." Pat blinked. "Are you serious?" "Couldn't be more," replied Greg with a grin. "Who better?" Blaine grew serious. "How do we make it happen?" "Well, my old friend Shel Friedman will agree to anything or anyone I endorse. He's aware of my track record. We're just a few weeks away from our final financial contract on the project. We're sole backers on this baby!" "This is beyond fabulous," said Pat, delirious with the possibility. "I think this calls for a toast," exclaimed Greg, raising his glass. The three toasted and continued eating.

Owen heard the commotion and turned. Spotting Pat with Blaine and the other rich guy he'd met briefly, he excused himself and strolled over to their table. "Hi Pat!" She barely made eye contact. "Owen. How are you?" Blaine, noting the awkward moment, extended his hand to Owen. "Good to see you. I believe you've met Greg Morgan from Houston. Reaching his hand past her, Owen shook Morgan's hand." Turning back to Pat, his eyes fastened on her. 'This contemptuous bitch needs to be put in her place,' he thought, caustically. "I understand you'll be leaving us at the end of the month, Pat." "That's correct." "That's a shame." Then, as if baiting her brought him utter pleasure, he added a barb. "Can you imagine gentleman, I made this stunning lady a star on Broadway and she's bailing on a mega hit? What kind of person does that?" Blaine caught the insult and volleyed back. "Well, Mr. Matthews, I believe this person has other plans." "Oh, so you're behind this decision!" "Not at all. It's solely Patricia's and I'm backing her 100%." Greg interceded. "Would you and your dining companion care to join us in a toast?" "I don't know, what are we toasting?" Pat had had enough, turning to Blaine. "Darling, will you share our news with Mr. Matthews?" "Certainly, beautiful girl, I'm happy to. Patricia and I are to be married next month." The sudden news caught Owen off guard, bruising his psyche and ego all at once. Trying not to miss a beat, he thanked Greg and excused himself, finding his footing back to the table and Diana. He was bewildered, unglued and worst of all, betrayed by the women he had once touted.

"Who are those people?" Diana was slightly bent, not used to being ignored. "Backers and a dancer I once knew," he said, absently. "How about another drink?" "I need fuel," said Diana, emphatically. "You invited me to dine with you. May we order?" Owen signaled a server who promptly arrived. "What are you having?" "I'd love the salmon filet, please." "Certainly, Miss. Would you care for a salad?" "Yes, I'd like a Caesar, with extra anchovies on the side." "Very good and for you, Mr. Matthews?" "A filet, the largest you have, rare with a tossed, blue cheese dressing." "Your dinners come with a choice of potato and a vegetable accompaniment." "I'll have twice baked and do you have asparagus?" "Yes, we do," Miss. "Sir, would you care for a potato and vegetable?" But Owen wasn't listening. He was fixated on the trio across the room. "Sir?" Diana reached across the table, giving him a well-placed nudge. "What?" "Our waiter would like to know if you want a potato or vegetable." "I'll take fries and sautéed mushrooms. You still serve them, right?" "Yes, Mr. Matthews, one of our most requested. "Fine." "I'll put in the order right away."

Silence ensued. Broaching conversation, she was curious about her dinner date. "Everyone acts like you're some kind of celebrity around here. Who are you?" "I'm the most respected director-choreographer on the Broadway scene today. That's who the hell I am!" "Oh, for real? That's impressive. I had no idea! What shows are you famous for?" "You've got to be kidding! You're putting me on, right?" "Honestly, no, I don't get out of Seattle much." "Don't you read the trades or watch talk shows?" "Not really, I'm serious about building an acting career and viable resume. I do spend most of my time rehearsing and performing." "Well, to edify your surprising lack of exposure, I've 10 hit shows to my credit over the last 20 years. My latest, *Centipede,* is the runaway hit of last season and is still playing to packed houses." "That's impressive. I had no idea." "Obviously not," he returned with an edge. "Dinner and free drinks doesn't give you leeway to be rude, Mr. Matthews. Please, could we just enjoy each other's company and get past the facetious tone?" Owen softened. "I'm game."

Their dinners arrived and Diana dove in, sighing at the first bite. "This food is incredible, so perfectly done." 'She's definitely a neophyte, but has possibility,' he thought. The rest of dinner went pleasantly as Owen upped his game to get what he wanted. So preoccupied with scoring, he didn't notice Pat and her companions passing by. At the end of the meal, he paid the check. "What happens now, Diana?" "I don't know. What do you have in mind?" Her eyes held attraction to him, so he decided to make his play. "You're a lovely woman. May I see you to your hotel?" She smiled faintly, realizing where this might be leading. Curious and turned on by his apparent notoriety, she accepted. Grabbing their coats and a cab, they headed to the Abbey. Owen was anticipating a delightful romp with Diana Corliss of Seattle.

Jeff and Nora had settled in, though he was experiencing intense culture shock. He was quieter than usual the first few days they were back. Nora sensed her husband was still in Japan and, accepting his rumination, stepped back, waiting. She was aware how profoundly moved he was toward Japanese culture and people. Seldom if ever moody, Jeff had withdrawn for the time being. She would take matters into her own hands. Being a voracious cook she decided to prepare Jeff's favorite meal, Yankee Pot Roast with all the fixings. She allowed it to cook all day, occasionally stirring the contents in a big iron pot she'd found second hand in the Village. As the evening drew closer, she added chopped carrots, celery, onions and a bottle of beer to flavor the juices. Having a taste, she was delighted how good it was and began setting the table.

Jeff had been gone for hours; trips to the bank, post office and the neighborhood liquor store, where a wine sale was in progress. He decided to treat his lovely bride to her favorite Riesling, though he preferred a good Cabernet or Pinot Noir. Included in his purchase, a six pack of Heineken's and some snack foods. As he rounded the corner of Broadway and 86th, he spotted a familiar sight at the corner grocery. Rows and rows of floral bouquets on display popped out, drawing him to lovely colors and fragrance. 'I have to get my love some flowers!' Stopping in, he selected her favorite; Stargazer lilies mixed with greens, paid the clerk and continued back to their sublet. His longtime friend, Hank Cassidy was on tour and had sublet his flat to them. The cozy one-bedroom had a kitchen, bath and living room on the basement level. The most attractive aspect was the working fireplace. How they loved to snuggle on the sofa and discuss their day, often sharing a glass of wine! The place was their love nest, a perfect hideaway from the pace and congestion of the city. Living in New York was a means to an end. It was the center of the musical theatre world and at present, their career path.

As Jeff walked into the apartment, the smell of something incredible reached his nose, causing a sigh. Putting packages down, he stood enjoying their kingdom. "Nora? When do we eat?" She burst from the kitchen, running to embrace him. "Hi Love, we'll eat a little later. I want to be sure the veggies are cooked through." "I brought you a surprise," he whispered, kissing her gently on the lips. "Oh, tell me! I love surprises!" "And I love you, more than anything on this earth," he soothed, handing her the bouquet. "Goodness, flowers! You sure know how to spoil a girl, Mr. Jenkins!" "Not just any girl," he whispered, nuzzling her neck. "How long until we eat?" "An hour, why?" "Because I know a splendid way to pass the time!" Nora took the hint, a broad smile forming. "Ok, lover, but I need to put these in something first," she insisted, taking the flowers to the kitchen in search of a serviceable vase. Once the lilies were placed in water, she turned down the heat under the pot and joined him. Dinner would wait.

The large aluminum bird dipped over azure-blue water, as the Edwards' flight descended on Hamilton, Bermuda. The day was perfect, the landing thrilling as always. Exiting, they descended the stair ramp and walked a short distance to the small terminal, passport control, and baggage claim. Bags in hand they headed for Customs, a procedure before they could continue. That out of the way, they looked for the taxi-cab stand. Spotting a man holding a sign reading *Mr. and Mrs. Edwards*, they approached. "We are the Edwards," announced Griff. "I am Quinn, Mr. Kaplan's driver. I am to see you to his home, Grand Bienvenue. May I take your luggage? "Certainly and thank you," said Griff. Quinn was double-parked as they walked to the car, a sparkling black Rover. He placed bags in the trunk and stood back, waiting for them to enter. "We'll be there in 20 minutes. Please sit back and enjoy." He pulled away and headed to the countryside. The intensely blue sea stretched parallel along the two-lane road. White surf spilled over continuous sandy beach and natives in colorful attire, hiked along the road to and from town. Each turn brought new vistas, rolling hills, intense greenery, fruit tree groves and carpets of flowers. As they sped along, the warmth of sun and gentle wind off the sea was a feast for the senses. Jackets off, they held hands and absorbed the views. At the top of a hill they left the main road entered a gated compound and stopped in front of a magnificent home.

Griff's excitement was in high gear. "Darling, take a look!" From the top of the hill was an expansive and breathtaking view! The entire house had floor to ceiling glass windows, with a wrap-around veranda. Quinn led the way, announcing: "Mr. Kaplan employs a small staff year 'round, including chef and housekeeper. I will be your chauffeur for any sightseeing and shopping you wish to do. For whatever you need, please use the service phones, our numbers are listed nearby."

The main room was impressive and impeccably furnished with a tropical flair of citrus colors and wicker. "You can see the ocean all the way through the house, Griff!" The Edwards' were speechless. A dining room, kitchen, guest bathroom, second bedroom and study formed a circle around the main room at center. The master suite had it all; king-size bed, fireplace, wet bar and bookcases filled with current best sellers. The bathroom featured a glassed-in duo shower, sunken tub with Jacuzzi, bidet and vanity.

The most enticing feature was the veranda, encircling the entire house, with access from every room. As Griff and Mally followed Quinn outside, they noticed a swimming pool, cabana, changing area and pathway to the beach below. "Our resident chef, Alan Bernard is preparing a special meal, following Mr. Kaplan's request. Dinner will be served at 8:00. It will be brought to the villa." "This is too much, Quinn, but greatly appreciated," said Griff. "And now, if you will excuse me, I will leave you to your leisure." "Thank you so much, Quinn. Where are you originally from?" "I'm from London, Milady. My family settled here decades ago. You may reach me at extension 4!" When he'd left, Griff reached for Mally, hugging her close. "This island is paradise," she murmured, pressing against him. "No my darling Mally, paradise is holding you!"

The night of their chance meeting at Sardi's, Owen was determined to score with Diana Corliss. She was beautiful, coltish and intelligent. Her figure stirred his desire to do her and the Abbey seemed a convenient place. Suggesting he see her to the hotel appealed to her. A perfect gentleman! Hailing a cab was the easy part; sitting close to her was tough. Her fragrance was intoxicating. The warmth of her body next to him, her thighs brushing his, her sweet breath and her compelling glances were creating an excruciating hard on, which he would have to endure. He preferred taking his time, enjoying his brand of seduction, easing into his best play. He would ready her for sex with him, her next role. Subtext based on reality was a beautiful thing! Owen paid the driver when they arrived. In the lobby, Diana stopped at the front desk for messages. The concierge handed her a note. "It's from my brother. I'll call him in the morning," she said. "He wants to meet for breakfast tomorrow before he goes to work." "Let's go," said Owen, ready to plunge. Do you have your key?" Diana smiled as she fished in her bag. "Here it is. I'm on the fifth floor." Entering the elevator, the silence between them was awkward, but only for a moment. Exiting, they walked down the hall to room 525. "Here, let me do this," said Owen, playing the gentleman. They entered the darkened room, with only a nightlight in the bathroom to light their way. Removing her coat, he slipped out of his, tossing it on a nearby chair. "Would you care for a drink, Owen? There's a choice of beverages in the small fridge over there," she said pointing. "Sure, what have you got?" "Well, let's see." Kneeling, she opened the door and checked the inventory. "Looks like beer and soft drinks only. Will either do?" "Yes, I'll have a beer. Care to join me?" "Yes, I will. Why don't you open two and I'll be right back," she headed for the bathroom.

He watched her go, his interest growing, his libido slapping his senses. Opening two chilled Heinekens, he found glasses and poured. As he waited, he imagined her nude. With any luck, she'd go down on him. He preferred fellatio to intercourse, loved watching a woman giving head, the more aggressive the better! The thought made him shudder with want. As he ruminated, the door opened and Diana returned in a white slip which outlined her body to perfection. "Come, let's drink," he said, his eyes fastened to what he imagined under the fabric. She joined him on the sofa. Handing her a glass, he clinked and murmured, "Here's to a good time!" She winked, took a swig, running her tongue around the rim. Her gaze stayed locked on him. In a matter of moments they had finished their drinks. Diana rose and moved to the bed. "Come here, Owen," she purred, patting the coverlet. He joined her, his pulse starting to accelerate. Slowly, she began removing his sport coat, one sleeve at a time. He was cooperative, curious. Next, she loosened his tie and slipped it off; his shirt was next. "What do you want, Diana? I'll make you feel so fucking good," he whispered hoarsely, his mind in overdrive. She continued to undress him, as if she hadn't heard. "Be still, Owen. I want to finish this first," she insisted, removing his belt. She was persistent as she slid down his pants, tossing them to the side. He was excited, thinking, 'Where is this going?' Only his jockeys remained. He was obviously hard as she looked him over, obviously relishing his hardened shaft clearly visible through the white cotton. Delightful! Her hands traced the outline of his equipment as he sighed under her touch. 'Hmmm, nicely endowed,' she thought, continuing. "Now, lie down Owen!" Her voice was aggressive, compelling and persistent! "What do you have in mind, Diana?" "You'll see. Do as I say," she insisted.

Now prone, Owen waited, more turned on than he had been in recent memory. 'How many months had it been since his last score?' Breathless, he mused, 'Whatever is going on in this Seattle broad's head, I dig.' Strong women were definitely a turn on and this one was stronger than most. What happened next surprised him. One wrist at a time, she tied him to the bed posts. 'Wow, little Miss Seattle likes it kinky,' he mused, delighted and ready for more. With finesse she slid his underwear off. "You'll like this Owen! You do want me to do you, don't you?" By now he was beside himself with want. "Oh yes, do me hard, Diana!" "Don't worry, I have every intention," she flipped, slipping off her slip. Her perfect body was moist, glistening with oil, apparently applied while in the bathroom. "First, I want you to beg to get off!"

Anticipating heaven, he felt the first move of her mouth, closing around him. Her hands moved up and down, light at first then hard and fast. All the while, her tongue moved rhythmically, her saliva keeping the action fluid. Owen moaned and begged, all the while twisting through waves of pleasure. Being tied made it all the more erotic, the build-up more intense. As he was about to peak, she stopped. Sitting back, she eyed him with glee, enjoying her control. "Fuck Diana, I want to come," he shouted. "Oh no, I'm not nearly ready, Brick." Then, as reality hit, he remembered their previous conversation at the restaurant. It was obvious she was using him for sex to prepare for her next role! "Wait a minute, wait a minute, what are you saying? I'm not some fucking character in a Tennessee Williams play, I'm Owen!" "Shut up, and submit, you fucker!" It was then he became concerned. "Stop, Diana," he begged. In a startling move she stuffed a scarf in his mouth. "You need to shut the fuck up," she demanded. It was a no-win situation. Owen stopped struggling and tried to relax. He was hard and decidedly ready as she mounted him. Slipping his throbbing shaft inside, she rode him like a stud horse. The oil on her body made the ride smooth, pleasurable. Owen lay tied, trussed like a slave. Sexual servitude was a mixed bag. He loved kinky sex to a point, but Diana's aggression bordered on sadistic.

When he came, it was wild, his climax all-consuming. Then, it was over. Without a word, she slipped off, untied him and removed the gag from his mouth. "Get dressed and get out. You're not Brick, you're an imposter," she snapped, clearly in another zone. Owen felt a chill, trying to process what just happened. Who was this woman who believed she was living in a play? The broad clearly had duped him from the get-go and got off on her terms. He felt used and cheap. Gathering his clothes he dressed and left as quickly as he could. The evening had been surreal and Diana Corliss from Seattle was not who she appeared to be.

Mally and Griff's week in Bermuda was about to end. They had toured the island, shopped and, after dinner they thought it would be fun to check out some night life. Quinn came in the Rover and suggested a club, "The Conch," he said, was the best in town. The drive down the hill at night had a new appeal and such a different ambience from the ride on their arrival. The sky was clear, revealing a vast wash of stars. A full moon sent light over the rolling hills, along the roadway and cut a swath through the sea below. In the distance, Hamilton was a golden glow in the sky.

The week had flown by quickly, every day and night a special dive into utter luxury and comfort. They marveled at Joe's generosity and his largess, which he never flaunted publically. Each detail was carefully worked out for their benefit, each favor and gesture, so thoughtful. It was a trip they would never forget.

Quinn pulled up to the club and opened the door for their exit. "I will come by when you are ready Mr. Edwards, what time would you like me to return?" Griff checked his watch. It was 9:00 PM. "How about 10:30? Mally and I aren't big club people," he admitted with a smile. "Very good, Mr. Edwards, I'll see you then." The interior of the Conch was surprisingly plush. The main room held several tables, a bar at one end and small stage at the other. Miniature white lights hung throughout, adding a soft glow to the ambience. In the center, a small portion of roof was open to the sky and lush vegetation was displayed throughout. Floral arrangements and candles adorned each table, adding an air of welcome. A host greeted and directed them to a table near the stage. Rum was the preferred libation on the Island and a table sign noted Mojitos as a house special. Mally and Griff had fun all week trying new tropical concoctions, neither were connoisseurs so tonight would be something new again. "Waiter, two Mojitos please."

An announcement caught their attention. "Ladies and gentlemen, the Conch is proud to present the vocal styling of Lise Reynard." A soft spot moved through the room and stopped at the piano, highlighting a gentleman seated at the keyboard and, next to him, a statuesque redhead, with mic in hand. "Ladies and gentleman, good evening and welcome to the Conch. We're so glad you stopped in! Tonight I want to share a medley of my favorite, the great Cole Porter and I'd like you to meet my great accompanist, Jimmy Martinez. Jimmy?" The light narrowed to her face as Jimmy began the introduction to *Night and Day.* As she started the song, Griff stopped drinking for a moment, watching her intently. Mally noticed and nudged him. "Griff, what is it?" "She looks and sounds very familiar," he whispered. She was unusually attractive and seemed far too sophisticated for this tourist setting. Mally agreed. "I think I've seen her before, maybe on tour."

Song after song continued and, at the end, the audience applauded with enthusiasm. She bowed and exited the stage. "She's good, Griff! I wonder what she's doing down here?" But he wasn't listening. He was restless, distracted. "Griff, what's wrong?" He turned to her, a scowl on his face. "She reminds me of someone I once knew." "Really, who is that?" "Elise Mitchell, my ex- wife!" "What? The woman we ran into in Indianapolis that time?" "Yes," he murmured, with irritation. His entire demeanor had changed. "I'd like to get out of here." He signaled the waiter, but instead was greeted by a handsome fellow, who approached him with an affable air. "Good evening. Are you enjoying the show?" "Yes, thank you," said Mally, trying to lighten the moment. "You're Americans?" "Yes." "May I introduce myself? I am Jacques Reynard, the owner. My wife and I would like you to join us for a drink." Griff showed complete surprise. "Well, we were just leaving," said Griff, lamely. "She'll be out in a moment, please stay." "Thank you," said Mally, we would love to. " She nudged Griff with her foot under the table. Her eyes spoke volumes in one phrase: *Make the most of this. We'll get through it.*

"What would you like to drink?" Griff was stuck with no choice but to be cordial and needed something stronger. "Thank you. I'll have a vodka martini, straight up with a twist, please." "Certainly!" "And for you, Madame?" Somewhat charmed by the gentleman's continental demeanor and tired of tropical toy and fruit drinks, she ordered her preference, a glass of Chablis. "I'll have that for you in a moment," he said, with his soft French accent. When he stepped away, Griff was piqued. "Why did you accept? I'm uncomfortable here," he muttered. "You're anticipating someone who may not be who you think she is," Mally whispered irritably. "If it becomes too intense, we'll excuse

ourselves, all right?" Griff could always count on her forthright thinking. "All right, you win. I'll be sociable!" Mally giggled. "Well, don't let
a smile break that handsome face of yours," she said, kissing his nose.
"What is it about you makes me feel like a set-in-my-ways old poop?"
"I don't know, are you that old?" Reynard returned and joined them.

"May I know who I'm drinking with?" "Griff and Mally Edwards,
Mr. Reynard." "Jacques, please," he said reaching for Mally's hand, kissing it gently. 'A little too smooth to the core,' thought Griff, trying not
to be an old poop. As they chatted the singer joined them. Reynard
reacted like a school boy, about to melt into the floor. He stood and
kissed her cheek. "Mon Cheri, may I present Monsieur and Madame
Edwards. This is my wife, Lise Reynard. Griff's stomach tightened,
but he remained collected. She was definitely his ex, the former Elise
Mitchell, no denying it. He wondered what her next move would be.
She smiled, sat down, next to her husband and said, "Enchanted!" At
this moment, Griff tapped Mally's foot. She could tell by the look on his
face, his assumption was correct! His ex was posing as someone else.

Reynard continued small talk. "Lise and I have been married six
months. I brought her here three months ago and opened this club for
her." Mally decided to keep the dialogue light and pleasant. "How did you
two meet?" "Cheri, let me tell the story," suggested Jacques, his enthusiasm obvious. "I met my angel in Paris by chance. I was in Printemps
buying a shirt. This lovely woman literally bumped into me! Our eyes
locked and that was it! We were married in three weeks." "How did you
happen to be in Paris, Lise?" Mrs. Reynard eyed Mally suspiciously. "I
was visiting a friend." The phony accent gave her away. "Where are you
from, originally?" Again, Lise gazed sharply at Mally, not enjoying the
interrogation. "I was born in the U.S. to French parents, my father was a
diplomat, the Ambassador from France," she recited.

Mally persisted, enjoying the charade. "You know, you remind me
of someone I met in Indianapolis a couple of years ago. Great singer!
She could pass as your sister," her Minnesota perkiness in high gear.
Griff watched, a small grin forming. "Really, I have never been to
Indianapolis. Where is it?" "It's in Indiana," replied Griff, barely able to
stifle a laugh. "You must have me confused with someone else. I have
no sister, I am French." Turning to her husband, she oozed a request.

"Jacques, Mon Chou, I'll have a double scotch on the rocks, neat." The air was awkward, as Jacques went to the bar.

"You've got a nice set-up here, Elise, how do you do it?" "I beg your pardon, Monsieur?" "Oh come on, Elise, cut the crap, I'm on to you. Don't pretend you're someone else. A nose job and new hair color, doesn't disguise your voice. I'd know you anywhere!" Madame Reynard's demeanor changed in an instant. Lowering her voice, she sent daggers toward Griff. "You listen to me you fucker! Don't screw this up for me, you understand? I've got this gig and I mean to keep it!" Mally became alarmed. "Griff, I think we should go." "Damn straight, Darling. Say goodbye to Madame Reynard." They stood and walked toward the door. Reynard spotted them and hurried over. "Monsieur Edwards, must you go?" "Yes, we must, Monsieur Reynard. Thank you for your hospitality and bon chance to you." Griff took Mally's hand.

Making their exit, they broke into laughter. "Darling, you were a champ back there! Thank you for being so brilliant!" "Griff, I love you. It appears you have your ex out of your system at long last!" "And I love you. Have you any idea how much?" They kissed, the night air filling their senses. "What time is it? Quinn won't be here until 10:30." "It's 10:00. Come on, there's a little bistro shack down on the beach. Let's end the week with toy and fruit drinks!" They continued holding hands walking to the beachfront. Removing their shoes, they strolled through the warm sand to the thatched roof bar. Tonight, Banana Coladas, would be their nightcaps.

Quinn was prompt. On the way to the villa, Griff broached the subject of Monsieur Reynard and his wife. "What can you tell me about the owner of the Conch, Quinn? None of this leaves the car." "Well, it's very cut and dried. Jacques Reynard is a multi millionaire, an ex patriot of France who favors island living. He brought his new wife here about three months ago and purchased the Conch. I'm told Madame Reynard is a very good vocalist." "Yes, you could say that," Griff remarked with a chuckle. "The gentleman has other real estate on the island as well." "Oh?" "Yes, indeed! His largess includes a resort hotel, the finest on the island, a villa, a compound of ten condos on the beach and boat charter service. I believe he has four in his fleet." "What do you know about Madame Reynard?" Quinn paused for a moment. "Very little. She's a bit of a mystery around here. Reynard has lived here a number of years. He travels back to France on occasion to see family, but considers Bermuda home. Rumor has it he's mad for her and she's the favorite of his previous wives." "Previous wives?" "Yes, he has had several. All gold diggers, but this one he claims is his last." "I'll bet," tossed Griff, winking at Mally. "I know little else about her." They exchanged looks. "That's the way she wants it, Quinn." "How so, sir?" "Just a hunch!" The ride back brought closure to a very strange evening, but pleasurable week in Bermuda.

Chapter 26

Putting It All Together

With a game plan developing and backers committed, Joe Kaplan called his production team together after the Edwards' return from Bermuda. The group included Kaplan, Maggli, their assistants Janice and Gary, Owen, Griff, Jonas, Phillipe, Joe Pinto and Dick Landry. Dates for auditions and rehearsals would be discussed and settled. The meeting was called for 10:00 Monday morning, one week before Pat's contract extension would end. Kaplan ordered coffee, tea, Danish pastry and gathered the group in his conference room. "Gentlemen, we have a lot of details to work out. I would first like to discuss the particulars regarding *Centipede* national. We must have it readied and launched by March 29th. How do we want to cast this tour? Griff, do you have any suggestions?" "Yes. I think we should consult with our Broadway people and also our international cast. Find out who will make a definite commitment, have contacts drawn and signed by those willing to tour for six months. We will renew contracts for those who wish to remain in New York, a sort of cut and paste process." "We must offer our most seasoned performers, those with longevity, first refusal and add additional people as needed," said Kaplan. "In other words, hold Equity and open calls for replacements once the others are in place," added Jonas. "Correct! I want the best people for this tour," said Owen. "Good! Let's go down the roster and speculate on our preferred," suggested Maggli.

"We're losing Pat in another week," said Jonas, obvious regret in his voice. "Who's replacing her?" "Mally Edwards is the best choice. She is the most qualified and experienced." "Owen, what about Catherine Andrews? I thought you were grooming her for this," said Joe Pinto, cutting in. "I put her into the show when Mally was assigned the lead in Japan. She's beautiful, conscientious and a solid technician," he insisted. Kaplan looked to Owen. "What are your thoughts on this?" "I would possibly use her for the road company," said Owen, flatly. "I thought you were planning to move her up if Mally takes the lead on tour." "I'll consider it," said Owen, an edge in his voice. "Well, this will depend on the Edwards' decision. Griff have you discussed this with Mally yet?" "Joe, we just returned from Bermuda. I'll discuss it with her tonight."

"Thanks Griff. Assuming that you and Mally agree to tour, she is perfect for the lead," Kaplan agreed. "Who would be her partner?" "Chad Chapman is the obvious choice. They've done three productions as partners. They work like one!" "How about the second lead and covers for Mally and Chad?" "No contest there. Nora Blake and Jeff Jenkins are superb and literally know the entire structure of *Centipede*. They were our original swings and second leads in Japan," said Jonas. "Well, someone convince them to take the road, ok?" "I think I can persuade them. They're now Mr. and Mrs.," said Griff. "Good! You're the voice of reason around here and our most trusted!" "Thanks, Joe. I appreciate your confidence!" "Once we have the potential company, I'll let you do the talking," chuckled Kaplan. "Ok, let's begin!"

Griff pulled out the New York cast list. "When Miss Byrne leaves, Mally will go on for the time being, partnered by Joe Pinto. Catherine Andrews will be with Phillipe, Fran Fairchild with Jim Sorenson, Cynthia Charles and Danny Bartlett, Kathy Olson and Ray Nordeen, Marcy White and Gerry Granger, Liz Gunther with Fred Norris. Are we agreed?" "If they all wish to remain, it makes sense to me," said Owen. "Who are your swings, Dick?" "Julie Jensen and Hal Royce and they've been solid!" "Well, let's hope we can contain everyone we have presently," said Kaplan.

"If most of the cast remains intact here in New York, who and what are our options for the road?" "That's an easy one," said Griff, pulling out the Tokyo file. Assigning Mally, Chad, Nora and Jeff for the tour leaves six couples intact, that is if they're willing to go out for six months." "Which people?" "Here's the bunch, everyone a winner," declared Griff, handing Kaplan the list with copies for the others. After checking the list, Jonas spoke up. "Assuming everyone agrees, we still need to be prepared for two-week notices here and there." "That's an easy fix, Jonas. I'm aware you're ready to move to my side full time, but for now I need your ability and experience on stage. You can still mount the road production with Phillipe's assistance, stay in town and keep bringing in the bread." Jonas beamed. "Wow, the old dog still has some tricks to offer?" "In a manner of speaking, Jonas," said Owen, smiling. Phillipe didn't miss the reference, giving Jonas a playful poke. And when the time comes, I will expect you and your pal to accompany me to L.A. We still have to cast a film and shoot it. Agreed?" "Absolutely, boss."

"Next, we need to finalize dates for the national," continued Kaplan. We hold auditions the first week in February, cast replacements and begin rehearsals mid month. Prior to this, I need verbal commitments followed by signed contracts, Griff." "Done, Joe!" "In addition to having our casts firmly set, we'll need time to finalize theatre venues en route with the written agreements, signed and ready for us. Our advance man and company manager is Dwight Procter, who will locate accommodations in each city for our cast, crew and arrange professional discounts. Gary, would you mind Xeroxing our route sheet so we can follow along with Janice?" "Certainly Joe, be right back." Maggli suggested seconds on coffee and Danish while the group waited.

Back in five, Gary handed out the *Centipede* route sheet. Kaplan continued. "If you gentleman will follow along, Janice will go over this with us." "As you can see, the show will open in Cleveland March 29-April 3 at the Hanna. Toronto, Canada will be next at the O'Keefe Center from April 5-April 17. Next will be Philadelphia, at the Shubert April 19-22. There will be a longer engagement in Washington, D.C.

at the National April 25-June 5. "Nice run Joe," remarked Griff, who always enjoyed working a show in the nation's capital, especially in springtime. Following D.C., the show will head north to Detroit, Michigan from June 7-June 19." "What venue?" "Why the Fisher of course," said Janice, who went on. "After Detroit, the production will have a few days off to travel and set up in Los Angeles. The engagement is scheduled for June 24-July 11." "What theatre, Janice?" "I believe it's the Greek Theatre in Griffith Park, Sir." "Great, it's one of my favorites," exclaimed Griff. "It's a pleasure to work in that venue, amphitheatre at its best!" "The cast will be bused from the Hollywood and Vine area, where we're setting up a range of hotels and prices," added Janice, continuing. "You're in San Diego from July 14-July 24 at the Community Concourse. And finally, an open end in San Francisco at the Curran from July 26 until business drops." "Nice route, good theatres," remarked Griff. "Joe, I think you can guess my decision. I just need approval from my beautiful wife." "Understood, Griff. Work on her fast!" "Not to worry Joe, I'll talk to her tonight."

"Moving on, we'll need commitments right away. The production departs New York Friday, the 26th of March in order to arrive, set up, rehearse and open in Cleveland, March 29th. "Let's back track for a moment, Joe," said Owen, already charting his course. "We'll have to begin rehearsals by February 28th." "Yes, we'll need a month to remount with hopefully most of our current cast intact," added Jonas. "Let's set calls for replacements only if necessary, in keeping with rules of Equity," said Griff. "Will you contact our people immediately?" "Done!" "That's why we pay you the big bucks, Griff," said Maggli, chuckling. "Well, we all have plenty to do, so if there are no concerns or questions, let's finish up!" The meeting broke up at noon.

Griff headed home immediately to discuss Joe's offer with Mally. He didn't consider his beautiful wife a tough sell, but it was important she be 100% on board. When he told her the news, she squealed with delight. "Oh Griff, I've always wanted to play California!" "You're sure, Darling?" "Absolutely, when do we pack?" They hugged, kissed and broke out a bottle of a favorite wine they'd been saving for a special day. Any day they could travel and work together was special. That's how their journey began and that's how it would continue.

Owen Matthews had created Pat's star turn and her time was winding down. The last week in *Centipede* was drawing to a close. She would miss the cast, but although she was gifted, strong and young, her body was starting to resist the physical punishment of eight shows a week. As she sat at the mirror the group expressed regret over her departure. Kathy Olson and Marcy White had known her as far back as the *Bravo Business* tour. "Pat, are you sure you have to bail?" "Kath, you know it's time. With so much water under the Owen bridge, bailing is what I need." They hugged. Marcy suggested they go to Allen's for a farewell drink and everyone agreed to do just that. Liz, Fran, Cynthia had been with her from the beginning, all original cast mates. Catherine and Julie were add-ins when Mally and Nora were selected for Japan. Julie looked up to Pat, wanted to emulate her as did Catherine, who was by far the more ambitious of the two. She was unusually quiet tonight as they prepared. Pat noticed as she caught her eye in the mirror.

"Catherine, are you all right?" No response. "Cath, what's up?" Pat noticed the welling of tears. "I'm going to miss you so much! You've been my one true friend here in the company besides Julie." "For heaven's sake, I'm not moving to Rangoon! I'll be around," she said soothingly. "I know, but there are so few I can trust in this business!" "True enough, but there's something more. What's really going on with you? Are you and Danny ok?" "Yes, we're fine. He's the best!" Barely able to stifle a sob, she suddenly stood up. "Come on, let's get some privacy," suggested Pat. She quickly led her down the hall to the girl's room. Closing the door and locking it, she turned. "All right, spill!" Catherine tried to put her thoughts into words. "Pat, I feel passed over, ignored!" "Why?" "Well, I honestly thought I would replace you when your contract ended!" "Who gave you that impression, management?" "No!" "Well then, who?" "The director," she said, starting to cry all over again. The dawn hit! 'That son-of-a-bitch, I should have known,' Pat realized, her contempt rising. Hugging Catherine she tried diplomacy. "I can't speak for Mr. Matthews, but I can confirm that Mally is my replacement. But there's something else you may not know. When my dad was seriously ill, they gave me leave for weeks and Mally took my role. She has earned the lead, fair and square, Cath." "I know, but he assured me I would be the next in line." Pat was tempted to let on about her own disappointment with Owen, but resisted. Instead, she tried a different tact. "There's a national company, a six-month tour of *Centipede* coming up soon." "You think I'd have a shot at the lead?" "I can't say, but if Mally goes on tour, there's a strong possibility they'll need a replacement here in New York. Why don't I suggest this to management on your behalf?" "You'd do that for me?" "Are you kidding, Cath? You're a terrific dancer and have worked hard!" "Oh Pat, thank you so much. I didn't know who to turn to." "I understand more than you can possibly imagine. I'll see what I can do. Now dry those baby blues and let's do a show!" Returning to the dressing room they heard Dick call, "Places, please!" The show was about to begin.

Patricia Byrnes's last *Centipede* was flawless. Joe's partnering was superb as she, on fire, delivered her finest performance! The entire cast rose to the occasion, displaying their best. They were unstoppable. When the finale came and bows taken, the company turned and applauded. The entire audience joined forces, rising in ovation to her. From the wings, Dick Landry emerged carrying two dozen long stem red roses. Handing them to Pat he kissed her on the cheek and joined the applause. Speechless and letting down, she cried and waved to the audience, as the show curtain came down slowly. The on-stage throng surrounded her with hugs and kisses. She took it all in, feeling the love and respect. Most had been together since *Centipede's* birth, January 15, 1965. Dick called for order. His hands shaking, he produced a note as the group quieted.

"Pat, we, the company want to thank you for your commitment, devotion and friendship. Each one of us will take away a lasting memory of your absolute professionalism. We will miss you, but will always be a part of your journey and hopefully, your life." Applause rang out as Jonas worked his way through the group. They hugged and wept, holding each other. Jonas had something to say. "My dear friend you'll always be my main girl!" "We couldn't let you go without giving you this," Mally and Griff shouted, their arrival unexpected. "Oh my God, you're here," cried Pat, embracing them both. "Wouldn't miss it, Miss Byrne," said Griff with a wide grin. For a long moment, Mally and Pat embraced. With a shaky voice she produced a package, handing it to her.

"Pat, we wanted you to have this token from the *Centipede!*" "Open it," shouted the gypsies. Pat removed the paper, handing it to Jonas. Inside, she saw an album and took it out. "We decided that memories are always the most precious, so we each wrote you a remembrance and added some fun photos and mementos." Mally braced the large book, as Pat quickly paged through it. All around the gypsies stood, some on tiptoe, jockeying for a closer look. Page after page contained hand-written letters from each company member with photos throughout. Pat's eyes tearing as she glanced at the contents; tour snapshots, party poses, cocktail napkins from out-of-town bars, press clippings, headshots, even an original Playbill on which each had added a signature. "Oh my God, I don't know what to say!" "Say you won't move to Rangoon," said Catherine, giving a big hug. "I love you all so much and will never forget you!" Applause rang out once more as the women crowded in. "Time for some liquid relief from all this mush," said Kathy. "Let's go," added Julie. "Hey, are the boys included?" Jonas piped up. "But of course! What's a celebration without a bunch of queens?" Kathy laughed and suggested they all meet up at Allen's. "Ok, y'all, see you at our favorite spot. Gypsies rule tonight!" Dick interrupted, catching everyone's attention momentarily.

"Ladies and gentleman, the call for Mally's put-in will be Monday at 1:00. Everyone must attend. Please arrive warmed up and ready to go. We will focus on placements and traffic patterns, only. Joe, I'll have Jonas take over while you run choreography with Mal." "Glad to, boss." "Ok, now go celebrate," ordered Dick. The gang dispersed to change and get to the party. Before Pat took off, Dick caught up. "Pat, Dana wanted to be here in the worse way, but she's having some nausea issues." "Whoa, could it be?" "Yes, we're expecting." "Fabulous, Dick!" When's Dana due?" "As near as we can determine around the first week in October!" "Griff told me, Dick. What wonderful news," added Mally. The two hurried off. Mally joined Pat on the way to the dressing room. "I thought I'd tag along, come upstairs." "Of course Mal, might as well try out my chair." "My dearest pal, it will be a hard chair to fill." "Well, I beg to differ! And besides you need to meet someone." They entered the room. "Hey girls, look who's here!" All eyes turned toward Mally and Pat. A cheer went up. "Catherine, come here please." She rose and approached. "Mally, I want you to meet a terrific lady, Catherine Andrews. Cath, this is Mally, who you'll be working with next week." "I've attempted to fill your shoes while you were in Tokyo." "And she did, very handily," remarked Pat, with a reassuring tone. "It's lovely to meet you," said Mally, graciously. "I look forward to working with you." "Jules, come here! Mal, this is Julie Jensen, who took over Nora's swing. She's tough and tops!" "The most important job in the show," said Mally, smiling and extending her hand. "Yes, Mal was swing on tour, so she appreciates what you put up with night after night!" "Welcome, Mally!" Kathy shouted for attention. "Come on you tarts, let's party. And party they did!

Mally's rehearsal went smooth as glass. The put-in took only two hours as the gypsies ran through the show cue-to-cue. Jonas was at the helm along with Pat, who was there to fine-tune any discrepancies in staging or style. Julie sat out, observing Mally with awe. Griff stopped by to observe only. Dick predictably ran the rehearsal to his satisfaction. "Okay, please be back at half hour. Good rehearsal, gang!" Everyone applauded Mally, some hugging her. The company left with the exception of Dick, Griff, Jonas, Mally and Pat, who huddled. When the others were gone, Pat approached Dick. "I understand there's a national going out at the end of March." "That's correct." "Griff are you and Mal planning to take the show?" "Yes, we discussed it over the weekend and we've decided to go one last time!" "Here's the deal, guys. With Mal in the New York show for only a few weeks, we need someone who is strong enough to take over." "Any suggestion coming from you, Pat, is a bonus," said Griff. "Has management made arrangements for this, Dick?" "Nothing has been firmed as yet. It's customary to hold a replacement call through Equity." "Well, with time of the essence, may I make a recommendation?" "Of course, Pat. Who do you have in mind?" "Well, isn't it a bit obvious? Catherine Andrews should take over" "Hey Irish, why are you partial to Catherine?" "Jonas, come on, she covered for Mal and has worked alongside me for three months. I'm a pretty good judge at this point. The lady is breathtakingly beautiful, a wonderful technician and savvy performer." "That's high praise coming from you, Irish." "Well, to replace Mal with an outsider is totally bogus, in my opinion, when you have someone right under your noses! Can't you bend Owen a bit, guys? Come on; slip her into the lead when the time comes." "Boy, what's lit your fire, Irish?" "Jonas, I'm keenly aware that Mr. Matthews runs the show around here, but he's out of the picture, hasn't been by for months. He's gone Hollywood and you're all too careful to admit it!" Griff spoke up.

"It's true. Owen and I are in the throes of planning the national and he is starting pre-production meetings in L.A. regarding the film for the next few months." "Well then, how about it? I mean that's why they pay you PSMs the big bucks," said Pat with a grin. "Let us run this by Kaplan. With his approval, we'll notify Miss Andrews to prepare to take over," Griff reassured. "Atta boy, Edwards, the man they pay the big bucks," said Jonas with a chuckle. Then another thought occurred. "Ok, next question, who takes over Catherine's?" "That's easy. One of our old-timers should have a crack at it. Then we can still hold a legitimate call for replacement," said Dick. "Are we all on the same page?" "Thanks, guys. Fair play is awfully nice," said Pat, remembering other days.

The huddle broke and Pat walked out with Mally and Griff. "Pat, why is this so important to you? Has it to do with old wounds?" Pat stopped and faced Mally. "You've got to be kidding, Mal. It's obvious that an affair between Mr. Matthews and Miss Andrews was going on. Catherine so much as confessed that he promised her the spot. She was distraught, so it was easy to figure out. I've had some experience with the great one, you may recall." "You've given this a lot of thought, haven't you?" "Fair is fair and it's time someone had a chance without strings attached!" "I'll take care of this, Pat. I'll give Joe a call tomorrow morning." "Thanks Griff." Before they parted, they hugged each other. "Break a leg, my dearest friend, you'll be fabulous tonight," said Pat. And indeed, Mally Edwards was!

Joe Kaplan gave Griff, his top PSM, leave-of-absence to work logistics for the *Centipede* national tour. Getting commitments from those who were already known to management was the first order of business. Some might be seeking other jobs or staying in town to continue auditioning. Honing one's craft taking classes was another consideration. There were those who didn't enjoy the rigors of suitcase living while performing. In addition, Griff's work also involved details of hiring base orchestra and crew, committed to travel length of contract. He smiled considering some past hires, those preferring the road, higher salaries being the hook. Transportation was covered, but per diems were not available or offered. Personnel had to pay out of pocket for lodging and food. The experienced travelers knew to sock away earnings, sending a portion of weekly pay back to New York bank accounts.

Less costly lodging choices and no frivolous spending meant more money saved, a necessary component for survival upon return to the city and unemployment.

Griff spent three days tying it all together. Joe Pinto decided to leave the New York cast. He wanted to get back on the road for a change of scene. Though Chad would partner Mally, he decided to fall back into the general ensemble, taking the dance captain position as well. Another inducement was Griff's offer of an assistant stage management, or ASM position, with the producer's approval. Joe jumped at the chance. Like Jonas, the time was coming to hang up his jazz shoes. He had turned 35 and every year of dancing was felt in his knees and back. Andy Wendt, of the Japanese company, had moved on to another Broadway show and preferred to stay in New York. Joe would partner Neely Sorenson.

Going down the roster, everyone in the Broadway cast wanted to stay put. The only change was Jonas taking over his old position partnering Mally until she left on tour. He would be able to keep an eye on the show as always. Chad was taking break until the national rehearsals began. Jeff and Nora did the same. Griff continued calling as he scanned the list. With Mally and Chad in the leads, Jeff and Nora, second leads and the addition of Pinto, the cast was complete. Everyone from the Japan cast had agreed to stay on and go on tour! Amazing! While Griff was at it, he considered his promise to Pat. He would suggest Miss Andrews for the lead in New York. Dialing Joe Kaplan's office, Janice picked up. "Good morning, Janice, is Joe available?" "Hi Griff, one moment, please." As Griff waited he continued perusing the rosters and writing copious notes.

"Greetings, Griff. How goes it?" "Fine, Joe. We have everyone's commitment! Both the Broadway and Japan cast remain pretty much intact." "That's why we pay you the big bucks, Griff. Nice work!" "I do, however, have something to run by you." "Of course, shoot!" Mally will be the lead in New York until we pull out on March 26th. That said, I think we should seriously consider Catherine Andrews to take over her spot." "Catherine. Which one is she?" "Joe, she's been second lead for over three months on Broadway. She's covered Pat and knows it complete." "Is she that gorgeous redhead with the amazing legs?" Griff smiled. "Yes, Joe. She's a stunning lady and an excellent dancer."

"I have no objection at all, Griff. I trust your judgment completely. Be sure Owen is informed." "I'll take care of Owen. He'll be kept in the loop. Frankly he's so busy these days, I'm sure he'll welcome the ease of this." "Great! Keep me in the loop, Ok?" "Absolutely, Joe." They hung up. With personnel bases covered, Griff followed-up details of dates, lodging and venues for the tour. This was his métier and he thrived on it!

Owen was immersed with thoughts of his upcoming stint in Hollywood. He would achieve his biggest dream, that of becoming a recognized Hollywood A-list director. These and other thoughts swam in his head. The ringing of the phone pulled his attention for a moment. Picking up, he immediately recognized the best PSM in the business.

"Griff, what's doing?" "I wanted to bring you up to date on a few things, Owen." "I appreciate it. First off are you and the missus a done deal for the national?" "Absolutely, we're looking forward to it! Mally's never played the west coast and performing at the Greek Theatre in L.A. and the Curran in San Francisco was the hook." "I find that a stretch, Griff. You two are like bookends! One doesn't hold up without the other!" "Well, yes, you're right. We're held together by invisible Velcro!" "Nice image, I like it!" "To get back to business, I wanted you to be aware that we have all personnel in place for both New York and tour." "Christ, you amaze me. How long did it take you?" It's been a cut and paste job for the past three days, but we're set. I have one other suggestion for you." Oh, what's that?" "As you are probably aware, my wife has taken over Miss Byrne's spot. However, she'll be leaving on March 26th. I've spoken with a number of our colleagues who've suggested Catherine Andrews taking over. After all, she was swing for Pat over three months while we were in Japan. She's the logical choice in looks, technique and experience. I'm calling for your approval. With Miss Andrews set, we can move one of our female ensemble to her former spot, which makes a replacement call legit." It makes sense, Griff." "This eliminates your involvement so you can fully concentrate on your film project." "I like your style, Griff. That's why Kaplan-Maggli pays you the big bucks," he chuckled. "Thanks, Owen. I'll inform Miss Andrews." "You're the best, Griff. Thanks for your follow-up. Talk soon, Ok?" "Thanks, Owen, will do." Hanging up, Griff quickly checked the cast list and dialed Catherine. A sleepy voice answered.

"Catherine?" "Yes?" "This is Griff Edwards calling." She quickly shot awake, rubbing her eyes and checking the clock. 'Good grief, it's almost noon,' she thought, trying to focus. "I'm calling to inform you that you will take over the lead in our Broadway company of *Centipede*, the last week in March. My wife, Mally Edwards will be joining the national and you are the obvious choice to replace her."

Catherine held the phone close, her hand trembling as she processed Griff's news. Tears sprang to her eyes. 'Am I dreaming?' "Catherine, are you there?" Slowly she returned to the reality zone. "We would like your approval and commitment at this time." "How did this come about?" "You have people who believe in you and their firm endorsement assured this decision." "Was Mr. Matthews 100% on this?" Griff weighed his words carefully. "This decision must come from the director and yes, he did fully approve." Reality hit hard. "Of course I will! Thank you so much for calling!" "You're welcome and congratulations, Catherine!" As she put down the phone, she fell back on the bed, a mix of laughter and sobs coming from the depths of her being. 'Maybe speaking up has finally paid off,' she thought, hugging herself.

Chapter 27

Celebration

The time was coming! Blaine and Pat's wedding day was only days away. Arrangements were made with John Lindsay, recently elected mayor of New York, to be married in his chambers. They picked a weekday morning and told Greg Morgan and Mally Edwards the date and time. They would hold off the reception, being planned by Pat's family at The Blarney in the Bronx. The party would take place the following Sunday evening, in order for Pat's friends from the *Centipede* cast to join the celebration. Alan Byrne's only daughter Patricia would have only the best for her reception! Byrne was sparing no expense hiring

Patrick McNally, an old pal to cater the affair. McNally was a successful restaurant owner and caterer, whose business had thrived for decades in the Bronx. The Irish liked to party and Patrick's business was never at a standstill for all the anniversaries, birthdays, weddings and other events he provided the families in his community. His large staff was kept busy and employed 365 days a year. Alan brought every one of his close business pals on board, including George Duffy, the neighborhood florist and his second cousin. Frank Flynn, a noted printer in the Bronx, offered to take care of invitations, with Alan and Maureen's approval. Included on the invitation was Pat's request for donations to the Actor's Fund, in lieu of gifts. Blaine was touched by her suggestion, feeling it appropriate. Alan's closest neighbor, photographer Jack O'Reilly, offered to lend his photography to the proceedings. Pat and Blaine had only to work out details of their honeymoon in Paris.

For the ceremony Pat would wear a tea length crème velveteen suit with modest neckline and soft pearl accents. Hair up in a chignon under a small pillbox hat and veil would complete her look. Pat found a soft wool sheath and matching bolero jacket in a delicate shade of pink for Mally. Her hair had grown beyond her shoulders and a French twist would be flattering and easily put in a matching cloche, a fun style for her. Blaine chose a double-breasted black silk suit with white shirt and cufflinks to match Pat's pearl accents. His conservative tie was gray silk with a matching pocket handkerchief. Best man, Greg Morgan was advised of their color scheme, knowing he would be dressed impeccably. Pat selected her favorite; red sweetheart roses in a nosegay arrangement. Mally would carry a similar arrangement with pink roses. The Edwards, Greg, Alan and Maureen, and Blaine's two brothers, Wallace and Stuart, were the only witnesses. Other family members would be introduced at the reception on Sunday, including the entire Byrne clan. Blaine's sister and French-born brother-in-law, long-time Paris residents, were on holiday in Asia and unable to attend. The vows would take place at 10:00 on Friday morning, February 14th, the reception following on Sunday, the 16th from 4 to 8. All was in readiness for the joining of two incredible people.

As Valentines' Day arrived the wedding party gathered at New York City Hall. Pat and Blaine looked stunning, as though they'd stepped from the pages *Harper's Bazaar*. Mally was beautiful in pink, escorted by Griff, who always dressed well on special occasions, a contrast to his work clothes backstage. He wore a dark navy suit of worsted wool. Though he would not be participating in the ceremony, he wore matching accessories to coordinate with his wife.

The group was shown to Mayor Lindsay's outer reception room and gathered, waiting for proceedings to begin. Blaine introduced his two brothers, Wallace and Stuart. They were friendly and unpretentious, considering their lifestyle and formidable wealth. Greg Morgan arrived and immediately greeted everyone with enthusiasm. The man, handsome and fit for his fifty plus years was impressive, impeccably dressed in grey Harris Tweed. He was given a red rose boutonniere for his lapel to match one worn by Blaine. The Byrnes embraced the bride and groom and were delighted to meet Griff and Mally, face-to-face at last. Well aware of Pat's strong friendship with Mally, they were happy to meet Griff, who always looked out for their daughter's interest. Pat was living at home in the Bronx during the first year run of *Centipede*. Having to commute back and forth between shows on matinee days proved time-consuming and tedious. The Edward's open invitation to Pat anytime was appreciated, whether to nap or spend the night.

Promptly at 10:00, Lindsay's assistant appeared and welcomed them. "If you will follow me, please, the mayor will see you now." The group followed her into an impressive room; dark walnut-paneled walls, conservative drapes in forest green velvet, a working fireplace, mammoth marble top desk and over-stuffed furniture, tastefully upholstered in leather. At the center of the room John Lindsay stood tall, conservatively dressed and cordial as he greeted each one. "Ladies and gentlemen, Mayor Lindsay," the woman announced. Without the expected formality of a public official, Lindsay approached. "Blaine, please introduce me to your lovely bride," he enthused, as he shook hands. "John, I'd like you to meet Patricia, Patricia this is Mayor Lindsay." "John, please!" "How do you do," she said, extending her hand. "And these are my parents, Alan and Maureen Byrne." Lindsay smiled, extending his hand to both. Pat turned her attention toward the Edwards. "May I introduce my best friend and husband, Mally and Griff Edwards?" "Of course, please!" Introductions continued until at last, Blaine introduced Greg. "Ah, Gregory Morgan, Blaine has spoken so highly of you over the years, welcome!" "The pleasure is mine, Mr. Mayor. It's an honor to be here." "John, please," he said, pleasantly.

Without further delay, Lindsay got to the business at hand. "Shall we begin? Blaine and Patricia please step forward. Mr. Morgan and Mrs. Edwards, kindly stand on either side of the bride and groom." Greg and Mally took their places. Stuart and Wallace Courtman stood to the side as did the Byrnes. "Let us begin. Dear friends, we gather today to witness the joining of this lovely couple in matrimony. Blaine, I have known you and your family a number of years. I hold you with great affection and respect. It is my pleasure to marry you and your lovely Patricia. Patricia, Blaine has shared with me his unconditional love and total commitment to you. Some might refer to you two as a match made in heaven. I prefer to think of this as perfect timing in bringing two exceptional people together to share a lifetime on earth." "Blaine, please take your bride's hand and repeat after me." At that moment, Pat handed her flowers to Mally. "I Blaine, take you, Patricia for my lawfully wedded wife. To have and to hold in good times and bad, in sickness and health, to cherish, love and protect for the rest of my life." Blaine repeated Lindsay's words to perfection, his gaze never leaving Pat. Lindsay turned to Pat. "Patricia, please repeat after me. "I, Patricia, take you, Blaine for my lawfully wedded husband. To have and to hold in good times and bad, in sickness and health, to cherish, love and protect for the rest of my life." Pat hardly got through it, her voice faltering with emotion as she repeated the words. "May I have the rings, please?" Greg stepped in and handed them to Lindsay. The mayor gave one to Blaine and the other to Patricia. "Blaine?" "With this ring, I thee wed." As he spoke, he slipped the ring on Pat's finger. "Patricia?" "With this ring, I thee wed," said Pat, gently sliding the ring on Blaine. Tears welled as they looked into each other's eyes. One heard soft sobs coming from Maureen, as Alan slipped an arm around his wife. Mally reached up and brushed a tear away at that moment. "Now by the power vested in me by the State of New York, I now pronounce you man and wife. Blaine, you may kiss your beautiful wife." Slowly as if to savor the moment forever, Blaine lifted the small veil covering Pat's face. The kiss was gentle and prolonged. Lindsay added, cheerfully, "Congratulations! Ladies and gentleman, may I present Mr. and Mrs. Blaine Courtman!"

Applause broke out as they turned to their guests. Mally was the first to hug Pat, then Blaine. "You're getting the very best woman in the world, you know!" "How well I do," he responded, kissing her cheek. Griff added his congratulations. Greg was next. "Congratulations, my friend," giving him an uncharacteristic embrace. "Thank you for being here, Greg. It means so much to us!" Stuart and Wallace stepped in, hugging their brother and new sister-in-law. The Byrnes stood quietly by, waiting for their moment. At last, Alan reached for his daughter, embracing her with all the love he held. "My dearest child, I am so happy for you and Blaine. May your years together be as gentle and loving as they've been for your mother and me." Maureen took hold of Pat and held her firmly, weeping. For a few moments there were no words, only tears. When at last she could speak, she took Pat's face in her hands. "Oh Patricia, I love you so! I pray you and Blaine will always be as happy as you are at this moment!" "Thanks, Ma. I love you too!" Greg and Mally signed the marriage certificate. Blaine had arranged luncheon for the wedding party at the St. Moritz in a private suite, hiring an extra limo to accommodate their group. Before departing, he took Lindsay aside. "Thank you, John. This is so special to have you marry us." "It's my pleasure and my gift to you both, Blaine." "That's very generous of you, John. I'm deeply grateful!" "You're welcome! Have a wonderful day and life." They shook hands. When everyone had gathered together the group departed to celebrate.

Late Sunday afternoon, Blaine's driver, Keith Noonan drove the newly-weds to the Bronx and the Blarney, where a reception was about to take place. Pat was dressed in a simple, form-fitting dress of wool jersey in Burgundy with a gathered t-neckline and long sleeves. A single strand of pearls and matching pearl posts were her chosen accessories. Blaine had on dress slacks, sports coat and open collared shirt without a tie. The couple entered the bar, decorated for a holiday. The family scurried about, taking care of last minute details, as they approached. "Ah, my girl and our new son welcome," shouted Alan, rushing to them. Hugging Pat and embracing Blaine, he beamed, as he took their coats. "You look beautiful, my girl and what a handsome lad you've chosen!" Just then, Maureen spotted them. "Saints preserve us, the newlyweds are here at last! You two look wonderful!" "Thanks, Mrs. Byrne," said

Blaine, giving her a kiss on the cheek. "Now just a minute my boy, you must drop the formality immediately and call me Maureen to be a permanent fixture in this clan," she said, with a mock serious tone. "Very well, Maureen!"

Pat's twin, Patrick and her two older brothers Mickey and Sean joined the group. Introductions were offered, handshaking and compliments were exchanged, as guests began to arrive. Greg Morgan, Wallace and Stuart Courtman and the Edwards were the first to join in the festivity. Mally and Griff hugged Pat with enthusiasm and greeted Blaine cordially. Jonas and Phillipe followed them in along with Joe Kaplan, Leonard Maggli, Gary Hanson and his partner, Steve Jackson. Well wishes flowed as coats were taken and drinks offered. "This is the absolute best, Irish," Jonas exclaimed, hugging Pat with such fervor he practically knocked the wind out of her. Phillipe waited his turn, taking her hand, kissing it and dipping her in an embrace, his greeting French and fervent. "Bon chance mon chere et fete du jour!" "Merci, Mon Amie," Pat returned followed by, "Je t'aime aussi!" They held the embrace until Jonas pulled Phillipe away. "You bagged your man, Madame! You can't have mine!" "Pardon, Monsieur," said Pat, giggling. The Blarney continued to fill.

At one end of the room a small group of local musicians began setting up; accordions, bass, drums and fiddle. The Byrne's owned an old upright piano that stood in one corner, newly tuned. In minutes, Irish music filled the air, mixed with a cacophony of chatter and laughter. Guests were offered drinks and food. As the first hour passed, *Centipede* cast members joined the throng, including Chad Chapman, Jeff and Nora Jenkins. Others included Catherine Andrews and Danny Bartlett, Julie Jensen and her new man, Nicholas Pappas and a host of old-timers; Kathy Olson and her partner, Sonja Berger, Joe Pinto and his old friend and occasional lover, Jordan Hendrix. The rest of original cast, including Liz Gunther, Cynthia Charles, Fran Fairchild, Jim Sorenson and a former cast mate, Jerry Thompson stopped in.

Delicious food and abundant drinks were offered. The band played with such gusto and zest, that even the non-dancers in the room couldn't resist. Blaine and Pat held court, greeting friends and associates as the party continued. Alan's three brothers, wives, nieces and nephews were in attendance. Pat had moved away from home and lifestyle in the past year, but now, having the entire Byrne clan there completed the day. Blaine was the object of curiosity, standing in the midst of the group, his personality and presence obvious. At the half-way point, Alan called everyone's attention, proposing a toast. "Please everyone, raise your glasses and join me!" As the throng followed, the room fell silent. "To our beautiful girl and her new husband: "May the blessing of light be with you always, light without and light within. May the sun shine upon you and warm your heart until it glows like a great fire so that others may feel the warmth of your love for one another." Applause followed as Alan's toast concluded, tears of joy in evidence as guests sipped en masse. Following the toast, the music drew some of the gypsies to the dance floor to begin a melodious jig. Stomping and clapping while others cheered and applauded from the sidelines, Jonas and Phillipe reached for Pat and pulled her to the center of the circle. The spirit of the moment was all-consuming! The new Mrs. Courtman kicked off her heels and joined her boys! Others moved to the sidelines in a wave, as the incredible three began to dance. Their footwork was a marvel to see, captivating and flawless! The sheer spontaneity and spirit of the moment brought a roar from guests crowding around! As the music grew faster and faster, the three never missed a beat! They headed toward a wild finish, the tempo growing impossibly fast, but on the last note they stopped on a dime, a grand pose following. The throng went wild, as the three hugged and laughed, applause deafen-ing. Blaine made his way through the crowd, handing his wife a bar towel. Kissing gently, they were oblivious to all. As Pat blotted moisture off, he moved closer. "Are you sure you can stop dancing, my beauti-ful bride? You don't have to give this up you know," he whispered. Pat smiled, knowing her career decision was for keeps and so was he.

The party wound down about eight PM. Pat and Blaine chatted cordially, thanking everyone as they approached. Greg stopped and hugged them both. "I know you have connections in Paris, Blaine. Is your brother-in-law arranging your lodging?" "Pierre and Yvonne are on extended holiday at the moment." "Where were you thinking?" "I was leaning toward the Ritz, but Patricia would prefer a little roman-tic hideaway down a side street!" "Absolutely," said Pat. "Well, I would like you to stay at Hotel de Villier! Please allow me to share in your joy by offering you that "little romantic hideaway down a side street!"

"Really Greg, I can't let you do that!" "Why the hell not? I own the place!" "I didn't know you had property in Paris." "I invested in a small hotel in the 17th district a few years ago. It seemed like a good move at the time and business has been steady year round. I want you to have a week on me. Consider it my wedding gift." "I don't know what to say, Greg." "You are so kind," said Pat, fighting tears. "Come, come, my dear girl. You have made my best friend very happy. It's the least I can do!" "Thanks, Greg. This is quite unexpected." "Well, it fits the request of your bride. The setting is outrageously romantic, allowing you to stay in bed all day undisturbed." They laughed as Greg put on his coat. "Well you two, let's talk in a few days. I will make all the arrangements when I know your exact dates." "Thanks, Greg. Thanks for everything," said Blaine hugging him. "You're a lucky man," he added, giving Pat a gentle kiss on the cheek. "Goodbye for now, my friends.

At the end of the crowd's departure, Mally and Griff stopped to say goodnight. "What are your immediate plans now that you aren't doing eight shows a week?" "Well, first we'll be working on details of our honeymoon." "Where are you going?" "I've always wanted to go to Paris in April!" "That's incredible! How long will you be away?" "We are thinking of at least a week, said Blaine." "It's an absolutely wonderful idea." "Pat and I are discussing what direction she wants to go next," added Blaine. "Really? Are you giving up performing, Pat?" "I want to move in a new direction within the business, Griff." "When you return, let's have dinner, our place." "We'd love that. Thanks, you two," said Pat, embracing them. Blaine and Griff shook hands before they headed out.

With the Blarney now cleared of guests, the immediate family sat down for a night cap. Exhausted, but obviously thrilled, Pat raised her glass to Alan and Maureen. "Dad and Mom, thank you for the beautiful party, but most of all, for being the best parents in the world," her voice catching. "May I add my gratitude for your support and raising such a special woman, my beautiful wife!" Glasses clinked, accompanied by the Byrne brothers whistling. "Faith and Begorra, another male in the Byrne clan," laughed Alan. "The more the merrier," Maureen chuckled, thinking of her three boys and Alan's three brothers. "Irish rule," shouted Patrick. "And you are?" Pat loved to tease her twin. Merriment continued as two more rounds were enjoyed. It was well past midnight when Keith pulled up to the Blarney. Entering he found Blaine and Pat ready to depart. A round of hugs later and the newlyweds left. A joyful beginning was about to launch an exceptional partnership. With the wedding and reception over, Mr. and Mrs. Blaine Courtman determined it was high time to spend the next weeks relaxing and doing whatever pleased them, including their anticipated honeymoon in Paris, mid April.

Chapter 28

New Horizons

All business appointments were on hold for a few weeks, Blaine delegating projects to his brothers Stuart and Wallace. Wallace would handle U.S. business, while Stuart scheduled meetings in the U.K. and Europe. Courtman Enterprises was on the verge of branching out. For months, the brothers worked to establish contacts. Their search began with a request of the U.S. Department of Commerce to identify potential suppliers. Blaine was hoping to find new styles of shoes and expand product offerings for the American market and establishing European partnerships.

In the meantime, Mrs. Courtman needed some serious spoilage. For the first week, following their wedding weekend, Pat decompressed from her former life of working dancer. A day at Elizabeth Arden was high priority at the insistence of her husband. She was booked for the works; sauna, body peeling, facial, full body massage, hair styling and cut, manicure and pedicure. Keith delivered her to the Arden salon on Fifth Avenue. Pat's eyes popped as she walked into a different world. The receptionist did everything but bow and scrape. "Ah, Mrs. Courtman, welcome to Elizabeth Arden. Please make yourself at home!" Gesturing to another, smartly dressed assistant, Pat's coat was taken. Shown to one of several luxurious chairs in the reception area, Marietta, the suave receptionist, continued. "An Arden associate will be with you momentarily. In the meantime would you care for Cappuccino or perhaps a Pellegrino?" "A Cappuccino sounds delightful, thank you!" Marietta waved to her lackey, Cecile. "Please bring Mrs. Courtman a Cappuccino!" Turning to Pat, she smiled. "Would you care for Biscotti or Scone? Our selection features plain or Almond Biscotti, Blueberry-Lemon, Raspberry-White Chocolate, or Ginger-Macadamia scones." 'God, so many choices,' she marveled. "I'd love the Raspberry-White Chocolate, please." "Certainly, Mrs. Courtman," she soothed, shooing Cecile away.

Pat sat, observing the scene, marveling how the other half spends free time. Following the refreshments offered, Marietta picked up the intercom. "Francine, please report to the reception room." In moments, an attractive young woman appeared in a pink smock. "Please follow me, Madame." Pat rose, stifling an impending giggle. Barely able to stay composed, she thanked Marietta and followed. "I'm Francine, your hostess today." "Please call me Pat." She was led through a door to a darkened room and asked to remove her clothes. "You may put on this robe. What shoe size, please?" "I wear an 8 narrow." Francine went to a cabinet and fished around for a moment. Handing Pat a pair of terry cloth slippers, she indicated they were to be worn at all times in the salon. "You will be given a sauna, followed by a facial and body mask peel." "A what?" "Celeste will be putting an Arden product on you. When it dries you will feel a slight pulling. It revitalizes your complexion and tightens your pores. Once she removes it you will receive a full body massage. Following a shower, you will dress and follow me to our top stylist, Richard. He will style and cut your hair to your specifications." Pat was trying to take Francine's narrative in, the routine so foreign to her. "Shall we begin?" "Yes, by all means!"

The sauna was just the thing for her tired muscles. The facial and body mask was a new experience and all the while she marveled what women go through to look perfect. Following the peel, she was taken to a small room where the essence of eucalyptus, low lighting and soft music set a relaxing scene. Left alone, a large Brunhilda woman entered and instructed Pat to remove her robe and lay face-up on the table. "Do you wish to be covered?" "By all means, please." "You have a choice of oil; almond, lavender or rose." "Do you have unscented? I'm not a fan of fragrance." The overly-ample masseuse, Olga, frowned. "Yes, I may have. One moment." When she returned, she asked the type of pressure Pat preferred. "I like to feel the massage," said Pat, wondering what to expect. Olga began her work, big fat hands pressing into Pat with intuitive skill. Her work was deep, thorough, causing a sigh. "You like Olga's work, yes?" "Yes," said Pat, barely audible, slurring her words. "You are very tight! What have you been doing?" "I'm a dancer, newly retired!" "It would be good idea to come see Olga more often!" "Am I that bad?" "You need lots of deep tissue work. I can accommodate you." "You're very good! Where are you from, Olga?" "I am from Minsk, in Soviet Union. Do you know Minsk?" "No, I'm afraid not," confessed Pat. "Is all right, I think you not like." "Why do you say that?" "People poor, not like here. I see rich all day long. There's no appreciation or awareness in America. I come from a family of 12, my parents were farmers. They sent me here to live with relatives when I was fifteen. I had no English." "You speak very well." "I went to American school and then went to work to send money home." Following the massage, she smiled, warmly. "Do come back and see me again, Mrs. Courtman." "Please call me Pat and I yes, I will." "The shower is in there," she said, pointing to the next room. "Good day."

The shower felt heaven-sent as Pat washed the oil from her skin. Reaching for an Arden brand shampoo, she worked it through her hair creating lather, a challenge given how relaxed she was. As she washed the long strands, her arms resisted. 'Long hair is old news, Irish. You could use a change!' Drying off, she found her street clothes neatly laid out. There was a knock on the door. "Mrs. Courtman, are you ready?" "I will be in a minute, Francine." "Very good, I will be nearby." As Pat dressed she thought, 'Stylist? In my old neighborhood, it's a barber.' She was escorted to Arden's top stylist. "He's a first cousin of Kenneth, imagine," purred Francine. "Who's Kenneth?" A shocked look crossed her face. "Why Kenneth is one of the top hair designers in the world, let alone New York. He's every bit as fabulous as Vidal Sassoon!" The news was lost on Pat, who was approached by a gorgeous fellow. Lean, dark and terribly sexy, he reminded her of Phillipe. She guessed he was one of the boys. Greeting her with enthusiasm, he was flamboyant, but sincere. "Good afternoon, I'm Richard!" "I'm Pat," she said, feeling immediately at home. "Please sit and enjoy, I'm here for you."

Running his hands through her long red tresses, he sighed. "You have magnificent hair and lots of it! What are we doing today?" "I'm a dancer and have worn my hair long all my life. I just got married and I'd like to surprise my husband. Frankly, I'm ready for a major change!" "How major, my sweet?" "Drastic comes to mind," giggled Pat. "Well girl, your features, color and bone structure cries for chin length!" "No, really?" "Absolutely, my darling, you can wear it. You're stunning!" "But what if I want to wear it up sometimes?" "I will cut it a perfect length so you have versatility at your fingertips! How long has it been since your last cut? Your hair is in very good condition." "Well thank you, maybe a year. I had 8 inches off!" "Where have you been, my darling?" "On a Broadway stage, in a chignon," she chuckled. "Mercy, a gypsy in my chair! How thrilling! What show, may I ask?" "Of course you may, *Centipede*." "For real?" "Yes, I was the lead dancer." "This is too much! My boyfriend and I saw *Centipede* this past year. We could only get standing room, but it was worth every cent! That director's work is to die for!" 'Not for this kid,' thought Pat with humor. "Are you still in it?" "No, I retired last weekend." "Sadie, Sadie, married lady, eh?" "Yes and happily so." "Well, he must be some kind of catch for you to abandon Broadway!" "Richard, you have no idea!" "Well, onward, let's do it!"

The cut took a full hour. Pat, watched, mesmerized with Richard's work. He was every bit as brilliant with hair as Owen with staging. Hair fell to either side, piling in heaps at the foot of the chair. When at last Richard finished, he handed her a mirror. "Darling, check the back, see if it's a good length," he instructed, turning the chair. "This will take some getting used to, but I absolutely love it!" "Let me blow dry the rest and you'll be good to go!" Putting the finishing touches on her, he had her take one more look. "Blaine is going to faint!" "Is Blaine the lucky one?" "Yes, the best thing that's ever happened to me!" "What a lucky lady and what a beautiful one," he cooed, running his hands through her shortened hair. "I think he'll love it. He'll still have something to run his hands through during sex!" "Monsieur, you are bold," laughed Pat. "True, the boldest and most brazen queen you'll ever meet! Please, let me know how your husband likes it!" "Richard, I'll be seeing you again, I promise. And thank you," she whispered, kissing his cheek. "Jeez, you could make me go straight," he giggled. "Bye!"

Next, Francine escorted Pat to the nail specialist. "Barbara, this is Mrs. Courtman. She is to receive the deluxe manicure-pedicure." "Of course, please have a seat there, next to the large foot tub." Pat removed her slippers, rolled up her slacks and settled, gingerly slipping her feet into the warm, bubbly froth. "What type of manicure do you prefer?" "I like my nails short and buffed with clear polish." "Very good! And what about your feet, toes?" "My feet are heavily calloused from the work I do. So you have your work cut out for you. I like my toenails short, but a fun color would be nice!" "I'm having you soak your feet for a few minutes. May I bring you something to read?" "Yes, thank you!" Barbara brought over a rack of current magazines. "Here's a selection. Enjoy! I'll be back in soon."

Pat thumbed through the selection. Choosing a current copy of *Modern Screen,* she began paging through show biz gossip. Suddenly, her eyes spotted a familiar face, a grin coming at her! 'Jesus, I don't believe this!' Clearly, it was Owen standing next to a Hollywood suit! The caption read: *Owen Matthews, noted Broadway Director-Choreographer with Vice President, of project development, Shel Friedman, Universal Pictures, sealing the deal for Matthews' upcoming film, Broadway Business.* 'Atta boy, work the room,' thought Pat. Barbara returned to begin work on her. She set the magazine aside and closed her eyes. Pushing Owen out of her mind was easier now. 'You're not ruining this treat for me, asshole!'

The foot treatment was delightful. Hands and feet as fresh as her new hairdo, she thanked Barbara and headed to the reception area. Mrs. Courtman, you look stunning!" "Thank you, so much! I feel like a new woman," Pat chortled, stopping at the desk. "Very becoming," said, Marietta. "Thank you so much for coming. Mr. Courtman has taken care of your spa visit. I believe your car is waiting." "Thank you for everything," said Pat, her enthusiasm impossible to miss. Walking out of Arden, she spotted Keith waiting at the curb. "Mrs. Courtman?" "Yes, Keith. It's me! If you don't mind, I feel like walking to the Plaza. It's such a lovely day in New York!" "Very good, Madame. I will inform Mr. Courtman." The two parted as Pat, a spring in her step, practically danced up Fifth Avenue.

Blaine was sipping a Martini, buried in a copy of *The Economist* when Pat walked in. Looking up he gasped at the new woman crossing the room. "My God, Patricia, what have you done?" Not the reaction Pat imagined, tears began to well. "Don't you like it?" He rose slowly, taking her in his arms. Choking back emotion she waited until a moment later, his soothing voice brought reassurance. "Beautiful girl, I absolutely love it!" Pat blinked. "Do you mean it?" "My darling Patricia, have I ever not meant what I say?" "Well, no, but you looked so shocked when I walked in!" "The shock is absolute delight! You look stunning! He kissed her deeply, playfully running his hands through her new hair. "This still works for me," he whispered, already turned on. "I need to make love to you! But first, let's have a drink while you tell me about your day. I have a lovely Vouvray chilled and waiting just for you. Come." They sat down in front of a crackling fire. Blaine uncorked the wine and poured Pat a glass. After touching glasses they sipped, Blaine glued to his bride. Pat snuggled next to him. Reaching up she stroked his cheek. He felt he would melt. "Blaine, Arden is such a wonderful place. Everyone was so kind and accommodating. It was truly a special treat!" "Well my beauty, you may visit anytime you wish. The Courtman's have had an account there for years. My mother and sister were regulars." "Yvonne?" "Yes, from puberty she insisted on being a princess. She and my mother were like bookends. You never saw one without the other. They especially enjoyed their joint trips to Elizabeth Arden Red Door!" "Blaine, you've never spoken of your mother." "I don't like to talk about my family." "How come?" "Both of my parents are gone. They were soul mates, inseparable. We kids grew up in a Robert Young fantasy." "What do you mean?" "Did you ever watch the TV show *Father Knows Best?* "Sorry to say I never did." "Never, why not?" "We had TV, but weren't allowed to watch during the week. There was school, homework and helping my dad with chores at the Blarney. For me, any free time was spent in a dance studio. The one exception was live variety TV shows on the weekend, provided my chores were done. My favorites were *Colgate Comedy Hour, Your Show of Shows* and *Hit Parade.*" Blaine continued.

"The Robert Young reference applies to the life my parents created and insisted on; ideal, perfect and tidy! They lived by the highest standard possible and there was no place for less. When my mother had a catastrophic stroke everything changed. She was reduced to a state of total dependency, practically vegetative. My father was heartbroken. She was the center of his world. As she became more infirm and unable to survive without machines hooked into her, my father began drinking heavily. Then it was other women and drugs. My brothers Wallace and Stuart chipped in and helped me keep the company running. The first few years were difficult. My sister Yvonne went to pieces and was institutionalized for a couple of years. Mother passed away leaving my father inconsolable. One night, after drinking heavily, he got into his Mercedes completely wasted and drove off a bridge. It took divers three days to recover his body. The unfortunate part was he wasn't alone. His mistress was with him at the time and died with him. The family legal counsel managed to contain the potential damage to Courtman Enterprises. Eventually Yvonne recovered and left the country to find a new life, with the help of permanent antidepressants. I was named CEO of the company with Wallace as VP and Stuart, Treasurer. When all was said and done, we siblings were left to glue the pieces back together. The father and mother who knew best were gone." Pat reached for Blaine and hugged him close. "I'm so sorry for your loss. Is there anything I can do?" "My beautiful girl, just hold me." And hold him she did until the last flicker of embers died.

The national tour of *Centipede* was cast and rehearsals underway. Mally was doubling as lead in the Broadway Company and would take that position on tour. That meant double days of rehearsals and performances, rigorous, considering the demanding choreography. Owen's work raised the bar higher than any other director in New York. He hired only the best dancers to achieve his inspiration. At the moment, Joe Pinto was partnering Mally until he joined the road company. Multitasking on tour would require him to work as ensemble dancer, dance captain and assistant stage manager. He looked forward to wearing all three hats, pleased that management had such faith in him. Nora and Jeff were psyched to be going on tour again, having grown fond of traveling together. Chad Chapman had taken a few weeks off and was now raring to get started. All other members of the Tokyo company were on board and grateful for continued employment, with the exception of Neely Sorenson's partner, Andy Wendt. In the interim he had auditioned for another Broadway show, was cast and moved on. Joe Pinto would now partner Neely. Jonas and Phillipe would remount and review the entire show, fine tuning it as they had done in Tokyo. There would be little to do in terms of teaching staging, as everyone involved were already veterans. The partners were back on Broadway together.

Griff was busy, finalizing details for the six-month tour. It would be old home week in several locations for he knew the circuit well and the best stagehands for hire from previous tours. His base crew included his new ASM, Joe Pinto. He hired old-timers Ed Franklin and Fred Duncan, his two transit drivers. His key grip, Larry Armstrong had worked six tours alongside him. Chief electrician, Harry Diller came highly recommended by Joe Kaplan. Though Griff had not worked with Diller previously, the man was regarded by many as the best in New York. Griff's team took any opportunity to work with him. Known for great working relationships, he favored those with commitment and strong work ethics. Skill was a prerequisite. As March 26th grew near, Kaplan called a meeting to be updated before the Cleveland opening, just a week away. Gathering in the producer's conference room, a light breakfast was offered.

"Good morning, gentleman. Thanks for coming in, I thought it time to finalize details. "Janice, will Owen be joining us?" "He will be in shortly. He leaves tomorrow for L.A. and had errands to attend to." "How long will he be gone?" "I believe he said a week this time; Universal wants to review the project schedule with him. "Yes, I understand they were waiting on Vincent Lehrman's agreement to license the rights of *Bravo Business* to Universal Pictures. His representative is taking care of the contract. Since Vinny's retirement, he has spent most of his time abroad. Talk about the good life!" The intercom sounded abruptly. "Yes, Phyllis?" "Mr. Kaplan, Mr. Matthews is here." "Please show him back, Phyllis." "Yes sir!" Kaplan smiled. "Phyllis is training to replace Janice during her maternity leave. She's bright-eyed and eager. We like that around here!" Owen walked in.

"Good morning, Owen! We were about to begin. Please help yourself to coffee and Danish." "Coffee sounds good. Do you have my ashtray handy?" "Of course! Janice, would you mind getting it for Owen? It's in the cabinet over there." "Certainly, sir," she said, with a tone of annoyance. Cigarette smoke was nauseating during her pregnancy. Owen pulled out a pack, shook out a smoke and lit up, inhaling deeply. The air around him turned blue as Kaplan spoke. "Griff, why don't you start?"

"Certainly, Joe. Everything is in place. Dwight Procter, our company manager, has all hotels and rates worked out for each city. Our venues are ready and dates are firm. My base crew is set. Sandy Irvin is musical director and conductor. He's hungry for another road stint and after a brief hiatus, is joining us. He's picked his four; associate conductor and pianist, Jimmy Swanks, Jack Henry, drummer, Teddy Lewis, string bassist and Ben Phillips, trombonist. This group traveled with us on *Bravo Business*. They are among the finest around." "Well, Sandy certainly has his standards and only the best may apply." They all chuckled. "As always we'll pick locals to fill in both on running crew and in the pit, standard stuff." "That's why we pay you the big bucks, Griff. You're a marvel!" "Thanks Joe, I certainly appreciate your trust." Joe shifted gears. "I'd like to hear from our remount guys. Jonas anything to add?" "The company is seamless and every bit as sharp as they were in Tokyo. I'm confident they will be tops on tour." "Great!" "Owen?" "That's why I only work with the best. Jonas, you and Phillipe have done me proud. Joe, when I dropped by rehearsal the other day, the work was as tight as the day we opened on Broadway. I think we best keep these two around indefinitely!" "Absolutely, boss, we're in," laughed Jonas.

"Are travel arrangements in place, Griff?" "Yes, Joe, we depart on March 26th for Cleveland, opening March 29. Our transit drivers will be leaving ahead of us, giving them time to arrive and unload. We'll need a couple of days to set up for tech and dress runs. The cast has already selected their first accommodations. The Hanna is downtown and accessible to all three choices. "Excellent!" "Is there anything else we need to discuss or does this cover it?" Owen stepped in.

"I want to thank all of you for being on top of this. I'm currently in the throes of film details. As near as I can estimate, auditions will begin June 1st for the ensemble. Following, we'll look for our leads, seen through agents only. Those strongly considered will be given screen tests. Filming begins late August, date to be determined by the suits! The backers are firm and contracts have been drawn up. There is a final meeting in early May to determine any overlooked or last minute details. Vinny Lehrman has released the rights to Universal and is on board in an advisory capacity only." "It sounds like things are moving along, Owen." "Yes, and Hollywood is another world, Joe. It's going to take some getting used to. It's all about money, clout and who's the best lay!" 'He's got the lay part covered,' thought Janice, smiling through her shorthand. The meeting broke up around noon.

Chapter 29

Certain Plans

Pat and Blaine were enjoying every moment together catching up. Such luxury following his constant business travel over the past months and her eight shows a week! They spent their days walking the length and breadth of Manhattan, shopping, taking the Circle Line like regular tourists. Evenings were active; going to the latest films, attending theatre, dining and dancing at some of New York's hot spots. Disco had arrived on the scene and clubs were popping up all over town. One in particular was considered the best. Arthur at 154 East 54th Street was owned by Sybil Burton. Her highly publicized divorce and hefty million dollar settlement from Richard Burton made it possible to open the club with the help of investors including Julie Andrews, Roddy McDowell, Leonard Bernstein, Stephen Sondheim and many other celebrities. It quickly turned into a gold mine.

Arthur Discotheque was top notch, the ultimate in trendy and constantly pulling in the rich and famous. TV and nightclub entertainer Steve Lawrence often taped his variety show from there, bringing in the crème of show biz pals to share the stage; Sammy Davis Jr., Liza Minnelli and the chairman of the board himself, Frank Sinatra often showed up to wow patrons. It was rumored that Andy Warhol, Jackie Kennedy, Gore Vidal, Truman Capote, Rudolf Nureyev and Tennessee

Williams were regulars. Night after night crowds of celebrity watchers stood outside, in all weather conditions, hoping to catch a glimpse of their favorites.

Blaine and Pat wanted to check out Arthur based on all the hype. Arriving by limo, they were admitted through a private entrance and seated at a VIP table. On the dance floor couples, in haute couture, moved to the beat provided by the club's band. Pat had heard about a new form of dance, the Frug. Looking improvised, the movements were funky, studied and ultra unique. Movement styles such as the Monkey, Watusi, Bunny Slope, Latin Hustle and Groovy One-Two were initiated and performed. Competition was keen, as couples tried to out-dance others on the floor. To Pat's trained eye the movements were unlike any she had seen or attempted. After ordering their drinks, they continued to watch with fascination. "Beautiful girl, do you want to give this a whirl?" "Are you serious, Blaine?" "Absolutely, let's go!" Without pause he stood, leading her through the gyrating throng. Finding a safe pocket near the stage, they tried to copy a couple next to them. Blaine's acumen astounded his bride, as he jived, gyrated, turned, wriggled and shouted to the beat! Pat could hardly keep up with her husband's spontaneity and enthusiasm! Her training kept her contained, disciplined and too precise to get down and groovy. Instead she followed, trying to ape his improvisation, amazed at his pleasure dancing disco. He let go, releasing months of work-related decisions and issues. Tonight, his free spirit was unrestrained.

As the music stopped, Pat grabbed and steered him off the dance floor, breathless and soaked! As they settled at the table, she pulled Blaine's pocket hanky out and dabbed his face. "You were sensational, absolutely amazing," she shouted over the noise. "I didn't know you could dance like that!" "You never asked," said Blaine trying to catch his breath. "Patricia, let's finish our drinks and head to Christos off Madison for a quiet dinner." "Sounds lovely! This place is too noisy for these ears." "Agreed!" Finishing, Blaine paid the tab and they left quickly. Keith was parked nearby and spotted them in the rearview mirror. Without hesitation, he stepped out and opened the back door. "I'm so ready for some quiet," said Pat, getting in. Blaine settled close to her. Nuzzling her he whispered softly, "And I'm so ready for you later, Mrs. Courtman. His kiss was deep, promising, as the car pulled away.

The flight from New York's JFK took four and a half hours. Owen's plane landed at LAX International on schedule. He had slept most of the way, having read *Variety* cover to cover. He'd polished off four scotches and scrutinized the first class stewardesses, none of which were appealing. He admittedly was spoiled by theatre women; beautiful, fit, choices of interest. Descending the mobile staircase, he made his way across the tarmac to the terminal.

Luggage in hand, he looked for a cab. Suddenly he spotted a knockout holding a sign reading, *Mr. Owens Matthews*. Approaching, he liked what he saw. "Hi, I'm Owen Matthews." "Oh, Mr. Matthews, welcome to L.A. I'm Trisha Connolly, Mr. Friedman's assistant. He asked me to meet and see you to the hotel." "Well, this is unexpected," he said, looking her over. "Please follow me," she said, walking toward the exit. "Did Mr. Friedman tell you you'll be staying at the Beverly Wilshire? The ride will take a few minutes." "Yes, I was headed there when I spotted you. I must say, you're a lovely surprise." She was all business. "Please, the car is waiting," she said, pointing to the stretch limo nearby. "Mr. Matthews, this is Mack Kennedy, your driver." "Hello, Sir." "Hi Mack, please call me Owen." "Yes Sir." They got in the back and Mack closed the door. A faint trace of lavender was evident in her hair. Her long, shapely legs were noticeable as her skirt hitched up slightly. Mack pulled into traffic. 'A nice welcome,' thought Owen, fixed on Trish. When they were well on the way, Owen started a conversation.

"What happened to Karen Eliot, Mr. Friedman's personal assistant?" "Miss Eliot resigned. She's expecting a baby in September! She and her husband are ecstatic!" 'That was quick,' mused Owen, still slightly bent by Eliot's surprise marriage. Previously, she had been an excellent distraction for him while in town and one of his better lays. "Good for them," he mumbled, with forced sincerity. In a few minutes, they were in front of the Beverly Wilshire. Mack opened the door helping Trisha out, followed by Owen. "Here's my card, Mr. Matthews. I will be assisting you this week. Please don't hesitate to contact me if there is anything you require." 'Oh baby, you have no idea,' he thought wickedly. "Thank you, Miss Connolly. I'm sure there will be something." He watched her turn and go to the car. She had an ass worthy of exploration and legs to wrap around him. For the moment, he would check in and enjoy the accommodations.

Hollywood was starting to feel like the place to be; meetings would start tomorrow, it was time to relax. Once in his suite he showered and ordered a steak sandwich and cheesecake from room service; cigarettes, scotch and a bit of TV would finish taking the edge off. He was horny as hell, that sweet cupcake, Trisha, had increased his desire for sex. After several drinks, he switched channels, finding an old favorite, *Never On Sunday*, starring Melina Mercouri. Soon, the screen became fuzzy, his eyes began to close, his thoughts in a jumbled blur. Sleep came very quickly.

The following morning, Mack arrived to drive Owen to Universal. It was a beautiful day, typical of Southern California in March. The stretch pulled up to the studio gate, the guard approached, Mack showed his security pass and given clearance to continue. Driving through the entrance, Mack turned down one of many side streets on the lot and drove for several blocks, past sound stages, actors in costumes and techies carrying lighting and sound equipment. Friedman's building was number 57, a gleaming white structure with high windows, colorful bricks in pastel colors laid in the masonry. Lining the front of the building, various palm trees and beds of colorful Impatience beckoned. Mack opened the door for Owen, who strolled in to be greeted by an older receptionist. "Good morning! How may I help you?" "Owen Matthews to see Shel Friedman," he said with a snap! "Yes sir, one moment." Momentarily, Trish Connolly appeared, looking bright eyed. "Mr. Matthews, good morning. If you will just follow me," she said, cheerfully. "Anywhere you like, Miss Connolly." She was wearing a tight outfit, displaying all her natural assets. 'Stay focused, Matthews,' he mused, reigning in his libido. "In here, Mr. Matthews," she said, knocking on a door. "Come in!"

Shel Friedman's office was grand. 'This power boy lives like a mogul,' thought Owen, extending his hand to Friedman. "Welcome, Owen!" "Good to see you, Shel." "You've met my new assistant, Trish. She's taken over Karen's position." "Yes, that's what I understand and every bit as attractive I might add," he said glancing her way. "It's more productive when the scenery is top notch! Don't you agree?" "Indeed!" "Have a seat, please. Trish, would you get Mr. Matthews coffee and an ashtray!" "Certainly, Sir." She smiled in passing, heading to a side room. "Your new assistant is lovely! How long has she been with you?"

"Long enough to know the score," he said. "Really? Is she as good as Karen?" Shel picked up the inference toward his former mistress and secretary. "Karen is the salt of the earth. I hated losing her, but she's truly happy and very pregnant! If it's a boy, she has asked me to be godfather!" 'How cozy,' Owen thought.

Shel pulled out a box of cigars. "Havana! I have connections. Care to join me, Owen? I think our collaboration deserves a topnotch smoke!" "Great, Shel, don't mind if I do," he said, putting away his cigarettes and selecting a cigar. "Help yourself to that lighter," Shel suggested, pointing to a beautifully carved Ivory on his desk. Trish returned with two cups and decanter of coffee on a tray. "How do you like your coffee, Owen?" "I like it very sweet and on the light side," he said, eyeballing her. "Trish, please add sugar to Owen's coffee. Does half and half work?" "Just fine, Shel, thanks!" Trish did his bidding, completing the coffee. Stepping aside, she took a chair across from them.

Cigar smoke began to fill the room, something Trish had learned to cope with. The smell made her nauseous and her eyes burned. As Owen gazed continually, he imagined her under the sheets. A certain portion of his anatomy began to awaken. Shel cut through the blue air. "Let's begin, shall we?"

"As you are probably aware, we have a guarantee on our financing for *Bravo Business*. My good friend, Greg Morgan out of Houston and his financial partner, Blaine Courtman are on board, signed, sealed and delivered. They are our only investors and excellent for us. The fact that they like the project is a plus. They will be bringing on an additional partner as well, but that person hasn't been named yet, though I believe it's someone very familiar with musicals." "Sounds intriguing," said Owen, feeling at ease for the first time. "We can't go wrong with this one, Owen. I'm counting on you!" There's been a renewed interest in movie musicals of late, perhaps not as prolific as MGM days, but certainly resurgence.

Viewer surveys and test marketing reveals the public is getting weary of cop, war and western themes. The conflict growing in Vietnam, war protestors and political unrest since the demise of JFK, cries for something entertaining and light. I think we have a product that will satisfy this need." "Can't think of something I'd rather do," said Owen, suddenly feeling pressure. Shel continued. "The way I see it, perfect casting, filming and a mega publicity campaign on our part will guarantee success. I want that success, Owen. Do we understand each other?" "Of course, Shel," said Owen, slightly nervous. "You'll be sitting pretty with the potential of other directing projects for us." "Thank you, Shel." "Enjoying your smoke, Owen?" "Yes, thank you!" Shel continued the business portion.

"We need to set a definite time-line for the project. When do we hold auditions?" "Let's set an open call for strictly west coast performers; singers, dancers, actors camera-worthy by June first." "No problem I assume you know we require a screen test of those submitted by agents for the leads." "It stands to reason, considering the project is film not theatre." "Exactly." "Casting should be complete no later than the first of July, filming to commence mid August. I'll be setting another meeting once casting begins. I'm asking our two investors to join us. I trust your schedule will be clear." "Certainly Shel, I'm on board all the way." "Good to know. Trish, take Owen out to lunch on me. Take my car, dear." Owen lighted up. "How can I refuse such a pleasant offer?" "You won't. I'll see you tomorrow at 10:00 to set production guidelines. Let's make productive use of your time here." "Fine with me! Thanks for everything!" "You're entirely welcome." The meeting ended on an encouraging note.

Owen had something in mind all right, but it wasn't lunch. Trish led the way through the building to a back entrance. "The car's over there," she said, pointing to a stunning Ferrari convertible. The California license plate simply read *Number One.* "Get in, Owen. You're in for a treat!" Settling, Owen glanced at his hostess and grinned like a school boy. "I can hardly wait." Trish stepped on the accelerator and sped off, slowing only to pass through the main gate. Off the lot, she accelerated until she accessed Hollywood Freeway toward Beverly Hills, Santa Monica and the Pacific Coast Highway to Malibu. The coastline drive was breathtaking, the Pacific stretched out as far as one could see and beyond. "The little lady likes fast," said Owen, winking at Trisha. "I like this," she tossed, turning into a parking lot next to a typical California restaurant. "The food here's the best on the coast. Come on!" She grabbed her bag and headed in, Owen close in stride. An attractive sun-bronzed hostess greeted them.

"Miss Connolly, how good to see you." "Thanks, Alana; could you seat us on the deck today?" "Certainly, if you just wait here a moment. I'll make sure we have one set-up up for you." Owen's eyes followed her across the room. "Do you like the scene, Owen?" "Yes, you might say that. You California girls look healthy!" "I meant the location. I thought you might enjoy an ocean view during lunch." Alana returned with menus and a smile. "Follow me please." 'As far as you let me,' he thought, taking up the rear. "Teddy will be your server today. Can I start you out with a beverage?" "Do you have Glenfiddich?" "Of course, how would you like it" "On the rocks, neat, please." "And for you, Miss Connolly?" "I'll have a glass of your house red. What is your feature today?" "We have a nice Cabernet." "That sounds fine." "Very good, I'll have those up for you shortly." Alana stepped away, Owen's eyes fastened to her. "Do you fancy, Alana?" "Not particularly. However, I do appreciate attractive women." "So do I," remarked Trish, casually. At that moment, Teddy approached, another California-type. "Good afternoon, Miss Connolly." "Hi Teddy, how've you been?" "Very well, thanks. You're drinks are on the way. May I interest you in an appetizer?" "Owen?" "No, I'll wait." "I guess not, Teddy. What are your house specials?" "We have a lovely grilled Swordfish filet with spring vegetables, served on rice pilaf for $12.95. Or Shrimp Alfredo Linguini and a house salad for $9.95. Our usual daily special is the steak sandwich served with fries and our soups of the day, New England clam chowder or tomato bisque. We also have our regular menu items if you'd prefer." "The swordfish sounds good. I'll have that. Owen?" "I'm an eastern boy. The steak sandwich works for me, medium rare." "Very good, sir. I'll bring our bread basket right away." Just then, Alana returned. "Glenfiddich for you and the Cabernet," she recited, placing napkins and drinks in front of them. "Enjoy!" Trish picked up the glass and took a whiff. "I adore California wines." Owen took a sip of scotch. "Do you mind if I smoke?" "It's ok I guess, we're out in the fresh air. Normally, I can't stand it." He pulled out a pack and plucked a cigarette. Lighting it, he reached across the table for the ashtray. Taking a long drag, he allowed the smoke to trail out his nostrils as he studied her.

"How long have you been with Shel? About two months. He's a dream. He takes very good care of me." "I can imagine," murmured Owen, a sly smile visible. "What are you inferring?" "Nothing, I can see he's generous." "Yes, he definitely is. He was good to Karen as well."

"Yes, I know all about that." Owen thought it was time to change the subject. "Are you with anyone?" "No, my lover left me for another woman. I'm not looking at the moment." "You're very attractive, Trish. You could use some attention." "What do you mean by that?" "While I'm in town, I thought we could get together and have some fun." "Oh, I don't think so. Shel doesn't allow fraternizing with clients." "What is this we're doing?" "Having lunch." Teddy arrived with their orders. "This looks great, Teddy." "Will there be anything else?" "No, I think this covers it, thanks." Owen, a little bent, tried another approach.

"Does Shel tell you who to see?" "Not at all, I tell me who to see." "I could make you feel very good this week." "Are you sure about that?" "Do you like to fuck?" "Who doesn't?" She was growing impatient with Owen's come-on. "Trish, honestly what do you like?" "Let's set something straight here and now, Owen. My answer is simple. I don't do dick, I do Jane!" Owen practically choked on a French fry. "Never? You never do dick?" "Not if I can help it." "Does Shel know your preference?" "Are you kidding me? This is Hollywood! Everyone does everyone up, down and sideways!" "I must say, you don't look like a lesbian!" "That's an archaic comment, I must say!" "I mean you're very pretty, feminine. You don't look like a diesel dyke." "Look, this is a ridiculous conversation. Let's just enjoy the food, the view and let it go at that." "Sorry, I didn't mean to insult you, Trish." "No, but you're way off. When I want sex, I always choose a feminine, sexy, woman. I don't want one who looks like a linebacker for the Chicago Bears!" "Well put. I'm backing off." "Good. I'm glad we understand each other."

The rest of the lunch was in silence. Owen ordered two more scotches and tried to process the fact that Trish preferred women. 'What a ball buster,' he thought, irritably. Following lunch, they drove back to Beverly Hills. Pulling up in front of the hotel, Owen got out without a word. "Sorry to disappoint you, Owen. If I were a straight swinger, you'd be at the top of my list!" "Thanks, I think," he mumbled. "I'll have Mack pick you up at 9:30 tomorrow morning. See you then." She peeled off and disappeared down Wilshire. After his ill-fated attempt on Trish Connolly, Owen was ready to get back to New York, where he'd find someone willing to suit his sexual needs. Hooray for Hollywood? Not likely. The rest of the week was spent finalizing details for *Bravo Business* with Friedman and working on a tan.

Back in New York, Blaine was busy. He called Greg Morgan to finalize the accommodations in Paris. Greg's gracious offer of a complimentary stay at his hotel had come as a complete surprise. Pat's desire for an intimate, out-of-the-way back street place fit Greg's property in Villiers, in the seventeenth arrondissment of the city. After confirming dates, Greg surprised Blaine once again, announcing that his 'Honeymoon Hotel' offer also included first class travel to and from Paris on Air France. They would depart on April 15th.

Since the night the three had dined at Sardi's, Blaine was intent on Pat's future, finding the right fit for her, a new career interest. Greg would be the one to consult in the matter. He was immediately met with an invitation to come to Houston with Patricia. "I insist you two stay at my place. When are you free to fly down?" "My lady and I are taking some time off the proverbial merry-go-'round to just be together." "Excellent idea, Blaine my boy! Let me fly you to Houston next weekend. Let's get your beautiful wife on a new career track. I'll make arrangements for you at Teterboro. Let's aim for next Friday, say 9:00 AM. I'll phone you the night before when I see the radar." "Thanks, my friend. We'll look forward to it!" The conversation ended. For Blaine Courtman, what started as a chance meeting in Jacksonville two years before, with a beautiful dancer in a touring show, had morphed into a journey of continual miracles; Patricia Byrne Courtman being the biggest and best of all!

Chapter 30

A New Role

The Lear descended at a private airfield on the outskirts of Houston. Greg's pilot, Mel Jacobson was a veteran flyer, having served as fighter pilot during the Korean War. He had replaced Greg's previous pilot, when Morgan learned of his former employee's drinking problem. Taciturn but courteous by nature, Mel was excellent and reliable, a man Morgan relied on for both overseas and domestic travels. Following the landing, a stretch limo stood waiting to take Blaine and Pat to Morgan Towers, Greg's privately owned luxury building in the heart of the city. Upon arrival, driver Cy Jackson saw them to a private entrance, sliding a card for admittance. Pressing a button in the vestibule, Greg's voice was heard. "Yes, Cy?" "Mr. Morgan, the Courtmans have arrived." "Very good, please send them up." The elevator ride took them past thirty-nine floors until it stopped, the door opening slowly. A uniformed maid stood, her warm smile, welcoming. "Good day, please come in!" Entering a vast alcove, Greg approached, his arms open wide. "Blaine, Patricia welcome to my home. By God, you both put a shine on the day. Please, allow Daisy to take your things. You're just in time for lunch!" Daisy took their bags, coats and disappeared.

The vast apartment was done brilliantly; Parquet floors, Persian throw rugs throughout, leather furniture grouped around a fireplace that stood at the center of the main room. The far side of the unit had floor to ceiling glass, with a balcony beyond. Tropical plants, original paintings and sculpture pieces added a finished look. Blaine stopped for a moment. "Does Greg's place look familiar, Patricia?" "Yes, but how?" "I brought you here following your performance of

Bravo Business to meet Greg, who was hosting a party that night. Remember?" Pat remembered all right. The blush on her face caused a faint smile on her husband's. It was on this balcony they first had sex, hidden only by a thicket of landscaping. The dangerously close proximity of other guests a few feet away had interrupted their oral play. "It's a stunning apartment, Greg," said Pat, breaking from the luscious memory. "Come, let's sit here."

The all-glass dining table was set to perfection; Fresh flowers, Limoges china, Waterford crystal and table linens by designer Emilio Pucci added a touch of luxury. "I'd like you to meet Arnold, who will serve lunch today. "Hello, Arnold," Pat said, with enthusiasm. "Good afternoon, Madame." "Please, call me Pat!" "Thank you Madame!" Arnold brought wine, a Saint-Emilion Claret, pouring a glass for each. Greg raised his to toast. "To you both! May your future be beautiful and bright." "Here, here," echoed Blaine, taking a generous sip.

Lunch was served with style, typical of someone who knew how. The first course was a Caesar salad, dressed with Greg's secret recipe and topped with his homemade garlic, herb and parmesan croutons. "Patricia, how do you like my salad? "Your salad?" "Yes, my passion is cooking!" He's a graduate of the Cordon Bleu in Paris," said Blaine, admiringly. "That's amazing! I mean that you have time to cook!" "Cooking relaxes me after a long trip or challenging day." "I was the envy of every one of my ex-wives," he said, chuckling.

Arnold removed the salad plates as they finished. Returning, he brought the main course and placed luncheon plates in front of them. "Beef Tournedos," explained Greg to Pat. For a few moments they ate in silence. This beef is like butter," said Pat, never one to pass on something tasty. "These tournedos are incredible, Greg" remarked Blaine after a few bites. "Thank you. You're eating a choice filet from my cattle herd. We only raise the finest beef. My ranch is located near Lubbock. "This meat is the tenderest and most flavorful I've ever had," declared Pat between bites.

"Ah, I'm now going to impart the secret of success with tenderizing, learned from friends in Kobe, Japan. Their meat is the best on the planet. I watched the process, very impressive and simply done." "What makes it so unique?" "They serve the cattle beer by the bottle!" "Oh come on, Greg!" "No, I'm serious! While one worker serves the steer in a nipple bottle, others massage the sides of the animal, producing tenderization. As a result, they have earned the reputation for producing the world's most tender beef." "I believe you judging from this!" At the end of the main course, coffee and cognac was offered. Greg had thought of everything, including his own Crème Brulee, served with fresh raspberries. The lunch was smashing and a great start to their visit. Following, they retired to the living room to allow lunch to settle. Greg offered a suggestion.

"Would you two like a little spa time? I have a pool, sauna and hot tub for your convenience, right next door." "Well, we didn't bring suits," said Blaine. "Nonsense, the spa is mine and I assure you, private. Your birthday suits will be sufficient. In fact, I insist on it! There are towels and guest robes in your bathroom. Daisy will acquaint you with the guest suite. Please help yourself to anything you wish. Enjoy! We'll talk business in the morning! This evening I insist you join me for dinner at my restaurant!" "Greg, you never cease to amaze and surprise," said Blaine. "Life's to be enjoyed fully," he chuckled. "We'll depart for the Silver Horse at 7:30. See you then." Daisy returned to show them around. For as long as Blaine had known Greg, he had never been this dazzled by his business associate and friend. He'd always considered him a mentor and close friend, but now he felt like family. Greg saw to it. It was pure joy to share their friendship with his beautiful Patricia. From the moment of arrival, it felt like home.

Blaine and Pat got settled, unpacked and changed into robes provided. They followed Daisy's instructions to exit their suite through the changing room, down a long hallway to the pool area. What they found in addition to a pool was a workout room, whirlpool and sauna. What more could one ask for? "This definitely is the good life," tossed Blaine, disrobing and diving into the pool. "Hey, wait for me, lover," shouted Pat, joining him. They met in the center, arms reaching for each other. Pat wrapped her legs around Blaine's waist, as they bobbed up and down. "Be careful, Mrs. Courtman, I feel a boner coming on!" "Good, that's the idea," she giggled. "Come closer," he whispered, pulling her in. The kiss was long and sexy. "Ever made love in a sauna?" "Can't say that I have, but is it such a good idea with the intense heat?" They pondered the notion for a moment. A wicked smile appeared on Blaine's face. "Let me do a few laps to loosen up and I'll loosen you up!" "Naughty boy, hurry!" Pat hung on the end of the pool working her legs. The warm water felt incredible as she sliced through the water. Blaine did several laps, never bothering to stop until at last he came to where Pat was waiting. "I had no idea you could swim so well." "I was state champ in high school, believe it or not," he remarked, climbing up the pool stairs. Pat followed close behind.

They entered the sauna. Blaine reached for the temperature control gauge and turned it on. The sauna had a drop shade for privacy on the door. Finding a fresh stack of towels he placed them on the bench for cushioning and reached for her. "Come here, my precious." "You forgot something," she teased. Taking a ladle, she filled it from a nearby bucket of water. Pouring the liquid over heating rocks, she enjoyed the hissing sound. Soon the sauna began to fill with steam, creating a vaporous cloud of humidity. Through the fog, Blaine reached for her. Plunging his tongue deep in her mouth, his hands played with her breasts and continued south. Pat's insistence was a complete turn on as his hand explored her mound, stopping at her favorite spot. "Yes," she whispered hoarsely. Feeling the first thrust of his finger entering her, her breathing quickened as she moaned her approval, the heat wrapping her in pure pleasure! "What now, my precious?" "Come inside Blaine, please!" The heat and wetness felt sumptuous, as Blaine, now hard, eased in gently. As he kissed her deeply, he found the familiar fit. Sliding in and out, his rhythm became faster, the intensity overpowering. Together they let go, screaming through the release. Their bodies gleaming sweat, their hearts beating rapidly, the two lay in languid rapture, waiting for equilibrium. "Oh my God, maybe we need our own sauna," whispered Pat, completely spent. "My beautiful girl, you are beyond everything!" Minutes passed before the two could get up. "Let's step outside and get some cool air," he suggested. "We'd better or I'll melt." "Can't have that, so I think it's time for another dip. How does a shower and a nap sound before dinner?" "Heavenly!" Easing back into the pool they clung together, the water cooling them.

Dinner at Greg's Silver Horse proved a memorable experience, the food and service beyond measure. Seated at the owner's table, Blaine and Pat felt like royalty second only to King Morgan! The staff treated them like gold, filling every request. The repartee was delightful as the staff aimed to please, making their dining experience one of the best.

It was long after midnight when chauffeur Jackson returned to drive them back. As they walked in, they immediately noticed that Arnold had been busy; candles flickering throughout the room, a crackling fire in the fireplace and on the sound system, the melodious voice of Sarah Vaughn filling the air. "Would you two like a nightcap?" "A cognac sounds perfect," suggested Blaine. "Patricia?" "Do you have Dubonnet?" "Indeed!" "I would love it." Arnold appeared. Would you bring us a Courvoisier, a Dubonnet and a Drambuie, please?" "Right away, sir." They settled, relaxed and enjoyed the silence of the evening. Pat slipped off her heels and snuggled next to Blaine on the love seat. "You two are the epitome of contentment. It's good to see you so happy." "I never dreamed I could be this happy," said Pat, smiling at Greg. "What's your secret, Blaine? How do I find a woman as good for me as Patricia is for you?" "I'm just lucky, Greg," he chuckled, kissing Pat's nose. Arnold returned and served drinks. "Will there be anything else, sir?" "No Arnold, thank you so much. We'll have breakfast at 10:00. Have a good night." "Thank you and goodnight!"

The three sipped quietly, enjoying Vaughn's singing. Minutes passed before Greg spoke. "Tomorrow let's get started discussing Patricia's future to find the right fit for you, dear. I have been thinking about this and have some ideas to run by you." Blaine perked up. "Sounds intriguing, Greg. Care to share?" "I owe you two a good night's sleep. Let's get to it in the morning." He rose and set his glass on a side table. Pat stood and hugged Greg. "Thank you for everything. You are so very dear." "You know the way to your bedroom. Daisy will have turned down the bed." "Thanks, Greg. You're the best," said Blaine, giving a shoulder pat. "My pleasure, kids. Good night!" Greg left them in the soft glow of remaining candlelight. Finishing drinks, they set the glasses aside and walked hand in hand to bed, the end of a perfect day in Houston.

The Texas morning was sun bright. Blaine and Pat emerged and joined Greg in the breakfast room. Arnold was at his post, ready to offer coffee, tea and a variety of juices. "Good morning you two, how did you sleep?" "Like we'd been knocked out," Blaine chuckled, pulling out a chair for Pat. "My beautiful girl can sleep anywhere, but I'm a tougher case! What did you add to this Texas air?" "It's called unwinding,

Blaine my boy," Greg chuckled. "What are you drinking this morning?" "I'll take my coffee, black." "And for the lady?" "Definitely coffee regular," said Pat, still waking up. Arnold looked puzzled as Greg explained."Coffee regular is coffee light; with cream and added sugar, Arnold." "Am I right, Mrs. Courtman?" "Yes, just ask anyone born and raised anywhere in the five boroughs!"

The breakfast selection was wonderful. Arnold offered a choice of eggs any style, including three types of Benedict. There was a selection of bacon, ham or sausage, a variety of breads; croissants, brioche and Danish. Fresh fruit of every variety was available. Mimosas and Bloody Marys were suggested to start off. "Not dancing and eating like this, I'll need a hoist!" "I beg to differ. You have the digestive track of a Chickadee, my pretty," laughed Blaine. "Greg, the first time I dined with Pat on my boat following a show in Jacksonville, she out ate everyone in the room. I never saw such an appetite given her svelte figure." "That's my point, Blaine. I was dancing off calories back then, remember?" "How could I forget? I marveled then and I still marvel," he said, reaching for her hand and kissing gently. Greg observed closely. "Your Patricia is bewitching and bright as a new penny! What should we do with her, eh?" "Let's find her a new career track, she's ready!" Greg stood up, asked Arnold to clear and invited Blaine and Pat to settle in front of the fire. He carried a pad and pen and sat across from them.

"Patricia, how do you see yourself? What area would you find satisfying enough to take you from the stage?" "I've been thinking about this and would like to try my hand at coordinating a project." "Bingo! You know we are financing Owen Matthews' film project for Universal Pictures. We are involved strictly on the financial end and need someone on our team who understands the artistic side. What better way to include you? I have complete faith and respect in Shel Friedman, spearheading the project." "Patricia, did you know that Friedman and Greg were close friends with a long history?" "You couldn't ask for a better friend than Shel," said Greg earnestly. "He'll go along with this. Given your history with the show, he'll be elated." Pat sat for a moment, a frown forming. "Does Owen Matthews have a say in this?" "Why do you ask, Patricia?" "Well it's simple, really. I think Mr. Matthews expected me to stay indefinitely when he gave me the lead in *Centipede*. My giving notice at the end of the first year came as a shock." "Are you sure?" "Oh, most definitely. When he found out I wouldn't be renewing for a second year he practically threatened me!" "How so?" "He inferred that he could make it difficult for me to get hired by anyone else in New York." "That's ridiculous," said Blaine, impatience growing. "I just want to be up front about his viewpoint," said Pat. "You needn't worry. Owen Matthews must answer to Friedman, who will answer to us, knowing we are carrying the financial ball," assured Greg. "Matthews will adhere to your decisions, believe me!"

"How will you broach this, Greg?" "It's simple. I'll fly out to see Shel, advise him of Patricia's knowledge of *Bravo Business* and recommend her for our film team. When he meets you, he'll be sold." "It's as easy as that?" "Money talks, especially with Shel. I'll work on him, you work on Paris. Enjoy your honeymoon and when you return, we'll shake up Hollywood!" "Thank you for everything," said Blaine, Pat joining in a group hug. On the flight back to New York, they discussed Greg's proposal. With a strong sense they realized Pat's future was wide open with limitless possibilities. As a couple, they were becoming unstoppable.

Chapter 31

On The Move Again

The national production of *Centipede* was about to launch. March 26, 1966 was departure day for a six-month, crème de la crème tour. Broadway's biggest hit was still playing to packed houses on the Great White Way! Kaplan-Maggli instinctively knew it was time to send out its Broadway clone. Why not share the wealth with the hinterlands? Cast, crew and orchestra were readied for the opening city, Cleveland. The Hanna Theatre, the city's most popular and best-equipped venue would welcome them. Griff had completed all details of the tour. The

Edwards were looking forward to another round of traveling. They'd be covering cities not previously worked together. Packing two steamer trunks, they each took a smaller bag for immediate use. The company was advised to have trunks labeled, locked and ready for Ed Franklin and his crew. The trunks would be transported from city to city, delivered to the cast's chosen hotels. The company call was 9:00 AM in front of the Royal Theater, where they would be bused to JFK. Their flight would depart at 12:00. As the group gathered, excitement was obvious throughout. Jonas and Phillipe came to see them off. Jonas was his usual contrite, sipping coffee and chatting with Joe Pinto. Meanwhile, Phillipe conversed with Mally, Chad, Jeff and Nora. Jonas and Phillipe would remain until called to California to assist Owen on *Bravo Business.*

Joe Pinto was looking forward to touring with a show he considered technically challenging but artistically fulfilling. Deep down, he had missed the road for some time. He and Jordan Hendrix had drifted apart over the past year and Joe was hungry for new conquests. On the road, chances were good he'd find action. He'd never lost his need for variety. Performers, specifically male dancers, attracted attention. It was easy to secure dates with local men, those waiting at stage doors from coast to coast. Getting lucky was not difficult for Joe and never had been. He was stunning; a firm physique, sensuous features and confidence that was irresistible. He loved sex; relentlessly, sometimes recklessly. He enjoyed multiples, but never repeats, unless he favored a current trick. Jim Sorenson had been a companion on tour, but with the understanding that theirs was an open relationship.

Jeff, Nora and Chad stood in a huddle, sipping coffee. Neely and Maddy chatted, waiting to board and find seats together. Terry Becker and Jeff Boyd had hooked up during rehearsals and were now lovers. Joe observed their body language with interest. 'Maybe they'd consider a three-way,' he mused, the thought making him horny. Georgia Kemper and Tom Sutton had been steady since opening night in Japan, attempting to keep their relationship private. They had succeeded, as no one in the company caught on until now. They planned to save money and get an apartment together upon return. Candy Roth and Daria Douglas were inseparable. It was rumored they were lovers, but no one knew for sure. Both extremely attractive women, they never seemed to be without the other. Only Betsy Allan seemed a loner. She was friendly to a point, but kept her distance when it came to group interaction. Jim Jaris and Kent Freeman were both gay and single. Like Joe Pinto, each was game for action when someone of like interest showed up.

Dwight Procter, the new company manager, arrived just as a large Carey transport bus pulled up. The driver opened the door and came down the steps. He and Dwight exchanged a few words before he began putting bags into the outside luggage bay. Dwight had trouble at first trying to get the group's attention until Griff whistled. Everyone stopped chatting immediately. "I'd like you all to meet our company manager, Dwight Procter, who likes to be called, Doc. Am I right?" "Absolutely!" Applause broke out. "Doc will take care of us for the next six months. He'll post hotel choices each week for the coming city, hand out your weekly pay and report any problems to me. I expect you to treat him with the respect he deserves. Anything you want to add, Doc?" "Glad to be among you! This is a great tour we have ahead of us. Happy trails!" "Time to board," added Griff, taking a head count. The gypsies lined up, ready to go! Jonas and Phillipe hugged Mally and Nora and then stood back. One by one, the company members boarded, Dwight and Griff on last. The door swooshed shut and the bus slowly pulled into the morning traffic. Jonas and Phillipe waved to dancers pressed against windows, waving back. *Centipede* was under-way! The itinerary was choice, with places unknown to some, save for a few, those true gypsies on board.

Owen returned to Manhattan, happy to be free of sun, studio bosses and uncooperative women. Since his ill-fated tryst with Karen Eliot, he had come up empty, had yet to score. The lack of coitus was getting to him. He needed to get laid and soon. Flopping down on his sofa, he sipped a double shot of Glenfiddich on the rocks. Grabbing a smoke and inhaling deeply, he slowly felt nicotine calming his nerves. He was bored, restless. He wasn't in the mood to go bar hopping, but he felt the need for release. Closing his eyes, he imagined having sex. Sliding down the zipper of his fly, he felt warmth and outline of his equipment, hardening to the touch. Reaching inside his shorts he took hold of his erection and began massaging himself, slowly at first until accelerating his moves brought excruciating pleasure and build-up. Moaning through the ecstasy of his own creation, he let go. The release was necessary to quell the frustration he was feeling. 'I need a regular,' he thought. It was time to check out the landscape, maybe stop by the theatre after a hot shower and shave.

Catherine was enjoying her new role in *Centipede*. Because of Pat Byrne's support and good word, she had moved up to the lead! In her wild imaging she never dreamed it would happen after her ill-fated affair with Owen. After all, she had walked out of his bedroom and their relationship, such as it was. She and Danny Bartlett were now involved, growing more serious in recent weeks. He was kind, protective, interested in her ideas and opinions. They discussed getting a place together soon. Meanwhile, her best friend Julie was faring well with her Greek squeeze, Nicholas. He, too, was heads above most guys. Being from a culture respectful of women and family, Nick captivated Julie with his calm, quiet strength. Julie brought humor and effervescence to their dating. She hoped being with him would eventually develop into a mutual commitment.

Owen grabbed a cab to the theater. A light spring rain was starting as he hurried to the stage door. Once inside, he checked the sign-in sheet. Catherine's name was the first on the cast list. He would check her out during the second act from the back of the house. For a moment he thought of his original star, Pat Byrne. Regret washed over him as he remembered her flawless dancing and her incredible body, one he'd been privy to until he screwed things up. His infidelity had been his downfall. Now, he was alone, dropping by like a stranger, a stage door Johnny! At intermission's end, he made his way up an aisle to the back of the house, just as the house lights dimmed. At the top of act two, the show drop rose on his favorite number, *Sailors-on-Leave*. Three sailors stood in tableau; Jonas, Phillipe and Danny were the trio of gobs looking for action on leave. Their counterparts; Catherine, Liz and Cynthia were their women of interest. As the choreography unfolded, Owen was mesmerized by the pairings and especially taken with the chemistry between Catherine and Jonas. It was like looking at Pat's twin, partnered by the best dancer in town. Jonas, Owen's clone in look, style and dance technique, understood the concept of line, sensuality and timing like no other. Owen had singled him out and groomed him to be his assistant and future artistic heir. With the *Bravo Business* film only months away, Jonas was glad to be keeping in shape. Physically he had to be ready, sharp. The timing on the film couldn't be better. He and Phillipe would be in Los Angeles about the time that *Centipede* would be in town. The show was scheduled to play the Greek Theatre for two weeks before heading to San Diego. Jonas could look in on the show, perhaps hold a brush-up rehearsal. He also hoped for a break from the picture to go visit his father in San Francisco. Every since he'd come out to his father, he longed to introduce Phillipe. This might finally be a perfect opportunity.

As the show came down, Owen made his way backstage to visit Dick Landry, who continued as PSM. Dick was in post show details when he spotted Owen. "Hey! This is a pleasant surprise. What brings you back to the boards?" "I thought I'd stop in to see how our Anthropod is behaving." "Never better. The cast is solid, seamless!" "So I see. It's good to have Jonas and Phillipe back in for the time being. How do you plan to replace them in June?" "We'll hold an Equity replacement call well in advance of their departure. When are your film auditions?" "We're aiming for June first." "Not long from now. We'll be on it. I think everyone else plans to stay another year." "Good to know." Changing the subject, he brought up Catherine. "How is Miss Andrews?" "She's excellent!" "Great! Please tell her I stopped by, will you?" "Will do. Where are you headed?" "I thought I'd drop over to Allen's. Care to join me, Dick?" "Normally yes, but my missus is expecting our second and I like to get home. Her pregnancies have proven touchy." "Hey, I didn't know Dana's pregnant! Please give her my best." "I will Owen, thanks. Do you have any notes for the cast?" "Not a one." The two shook hands and Owen headed out. As he exited the stage door a heavy downpour caught him off guard. Pulling up his collar, he hurried toward Eighth Avenue, each step an effort to stay upright through the gusts of wind. 'A couple of scotches will hit the spot,' he thought, the chill running through him.

Joe Allen's was a quarter full. Those imbibing were mostly at the bar or scattered at tables near the rear. Shaking the moisture from his coat, he placed it on the back of a stool and took a seat. Reaching for an ashtray, he pulled the familiar pack from his pocket and shook out a cigarette.

The first drag was always the best and his first since he left home. Ordering a scotch on the rocks, he stared into the mirror behind the bar. Suddenly he spotted a familiar figure. 'Catherine? What the fuck! And she's solo,' he thought, getting up. "I'd like to run a tab, Larry." The bartender nodded and continuing helping another customer.

Owen picked up his drink and sauntered across the room, eyes fixed on his ex. When within range, he spoke. "Catherine, this is a coincidence." As she looked up, her stomach clenched. "Hello, Owen." "How are you?" "I'm fine." "I caught the second act tonight. You looked wonderful." "Thank you." The tension was building, the small talk, awkward. "May I sit down?" "Well, I'm expecting someone." "Oh?" "Yes." Owen moved closer taking her hand in his. "Catherine, I've missed you so much," he oozed. Catherine pulled away. "Please, Owen." "Don't be that way, Baby," he murmured, feigning hurt. "There's nothing further to discuss. You and I never had a chance from the start." "What do you mean?" "We wanted different things." He sat quietly for a few moments, processing her words. Crushing out his smoke he took a sip of scotch and stood, pushing the chair into the table. "I'm sorry you feel this way." "I think its best," she murmured, looking straight at him. Her gaze cut hard. How he wanted her! "Well, I guess I'll see you around, kid." Putting another cigarette in his mouth, he turned and walked away. Returning to the bar, he gestured to Larry. "Set me up again, will you?"

Danny entered Allen's and scanned the room for Catherine. Spotting her at the back, he waved and headed toward her. She sat stone-faced and teary. "Honey, what's wrong?" He sat down quickly and took her hand. Avoiding his eyes, she stared at the table, attempting to recover. "Oh, I just had some bad news." "What, for heaven's sake?" "There's been a death, someone I used to know." Danny moved over and put his arm around her. "Cath, I'm so sorry. Anyone I know?" "Not at all, someone from my past." "Are you okay?" She half smiled and kissed him. "I'm just fine, Danny. "I love you so much!" They kissed again. From across the room, Owen stared into the mirror, not quite believing he'd thrown her away. As with Pat Byrne he had blown it big time. 'You're an asshole, Matthews, a big one,' he thought, ordering another drink.

Centipede hit the Hanna Theatre in Cleveland with full force! Opening night brought a standing ovation, the cast taking bow after bow. Once again, the show's innovation and execution brought raves from the public and critics alike. The cast was invited to a press party at one of the city's most popular hotels, the Hollenden House. The giant ballroom was filled to capacity with press, VIP guests, Mayor Ralph Locher, his entourage and various theatre patrons with or without financial clout. A jazz trio entertained as waiters strolled through the throng, offering complimentary champagne, a variety of Hors d'oeuvres and affable greetings to cast and crew.

The gypsies were an impressive group, dazzling the locals with their outstanding looks and deportment. Hangers on grouped around several dancers, eager to talk about life upon the wicked stage. Joe Pinto stood at the bar enjoying a beer when approached by a local reporter from the *Cleveland Plain Dealer*. The guy seemed more interested in him than the show. Joe's instinct for birds of a feather kicked in. The reporter gave him a big smile. "You're in the show, right?" "How did you guess?" Joe's ability to flirt was in high gear, as he worked on his beer. "What a great production! How long have you been in it?" "About three hours," tossed Joe, winking at this possible trick. "No kidding?" Joe laughed. "Actually, I was with the original show on Broadway, but I decided touring would be a nice change, so I took this job." "How long will you be in town?" "One week here, then off to Toronto for two." "I envy your life," the fellow admitted. "I don't travel much with my job. I cover mostly local stories." "What's your name?" "Jim, Jim Ackerman." "Well, Jim Ackerman can I buy you a drink?" "Thanks. I'd like that." Joe was spinning a web for this eager fly. He just might get lucky! He was horny as hell and this guy was a cutie, a real innocent. He loved the conquest, especially of one less experienced. Jordan Hendrix, his former lover, had been that way when they first got together, a real turn-on.

Across the room, Mally and Griff chatted with Mayor Locher and his wife, Denise. They were impressed with the production and had so many questions about the tour. Jeff, Nora and Chad huddled, watching the locals, while Chad perused the women. He hadn't been interested in dating since his ill-fated romance with Myoshi Watanabe in Tokyo, but now he felt ready to socialize. However, most of the women in the room were dowager types, or part of a couple, or pushy females. One might find a one-night stand something to write about in a diary or share at the office the next day. No, he would keep his distance. Just as the thought ran through his head he noticed Betsy Allan sitting by herself. She looked pensive and a little sad. Funny, he hadn't noticed her during the Tokyo run. He'd been so in love with Myoshi, he'd thought of no one else. Excusing himself, he crossed the room toward her.

"Hi, Betsy!" She startled until she realized it was Chad. "Hello." "What are you drinking?" "White wine, why?" "Would you care for another?" She thought about it for a second and nodded. "That would be nice, thank you!" She was cuter than he remembered; with a short pixie haircut, a spill of freckles over her nose and big, blue eyes, framed by long lashes. "Be right back," he said, smiling at her. Ordering a house white for her and a Heineken, he waited patiently for the barman. Glancing over his shoulder, he liked what he saw. 'Betsy, how could I have missed noticing you?' Returning, he handed her a glass and touched the rim with his beer. Her eyes never left his as she took a sip. "How do you like touring so far?" "I don't know yet, it's my first!" He chuckled as he took a swig. "What was Japan?" "Well, we stayed put. It was nice. I loved being there. It was my first time out of the United States." "Mine, too."

For a few minutes neither spoke. Chad felt drawn to her and wasn't fighting it. She wasn't a typical chorus girl; competitive, knowing, self-possessed. He would have to work hard for conversation with her, but he didn't mind at all. Soft-spoken, shy women had become preferable of late, remembering Myoshi's quiet demeanor. "What other shows have you done?" "Oh, the *Centipede* engagement in Japan was my first big job. I've done a couple of off-Broadway shows, all flops and a shoe industrial!" "Shoe industrial?" "Yes, a choreographed production where the only stars are shoes!" "Never heard of such thing," he chuckled. Her gentle enthusiasm began to grow on him. "Well, it was a one day job; a morning rehearsal and fitting and two shows in the afternoon. We modeled shoes in different scenes and danced to demonstrate. It paid really well and rehearsal time was short!" "Who saw it?" "Only buyers and manufacturers. You'd be amazed how many shoe brands there are. The best part was getting to keep the shoes we wore."

Betsy was adorable when she opened up; bubbly, personable and sweet. Chad was feeling a definite attraction. He took a leap. "Would you

care to dance?" "Dance on a ballroom floor?" She set down her glass.
"Yes, I really would." "Come on!" Chad took her hand and led her out
on the floor. She was petite and short, but her body fit right into his. He
liked that she was pressing against him. It had been a long time since
he felt this kind of pleasure. The music seemed to bring them closer.
He could feel her heart beat, her eyes locked on him. When the music
stopped, they stayed motionless, looking at each other. The band played
a Lindy next. "Can we sit this one out?" The moment was over. Chad
broke out of their hold. "Of course we can." Taking her hand, he walked
her back to the seating area. "Would you like to go somewhere quieter?"
She blushed. "Yes, I'd like that very much." "Let's get out of here, ok?"
They walked through the ballroom and out to the front door. "I don't
know Cleveland, but we could go back to the hotel. Where are you staying?" "The New Amsterdam, near the theatre." "You're kidding, that's
where I'm registered. It's only a few blocks from here and it's a nice night.
Care to walk?" "I'd like that very much, Chad." As they walked, he put his
arm around her. She cuddled next to him, doing the same. Something
was definitely beginning, he could feel it. 'This tour may turn out to be
some kind of terrific after all,' he mused, as they strolled to the hotel.

The next morning Griff woke up, stretched and carefully got out of
bed. Mally was still deep asleep, the last thing he wanted was to disturb. Putting on his robe, he went to the door; peeking under was
today's *The Plain Dealer*, Cleveland's major newspaper. Retrieving
it, he went to his bag for reading glasses and the makings for coffee.
Fishing inside, he found the jar of Folgers's instant and an immersion
heater. Filling a glass with tap water and heater, he plugged it in the
bathroom outlet. Water heating, a morning pee was next.

Shaking some crystals into the hot water, he stirred with his tooth-
brush handle and, 'Voila,' fuel to wake him up! Settling in a chair, he
turned on a table lamp and opened the paper. Finding the entertain-
ment section, he spotted a dated photo of *Centipede's* original cast,
taken by the New York Times, prior to the Broadway opening. The
headline caught his eye: *An Anthropod Takes Over Cleveland!* The
review was written by local theatre critic, Jane Scott:

*Clevelanders, long-devoted fans of musical theatre, have opened
their hearts to a most unusual visitor at the Hanna Theatre this week.*

"Centipede," the Tony award-winning Broadway show created by famed director-choreographer Owen Matthews,' has arrived in Cleveland, the first of eight cities on its national tour. This unique offering is an all-dance show, unusual for Matthews, who usually relies on a well-written libretto and score. Not this time! The much-touted production features a breathtaking ensemble; fourteen stunning men and women pulling all the stops out and delivering his concept to a breathless audience. This troupe parallels the original in talent, all phenomenally adept at carrying out Matthews' vision. Always the sensualist, Matthews doesn't disappoint, as his troupe executes suggestive and visually tantalizing choreography. No holds barred, one feels an arousal of the senses and experiences an intimacy of mind and body rarely seen on the legitimate stage. For an evening of feverish fantasy and indulgent pleasure, run don't saunter to the Hanna. "Centipede" runs through April 3rd. Take this reporter's advice. You don't want to miss a leg of it.

Griff put down the paper and called the hotel operator. "Yes, how may I help you?" "This is Griff Edwards in room 1510. May I have an outside line?" "Certainly sir, one moment." He waited until he heard a dial tone and phoned Joe Kaplan in New York. "Kaplan-Maggli, how may I direct your call?" "Hi, Jennifer, this is Griff Edwards calling from Cleveland. Is Mr.Kaplan in this morning?" "Yes, Mr. Edwards, he just came in. I will connect." As Griff waited, he looked over other parts of the paper, while enjoying his morning brew. "Well, this is a great way to start the day! How are you and the gang out there in Cleveland?" "Hi, Joe. We've done the deed and the local critic has given us a thumbs up!" "Terrific, this is great news." "I'll wager we'll be sold out by this evening until the end of the week." "Music to my ears, Griff. Say, send me a clipping of the review, will you?" "I will, Joe. How are things in New York?" "The weather is shitty, cold and wet, lots of wind, but as long as the numbers stay solid on the show, I should gripe?" "I'll phone you next week from Toronto." "I appreciate your checking in. You're always on top of it, Griff." "That's why you pay me the big bucks, Joe. Talk to you soon." As he hung up, Mally stirred. "Good morning, Darling!" He melted at the sight of her. Hurrying to her side, he took her in his arms, kissing her deeply. Breakfast could wait.

Nora and Jeff had settled in. They were already enjoying the tour as a married couple. Having sublet from a friend for a few months, the timing for vacating had worked well. Their friend's return from his travels had coincided perfectly. The tour would enable them to sock away enough money to return to New York in six months and get their own place. They both loved doing the show and had made a solid marriage. Neither wanted to start a family, at least not for awhile.

Nora had family in D.C. and was pleased they'd have six weeks at the National Theatre, time enough to introduce Jeff to her brother and sister-in-law, who were expecting their first child in early June. Nora hoped the blessed event would occur while they were in town. Her parents had died some years before, leaving her on her own at 15. At the time her brother Bobby was older by 10 years. He and his wife, Sharon had taken her in until she was 18 and able to pursue her dream, to dance professionally. She had spent a couple of years in New York, training and then took off for Europe, dancing with companies in Copenhagen and London. She'd hit some rough patches during her time abroad. Her affair with a married company manager in Copenhagen turned out messy and she was asked to resign. Her boyfriend of a year in London cheated repeatedly, leaving her frustrated and determined to play the field from then on. Following several men and some nasty breakups, she'd returned to New York and started auditioning, winding up one of Owen's choices for the original company. Her immense ability technically and her flexibility as a quick study led her to position of swing dancer.

Then, once again her lack of discernment led her to casual sex out-of-town, this time with a sexual predator. Raped and impregnated, she was fearful of the man who had assaulted her, so she kept the assault a secret. Terrified and worried in those first weeks following the rape, she wondered how she could keep her job. Jeff stepped in, gained her trust and referred her to an abortionist, through a friend. Though illegal, the procedure was necessary. Seeing her through the entire ordeal, he took care of her immediately following. She stayed with him while recovering until she could return to her swing post. He encouraged, nurtured and protected her. He was first a good friend, then lover. Now her husband, Jeff was the stabilizing force, changing her life from messy detours and traumatic affairs to a solid life, respectful and loving.

Clevelanders continued raving about *Centipede,* the show playing to sell-out audiences the rest of the week. Even standing room tickets were scarce through the run. The cast, encouraged by public response, looked forward to their second stop, the O'Keefe Center, a dazzling, state-of-the-art theatre complex, not unlike the Nissei Theatre in Tokyo. Located in Toronto, Ontario, the theatre featured closed circuit TV in dressing rooms with a lounge, fully-stocked concession in the green room, enough showers and toilets stalls to accommodate several dancers at once. In addition to the theatre; a coffee shop, upscale restaurant, piano bar, drugstore and cleaners on the main concourse was convenient. The set-up was reminiscent of the Fisher Theatre Complex in Detroit. These full-service venues were helpful to the gypsies on matinee days, when break time between shows was tight and going back to the hotel often required a cab ride.

The load out would start after the show Saturday night. Griff and his crew would strike the set; cyclorama, rigging, scrim and teasers. Costumes and shoes were to be collected by each gypsy and given to Elena Klein, veteran wardrobe mistress. Each gypsy was responsible for personal property; underwear, dance belts, make-up and other assorted items. Griff would remind them to have their trunks packed, locked and out by 2:00 AM for pick-up. This routine would take place at the end of each engagement. Ed Franklin and his assistant, Al Keen would pick-up, load, transport and deliver to the next hotel stop. Company manager, Dwight Proctor was detail-oriented to the letter, making sure nothing was overlooked either affecting the company or the crew. He and Griff had great rapport and respect for the other man's job. The trip to Toronto Pearson Airport from Cleveland Hopkins International was at noon, the shortest of the tour, the flight taking one hour. The call was 9:00 AM, curbside at their hotels. *Centipede* would run two weeks in Ontario, time enough to enjoy the Canucks' hospitality.

Chapter 32

April in Paris

Blaine and Pat left New York the afternoon of April 15th for their wedding trip to Paris. Pat picked the locale, fantasizing a honeymoon in the City of Lights. Greg had chosen the best carrier, Air France, and their flight was flawless. Sitting in first class they were attended by three stewardesses who were bi-lingual. Ever the business traveler, Blaine was fairly fluent and used their time aboard to practice, his exchanges with the attendants, charming. Pat was all ears.

During the early portion of their flight, dinner was served with typical French panache. The menu was: Pate de Fois Gras and Champagne to start, a choice of Boeuf Bourguignon or Filet of Sole Bonne Femme, with Haricots Verts and Frits followed. St-Emilion Claret or Sauvignon Blanc was offered. Next, a small salad with a tangy garlic-mustard dressing, rolls and butter. An assortment of cheeses, fruit, Crème Brule dessert, coffee, Grand Mariner or Cognac, the grand finale!

Pat ate each offering with unbridled enthusiasm, causing her husband to chuckle with each sigh. Never had she tasted such food! "Oh Blaine, if I keep this up, I'll weigh a ton by the time we get home!" "My beautiful girl, don't you worry, we'll find ways to burn it off," he whispered, leaning close. "Paris is made for walking and well, we'll have plenty of opportunity for some late night fun!" "Music to my ears," she murmured, taking a last bite of Crème Brule.

Later, lights were dimmed, blankets and pillows offered. Pressing their seats back and slouching down, Blaine covered them to their necks. As they cuddled, his hand traced Pat's nipples, causing a sigh.

Not to be outdone, she reached down and carefully unzipped his fly. "Two can play at this," she whispered, running her fingers over his underwear. "Careful now, I might be forced to do something not acceptable here," he chuckled, softly. As he hardened, she reluctantly stopped and removed her hand. "You win, but only for now," she murmured. The steady hum of engines, a darkened cabin and generous dinner caused Pat's eyelids to droop. Soon she was fast asleep, nestled next to her husband. Blaine joined her, the two deep in slumber.

Hours had passed and the morning sun began filtering through the cabin. Stewardesses passed through first class with breakfast trays laden; a choice of coffee, tea, juice, brioche and croissants with cheese and jam looked inviting. The smell of freshly brewed coffee stirred Pat as she slowly came to. Glancing over she noticed Blaine immersed in the airline magazine, *In Flight.* He stopped, looked over and smiled. "My beautiful girl, good morning!" He leaned over, kissing her gently. "How did you sleep?" "Like the dead! I was never able to relax on an airplane before. On tour I hated every minute of it. Just ask Mal!" "And now?" "Oh Blaine, this whole experience is delicious!" "How does a bite of breakfast sound?" "Fabulous! I'm famished." "Really," he deadpanned. "Why does this not surprise me?" "You know me well, my husband!" A stewardess stopped and placed their trays.

"Café, Monsieur?" "Oui, merci!" "Et Madame?" "Absolutely!" Coffee was immediately poured and handed to them. "This looks yummy," said Pat, perusing her tray. Picking up a croissant, the texture was buttery to the touch. "This is so flakey and moist. I won't need butter, but what is this cheese? It's so soft?" "It's Boursin, very popular in France." Spreading some on a piece of croissant, she quickly took a bite, closing her eyes, savoring the taste and texture. Blaine sat back, observing his ebullient, unspoiled wife with delight. How did he ever manage to make her his? She was irresistible and he deeply in love.

The plane touched down at Charles De Gaulle at 8:35 am. Disembarking, Blaine and Pat followed the lines of passengers to passport control. Immigration officials asked the usual questions about the nature and length of their visit and, when advised "Honeymoon," responded with "Congratulations Madame et Monsieur." Claiming their baggage and proceeding through customs was uneventful. The whole affair took about an hour, given that it was morning. Many inbound flights had arrived at the same time from all over the world. Having made it through, they were now free and clear. They stood in the cue, with dozens of others, waiting their turn for a taxi. Finally, it was their turn, as a driver pulled up, exited the car and helped them with bags, placing them in the trunk. The driver had no English but understood and appreciated Blaine's willingness to speak French. Blaine handed him a map, with the route from the airport to the Hotel Villiers, in the 17th district of Paris. It was direct and clearly marked in red ink. Greg had thought of everything!

The driver pulled out into the heavy morning traffic and headed toward the city. Bicycles, buses, limos, motor scooters, and small cars of every description zipped in and out of traffic lanes, drivers trying to cope with the heavy clog, all jockeying for the most expedient passage. Horns blasting, fists shaking and certain expletives heard through open windows added to the ambience of the French capitol. The morning was fresh and sunny following three days of spring rain, according to the affable driver. Trees along boulevards were in blossom, the sidewalks washed clean to accommodate café customers, who preferred service outdoors. Pedestrians moved along main thoroughfares and narrow side streets winding through the immense metropolis. Pat's eyes were fixed on the populace moving around her, going about their business; men, women, children, dogs, city workers and tourists, making their arrival exciting.

After a 45-minute ride the driver turned down a narrow side street and pulled up to a charming door front. The Hotel Villiers looked like any average inn, the front entrance protected by a dark green awning. The driver helped Blaine with bags and smiled as he collected the fare. "Merci et bonjour," he said, returning to the taxi. Pat waved as Blaine opened the door and together they each managed a bag into the lobby. The décor was simple but elegant. Maroon and gold upholstered furniture was situated at the far end of the room, a glass door leading out to a quaint garden area, was seen through a large picture window. Greenery was here and there and soft lighting, from a few lamps in the seating area, adding a welcome glow. A small elevator stood to one side. A front desk dominated the small lobby and behind it, two staffers were answering phones and helping other guests. The male clerk finished his business as Blaine and Pat approached. "Bon

Jour! How may I help you this morning?" His English was impeccable, tinged with a slight Charles Boyer accent. He was middle-aged and very pleasant in manner.

"We are Blaine and Patricia Courtman here to check in." "Oui, Monsieur, we have been expecting you. We received a Telex from Monsieur Morgan. Would you sign the register please?" "Merci, tres bon," said Blaine, picking up a pen and signing. "We have you on the sixth floor, number 615. Please don't hesitate to call if there's anything you require. My name is Alain." "Thank you, Alain." "You're welcome, Monsieur. Your accommodation includes a complimentary breakfast 7 to 9:30 daily, on our lower level. There is no lunch or dinner service, but if I may recommend a number of excellent restaurants in the Villiers, I will be happy to do so." "Wonderful," said Pat, already keen on French cuisine. "Here are your room keys, Monsieur. Take the elevator to floor six. When you exit the lift, turn left. Your room is at the end of the corridor and ready for use." "We appreciate your help." "You are most welcome! Please enjoy your stay."

On floor six, Blaine and Pat found room 615. Setting the bags down, he unlocked the door and motioned for Pat. "Come here, my beautiful girl!" Lifting her up in his arms, he carried her across the threshold and put her down gently. They kissed and stood motionless, savoring the moment. Blaine went back to the hall and brought in the luggage, setting it aside. The room was simple, but cozy. Two windows a few feet apart looked out onto the street, covered in dark blue drapes with gold-braided swags to hold them back. The bathroom was basic but complete with a tub, shower, sink, vanity, bidet and toilet. Stacks of fresh towels lined shelves and a third window overlooked the street as well. The bedroom featured a double bed, with matching linens in the same color scheme as the drapery. A large dresser, table model TV and wet bar with a small fridge completed the furnishings. A small closet was ample enough for the two of them. A table near the window held a beautiful arrangement of spring flowers, a box of chocolates and a silver bucket with champagne chilling. Blaine noticed a small envelope next to it and opened it, reading it aloud. *To my wonderful friends! May your honeymoon be memorable and your life together beyond compare! Enjoy your week in Paris! Congratulations and love, Greg.* Blaine passed the note to Pat and sat on the end of the bed, removing his shoes. "Best man I've ever known," he murmured, eyes welling. "Oh Blaine, you two are so blessed to share this friendship." "And now you, my love." "Yes, and now me!" In moments he took her in his arms holding her close, kissing her deeply. Soon, they were making love, feverishly, insatiably, an auspicious and passionate beginning in the City of Lights!

In the days to follow the Courtmans behaved like true tourists. Though Blaine had been to France often for business, he had little time for leisure. Occasionally he would visit his sister, Yvonne, married to a wealthy Frenchman, but more often than not, time was pressing and the opportunity lost. What a perfect opportunity, seeing it with and through the eyes of his beloved Patricia! Up early, they had a light breakfast of rolls, coffee and juice. Then, putting on walking shoes, they ventured along the streets of the 17th Arrondissement, poking through stalls in the local open market on Rue de Levis. It was such fun exploring a vast array of boutiques selling books, music, handbags, hats, jewelry and scarves. There were a few dress shops, which Pat eagerly checked out. Blaine got a kick out of the many shoe stalls, featuring knock-offs of famous brands. The market, a quarter mile in two directions was convenient to the locals, who shopped daily. French householders could choose from varieties of fresh produce, meats, seafood and from many Boulanger's, local bakeries, whose doors stood open. Walking by was a touch of heaven, their noses picking up the smell of fresh bread and pastries baking, then placed on display for locals and tourists alike.

Paris was alive with motion every minute of every day and night. Blaine wasted no time in planning a daily itinerary for them. The Villiers Metro stop only two blocks away, everything was convenient. A must was a visit to the Eiffel Tour, the most famous and popular landmark in Paris! There was the majestic Arc de Triumphe and The Champs Elysees along which you could find everything from movie houses and cafes to tourist shops. Just walking it was a thrill! One afternoon they discovered L' Avenue George-V. Pat was fascinated as they walked past world-famous couturier houses like Chanel, Givenchy, Cardin and Valentino! They noticed an austere, uniformed doorman at each pristine and polished entrance. "You'd need a blood test to get past these boys," tossed Pat. Blaine chuckled, her manner reminding him of his gypsy wife. "You can take this girl out of the chorus, but you can't take the chorus out of this girl," he chuckled, tickling her.

Museums were a must! One day they visited the Louvre, after spending the whole morning they decided it would take a week to see it all, a good reason to return. In the afternoon, they went to Musee d'Orsay. Blaine favored the Impressionists. It was amazing to see works of Monet, Cezanne and Degas. The sculpture was impressive, but one Pat insisted on was the home of Rodin. Pat asked Blaine to take her the following day. She loved the famed sculptor's awareness of movement, captured in each piece, especially *The Kiss* and *the Thinker,* her favorites.

A trip to Montmartre was a two stop Metro ride from Villiers. That section of Paris brought memories to Pat of the MGM film, *American in Paris,* starring Gene Kelly and his discovery, French ballerina Leslie Caron. As a young child she fell in love with the pair, dancing along the romantic Seine in the moonlight, increasing her desire for the same. And now, here she was with her incredible Blaine! As they strolled block after block, paintings and painters lined the narrow streets. At one point they spotted the famed Moulin Rouge. One look and Blaine knew it had to be one of their evening jaunts. When they returned to the hotel, the clerk arranged tickets for the following evening. Though exhausted from a full day of sightseeing, Blaine and Pat made love that night and every night, immersed in their inexhaustible desire for sex in the glow of their immeasurable love.

Paris at night proved magical! Blaine arranged dinner and a cruise along the Seine boarding the Bateaux Mouche, the traditional boats traveling the river. Symbolic of true romance in Paris, dinner cruises featured full-course meals as couples enjoyed the magnificent panorama of Paris lights clustered in the night sky. Following their cruise, they took the Metro back to Montmartre to catch the late show at the Moulin Rouge.

The hotel manager had booked premium seating; a bottle of chilled champagne was waiting. As the house lights dimmed, stage lights came up full on pure spectacle! The stage filled with exquisitely beautiful people! Men and women of every nationality moved regally as the overture finished. The guys were buff and shirtless partnering the girls, who were topless with only scanty g-strings to cover their most private selves. Number after number featured them in various modes of dress or undress and choreography for the girls dancing topless without a bounce! "I think they've had some work done! What do you think?"

Blaine sat riveted, enjoying the eye candy of bare-breasted show-girls. "Let's ask for a towel, you're drooling," giggled Pat. The men were fascinating, though more covered. However, tight pants couldn't hide considerable baskets, which Pat was obviously enjoying. Featured acts such as mimes, jugglers and aerialists added variety to the production. During the finale, the crowd went wild with appreciation, rising and shouting praise. Blaine took care of the bill and escorted Pat through the throng of tourists and locals alike. It had been a terrific evening! Their week in Paris was about to come to a close. They were scheduled to depart Charles De Gaulle for New York the following afternoon. So many impressions, so many firsts made up their dream honeymoon for which they owed endless gratitude to their good friend Greg Morgan. Soon, another new adventure would begin.

Chapter 33

Business is Business

While Blaine and Pat were away in Paris, Greg Morgan had been busy arranging Pat's future and furthering their investment in the film version of *Broadway Business*. He phoned his friend Shel Friedman at Universal. "Greg, good to hear from you. What's doing?" "Have you got time to see me next week?" "Why certainly! Is everything okay on your end?" "Couldn't be better! My partner is on his honeymoon at the moment, so I will be arriving alone. We are ready to offer you an added plus for the production. I'd like the opportunity to run it by you." "Really? Are you coming to the coast anyway? We could discuss this over the phone and save you a trip. After all, Universal is signed, sealed and ready, thanks to you and Courtman," he offered. "No, this is something I'd like to run by you personally. What is your time frame?" "Let's see, this coming Friday looks open," he said, flipping through his desk calendar. "Great, let's say about 1:00 on Friday. See you then, friend." "Sounds intriguing, Greg. I'll look forward to it. Would you care to stay at my place in Bel Air while in town?" "Very generous of you, Shel, but I'll be in and out. Thanks anyway!"

On Friday, Greg arrived at Universal, having hired his own limo. Walking into Friedman's outer office, Trish Connolly smiled and immediately showed him in. Shel was busy looking at scripts as Morgan entered the inner sanctum domain. Rising Shel grinned and extended a handshake. "Good to see you, my friend. Have a chair. May I offer you a drink?" "Coffee black sounds good at the moment," said Greg, settling. "Shel pushed the intercom. "Trish, baby, would you bring Mr. Morgan a carafe of coffee and Dewers on-the-rocks for me?" "Certainly sir, be right there."

"Nice secretary, Shel. Who is she?" "My new assistant, Trish Connolly. She's a honey!" Greg smiled to himself, aware of his friend Shel's fondness for attractive women, especially in the office. Shel continued. "She replaced my longtime girl, Karen Eliot. Do you remember Karen?" "Of course, she was with you for years. What happened?" "She fell in love with our chief cinematographer here at Universal and married the son-of-a-bitch! Can you beat that? Now, they're expecting! Talk about a 180!" "Well, if she's happy," added Greg. "Between you and me, Karen was the best piece of ass I ever had!" "Well, it's really none of my business, Shel" said Greg, clearly uncomfortable. "You know the irony of my new girl? She's a lesbian! I couldn't get to first base with her, but she's an excellent assistant, so I've kept her on." "Good for you, Shel. Good help is indispensible!"

Friedman changed gears. "To what do I owe this visit, Greg?" "I have a friend, in fact she's Courtman's new wife, Patricia. She's looking for a career change and she's a natural fit for our production staff." "Why are you sold on her?" "She's a former performer, actually. She was lead dancer on the national tour of *Bravo Business* and starred as Matthew's leading dancer in his highly successful *Centipede* on Broadway. I know her to be a consummate professional. She understands the ins and outs of the musical theatre and would be an excellent casting consultant and project associate for us. We could use someone on our team to keep tabs on creative, finances and personnel." "Has she worked in film?" "No, but as you know Shel, this can be learned.

She's got the best teacher in the world with you holding her hand. She's retired from dancing but a true veteran, who is not only street smart, but savvy when it comes to knowledge of the form. She would keep anyone in line, a real no-nonsense force." "When can I meet her?" "I can get her out here in a few days." "Wait, I have a better idea. She lives in New York, right?" "Yes, they have a place at the Plaza, why?" "I have business in New York the week after next with Matthews and others involved on the picture. Perhaps we could arrange a dinner meeting." "That's a great idea, Shel. I would appreciate your meeting her at your earliest convenience, get a chance to hear her out." "We could meet for cocktails, then involve Matthews." "Excellent. May I buy you dinner tonight at Chasen's, or would you prefer the Brown Derby?" "I'd love to join you Shel, but I have to get back to Houston tonight." "You're a regular jet-setter, my friend." "Thanks for your time, Shel. I'll look forward to our next meeting." "Hey, you never got that cup of coffee!" "Not to worry, Shel. I'm amped enough," he said with a chuckle. Trish hurried in just as Greg was about to leave. "Oh Mr. Morgan, I'm so sorry, the coffee maker broke down. Shel, do you still want that drink?" "Of course, Sweetness, bring me one, okay?" Greg chuckled, adding, "You're king around here, Shel. Keep up the good work!" Both men shared a laugh and embrace. Greg headed out, a grin growing. 'Step one's over,' he mused.

Toronto proved a welcome city. The Canadians received *Centipede* with open arms and two weeks of sold out shows. The cast enjoyed the venue, O'Keefe Center, centrally located and easy access to the Hotel York. Most of the company chose the same hotel for the decent rate and location. In cities where runs would be longer, apartment hotels with kitchens were ideal. It was a perfect opportunity for gypsies to cook and eat in, saving extra money for later at tour's end. Most would rely on savings accrued over the months. Stops in Washington, D.C., Detroit and San Francisco were longer runs. Dwight would have a choice list ready for each city. Philadelphia was the next stop for a two-week engagement. A favorite city on the itinerary, touring companies liked the sophisticated audiences in Philly and easy access to New York, commutable in two hours by bus or train. One could be in Manhattan for 24 hours and back to the Shubert Theater by half hour.

Centipede's pack-up and load-out commenced Saturday night following the show. The transit trucks were on the road by daylight and the cast flown to The City of Brotherly Love in a little over two hours on Sunday afternoon. Arriving at Philadelphia International, they boarded a bus to the center of town. Though it was their day off and used for travel, the gypsies enjoyed a change of pace; arriving in a new place, getting settled at the hotel and exploring the area for places to drink, eat and unwind. The Shubert was in the heart of downtown and walking distance to shopping, especially Wanamaker's, the famed department store. The restaurants were outstanding and known for the finest steaks and seafood. Though expensive, Bookbinder's was a favorite and the best eatery in Philly. The city, rich in American history, afforded the cast opportunity to visit Independence Hall Square, the Liberty Bell, National Constitution Center, the former site of Benjamin Franklin's home, the Betsy Ross House and Christ's Church, where many of the signers of the declaration were buried. A potpourri of choices for history buffs and enthusiasts, there was much to see. Yes, it would be two weeks well-spent in addition to performing.

Griff was comfortable at the Shubert. He and his base crew felt right at home in a venue he'd worked many times; countless national tours and more recently the out-of-town tryout for *Centipede,* prior to its Broadway birth. The Philly locals were technically experienced and pleasant to work with. The load-in and set-up was easy and quick. The boys had time to get acquainted, have a few beers and enjoy a bite of dinner at the end of the first day. Opening was delayed a day and would commence on Tuesday night. The pre-sale was promising, the first week of the run already sold-out. The following week was selling fast. Many patrons had seen the show in New York and were giving it another look with a new cast. Kaplan was more than pleased with financial totals reported from Cleveland and Toronto. He was ecstatic. He'd gambled on Owen's concept for an all-dance show from the very beginning. He'd taken a major risk and that risk proved a sure winner, a mega hit! Now he was enjoying the fruits of that risk; a Broadway hit, success in Tokyo and a first national tour.

The phone rang suddenly in Courtman's suite at the Plaza. Blaine picked up after a few rings.

"Hi Blaine, am I too early?" "No, your timing is perfect, Greg. Have the towers concierge bring you up to our place right away." He put down the phone and walked into the bedroom. Pat had a pile of clothing on the bed. "Decisions, decisions, I don't know what to wear!" "My beautiful girl, if you wore a gunny sack you'd beguile our pal Greg." "Which dress do you prefer?" I love the dark green one, with a slit that travels to your special place!" "Oh my God, that was one I wore when we first got together!" "Yes, I know," he said, pulling her to him, giving her a lingering kiss. The door bell rang. "The green one, definitely, Patricia," he said, hurrying away.

"I'll go let Greg in. Take your time." Blaine opened the door revealing a dapper Greg, who stood holding an impressive bouquet of long stem red roses. "Trying to steal my girl, eh? Welcome, my good friend. Come in!" Greg entered and received a warm hug. "These need a drink," he said, handing over the bouquet. "Make yourself comfortable, Greg, what are you drinking?" "A gin martini sounds great! Tell me, do you have Red Hills Dry?" "Yes, of course." "Make mine dirty, will you?" "Be right back. Patricia is about finished dressing."

Greg removed his jacket, loosened his tie and found a comfortable chair. While he waited he looked over the large room. 'That boy has impeccable taste!" "Good evening, Greg." He turned to see Pat, looking beyond stunning in the form-fitting sheath, the outline of her body hard to miss. She was quite simply, perfection. "You look beautiful, my dear," he said, taking her hand. "Thank you, Greg. How wonderful you were able to spend some time this trip." Blaine returned, handed Greg his drink and reached around Pat's waist. "You look ravishing, my beautiful girl," he whispered, nuzzling her neck. "What would you like?" She caught the reference and smiled. "Do you have Vouvray chilled?" "Yes, I put one away just for you!" Blaine uncorked the wine and poured a glass for Pat and one for himself. "Your place is delightful, Blaine. How long have you been here? Two years at the Plaza, six months in this place. Patricia and I took this larger space when we decided to live together."

Greg gazed at the pair. "You two make life extraordinary! Just look at you!" "Well, your generosity in Paris will never be forgotten. Talk about newlyweds off to the right start!" "So they took good care of you at Villiers?" "They were charming and very accommodating. Patricia and I loved the neighborhood, the ambience." "Yes, it was just what I hoped," said Pat, sipping wine. "So cozy and convenient to every place we wanted to see." "I bought it for the very reason you liked it. I wanted a little hideaway for guests; quiet, romantic, away from crowds and noise." "Well, it was perfect." Greg changed the subject, checking his watch.

"I made a reservation for us at the Rainbow Room for 8:00. We have some fine tuning to take care of for Patricia's new venture," said Greg. "I'll call down to Keith, who'll have the car ready." "Good, I want to sort out details, get a leg up. Shel Friedman will be in town next week. "He wants to meet Patricia." "I've never met a movie mogul. I'm a little nervous," admitted Pat. "Nonsense, you'll dazzle the king! That's what I call him, you know." "The king?" "Well, he's by far the most influential and respected suit in the industry. Nothing gets past Shel Friedman.

He's known for all three; savvy, shrewd, successful! There's no one like him in Hollywood, now or ever will be." "You're really sold on him, aren't you?" "Shel came up the hard way, no silver spoon in his mouth. Raised by adoptive parents, he worked three jobs to save for college while supporting younger siblings after his folks died. At first, he was hired at Universal as a messenger, then production go-fer and after some years, worked his way to the front office, becoming vice president of project development. He's driven, honest and most of all, smart, one of the smartest around." Pat and Blaine sat rapt, hearing Friedman's history. "Have you brought my wife up?" "Yes, I flew out to see him while you two were in Paris. He's intrigued with my idea of having an additional person on our team to handle the artistic side." "I'll look forward to meeting him," said Pat, still a little unsure. "He'll take one look at you, Patricia and melt!" "Good lord, I hope he'll see beyond this former gypsy's appearance and hire me for my talent!"

"Good as done, kids. Now, let's go to dinner. I'm famished," said Greg, rising. He straightened his tie and slipped on his jacket.

Dinner at the Rainbow Room was impeccable. Pat had never been and loved the food and service. The waiter brought an assortment of desserts, which Pat eyed eagerly. Blaine caught her stare. "Which one, beautiful girl?" "The most decadent one of course, the double chocolate cake!" "How about you, Blaine?" "No thanks on dessert! I'll settle for a Grand Marnier." "And you, Mr. Morgan?" "I'll have a Drambuie, warmed slightly." "Very good Sir, I'll have those for you in a moment. And for the young lady?" "Death by chocolate, of course," said Pat, pointing it out on the tray. "Very good!" In a few minutes the drinks and dessert were brought. Pat enjoyed the first bite of cake, then a second and third. "Do you believe this trim and fit woman?" Greg laughed. "From what I know of dancers and athletes, the rate of burn is incredible. And now for the business at hand," Greg said, sipping his drink. They huddled as coffee was offered and served. "Let's develop and fine tune Patricia's new role on the coming picture." Blaine took over the conversation.

"As I see it, my wife could serve as artistic consultant of our team. This will come naturally to her; overseeing details of the artistic content like approving casting, locations, use of time filming, viewing daily rushes, even working on the final edit. In short, making sure everyone involved is on the same page." "That works for me," said Greg. She will be liaison between our team and Shel's group. It will be as simple as one, two and three. Too many chiefs are never advisable or useful on the Hollywood playing field," added Greg. "Patricia, dear, do you have any questions or concerns?" "It's a lot to bite off all at once. I'm depending on you two to be my coaches." "What can I teach you about your business, my dear? You're the artiste," soothed Greg. "Please don't worry, my beautiful girl, you'll be wonderful," assured Blaine, taking her hand. "I'll love the casting, that part will be a blast!" "You know, Owen Matthews will be answering to you. In a sense, you'll be his boss. How do you feel about this role rehearsal?" "It will certainly be different," she remarked, smiling to herself. "Well, I'm glad we're agreed. Does anyone require another drink?" "No, but I think we should get going, it's late," said Greg. "I have to be in Houston tomorrow morning for a meeting." "You never stop, my friend." "Not if I can help it," he chuckled, waving over the server. "Ronald, may I have the check?" "Certainly, Mr. Morgan, right away!" Dinner had been perfect, like everything Greg touched.

The following week, Shel Friedman hit town running. His sole purpose was to iron out any last minute details for the film with his two exclusive backers, Morgan and Courtman. This was a choice opportunity to introduce Patricia Courtman into the mix. Greg was on hand at his usual haunt in New York, the St. Moritz Hotel. He invited Blaine and Pat to stop by for a drink before Friedman arrived. He liked working out details on his turf and suggested meeting in his suite, rather than at the Waldorf, Friedman's preferred stay. The three settled and were working on drinks, when the phone rang. "This is Greg Morgan. Yes of course, please have Mr. Friedman come up." A slow grin was forming, as he put down the phone. "This is our finest hour, kids. Get ready to dazzle, Patricia!" Minutes ticked by until the buzzer sounded. "I'll be right back."

Opening the door, he smiled warmly. "Shel, good evening, it's great to see you! Please come in!" Pat glanced over and spotted a dapper, well-dressed gentleman of average height, gray at the temples with a bald pate. He had a sporty pencil-thin mustache and a jocular presence. "We have to stop meeting like this, Morgan. It seems like days since our last confab!" "Actually, it was," returned Greg, the two shaking hands. "Shel I believe you know my partner, Blaine Courtman." "Yes, indeed. Good to see you again, Blaine!" "And you, Shel." Friedman's eyes suddenly found Pat and fixated on her, as if stapled. "And who is this lovely lady?" "I'd like you to meet my wife, Patricia Courtman," said Blaine, obvious pride in his voice. "My, some guys have all the luck! How nice to meet you," he said, eyes traveling a short distance to take in her incredible body. The moment was hardly lost as Greg caught a flicker of annoyance on Blaine's face and broke in. "Come, let's sit by the fire. What are you drinking, Shel?" "Dewers, rocks, neat," he replied, taking a seat across from Blaine and Pat. "Kids, would you like to continue with the same?" "Yes, I'd like another Vouvray," said Pat, slightly self-conscious as she noticed Friedman's eyes all over her. "Blaine?" "I'll stay with a perfect Manhattan, thanks, Greg!" Moments later, he returned with drinks including a martini for himself. "Welcome Shel! Here's to great movie making," he said, lifting his glass. The others followed suit.

Friedman wasted no time, cutting right to the chase. "I want to hear from this young lady," he said, smiling at Pat. She set down her drink, caught a smile and nod from her husband. "Mr. Friedman, I would like to offer my service to the *Bravo Business* film project. The show is dear to my heart and I feel qualified to assist with any creative aspect of it. I am very familiar with the content and structure of the piece." "How is that?" "I was Mr. Matthews' leading dancer on the national tour for nearly a year. I am familiar with how he thinks and works. In short, how he conceptualizes, casts, structures and executes choreography and direction." "That's a tall order. Wouldn't he have an assistant to work with him, another dancer?" "Of course and that gentleman's a colleague and friend of mine, Jonas Martin. Jonas is the best in the business and will be a tremendous asset to the project. I know how he thinks when he is working the process and is a perfect fit." "So where do you fit in, Mrs. Courtman?" "You need someone familiar enough with the show and Mr. Matthews to keep tabs on the day to day workings of the production, someone to make sure you're not over budget or out of time." "Have you ever done a film, Mrs. Courtman?" "No I have not, Mr. Friedman, but I know this show inside out. You could use an objective ally, with a history of this show. I will not be subject to studio drama, politics or whim. In short, I'm an outsider who understands the musical frame." Shel listened carefully, impressed with Pat's acumen and suggestions. Blaine stepped in.

"How will my wife's contract be handled?" "I imagine you will take care of details, Shel," offered Greg. "Mrs. Courtman will be paid by the studio and report to me." Pat politely raised her hand. "Mr. Friedman, will Mr. Matthews be made aware of this?" "Please call me Shel! You're not to worry your beautiful head, I will take care of this personally," he insisted, a shark-like grin forming. "How does this sit with you two?" Greg chuckled. "You're the king, Shel. What you say goes, right?" "You were always the brightest penny in the pile, Greg." The two enjoyed a mutual laugh. "Let's meet for lunch tomorrow at Sardi's, 1:00. I'll make the arrangements. In the meantime, welcome to the team, Mrs. Courtman."

That evening, Pat and Blaine shared wine in front of the fire. For Pat, their Plaza suite was a sanctuary, a place where she could shut out the world at large and tonight, unpleasant memories. Blaine noticed a growing frown. She was quiet, reflective; another sign that she was preoccupied. In truth Pat was worried and unsure of her coming stint in movie land. Separation from Owen Matthews and *Centipede* over the past months was a Godsend. Blaine's constant devotion and their marriage had instilled confidence and given her a peace. Now, with her former lover and mentor in the picture, she wasn't at all sure how to handle the situation. Blaine put down his glass, took hers and set it aside. Pulling her close he kissed her gently and nuzzled her neck.

"My beautiful girl, what's wrong? You're not yourself tonight," he murmured. "It's that obvious? Wow, I'm transparent!" "No, you're worried. What is it?" "You want the plain truth? I'm scared to death, Blaine. I've never worked on a film! I know nothing of Hollywood or how to play the game. Worst of all, Owen and I parted on a sour note." "Is that all?" "Isn't that enough?" "Do you know how much I love you, Patricia? I would never put you in jeopardy. Greg trusts and believes in you almost as much as I. We've got your back, Shel's approval and the bottom line? You know your way around *Bravo Business*. There's little Matthews can do except accept Friedman's decision and cooperate." "You make it sound so easy," she mumbled, her voice tight. "Why are you so worried about Matthews?" "We parted on a bad note. He was pissed when I left *Centipede* after the first year. He's a control freak when it comes to the work. And he resents us." "Why so?" "I think he was touting me for bigger and better things, roles in his future shows. I cut his water off when he saw that our relationship was more important to me than Broadway success. This is something he can't relate to. He's a theatre animal and from his known past, he was downright jealous of us. So when I up and quit a show he had conceptualized for me, he became hostile. I'm sure it's still there." "Are you sure? Are you convinced there will be trouble?" "I'm not sure, but there is irresolution between us." "Beautiful girl, I'm strictly a business man, but I know from experience, that sometimes we're given an opportunity to clear up conflict. You have a chance to shine on this picture, to prove you have the talent to succeed without his dictates or influence." Pat smiled for the first time that evening. Throwing her arms around her husband's neck she kissed him passionately, holding him tightly. The kiss continued, growing deeper, more sensuous. Without a word, they rose and took hands. There was only one place for them now, the bedroom.

Reaching the end of the bed, Blaine slipped Pat's robe off, covering her mouth with his. His hands moved down her body caressing her gently. Her sighs encouraged him further. Gently laying her on the bed, he did what she loved most. She felt his warm breath between her legs as his tongue took over. As he applied pressure her breathing quickened, her moans intensified. Barely able to control himself, Blaine slipped off his robe, joining her. He was hard, crazy with want. Positioning himself, he slipped inside, moving aggressively in and out. The depth of his passion was unstoppable, intensely erotic. In moments they burst in mutual explosion, writhing and rolling on the coverlet. Bathed in moisture, they lay entwined as they slowly calmed down.

Regaining his composure, his hand caressed her face, his gaze holding her rapt. "Feeling better, my beautiful girl?" She giggled, "What's not to like?" "Now, my wife is back," he teased. They crawled in and spooned, the ticking clock nearby lulling them into deep slumber. Tomorrow would matter. Pat was about to begin her journey as a business woman and partner. How different from dancing her feet off 8 shows a week, 52 weeks a year, for little pay or praise! Life with Blaine was sweet, close to perfection. And at last, Owen Matthews was persona non grata, another fact close to perfection!

Chapter 34

Showdown of Sorts

It was close to 1:00. Greg, Blaine and Pat arrived at Sardi's and were seated at Mr. Friedman's table. He was a popular guest of Vincent Sardi and always given special treatment when he called. Shel had not yet appeared, so they ordered a round. Blaine marveled how relaxed his wife was today. After her expressed concerns the previous evening, she was in charge, ready to take on Goliath, if need be. There was a part of Patricia's nature that Blaine had learned over time. His making love to her always had a calming effect. Last night was exceptionally intense and satisfying, coupled with words of support. They had fallen into a restful sleep. Today, she looked radiant and ready in a dark burgundy coat dress and matching cloche. Simple pearl posts and a tiny seed pearl necklace added a nice touch to her ensemble. Her hair was cut and styled by the incomparable Vidal Sassoon, the British hair designer. Taking New York by storm, he introduced his geometric haircuts, turning the fashion elite upside down beginning in the mid 60's. Pat had grown accustomed to shorter hair since her first visit at Elizabeth Arden. The style gave her sophistication and a no-nonsense appeal. No longer the chorine with ass-length tresses and an obvious naiveté, she appeared glamorous and self-assured.

As the trio sat sipping drinks, Greg glanced up, spotting Friedman and Matthews at the host station. Waving in their direction, Shel walked across the dining room toward their table, Owen at his heels. As he reached over to shake hands with Greg and Blaine, Pat came into plain view. Owen stopped, his face showing complete surprise. Shel was in great spirits and unusually effusive. "Good afternoon, Greg! Sorry for our delay. It was difficult finding a cab," explained Friedman. "Matthews, I believe you know Messrs. Morgan and Courtman, but may I present Mrs. Patricia Courtman? I believe you two know each other." "Hello, Owen," said Pat, with business-like tone. Dumbfounded, Owen blinked, nodded and took a seat. He fumbled for his smokes, pulling out a crumpled pack from his coat pocket. He was promptly offered a light by Anthony, Friedman's preferred waiter. Anthony immediately responded, offering a match. Lighting Owen's cigarette, he graciously handed him the matchbook with the famous Sardi's logo and stood back. "Owen, what are you drinking?" "My usual, Glenfiddich on the rocks, neat, he mumbled absently." He felt like the earth had shifted under his feet and he was fighting to maintain equilibrium. "And, I'll have a gin martini, straight up with an olive, Tony." "We'll have another round of the same," replied Greg. "I'll have those for you momentarily." "Thanks for meeting with us, guys. We have some details to run by Matthews here. June first is only a month away. So let's get to it." The silence was awkward as Owen smoked and Pat fiddled with her napkin. Owen looked at everyone except Pat. In a matter of minutes, Tony returned with drinks. Shel raised his glass, the others following. "To a winning picture!" Everyone sipped. Orders were taken for lunch and Shel continued.

"When the *Bravo Business* project first came across my desk I had my reservations whether Universal could make a film version of such

a behemoth Broadway hit! The studio specializes in drama, that's what
we're known for." Greg responded. "What convinced you, Shel?" "I
was itching to do something fresh and new. The biggest hurdle was the
financing. Substantial investment was needed to seal the deal, as musicals are costly from what I've researched. That's where you came in,
Greg. You and your associate here made it possible when you requested
sole investment." "We both happen to be big fans of this show, so it
seemed like a fit for us," added Blaine, winking at his wife. "Bringing
Owen on was the next step. Tell them Owen, how you jumped at the
opportunity," insisted Shel. Owen was immersed in scotch, nicotine,
thoughts lost to conversation. "Owen? Are you with us?" He jerked
to and sat straight, collecting himself quickly. "It was a no-brainer for
me. Of all my hits, this is by far my favorite," he said, shooting a look
of defiance toward Pat. "Really, I thought your present hit, *Centipede*
is your greatest triumph to date," said Shel, a little surprised. "Well, it
wouldn't make a good movie given there's no script, dialogue, or single
score. *Bravo Business* is perfect to translate to the screen." "Well, we
shall see," poked Shel, just as lunch arrived. The entrees looked inviting
as Tony served. Pat had ordered salmon, Blaine, the Tournedos, Shel,
Lobster Bisque and chef's salad and Owen, steak tartar and another
scotch. There was quiet temporarily as everyone enjoyed their entrees.
Coffee followed as dishes were cleared.

 "Getting back to business, I've asked you here Owen to introduce
you to a definite asset on the coming production. Because I'm new to
the musical format and considering the financial risks involved, I've
hired a personal assistant for myself and overall project coordinator. In
my absence for any reason, she's in charge." Owen, intrigued, crushed
out his present smoke and pulled out another. Lighting it, he inhaled
deeply and slowly let smoke curl out his nostrils. "It all sounds logical
to me, Shel. Who is it?" He took a swig of his third scotch. "You're
looking at her," said Shel, smiling like a kid at Christmas with a new
toy. "Pat?"

 The name scarcely left his mouth when scotch went down the
wrong way, burning Owen's throat intensely. Hastily putting out his
cigarette, he coughed repeatedly. Eyes watering profusely, he grabbed
a napkin, wiping his face. The coughing continued. "You all right,
Owen?" "Yes, I'll be back," he hissed, hastily heading to the men's

room. "Looks like Matthews' is a bit surprised," tossed Shel. "He's not fond of surprises," added Pat, trying to stifle a giggle. "He'll get over it. I will insist. Here, most of the big bosses are men, with few exceptions. We have female costume designers, speech coaches, secretaries and a couple of exceptional film editors, but that's as far as it goes. I'm looking forward to having your help, Patricia. You will be a great asset and I am pleased you've joined our team." "Thank you, Mr. Friedman!" "Shel, please. Let's skip the formality."

General small talk continued as Owen returned and sat down. "You had me worried there, Matthews. For a moment I thought you'd require an emergency tracheotomy!" "I'm fine," he muttered, gloomily. Shel continued. "We're aiming for the first week in June for auditions. I want your dance assistants there. Any problem with the timing?" "Both are currently in the Broadway production of *Centipede*. We'll have them out in L.A. as soon as you're set to go. We have swings ready to cover during filming." Shel looked puzzled. "Swings?" "Yes, people who understudy and cover dance spots," added Pat, triumphantly. "Fascinating! I see I have a lot to learn, so it's brilliant having Mrs. Courtman on board. Oh by the way, I assume you know she will have full approval on casting, Owen. She will handle the screen tests for the folks being submitted by agents only for principal roles." Owen felt a headache coming on. "Fine," he said, half-assed. "If there's nothing else to discuss, I need to leave. I have another meeting." "No, I think that about covers it, Matthews. I wanted you to meet the newest member of our team. We will convene with a final meeting in Los Angeles before shooting begins in four weeks. If I need to chat, I'll give you a shout." "Fine, I'll be around," he said, excusing himself. "Nice to see you again, Owen," said Blaine. "Yes," tossed Owen, glancing back at Pat. He wanted out the door as fast as possible. "Kind of a cold guy," remarked Greg. "He takes getting used to," added Shel. Greg addressed Pat. "Patricia, you worked with the guy on two shows. What's he like?" "He's tough and driven, a genius in his métier. He should be fine for you," said Pat, magnanimously. "Good to know, but I think he's a little out-of-his-depth when it comes to film," said Shel. "Yes, perhaps right now, but he will catch up. When Owen decides he's going to do something, he's 200 % full out. He'll come around." "You give him a lot of credit, don't you, Patricia?" "Only toward his work, Greg. As a human being, away from the stage, he's rather limited." "Well, none of us have to be in bed with the guy," declared Shel. 'I'd die first,' thought Pat, knowingly.

At the conclusion of lunch, they all shook hands, including Pat, who was beginning to like Shel Friedman. "We'll meet on the Coast next month. I'll set a date and call you." "Sounds good, Shel. Thanks for everything," said Greg. "You are so welcome, my friend. It's good to have you on board, Patricia. Blaine, take good care of her. I'm going to need her help!" "Certainly, Shel and thank you!" As they exited the restaurant, they spotted Blaine's driver, Keith curbside. "Greg, can we drop you?" "No, I think I'll walk back to the hotel, thanks! It's one of the true pleasures of being in Manhattan. See you two next month in fantasyland." They waved as Keith pulled away. Blaine pulled Pat close to him, cuddling her. "My beautiful girl, you were a knock out in there. I'm so proud of you!" Pat breathed a sigh of relief. "I think this is going to be good," she said, feeling a new sense of purpose. How far she'd come, how much she'd grown since her days with Owen. She was astonished at her good fortune, starting with a phenomenal husband, who meant the world to her.

Owen didn't have a meeting to get to following lunch at Sardi's. He just wanted to get the hell out of Dodge! Hailing a cab, he got in the first one pulling up. "Taft Hotel," he ordered and climbed in, angrily slamming the back door. The cabbie pulled away. "Hey, Mister, take it easy. I can't afford another door." En route, Owen's mind raced. 'That bitch, how did she pull this off?' By the time he arrived at the Taft, he was outraged and shaking. Handing the driver a twenty, he got out. The driver looked at the bill and rolled down the window. "Change?" "Keep it, ass hole!" The driver, surprised, shot him a look and volleyed, "Much obliged, ass hole." Owen found his way to the lounge and took a seat at the bar. 'I need a drink, maybe a few,' he thought, feeling cut to the quick. 'After all I did for that bitch,' he muttered. The bartender approached. "Hey, how've you been, Owen? You haven't been around lately." "Been busy, Harry. I'm doing a film." "No kidding, I didn't know you were an actor," he replied, with enthusiasm. "I'm not an actor, Harry. I'm a director," his impatience growing. "Better yet, I hear directors in Hollywood make a lot of bread," Harry offered. "What are you having?" "Glenfiddich, rocks, neat, Harry." "Ah, the usual, be right up." Owen needed nicotine, needed it badly. "The bitch, the bitch," he mumbled, pulling out a smoke and sticking it in his mouth."

"Have you another one of those?" The voice was throaty, sexy. Turning, he smiled when he saw the shapely brunette. 'The answer to a horn toad's dream,' he thought, zeroing in. She was older, but in good shape. Her breasts were full, neatly organized and on display, leaving little to the imagination; lips full and pouty, deep set violet eyes, lined with dark lashes and obvious eyeliner. Her skin tight dress was stretched; a curvaceous body, slight tummy, generous ass. She looked to be in her mid 30's. He liked her approach. She was pretty, in an offbeat way and possibly lonely. 'Definitely not a virgin,' he surmised, sizing her up. Pulling out a cigarette he handed it to her and reached for a lighter, lighting both. "Thanks, I really need this," she said, taking a drag, relishing the first hint of nicotine. "Would you buy me a drink?" 'This broad's not shy,' he thought signaling Harry. "What can I get you, Miss?" "Jack Daniels on the rocks, neat." 'A hefty drinker, I like that,' he mused. She sidled up to him, perching on the stool next to his.

"I'm Minnie, Minnie Kent." "Owen." "Owen, I like that! It's a different kind of name, not like Jim or Joe. What do you do?" "I'm in the theatre." "Oh, which one?" He smiled. 'What a twit, and probably fucks like a jack rabbit.' "No, I mean I work in theatre." "What do you do there, work in the box office, or are you a custodian?" "Jesus, do I look like a janitor?" "Hey, don't get sore. I'm just asking," she said, beginning to sulk. "I apologize, Minnie. Actually, I direct." "Really, what do you direct?" "Shows." "No shit? Have you ever worked on the Tonight Show? I just love Johnny Carson! Do you know him?" "No, can't say I do." "What a shame. He's adorable and so funny." Harry brought her drink. "Hit me up with another, okay?" "Certainly, Owen." "Boy, he must know you. Do you come here often?" "Not usually, I've been away." "Oh, away where?" "On the west coast. I'm doing a film this summer." "Oh my God, really? You're an actor! That's so exciting," she stammered, taking a sip. "I'm not a fucking actor! I told you I direct." Surprised, she pulled back. "Jeez, you're touchy. What's the matter with you anyway?" She appeared slightly bruised, her sad eyes never leaving her drink, which she finished quickly. "Could I have another?" "Jesus, do you have a hollow leg?" She giggled. "That's what my brothers used to ask me. Do you have a hollow leg, Minerva? That's my given name. Anyway, I could drink them under the table back home and never, ever got drunk," she said proudly. "Where's home, Minnie?" "I'm from Kalispell, Montana. Ever hear of it?" "Up in the northwest corner of the state, right?" "Wow, you're good! Most people think it's in Missouri or someplace like that." "So, you're a country girl at heart?" "No, not really. I left Montana ten years ago. I'd always wanted to visit New York so I came and never left." "What do you do?" He pulled out another smoke and lit it. "Want another?" "Sure. I love to smoke," she said, accepting it. Owen took out another for himself, lit up, inhaled deeply and studied her carefully. She was interesting in an odd way. "What do you do for a living, Minnie?" "What do you think I do, Owen?" "If I knew I wouldn't be asking you," he said, sipping his scotch. He waved at Harry. "Bring the lady another and hit me up as well." "Sure thing, Owen."

As they continued smoking and drinking, Owen's libido started kicking in. She wasn't exactly his type; dumb as a stump but at the moment, handy. "So Minnie, what are you doing later?" "I was going to ask you the same," she said, crushing out her cigarette and moving closer. "I could use some company. Care to join me?" Her smile was warm, her eyes lighting up. "That would be nice, Owen. Tell me, where are we headed?" "My place is uptown on west 67th between the Park and Columbus. How does that sound?" "That sounds fine, but I have to make a call first," she said, excusing herself. In minutes she was back. He paid the tab, helped her on with her coat and grabbed his. The cab ride to his flat took only minutes.

Entering the apartment, he wasted no time. Backing Minnie into the living room, he removed her coat and kissed her aggressively. She didn't budge, allowing him full access. Running his hands down her body, she didn't flinch, taking it all in stride. "Here, let me get this," he hastened, reaching for her zipper. As it slid down, he became more excited. His eyes fixed on her rounded belly, pendulous breasts and the v of her mound, the dress falling to the floor. "I'll be damned, no underwear?" "What for, it's so much easier without panties," she purred, now pulling at his fly. "Yeah, get it down, I want you all over me," he whispered hoarsely. "Oh, you want me to give you head! I was about to ask you what you like," she giggled. She proceeded to pull his slacks down, then his shorts. He was hard, gorged and ready to be taken. "You don't have to ask, Minnie, just do me," he insisted, lying on his back, pulling her down. "I'm supposed to ask first," she whispered. "And how long do you want me for?" Then, a large siren went off, as Owen caught on. "Jesus, you're a pro!" "Of course, what do you think?" She proceeded to go down on him. Owen sighed, closed his eyes and lay still, letting Minnie from Kalispell take over. Only one thought crossed his mind as he wallowed in her handy work. 'If I'm paying for this, it better be exceptional!' Minnie Kent did her best.

In late April *Centipede* made itself at home in the National Theatre, Washington, DC. The company would play the nation's capital for six weeks. The gypsies chose apartment hotels for the long run. Springtime was the perfect time to be there! The cherry trees were still in blossom and the air was warm and welcoming. The National Theatre was one of the country's most beloved venues for touring shows. The theatre's equipment was always up-to-date and access to the stage door was easy, through a wide alley between the theatre and a large restaurant across the way. Trucks could easily pass through, making loading and unloading a simple process. The trip from Philadelphia was short, only two hours driving time for Ed Franklin and his assistant. The load-in was equally quick and efficient, thanks to the locals. Griff thrived in D.C. He had called many shows there and considered the National one of the very best on the circuit. The stagehands always enjoyed Griff calling the shots. He treated his men like family, looking out for them. Safety was a first priority. He made it his business to make sure each crew member was comfortable and secure in his particular job during the run. He knew first and last names of each techie, names of their wives and kids. He remembered birthdays and anniversaries and gave each man courtesy, care and respect. His reputation as the best PSM in the business was well-known.

The cast was happy in Washington. Besides the friendly, savvy theatre-goers, there was time to be tourists, venturing to the many points of interest and history. They would perform eight shows a week, including a matinee on Wednesday and Saturdays, relax in the comfort of a home-like environment; buying groceries, cooking-in, entertaining off-hours and if need be, commute to New York on their day off; four hours by both bus and train. Most, however, wanted to just stay put. Life on the road was unlike home. In New York, one could leave the theatre following a performance, go home, stay there and lead a relatively normal life. The more seasoned gypsies did their best to make each stop on tour as home-like as possible. The newcomers had some adjusting to do. National tours carried a sense of non-permanence, truly a gypsy existence. If a road alliance was made, it was often with an awareness of how temporary it was. Affairs would last the length of the tour, but usually not carried back to New York. If one partner was on the road and one back home, show romances were often a welcome distraction from loneliness or boredom. Friendships made in those months on the move could and often did last a lifetime.

Such was the friendship between Mally Winthrop Edwards and Patricia Byrne Courtman. Their friendship began and continued from their first days of touring with the national company of *Bravo Business* to *Centipede,* their first original Broadway show. Through growing pains of romance, courtship, proposal and marriage, both women retained and cherished their friendship. Both were exceptional women, talented and true, each finding a niche in one of most challenging professions, that of professional dancer.

The jumbo jet lifted high in the sky over Queens, N.Y. On board, Blaine and Patricia Courtman settled back for the four hour trip to Los Angeles. Flying first class was a plus as the cabin crew waited on them generously, their every request accommodated. The trip marked a beginning of a new career move for Pat. No longer the chorus gypsy, subjected to the rigors of eight shows a week, for a director relentless in his demands, a user, minimally honest and disrespectful. This time, the shoe was on the other foot. Owen Matthews, the famous Broadway director-choreographer would answer to Patricia Byrne Courtman in her assigned job at her new home, Universal Pictures. Life was growing sweeter all the time.

Glossary of Show Business Terms

Audition: The process by which the production team of a show decides who will be cast in their project. The call can be for actors, dancers, or singers. Performers must execute a cold reading from a script, a dance combination, and/or sing their best 16-32 bars of a song.

ASM: Assistant Stage Manager, one or more persons assigned to coordinate specific off stage tasks during a performance.

Backer: Investors who provide the money necessary for a production to be birthed.

Call Back: The second audition call after a performer has made it through the first audition without being cut.

Dark: The one day a week off in professional theatre.

Dry Tech: The tech staff running the show from cue to cue (lighting and set changes) without the cast or orchestra; also known as a 'dry run.'

Green Room: The designated actor's off stage lounge.

Grip: A tech individual of the production staff working backstage to shift scenery, secure rigging and fly equipment before, during, and post production.

Hazard Pay: Additional compensation paid to performers executing dangerous activities.

House: Where the audience sits in a theater.

Jobbers: Crew members added to base staff in out-of-town cities, for run of the engagement.

Libretto: The script or book story of a musical show.

Pre-Production: May denote the planning of a show before it goes into rehearsal, or a pre-check by tech team before the run of a performance.

Process: Development and rehearsal as a show comes together.

Producer: Oversees the entire production financially, including investors, and all decisions regarding the operation of a Broadway show.

PSM: Production Stage Manager: Person in charge of all aspects of the production: calling the show, delegating tech assignments, handling details pertaining to company, crew and staff.

Reviews: Critiques, evaluations or notices by the press whether print, radio or TV assigned to attend the production.

Run-Through: Running through the entire production, usually without an audience.

Swing Girl/Boy: Understudy, stand-in covering in the event of illness, injury, or vacation time of the regular ensemble performers.

Travel Day: When a production travels from one city and venue to another.

Tryouts: Out of town cities where a production tries out the show material; also a period to make changes before returning to Broadway or the initial opening city.

The Gypsies' story continues in:

Gypsy Road—New Adventures

Here's a sneak preview:

Chapter 1

Hooray for Hollywood!

"Damn, look at this frigging crowd! Every out-of-work dancer on the west coast has to be here," shouted Margie Nash, tugging on her buddy Patrick Dorsey's sleeve. "Stop it, Margaret," he snapped, determined to proceed with steady nerves, ignoring the butterflies flying loosely in his gut. He didn't need a reminder that he and Margie were just two in a bunch of cattle, corralled for slaughter or in this case, being cut! "I can't believe we put ourselves through this auditioning shit," she groused. "What? And give up show biz?" Patrick, always acerbic and clever in his responses was feigning nonchalance, but in truth he was terrified. Lines upon lines of hopefuls, dancers of every demographic; age, gender, race; some attractive, many worn, but all relentless in pursuit of employment.

The gathering at the entrance of sound stage one, Universal Studios, June 1, 1966, would be a day of reckoning for most. Dance jobs were few and far between in Los Angeles. Movie musicals were a rarity these days, so an opportunity like this was golden! The call had brought throngs of dancers from the length and breadth of California and Nevada. Those who could afford the cost and time made the trip from New York to try their hand at being hired. The competition was fierce and frightening. Being hired for this film in particular was a long shot, given the numbers hoping for a crack at the upcoming movie version of Owen Matthews' Tony Award-winning hit, *Bravo Business*. Those holding SAG cards, members of Screen Actors Guild, would be seen first. Non union dancers would be allowed to audition following. If a non union dancer was hired, it was with the understanding he or she would have to join the union.

Margie and Patrick stood in line moving slowly forward. Just ahead, they could see dancers being put through their paces. The sound of a piano, shouts, shuffling feet and low ebb conversations bounced and ricocheted around the huge abyss. "I hate this, I fucking hate this," mumbled Patrick as he found a corner and removed his outerwear. He had underdressed a tank top, jazz pants and shoes. His slender form was already wet from the warmth of the typical June morning in Southern California, nerves adding sweat to his body. Margie was caught up in the excitement of the occasion, eyes darting all over the swarm as she slipped out of her jeans and blouse. Wearing a high cut pair of trunks and a sleeveless top that came to mid torso, she was minus a few pounds in recent months. She hadn't worked lately, although her agent had submitted her for extra work in a couple of national commercials and a pilot for a proposed series, nothing had materialized. Her first love was dancing and she hoped to impress the studio powers.

As the dancers filed through, they were required to show SAG cards, proving current and paid-up status. Once noted, they completed audition cards, the numbers on them noting the order in which they would dance. Those ready were placed in groups of 12, men and women separate. Two extremely attractive men were leading the group. Whispers indicated they were assistants to the director. Jonas Martin was lean, angular and breathtaking to watch. His every move was supremely clean and streamlined. His associate, Phillipe Danier was earthly, sensuous, spot on accurate to Martin's every dictate. They were an unbeatable team. From the sidelines, Patrick gazed longingly at both men. "Jesus, I'm moving to New York if the men out east are this attractive," he whispered to Margie. But she wasn't listening or watching them. Her eyes fixed on the man standing by, making notes with his eyes. "Patrick, it's him! It's Owen Matthews! Oh my God, can you believe it?" Patrick shifted his gaze, taking in the famed choreographer-director. His reputation made him an icon, his work revered even to those on the west coast. Dressed all in black, wearing boots and sporting a nub of cigarette in the corner of his mouth, he stood motionless, surveying the groups of whirling bodies, aiming to please. He was a lean, graceful cat; compelling and mysterious.

"Let's try the combination from the top. Ladies and gentleman, I want more precision in head accents and perfectly timed finger snaps. No spaghetti limbs or sloppy feet! I want 150% effort! Anything less is unacceptable! Okay Jonas, run them again!" The two groups on the floor repeated the combination until Owen had seen enough. "Thank you! Please wait a moment!" Owen, Jonas and Phillipe huddled, locked in a confab. An occasional glance at the waiting dancers produced extreme nerves. Following a lengthy discussion, Matthews began cutting. "Oh, oh, the cattle slaughter is starting," whispered Patrick, carefully. Most of the group was let go, with two exceptions; a tall blonde with legs up to her earlobes and a hunky, muscular wonder, whose look would attract any camera lens. Pete Norcross, the audition production assistant kept cards of those called back separate from those eliminated right away. Those not cut were asked to report back the following day at 10:00.

Meanwhile Margie and Patrick inched along in line, waiting to be called. One could hardly see over tops of heads, to get a take on what was being taught, what would be expected of them. The thicket of humanity was overwhelming, the numbers of hopefuls, mind blowing. Patrick sighed. "Maybe I should have accepted that stupid restaurant job. This is impossible, Margaret!" "Stop it, Pat! You have as good a chance as anyone here. You're technically one of the best dancers in L.A.!" He leaned in and gave her a hug. "Could you repeat that to Matthews' gorgeous assistant? I'll owe you for life!" Nudging him, Margie whispered, "I don't believe my endorsement will work at the moment. Perhaps you'd consider the casting couch," she said with a wink. Patrick shrugged and grinned. "Too true, Margaret, in a heartbeat!" Within moments they were moved to the front of the line. Jonas moved forward greeting them.

"Good morning, I'm Jonas Martin, Mr. Matthews' assistant and this is my associate, Phillipe Danier. Welcome! If you will place your dance bags to the side, we'll begin with the first combination. I would like six and six, please." The group was counted out until there were six men and six women ready to start. "Please spread out so that you each have a window through which I can see you work. Margie, Patrick and the others took their spots and waited for the next phase. As she glanced around she noticed women of every description. The showgirl types, via Las Vegas, were tall, stacked in skimpy attire, wearing too much make-up and attitude. The All-American looking women were definitely white bread and tidy. Some were ethnic; mostly Hispanic, Asian and some blacks. She wasn't quite sure what group she fit, but plain Jane came instantly to mind. Margie never considered herself a looker; attractive, maybe on a good day, but never beautiful. On occasion she wished she could have some work done if she could afford it. However, temp work, dog walking and house sitting or the occasional retail job wouldn't cover the cost, not by a long shot. No, Miss Margaret Nash would have to rely on personality and skill to get by. The sound of Jonas' voice cut through her fog.

"All right, let's begin. The combination I'm giving you is from the original Broadway production of *Bravo Business*. The movements are a combination of Marcel Marceau mime, ballet and soft shoe. I'm looking for those who can capture Mr. Matthews' style, which is paramount for this film. Starting facing forward in parallel first position, hands in the small of the back, turn your right foot in ballet turn out from the hip and close back to parallel. Repeat with the left foot. As the foot moves open, the head snaps in the direction of the foot, same foot as shoulder. Return to parallel, head is front. Ladies and gentlemen, the movements are sharp, snappy. The whole thing repeats a second time, so two counts of 8. On the third eight, you bend at the waist, toward your right foot, pointed and turned out at the hip. Lock into that left hip and draw three little circles with your toes going clockwise toward your body. On the 4th count, cross over the supporting leg's ankle, step out on five, cross back on six, step on the right foot on seven turn your left shoulder to the audience coming into a slight sit in profile by count 8. Step on right, brush hop left with a slightly straightened leg, step on left brush hop with right leg, repeat on left and sit, still in profile.

Hand jive moves are on counts of five and a six and a seven. Straighten, lock into right hip, cross left foot over ankle of supporting leg, lean out with left arm extended from the downstage shoulder and snap on 8. Are there any questions?" A hang sprang up. "Yes, girl in the hot pink leotard." "Those four counts of eight have a mechanical quality. Is that what Mr. Matthews wants?" Jonas and Phillipe exchanged looks. "Yes, the feet should be very sharp, staccato, but overall the movements must be fluid as well. The movements should transition seamlessly through each count of 8." Another hand went up.

"How can I become fluid and staccato all at the same time?" Owen, who had stepped out for a moment, had returned and overheard the question. Singling out the bodacious blonde he walked to her. "What's your name?" The group was still. "I'm Bernice, but my friends call me Bernie," she said with a wink. "Well, Bernice, watch this. Nodding at the accompanist, he shouted "A five, six, seven, and eight," performing the combination himself; a breathtaking display of perfection. His attention to style nuances and his fluidity throughout kept the mass of want-to-be-hired dancers riveted. Finishing the four sets of 8, he stopped on a dime to wild applause. Owen broke out of the last pose and turned to the young lady. "That's how I do it. That's how I want it. Jonas, let's go." Bernie, embarrassed, stepped back to her spot. 'What a showboat,' she thought, refocusing her intention. 'I can nail this, sucker! Just watch me!'

As Jonas explained the rest of the combination, his movements matched Owen's to perfection. After running over each portion of the combination he stepped out, allowing Phillipe to take over, while he watched the current 12 on the floor closely. West Coast dancers had a different vibe, bodies, looks and technique from their New York counterparts. Maybe their collective vibe was due to living year 'round, all the sunshine and ocean air. The huge numbers of unemployed indicated fewer opportunities to perform save for TV work. Maybe it was the style and training of west coast teachers, producing a different kind of dancer than he was used to seeing back east.

Originally from California, Jonas, became a professional dancer quite late, having been a superb soccer player in high school. Hiding his sexual orientation became impossible in that sporting life, so he turned instead to the dance world; a milieu where he would be accepted and safe! With agility, strength and timing, he trained vigorously in ballet, modern and jazz. After dancing on network TV, specifically Los Angeles-based variety shows, he was drawn to New York, where his dance career really took off. Spotted at an open call by Owen Matthews, he worked tirelessly to gain opportunity and his trust. Eventually his considerable drive and talent brought him the opportunity to assist the director, becoming his right hand. One day, he would become a choreographer-director himself, sharing his acumen and a tradition set by his boss and mentor.

Margie and Patrick danced the combination repeatedly. Jonas approached them with constructive notes, enlisting them to improve their performances. Margie's technique was exceptionally good, her ability to ape the combination shown her plus her bright, perky personality made her a keeper! She was called back the next day. Patrick, too, learned his fate when Jonas stopped by, complimenting his work. "What's your name?" He looked surprised at being singled out. "Pat, Pat Dorsey," he stammered. "Nice work. I like the way you move. You fill the space extremely well." "Thank you," he said, turning beet red. "Please come back tomorrow at 10:00." "I will! Thanks!" "Next group, please!"

As the morning wound down, group after group of SAG members and non-union dancers passed through the cattle drive. By 1:00, Owen had kept 30 union and 10 non-union dancers for the callback; different types and levels of talent. He had to look for an ensemble of would-be office workers of various demographics for the cast of *Bravo Business*. California offered a wide range of ethnicity and talent. Following the dance call and subsequent casting, there would be a call for principals, submitted through agents and managers only. There would be the inevitable crop of unknowns to Owen and his team, but so much the better. Perhaps through the Hollywood process they would acquire some new and unique actors. Following the morning cattle drive, Owen, Jonas, Phillipe and Pete Norcross, production assistant met to discuss the field of finalists. Lunch was brought in for their convenience. 'Wow, this is no noon rush at the Greeks,' said Jonas with enthusiasm, glancing over the impressive repast. The Greeks, a nickname referred to by neighborhood locals, was a popular but small diner next door to Dance Arts in the heart of the theatre district. Principally a one-counter wonder, folks would stop in, grab beverages and sandwiches made-to-order in a jiffy by owners, Nikko and Peter Drakos. The two brothers had thrived for decades on daily business brought by show biz types and others in the neighborhood.

"Let have lunch and then discuss," said Owen, lighting the familiar cigarette. The buffet had been catered by the studio kitchen on the lot. "I could get used to this treatment," sighed Jonas, scrutinizing the sumptuous array of sandwiches, sides and desserts. "Thank God I'm not hoofing this afternoon!" "No, but I need your brain in high gear, so easy on food," ordered Owen with a chuckle. "Please help yourselves!" Pete Norcross, production assistant, had come highly recommended by Universal. Shel Friedman, vice president of project development had chosen him personally. Friedman was the most influential and touted executive in movie town. A positive nod from him and there was no turning back! Waiting while Jonas and Phillipe helped themselves, he was more pleased than hungry to be working on *Bravo Business*. The opportunity to work on a musical was rare in Hollywood now. The days of making high caliber movie musicals, like those of Metro Goldwyn Mayer in the 40's and 50's, were long gone. This film was potential gold for the studio and Pete wanted in. A credit like this would open doors and he was more than ready!

Following lunch, Owen began the meeting. "Pete, hand me the audition cards, will you?" "Certainly, Sir!" "I prefer Owen, Pete." "Certainly, Owen." 'This guy's a brown nosing snake,' Jonas thought, scrutinizing him. Owen took the cards and began looking over names and comments about each. "It looks like we have an interesting assortment, Jonas. What's your take on these west coast kids?" "They have a different vibe from New York dancers, Boss." "How so?" "I think it's obvious in their experience level. The training out here is less intense than back east. Fewer opportunities to work makes for lack of edge. They don't appear as polished or quite as facile in technique. I'm just prejudiced, I guess." "Nothing wrong with your demand for excellence, my friend. This film has to be nothing short of spectacular and we need a topnotch cast to make it happen." Pete hung on Owen's every word. He also found himself attracted to the director. He liked older men, especially the powerful and rich. "Well, we'll have them back tomorrow and choose the best of the lot." "How many are you thinking, Boss? It looks like we've called 40 back." "I'm aiming for an ensemble of 28. I'm sure we can find that many in this bunch. What we lack here we'll scour New York for. New York dancers currently out-of-work would jump at three months in the sun and a major film credit." He turned to his newly-assigned assistant.

"Pete, in the morning, please handle the flow of finalists same as today, moving them along as quickly as you can. I'd like this wrapped as soon as possible." "Okay, Owen. I'll take care of it," he soothed. Jonas and Phillipe exchanged glances. "Jonas, let's give them a stronger combination. The Buccaneer is a good choice to see their stamina and performance value. Please teach them the final breakout, no holds barred. Got it?" "Ok, Boss." "Good job today. I'm lucky to have you guys here." "Thanks, Owen, we appreciate this," said Phillipe. "Take the rest of the day. Get some sun, check out the area. Pete jumped in. "Universal is providing your staff cars. Just check with Trish in Shel's office. She'll assign a vehicle for your use." "Thanks, Pete. We appreciate your help." "Glad to help, Sir." "Pete, forget the Sir. Owen is sufficient!" The meeting broke up.

Patricia and Blaine Courtman arrived in L.A. and quickly settled at the Beverly Wilshire. Pat was about to start her new job, that of production coordinator and casting consultant on behalf of her husband Blaine, his business partner, Greg Morgan, the sole investors and Shel Friedman. She was a bit nervous, given her ill-fated history with Owen Matthews. He had been obvious in his dislike of the decision to hire the former Pat Byrne. Here would be his former lover, muse and star now his superior and watchdog on the project. She would be around the shoot, breathing down his neck at callbacks to insure the right selection of ensemble people. Beyond that, she'd advise and assist in principal casting. During the shoot she would throw her weight around advising artistically, making Owen's blood boil. The pain in his ass was growing more intolerable as time grew closer and they would meet.

Pete Norcross was crazy for Owen Matthews. He wondered how to get to first base. After all, he was working for him. He liked everything about the director, especially his track record of success. He was another powerful man, one who could boost his career. But he'd bide his time, be cautious and not appear too obvious. A rumor of Owen's flagrant womanizing was all over the studio. Was Matthews straight or bi? Perhaps he'd give him a tumble! These and other thoughts collided as he hurried out of the building. He didn't see Jonas and Phillipe stop to observe him as he headed to his car behind the soundstage. Throwing his belongings in the backseat of the silver gray Porsche convertible, he climbed in, straightened the rear view mirror and ran his hands through his hair. He primped and preened, wiping his teeth with his fingers and admiring his face. Pete Norcross apparently had a hot date. He sped off, never noticing the New York gypsies watching his every move. "That brownnose could be trouble," muttered Jonas, searching the lot for slot number 16. "Cheri, don't take on. He's enthused, that's all." "We'll see, Babe. He has the smell of over-amped ambition all over him!"

The boys discovered their assigned car in slot 16. "This is the best," crooned Jonas, checking out the brand new wheels; a shiny turquoise blue Buick convertible, with crème leather interior. "Cheri, are you sure this is ours?" "Well, Trish said to look for parking spot 16, so voila my love! The keys are supposed to be under the mat on the driver's side." Jonas opened the door and slipped a hand under the mat. Feeling for and finding a key set he slid into the driver's seat. "Get in, handsome! I'm going to take you for a major spin in this baby!" "Are you sure, Cheri? How long has it been since you've driven?" "Lover, I'm a native Californian, remember? I was driving while teething," he chuckled. Phillipe settled, put his seat belt on and waited. Jonas put the key in the ignition and heard the smooth turnover instantly. "Let's go, Babe!" They pulled out of the parking space, drove the narrow streets of the back lot until they arrived at the main gate. Harvey Smith, the daytime security man, stepped out of the booth and approached. "Good afternoon, gentlemen. May I see your passes?" "Yes of course, we're here with the *Bravo Business* production." "Mr. Martin, Mr. Danier?" "Yes, how did you know?" "I cross checked the production list and license plates of assigned vehicles. It takes a while to familiarize with new personnel. Welcome to Universal. Be sure and keep your I.D. badges with you at all times whether coming to or going from the lot and during working hours." "Thanks so much!" "Have a good afternoon, gentlemen." Jonas pulled away as Phillipe glanced back at Harvey. "These Universal people are pleasant." "I agree, Babe! This place is classy, real classy!" I may go Hollywood," he said, driving through the gate. "Let's go to the ocean," he shouted driving off in the direction of Venice Beach. "This movie business is not hard to take," he shouted gleefully. "I like this job already!"

Chapter 2

Survival of the Fittest.

Patricia Courtman arrived at Universal fresh and ready to work. After a breakfast meeting with Shel Friedman and staff, she was escorted to callbacks by Pete Norcross, who oozed compliments to hopefully impress her. Her reputation as one of Broadway's finest dancers preceded her through the studio gate and Pete was going to make sure she took notice of him. "Miss Byrne, it is such a pleasure to meet you. I saw *Centipede* last year and your work put shine on the entire production." "Thank you so much!" "How exciting that you and Owen Matthews are teaming up again!" "Yes, isn't it?" Pat's acting skill kicked in as she worked with Pete's repartee. His behavior was a perfect example of Hollywood bullshit and nicety. 'I think Pete's Peter needs stroking,' she thought, stifling a giggle. "Right in here, Ms. Byrne," said Pete, leading the way.

The impressive size and cavernous feel of soundstage one was so different from a typical Broadway theater. As they strolled over to the production desk, Pat could see Jonas and Phillipe warming up. Jonas spotted his best gal pal first! "Irish, I can't believe you're here," he cried, picking her up and swinging her around. "Hi, my darling hunks!" Phillipe was next, taking her in his arms, dipping her back and planting a luscious kiss on her lips. "Some things never change. I love you Frenchie," she said, giggling as she grabbed his ass. Pete stood riveted watching the three obvious comrades carry on. Jonas noticed him staring. "Irish, you've met Pete Norcross, our production assistant?" "Yes, indeed. Mr. Norcross has been very helpful." Pete blushed and rushed away to find Pat a chair. Jonas followed with his eyes, a grin on his face. Pat caught on immediately to Jonas' dislike for this PA. Jonas refocused. "Have you seen the great one yet?" "Owen? Not yet. I'm sure he'll be thrilled to pieces," she said with an edge. "Irish, you're in charge of him. Karma's a bitch and payback is just the best," he chuckled. "We'll see, Twinkle toes, we'll see!" Pete returned with a chair, bottle of Avian, glass and a pillow. "Please make yourself comfortable, Ms. Byrne," he oozed. "I prefer Mrs. Courtman. When we know each other better call me Pat, okay?" Jonas bit his tongue to keep from laughing out loud. A little bent, Pete slouched away to set up the final cattle drive.

At 9:30 those called back arrived in bunches, a pack of hopefuls all praying to be cast. Pete took names and crosschecked the audition cards from the previous day. Filing in, several couldn't miss the striking redhead seated at the audition table. Murmurs spilled over from conversations here and there, as the group warmed up, ready for the final hurdle. The dancers were divided into groups of six, mixed male and female. Promptly at 10:00, Owen sauntered in, looking like the dazzling Broadway icon he was. He was dressed all in black, his customary dress for work. The ever present cigarette hung precariously from the corner of his mouth. For a moment he stopped, catching a glimpse of Pat, then continued nonchalantly toward her. "Miss. Byrne, welcome to Hollywood," he said with a flippant air. "Thank you, Mr. Matthews!" 'Miss, Mister, what gives with that?' Jonas already sensed a growing rivalry, two exes trying to gain the upper hand. Owen turned to Pete. "Have you met Miss Byrne?" Before his response, Pat slipped in. "I've suggested Mr. Norcross call me Mrs. Courtman for the time being." "Fine with me, Mrs. Courtman," snapped Owen, now edgy. "Let's start," he bellowed, turning to Jonas and Phillipe. "Jonas, please teach the Buccaneer breakout, all 8 sections of 8." And so it began.

As the groups readied themselves, Jonas went through counts of the biggest and most demanding number to be filmed. On the Broadway stage, *the Buccaneer* was known as the 5-minute ball buster, one challenging even the most facile. The choreographic style of movement in the number was exacting in detail, the energy output, daunting. The fittest flagged under the demands of doing it 8 times a week. In filming the screen version, the *Buccaneer* would require take after take for Owen to be satisfied and call, "Cut and print!" Auditioning was physically easier by comparison to what lay ahead for them under Owen's scrutiny. Group after group was taught, followed by a full out demonstration of their presence and technique. They were required to give 150%! Any less and they would be cut from the herd. From her vantage point Pat watched the dancers closely. Her trained eye and experience scrutinized everyone, noticing those with the 'it factor.' 'It' was indefinable and impossible to describe. The ones who stood out from the crowd had charisma and presence. In her heart she knew that Owen would settle for nothing less. Still, she needed to keep her eye on the ball, making her own observations, stating opinions and making decisions for the good of the project. She was prepared to handle Matthews anyway necessary. This was in her job description. She would uphold her position no matter what, personal feelings aside. Owen was a challenge, given his insufferable ego, temperament and their past history. However, he didn't realize his prior influence was now miniscule.

As the morning went by, the weakest dancers were cut until the very best remained. Twenty-eight men and women of every demographic stood before the production team. "Those here take a break and return at 1:00. Mr. Matthews and Mr. Martin will be with you at that time," announced Pete, his self-appointed importance intact. Owen, Jonas, Phillipe and Pat adjoined to the lounge, where lunch was already set up. Pete, now Owen's constant shadow, followed. His officious manner was annoying to say the least, prompting Jonas to roll his eyes toward Pat. Phillipe caught it too, and gave him a playful nudge. "Easy, Cheri, he's here for the long haul," he whispered. "He's your minion and must do your bidding," added Pat with a snicker.

Unaware of his ill favor with the gypsies, Pete pointed to the buffet at hand; sandwiches, salads, sides and desserts. "Who would like coffee, a soft drink, some water?" "Coffee regular, please," said Pat. Pete looked puzzled. "Coffee regular?" "Yes, it's strictly east coast, mind you. It's coffee with cream and sugar added." "Sure, right away. Anyone else?" "A regular coke sounds good," said Jonas. "You got it!" Phillipe was next. "I'd like a glass of ice water, thanks!" "Okay!" Pete was ready to take off, until Owen spoke up. "Pete, you wouldn't happen to have Glenfiddich handy, served on the rocks, neat?" He looked confused. "I don't know that one," he confessed. "It's my preferred brand of scotch. In the future, please make arrangements to have it here at lunch time?" "Certainly, sir, whatever you wish." "Pete, please for the last time, it's Owen." "Oh, that's right! Would you care for coffee instead for now?" "That would be fine, coffee black." "You got it," he chortled as he hurried off. Owen sighed and sat down. "Help yourselves, I'll wait for coffee." Jonas, Phillipe and Pat looked over the repast and began filling their plates. Owen watched them carefully, a grin forming. "You hoofers have the keenest appetites. I've never seen it otherwise." "Aren't you hungry, boss?" "Yeah, but coffee is a must, and this," he said, pulling a cigarette from a pack and lighting it. That first hit of nicotine was a necessary ally when it came to decisions. The others joined him at the table. Owen glanced at Pat, not able to hide his attraction. Though their break-up was ancient history, he'd never gotten over his desire for her. He was the one who had messed it up royally and that fact ate at him constantly. Now his gaze was locked on her.

"You cut your hair." "Yes, I did. Do you like it, Owen?" "You know I like long hair." "Well yes, but it was time for a change. Out with the old, in with the new, right?" He frowned as he took another drag, letting the smoke curl around his head. Pete returned with a tray of beverages. "Here you go, help yourself!" The group took their beverages and began eating. "Owen, may I get you a plate?" "That would be great, Pete. Is there a roast beef sandwich lurking over there by any chance?" "Yes sir, the best in town. The Brown Derby caters for us occasionally. Their beef is the best." "Sounds good. Bring me a roast beef sandwich, chips and some slaw." "Right away, Owen." 'Jeez, he does everything but snap his feet together,' thought Jonas, catching Phillipe's gaze. Lunch continued with very little conversation save for Pete's constant mouth in gear. Following, Owen asked for the audition cards. Pete handed them over then sat next to the director. He was ready to take notes on a steno pad that seemed permanently affixed to his arm. The others sipped and waited.

"I think we have an ensemble, gang. I have 28 remaining and it is a good number for the chorus.

"Who are you using?" Owen looked through the cards, spotting a few standouts. "I especially like Margie Nash and Bernice Douglas. I think they technically are the best of the bunch of women. The rest will be split up throughout the shoot, featured here and there. Having a few extras gives us flexibility and variety." "Which of the men stand out?" "I especially like that Pat Dorsey," said Owen. "I totally agree," added Jonas. "He seemed to pick up the steps fast and has a terrific personality and flair." "That's why I hired you, Jonas. We tend to see the same things."

"Mrs. Courtman, what is your take?" Pat took a breath and began. "I really liked Margie and Bernice, but the tall one with the fantastic smile was a standout too." If she can sing, we might feature her as the company vamp. She's certainly attractive enough." "You always were a leg man, boss." "You bet your ass!" "All right Pete, make up a list of these 28. We have 14 and 14 and that will work just fine for me." "Right away, Owen! Do you want me to announce to them? They were asked to come back at 1:00." "Absolutely not, Pete. I do the selecting and talking! Capiche?" The group exchanged looks. "Jonas, Phillipe and Mrs. Courtman, do you have anything to add?" "No, I think we're set, Boss. These 28 are the best of the bunch." "Let's go," said Owen, picking up his smokes. "Pete, grab me another cup of coffee, will you?"

The final group stood waiting for the powers to make or break them. Standing in small clumps of conversation, they looked up in waves as the production team entered. A hush descended over the huge abyss, the air thick with anticipation and dread. Pat took a seat next to Jonas and Phillipe. Pete stood by with his steno pad at the ready. Owen walked front and center. "Ladies and gentleman, thank you for your patience through this process. First of all, I want welcome each of you to the cast of *Bravo Business!* You've demonstrated here your ability to take direction, show initiative and have the dance technique to cut my work. Demographically, you are all interesting and camera-worthy." Applause rang out through the huge space. "Pete Norcross is our PA and will get all your particulars when I've finished. You've all met my right hand man, Jonas Martin. Working alongside him is Phillipe Danier, a splendid teacher and technician. Last but by no means least; I'd like to introduce Patricia Byrne Courtman. Mrs. Courtman was my

featured dancer on the national tour of *Bravo Business* and starred in
Centipede, my touted hit currently on Broadway." Again, enthusiastic
applause broke out.

"We will begin shooting in mid July, however, rehearsals will begin
July 1st. You'll be required to learn the entire choreography of this
piece before we break down sections for the camera lens. Mr. Norcross
will take your names, addresses and phone numbers and send your
contracts for signing. Are there any questions?" At the moment, the
group was silent, reverent; each caught up in thought. Owen broke the
silence. "Thank you for your tremendous effort! See you next month."
The group applauded once more and began to file out. Margie and
Patrick hugged through tears. "Oh my God, can you believe it Pat?
We're doing a picture together!" Pat glanced over at Jonas, who was
busy conferring with Matthews. "I can't wait to work with him," he
said, nodding toward Jonas. "Down boy, you're hired to dance, not
put out." "I wish this contract included both," he whispered. "Patrick,
for pity sake, you're trolling!" "I'm that obvious?" "Honey, you've been
obvious since birth. Settle down! This job is like pure gold, so don't
fuck up!" "Okay, Mom," he giggled. Gathering their belongings, they
grabbed hands and left the soundstage.

Meanwhile, the confab continued. "We need to set principal auditions." "That will be handled differently from this call, Owen." He
looked perturbed. "How so?" "The studio needs to run ads in all the
trades. The studio will have a list of the top agents, the A-listers with
the most clout. They will be notified regarding principal casting by
Universal. Those actors interested in being seen must be submitted by
an agent or manager. Then individual appointments are set for inter-
views and readings. Once the individual passes muster, the next step
is a screen test for only those in contention for starring roles." "Well,
Mrs. Courtman, one can see you've done your homework," he said,
drily. "Mr. Matthews, it's my job. Your next step is to spread the word
and set interview dates. Better get going if you want to start shooting
in a month." "Thanks for your advice, Mrs. Courtman. I'll take it under
advisement." "You've been advised, Mr. Matthews," said Pat, picking up
her things. "Pete, will you show Mrs. Courtman out?" "How very con-
siderate of you, Mr. Matthews. I do have to get to an appointment with
Mr. Friedman. See you around," she tossed, with a wave of her hand.

Jonas and Phillipe watched her leave the soundstage. Their best gal pal had grown beyond imagining since the heartbreak of Owen's betrayal. 'Irish, you are absolutely fabulous,' Jonas mused, a wide grin growing.

While Pat was meeting with Shel Friedman, Blaine was looking for a house to rent for the duration of filming. Universal was covering the cost as a courtesy to them. After looking at several properties, he chose a cozy bungalow in Laurel Canyon. The place had all the basic amenities needed, including a housekeeper. The Courtmans made their preference known for a private home rather than stay at a luxury hotel. Universal was only too happy to accommodate. The house came fully furnished with a majestic view of the valley below. They would move in the next day.

After Pat's departure from soundstage one, Owen, Jonas, Phillipe and Pete returned to the conference room. Pete was eager to please and organized the newly hired dancers by laying out audition cards in alphabetical order. It was an eclectic bunch. "Pete, draw up a list of our dancers for Shel. They'll need contracts. An interview of prospective principals is next, followed by a cold reading from the script. If we wish to pursue them further, a screen test will be set up. All our final decisions will come from this process. "I'll see that Shel has all these details today, Owen." "Thank you. I think that about covers it for now." Pete paused and then spoke.

"Where can I reach you? I mean, away from Universal." Jonas and Phillipe exchanged looks. "I'm not sure I follow you, Pete," said Owen, a puzzled look growing. "I mean, if I need to reach you, where might I call you," he said, slightly nervous. "I don't think it's necessary for you to contact me away from the lot. Only Friedman and my assistants need to find me. I think that about covers it. You'll receive any updates at the studio, Pete. Capiche? Now gentleman, enjoy your evening. I will see you on Friday morning."

He stood, shook out a smoke, lit it and sauntered out of the room. Jonas and Phillipe gathered their belongings and followed. "See you, Pete!" When they'd left, Pete Norcross stood alone, feeling put off. In truth, he was downright miffed. His first attempt to get to Owen Matthews alone hadn't panned out. 'There must be a way to gain his interest,' he thought, a fantasy seeking reality.

Owen Matthews had found his chorus. His next step was to cast the principals, an arduous job considering the numbers of actors in L.A. Whoever he cast had to be multi-talented; they had to sing, dance and act and, the camera had to love them. As he pondered the next step, he returned to the hotel, stopped in the bar and ordered a double scotch on the rocks, neat. Pulling out another cigarette he relished the first drag, allowing the smoke to train out of his nostrils. Through the low lighting he noticed several attractive women, unescorted. The landscape was getting better all the time. Hooray for Hollywood indeed.

Made in the USA
San Bernardino, CA
29 March 2014